Unsheltered

Also by Barbara Kingsolver

FICTION

Flight Behavior

The Lacuna

Prodigal Summer

The Poisonwood Bible

Pigs in Heaven

Animal Dreams

Homeland and Other Stories

The Bean Trees

ESSAYS

Small Wonder

High Tide in Tucson: Essays from Now or Never

POETRY

Another America

NONFICTION

Animal, Vegetable, Miracle: A Year of Food Life
(with Steven L. Hopp, Camille Kingsolver, and Lily Hopp Kingsolver)

Last Stand: America's Virgin Lands
(with photographs by Annie Griffiths Belt)

Holding the Line: Women in the Great Arizona Mine Strike of 1983

Unsheltered

A NOVEL

Barbara
Kingsolver

FABER & FABER

First published in the UK in 2018
by Faber & Faber Ltd
Bloomsbury House,
74–77 Great Russell Street
London WC1B 3DA

First published in the US in 2018
by HarperCollins Publishers,
195 Broadway, New York, NY 10007

Designed by Fritz Metsch
Printed in the UK by CPI Group (UK) Ltd, Croydon, CR0 4YY

The right of Barbara Kingsolver to be identified as author of this work
has been asserted in accordance with Section 77 of the Copyright, Designs
and Patents Act 1988

A CIP record for this book
is available from the British Library

ISBN 978–0–571–34698–1 (hardback)
ISBN 978–0–571–34701–8 (export)

For Lily Hopp Kingsolver

After the final no there comes a yes
And on that yes the future world depends.

—WALLACE STEVENS,
"The Well Dressed Man with a Beard"

Unsheltered

1

Falling House

"The simplest thing would be to tear it down," the man said. "The house is a shambles."

She took this news as a blood-rush to the ears: a roar of peasant ancestors with rocks in their fists, facing the evictor. But this man was a contractor. Willa had called him here and she could send him away. She waited out her panic while he stood looking at her shambles, appearing to nurse some satisfaction from his diagnosis. She picked out words.

"It's not a living thing. You don't just pronounce it dead. Anything that goes wrong with a structure can be replaced with another structure. Am I right?"

"Correct. What I am saying is that the structure needing to be replaced is all of it. I'm sorry. Your foundation is nonexistent."

Again the roar on her eardrums. She stared at the man's black coveralls, netted with cobwebs he'd collected in the crawl space. Petrofaccio was his name. Pete. "How could a house this old have a nonexistent foundation?"

"Not the entire house. You see where they put on this addition? Those walls have nothing substantial to rest on. And the addition entails your kitchen, your bathrooms, everything you basically need in a functional house."

Includes, she thought. *Entails* is the wrong word.

One of the neighbor kids slid out his back door. His glance hit Willa and bounced off quickly as he cut through the maze of cars in his yard and headed out to the alley. He and his brother worked on the vehicles mostly at night, sliding tools back and forth under portable utility lights. Their quiet banter and intermittent Spanish expletives of frustration or success drifted through Willa's bedroom windows as the night music of a new town. She had no hard feelings toward the vehicle boneyard, or these handsome boys and their friends, who all wore athletic shorts and plastic bath shoes as if life began in a locker room. The wrong here was a death sentence falling on her house while that one stood by, nonchalant, with its swaybacked roofline and vinyl siding peeling off in leprous shreds. Willa's house was brick. Not straw or sticks, not a thing to get blown away in a puff.

The silence had extended beyond her turn to speak. Mr. Petrofaccio courteously examined the two mammoth trees that shaded this yard and half the block. Willa had admired the pair of giants out her kitchen window and assumed they were as old as the house, but hadn't credited them with a better life expectancy.

"I have no idea why someone would do that," he finally offered. "Put up an addition with no foundation. No reputable contractor would do that."

It did seem to be sitting directly on the ground, now that she looked, with the bottom courses of bricks relaxing out of rank into wobbly rows. A carapace of rusted tin roofing stretched over the gabled third floor and the two-story addition cobbled on the back, apparently in haste. Two tall chimneys leaned in opposite directions. Cracks zigzagged lightningwise down the brick walls. How had she not seen all this? Willa was the one who raised her anxiety shield against every family medical checkup or late-night ring of the phone, expecting the worst so life couldn't blindside them. But she'd looked up contractors that morning with no real foreboding. Probably assuming her family had already used up its quota of misfortune.

"I can't hire you to tear down my house and start over." Willa ran her hands through her hair at the temples, and felt idiotic. Both-hands-on-the-temples was a nervous habit she'd been trying to break for about twenty years, since her kids told her it made her look like *The Scream.* She shoved her fists into the pockets of her khaki shorts. "We were thinking we'd fix it up, sell it, and get something closer to Philadelphia. We don't need this much room. *Nobody* needs this much room."

On the moral side of things, Mr. Petrofaccio gave no opinion.

"But you're saying we would have to repair it first to put it on the market. And I've noticed about every fourth house in this town has a For Sale sign. They're all in better shape than this one, is that what you're telling me?"

"Twenty five percent, that would be a high estimate. Ten percent is about right."

"And are they selling?"

"They are not."

"So that's also a reason not to tear down the house." She realized her logic in this moment was not watertight. "Okay, you know what? The main thing is we live here. We've got my husband's disabled father with us right now. And our daughter."

"Also a baby in the picture, am I right? I saw baby items, a crib and all. When I was inspecting the ruptures in the ductwork on the third floor."

Her jaw dropped, a little.

"Sorry," he said. "I had to get behind the crib to look at the duct-work. You said you are looking to downsize, so I just wondered. Seems like a lot of family."

She didn't respond. Pete extracted a handkerchief from his pocket, mopped his face, blew his nose, and put it away. He must have been braising inside those coveralls.

"That is a blessed event, ma'am," he suggested. "A baby."

"Thank you. It's my son's child, just born. We're driving up to Boston this weekend to meet the baby and bring them the crib."

Pete nodded thoughtfully. "Due respect, ma'am, people usually ask for an inspection before they purchase a house."

"We didn't *buy* it!" She wrestled her tone into neutral. "We inherited. We were in Virginia wondering what to do with some old mansion in New Jersey after my aunt died, and then out of the blue my husband got a job offer from Chancel. A half-hour commute, that's too good to be true, right?"

"Your husband is a professor up there?" Pete's nostrils flared, sniffing for money maybe, engaging the common misconception that academics have it.

"On a one-year contract that may not be renewed," she said, taking care of that. "My aunt had this place rented for quite a while. She was in a facility out in Ocean City."

"Sorry for your loss."

"It's been a year, all right. She and my mother died a week apart, same kind of rare cancer, and they were twins. Seventy-nine."

"Now that is something. Sad, I mean, but that is like a magazine story. Some of that crazy crap they make up and nobody believes."

She let out an unhappy laugh. "I'm a magazine editor."

"Oh yeah? *Newsweek, National Geographic,* like that?"

"Yeah, like that. Glossy, award winning. Mine went broke."

Pete clucked his tongue. "You hate to hear it."

"Sorry to keep you standing out here. Can I offer you some iced tea?"

"Thanks, no. Gotta go check a termite damage on Elmer."

"Right." Despite her wish to forget everything he'd told her, Willa found his accent intriguing. Before this move she'd dreaded having to listen to New Jerseyans walking out the *doo*-ah, driving to the *shoo*-ah, but South Jersey was full of linguistic surprises. This Pete was the homegrown deal, part long-voweled Philly lowball, part Pennsylvania Amish or something. She watched him scrutinize the garage on the property line: two stories, antique glass windows, thick pelt of English ivy. "You think that building goes with this house?" she asked. "The deed isn't very clear."

"That is not yours. That would be the stip house to the property next door."

"The stip house."

"Yes ma'am. When they sold these lots back in the day, they had stipulations. Improve the property in one year's time, show intent to reside, plant trees, and all like that. Folks put up these structures while they got it together to build their real house."

"Really."

"You look around this town you'll see a few, all built on the same plan. Trusses like a barn, fast and cheap. Some guy was doing well in the stip house business I figure."

"What era are we talking about?"

"Landis," he replied. "You don't know about Landis?"

"He's what, some real estate developer?"

"A king more like, back in the day. This is just a bunch of wild wilderness when he buys it, right? Thirty thousand acres and nobody but Indians and runaway slaves. So he makes this big plan to get people to come. Heaven-on-earth kind of thing."

"One of those utopian communities? You're kidding me."

"I am not. Farms like a picture book. You notice the streets are

Plum Peach Apple and all like that? Almond?" He pronounced it *owl*-mond. She also noted his resistance to contractions, and the recurrent *back inna day*. She wished for her pocket tape recorder.

"Yeah, I noticed. My daughter goes out to walk the dog and comes home wanting a snack."

Pete laughed. "Sounds like some healthy kid. All my girls want are those Sour Patch things and the diet pop. I am gonna tell you, it drives the wife crazy."

Willa had no intention of trying to explain Tig. "So he named it Vineland thinking people would swarm around like fruit flies?"

"Captain Landis was all about the fruit, is what I know. And who knows how to grow grapes but the Italians? So he starts up his own newspaper in the Italian language for attracting the right element. The Petrofaccios came from Palermo, Italy. My nonnie kept a scrapbook of that stuff."

Willa smiled. "Landis was a wino."

"No ma'am, that is the crazy thing, there was no drinking alcohol in Vineland whatsoever. That was a very significant rule, back in the day."

Willa saw holes in this story but still might look into it for a feature: Nineteenth-Century Utopias Gone to Hell. "You're sure the garage is theirs? Not that I need it." She laughed. "Unless you think we'll need a new place to live."

Unnervingly, he didn't laugh. "It's theirs. I can tell by the angle and the setback."

She assumed the neighbors didn't know this, or it would be crammed with collateral debris from their garden of broken cars. Pete gave their peeling ranch house a once-over. "Original structure came and went. That is a shame. Those originals were some beautiful old girls in their day. Like yours."

"Except for her weak foundation. The ruin of many a girl, I guess."

Pete looked at her, evidently finding this unsuitable material for a joke.

"If it's such a shame to lose them, shouldn't ours be saved? Isn't there grant money for this kind of thing? Historic preservation?"

He shrugged. "Our fair city has got real empty pockets at this moment in time."

"They must have been loaded at some point. It sounds like this place was built on an immigrant work ethic and old money coming out of the woodwork."

"Money," Mr. Petrofaccio said, staring over the dead Fords and Chevys at two girls pushing babies in strollers down the gravel alley, conversing in a musical Asian language. "Where does it all go?"

Willa had been asking the same question. In her family, in her profession and her husband's, in strained European economies and the whole damned world, where is the cash that once there was? Her husband had a PhD in global politics, her son was an economist, and neither of them seemed all that interested in this mystery that plagued her. Not as it specifically applied.

"That would be the thing here, government money," Pete offered. "Because no ordinary residential person is going to have what it takes here. There is a time for propping things up, and then there is past time."

Willa exhaled. "Okay. This isn't the straightforward consultation I expected. I think you're saying if we don't choose to demolish our home, our only other options would be stopgap measures, and none of them looks very good. I guess we'd better schedule another meeting when my husband can be here."

"Right." Pete offered her a business card and a condolent handshake. She already knew her gregarious husband would collect this man as a pal. All their married life she'd watched Iano swap phone numbers with plumbers and oil changers, the born Facebook friender, long before Facebook.

"We'll call you about the next step after I break the bad news. But I'll warn you, my husband is also going to give you a bunch of reasons why we can't tear down the house. And they're not all the same as mine. Between us we can filibuster you."

Mr. Petrofaccio nodded. "All due respect? I hear that kind of thing all the time. It does not ever get the house fixed."

✄

Willa spent a restless hour walking around the empty third floor trying to choose a room for her office. After a month in the house she'd gotten things decently organized downstairs but had made no inroads on the top story except for the room she'd nominated as an attic. Alongside the antique crib she'd stashed the usual junk, holiday decorations, underemployed sports equipment, plus boxes of the kids' keepsakes stretching from preschool finger paintings to Tig's wacked-out science fair posters and Zeke's high school yearbooks signed by all the girls who'd found him 2 cute 2 b 4gotten.

Willa now recalled the contractor's reason for stepping behind the stuff: To inspect ruptured ductwork? Christ. It sounded like an aneurism. What shook her was his cheerful demeanor as he delivered the awful prognosis. Exactly like her mother's last oncologist.

To steer out of a tailspin she staked her claim on the room that looked down on the automotive neighbors. A view to avoid, some might say, but the leafy afternoon light through the giant beech was gorgeous. And the hardwood floor was in pretty good shape except for the scarred, grayish path that ran the circuit of the four connected third-floor rooms. She remembered Zeke and Tig and one of their now-dead dogs chasing each other through a circular floor plan like this in one of their homes. Which one? Boulder, she thought, recalling mountains out the kitchen window. Hills to which she'd craved to flee, stuck at home with two preschoolers while Iano laboriously blew his first shot at tenure.

These top-floor rooms heated up like a furnace. All the windows in the house reached from floor to ceiling, and most so far had proved unopenable. She leveled a couple of kicks at a frame before giving up, then sat on the floor and unpacked a box of her books into categorical piles. Then angrily repacked them. Nesting was ludicrous, given the doomed state of the nest. She closed her eyes and leaned back against the wall, feeling the rhythmic thrum of Nick's oxygen compressor on the first floor. Lest she ever relax into solitude, the miasma of her father-in-law and his life support suffused the household. She wished Iano were home. Classes didn't begin for several weeks but already he had pressing duties galore at his new office.

The word *office* plucked a pang of nostalgia in her chest. Given her age and profession—midfifties, journalist—she might never again have a working life with colleagues, office gossip, and a regular incentive to get out of sweatpants. The remainder of her productive life revoked overnight felt like an amputation. In her last years at the magazine she was telecommuting more than not, but still the regular drives to the main office on the outskirts of DC had consumed so much life force she'd started envying her friends who were going freelance. Of this envy Willa was cured in no time flat. Now she understood an office had made her official. Her whole career was thrown into doubt retroactively. Did a professional wake up one day with no profession? For sanity's sake she needed to send out some freelance proposals, and step one was to claim a room of her own. Now even that simple project was tainted with calamity.

She lay on the floor and stared at the concentric brown stains on the ceiling. Iano had proposed they paint over the stain and forget it, because he was Iano. Willa had felt that if timbers up there were leaking their dark fluids, the trouble must run deep enough to warrant calling a contractor. Some tin would need patching, maybe they'd find rot in the roof beams. But the whole house a *shambles*?

The shock settled on Willa as a personal failure. As if she'd invited the disaster by failing to see it coming.

She forced herself up and went downstairs, rousing Dixie from her nap on the front hall rug, clipping on her leash and urging her out the door for a walk. Dixie, with the help of expensive doggie Prozac, had conquered a lifelong terror of car travel and coped with the move from Virginia, but now wanted to spend her remaining days sleeping off the dismay. Willa saw the merits of that program.

"Easy does it," she coached, wondering what Dixie's old eyes were making of these Vineland sidewalks that were broken everywhere, heaved up by the bunions of giant old trees. Every street offered a similar view of oak and maple trunks lined up like columns of the Parthenon. The contractor's utopia story made sense insofar as these trees suggested some thorough city planning over a century ago. She passed in front of the neighbor's house with its generous corner lot fully planted in autos, then turned south on Sixth and made tedious progress as Dixie inspected every tree trunk. The dog was finicky about emptying her bladder but eager to sniff out the local news, seeming to think it differed from yesterday's. Like the elderly Vinelanders Willa saw in diner booths poring over the town's weekly, as if something might have happened here since the last issue.

She crossed Landis Avenue, a bizarrely supersize main street, the width of a four-lane freeway at least. Iano had posed various entertaining theories, but the truth turned out to be mundane: Land Baron Landis had laid out a namesake street to match his ego. He might as well have paved the place in gold. He should see his dying little burg now, with its main drag so deserted Willa felt safe taking out her phone to check the time as she and her legally blind dog casually jaywalked.

She wanted to call Iano with the new installment of their family disaster so he could share her sensation of drowning. But he would be on his way home by now, and Iano was a highly distractible driver. Really it was her mother she'd wanted to call right after the bad news, or in the middle of it, while Mr. Petrofaccio was blowing his nose. First thing in the morning, last thing at night, whenever a fight with Tig left her in pieces, it had been her mother who put Willa back together. When someone mattered like that, you didn't lose her at death. You lost her as you kept living.

Willa and Dixie passed a pawn shop, the welfare office, a Thai restaurant, and the Number One Chinese Market before heading south again. After five leafy residential blocks, at the corner of Eighth and Quince, Dixie finally elected to pee on the foot of a maple. Most of the houses on this block dated from about the same Victorian era, variously run-down, two for sale. And sure enough, she spotted two garage-like buildings in the backyards, identical in design, disguised by years of divergent use: one sheltered a Honda sedan; the other was an epic man cave covered with old license plates. She pressed her brain for a second to recall the word, then got it: *stip*. Stipulation houses. Quickie predecessors of the more carefully constructed mansions that were now coming due for collapse.

Dixie waddled homeward and Willa followed, feeling the word *shambles* in her sternum. How could two hardworking people do everything right in life and arrive in their fifties essentially destitute? She felt angry at Iano for some infraction that wouldn't hold up to scrutiny, she knew. His serial failures at job security? Not his fault. Plenty of academics spent their careers chasing tenure from city to town. They were a new class of educated nomads, raising kids with no real answer to the question of where they'd grown up. In provisional homes one after another, with parents who worked ridiculous hours, that's where. Doing homework in a hallway outside a faculty meeting. Playing tag with the offspring of physicists and art historians on some dean's lawn while the adults swigged cheap Chablis and exchanged companionable gripes about their department heads. Now, without complaint, Iano had taken a teaching position that was an insult to someone with his credentials. As the family's sole surviving breadwinner, he should get a pass on the charge of being unfit to take a tough phone call while driving.

It never mattered before. Having a mother to shore up Willa had always left Iano free to be the fun, sexy one who didn't worry even about death or taxes, who brought her flowers picked from other peoples' yards, who once threw her pain-inflicting shoes out the car window on the way to a formal reception at the provost's. She couldn't expect him to be a new kind of person now. She was the crisis handler, he was the evader. Marriages tended to harden like arteries, and she and Iano were more than thirty years into this one. This evening he would come in the door like a blast of warm weather, give her a kiss in the kitchen before changing out of his office clothes, and they'd have no chance to talk before dinner.

So she would drop this bomb on everybody at once. They were all adults, entitled to share her concern about a house falling down on them. Old Nick with his oxygen tank and rabid contempt for the welfare state would be especially vulnerable to the challenges of homelessness. On the other hand, Tig might light a bonfire and dance in the yard as the bricks rained down. Willa had tried and failed to track her daughter's moral path, but collapse of some permanent structure always seemed to be part of the territory.

⋇

Willa's evening forecast evaporated as she was putting the spaghetti water on to boil. Iano had kissed her and disappeared into the bedroom, as predicted. But now he walked back into the kitchen looking stricken, carrying her phone. Answering her calls and texts was a habit she kept meaning to discuss, but this wasn't the time. He held the thing as if it were scorching him.

She recoiled. "What? Is it Zeke?"

He nodded, unreadably.

"Is he hurt? God, Iano. What?"

Iano set the phone on the counter and Willa picked it up, shaking. "Hello?"

"Mom, it's me."

"Oh Jesus, Zeke, you're okay. Is the baby okay?"

Zeke was sobbing. Choked. A level of desperation she couldn't associate with her levelheaded son. She waited without realizing she was holding her breath.

"The baby's fine," he said finally. "It's Helene."

"Oh no. Some problem from the C-section? It happens, honey. Did she have to go back to the hospital?"

Iano was looking at her with mournful eyes, shaking his head. His face behind the dark, trimmed beard looked scarily pale, and his foreknowledge was disorienting. She turned her back on him and listened to her son's silence, the gathering of his will.

"Mom, Helene's dead. She died."

"Jesus! How?"

The beat of his silence lasted long enough for Willa to wonder if she'd been rude to ask. Her mind battered itself like a trapped bird.

"She took pills," he finally said. "She killed herself."

"You had *pills* around? With a baby in the house?"

"He's not up to childproof caps, Mom."

The scolding sobered Willa, put them on solid ground. "Have you called 911?"

"Of course."

"I'm sorry, I'm just . . . I'm in shock. When did this happen?"

"What time is it now? I got home around a quarter to six. She's still here."

"*Who* is?"

"Mom, *Helene*. She died in the bedroom. There's a thing in her mouth. Ventilator. They tried to revive her even though it was hopeless I guess. They said they have to leave that thing in her until the coroner's report. It's kind of freaking me out, it pulls her face all out of shape and looks so painful. I guess that's a stupid thing to worry about."

"So the EMTs came. Are they still there? What happens now?"

"They left. They had another call that was, you know. Urgent. Now the coroner comes and then the mortuary, to take the body. The EMT gave me numbers to call."

"Oh, honey. Are you alone there in the apartment?"

"I'm with Aldus."

God, she thought. Aldus. A few weeks in the world, now this.

"I'm sitting on the couch," Zeke said, seeming now to want to produce words. "He's lying beside me, asleep. I guess it wore him out, waiting so long for . . . He was so hungry. And scared, I think. Jesus. How can he not ever know his mother? What does that do to a person?"

"I guess we take this an hour at a time, and right now you shouldn't be alone. As soon as we're off the phone, call somebody. I don't mean the coroner, I want you to have a friend there. Gosh, Helene's poor parents. How long will it take them to get to Boston?"

The sound he made startled her, an animal moan. The impossible task of calling them had not yet occurred to him.

"Do you want me to talk to them?"

"You've never met them. How would that feel, this, coming from a stranger?"

"Okay, but please get somebody there to be with you. You'll have to decide a lot of things. When Mama died I was shocked at all the practical stuff that has to happen immediately. Do you have any idea about . . . what she would want?"

She listened to Zeke's breathing as it caught in a sob, tried and caught again, like a halting engine. "We didn't talk about that, Mom," he managed. "When the subject of death came up, it was me telling her not to do it."

"What do you mean?" She turned around but Iano was gone. She stepped to the doorway and looked into the dining room. Tig was playing backgammon with Nick so he wouldn't throw a tantrum while he waited for dinner. They made an impossible pair facing off across the table: pixie Tig with her springy dreadlocks, hulking Nick with the oxygen tubes pressing his jowls in a permanent grimace.

"This morning she seemed, just, normal," Zeke was saying. "She took the baby for his checkup yesterday and was relieved he's, you know. Fine. Gaining weight. Today she was going to take him out in the stroller. We joked about whether she needed an owner's manual to drive it."

Willa was amazed at his coherence. People handled emergencies in many ways—she'd covered enough crime scenes to know—but they fell back on the habit of self. This reasonable, desperately sad man on the phone was the bare wood of her son beneath the bark. Willa saw her pasta water was boiling over. She clicked off the burner. "You said when death came up, it was you telling her not to do it. What does that mean, Zeke?"

"I didn't even kiss her goodbye, Mom. I mean, maybe I did, without knowing it. I can't even remember. That's so sad."

"Are you telling me she had threatened suicide?"

"She should never have gone off the antidepressants. I shouldn't have let her. Nobody should have asked her to do that."

"Don't blame yourself. The drugs were not your call. There must have been risks to the baby. What was she taking?"

"Paroxetine was the one they said she really needed to get away from. They tried her on Sarafem, I think, I don't remember exactly. They okayed some things after the first trimester but nothing ever worked, once she'd gone cold turkey. She was, like, paralyzed with fear about doing the wrong thing. They have black box warnings on those drugs, Mom. How could she look in the mirror, pregnant, and take a medicine like that? A black box is like 'Smoking gives you cancer,' that extreme level of warning."

Willa felt the weight of Helene transgressions she should have forgiven. The pregnancy whining, the lethargy. "I'm sorry. This must have been so hard for you."

"It was harder for her. Obviously."

"I'm sure you didn't tell her to stop taking her antidepressants."

"Maybe I expected too much from her. I do that, Mom, I feel like when things seem easy to me, they should be easy for other people. Maybe she felt guilty."

"I'm sure her doctors advised her. Knowing Helene, she was well informed."

"But what kind of choice did she have? You can't imagine what she's been through. Every day of the pregnancy was hell. She was obsessed with the idea that something was wrong, the baby was dead, or deformed. She memorized the possible side effects of SSRIs in pregnancy. Anencephaly, which is when the baby is born with no brain. Omphalocele, where the intestines protrude through a hole in the abdomen. The whole thing got to be like this monster. She just didn't want it."

"What are you saying? Of course she wanted the baby." Willa had assumed *he* hadn't wanted it. Zeke, who at age one put his toys away, the improbable straight-arrow child sprung from the mess of his itinerant parents' lives, would not gladly interrupt the order of his life's events with the chaos of an unplanned baby. Willa didn't even believe he'd neglected birth control. Boys will be boys, she'd heard, but she had only the one, and Zeke did the right thing every time. She and Iano had resisted lobbying for an abortion, but they saw this pregnancy as a duty imposed on their son, if not an ambush. Privately they'd worn out the tread on various speculations.

None of their scenarios held a role for a Helene who *just didn't want the baby*.

She tried to picture Zeke in his apartment. "Oh, God. Did you . . . find her?"

Tig appeared in the doorway, round eyed, looking painfully small in her baggy clothes, the corona of hair standing up around her head in a caricature of shock. She must have overheard some of this and was reading the rest in Willa's face.

Willa pointed at the package of pasta and jar of sauce and raised her eyebrows in a plea. With this daughter no wish was easily granted. Willa expected resistance as she stepped away from the stove, but Tig slid into the gap and began making dinner.

"Yeah, I did," Zeke said. "I got home from work and the baby was crying so hard he was choking. It freaked me out. I don't know how long he'd been . . . I changed his diaper, warmed up a bottle, fed him. I thought she was asleep. She's been sleeping so much, all these months. So I spent maybe an hour in the house like that, letting her sleep. *Jesus*, Mom. What if I'd gone in the bedroom sooner? What if I could have saved her?"

"The baby had been crying awhile when you got home, so she was gone already. Don't do that to yourself. Please, honey. You took care of your son."

The weight of these words hit Willa as she said them, a punch to the gut that must have produced a sound because Tig turned around, alarmed. It took effort for Willa to stay on her feet instead of sinking to the floor and pulling her knees to her chest as she cradled Zeke's voice in her ear. Her dutiful, promising son would be taking care of a child now, every day, marooned in the loneliness of single parenthood. Anger at the dead Helene rose like acid in her throat. So useless.

Tig stood watching her with the air of a fairy godmother, the wooden spoon tilting up from her fingers like a wand. Behind her the pot boiled. Willa closed her eyes and made herself speak calmly into the phone. "I can get there by morning."

※

Sitting in a grand Boston church trying to quiet a howling infant, wearing a designer suit that belonged to the girl in the coffin: even Willa's florid imagination hadn't seen this coming. The tight cut of the jacket constricted her movements. Mr. Armani wouldn't have had baby dandling in mind, not that any of this was his fault. Willa had thrown jeans into a duffel and headed out to rescue her son without giving a moment's thought to funeral wear. That was four, maybe five days earlier; she'd lost track. Aldus had made no advances on sorting out night versus day, and she was operating on less sleep than she'd thought humanly possible. Getting dressed for the funeral was a task she undertook about thirty minutes before the event, and it sent her with some urgency into Helene's closet. She found everything on wooden hangers, organized by color, and within that orderly place she glimpsed the bond between the dead girl and her son. But the stunner was Helene's expensive taste. Checking labels quickly for size, Willa hyperventilated: Fendi, Versace, Ralph Lauren. A couple of suits were in her ballpark, thank goodness. Helene must have nudged up a size before going into the chic maternity business wear.

Willa was so relieved to score something better than a T-shirt for the service, she hadn't thought ahead to a chapel packed with Zeke and Helene's friends. Now it dawned on her they might recognize this navy silk suit, last seen at some promotion party. Making her the creepy mother-in-law who didn't even wait till Helene was in the grave to poach on her couture. She could see awfulness in the situation but felt it at a distance, walled off by exhaustion. Anyway, the suit was probably camouflaged by the pinstripes of spit-up trailing down the lapels.

The baby's howl caught in a series of gasps and went quiet, providing a moment of funereal balm before he shattered it again. His wail rose and fell like a siren above the muted organ music. For all Helene's worries about pharmacological harm, she'd borne a son with a dandy set of pipes. And yet he felt insubstantial in Willa's arms, pink as a baby mouse. Willa hadn't consoled a newborn for decades and felt close to tears herself. Catching Zeke's eye, she nodded toward the aisle, then got up and made her awkward way out, squeezing between the wooden pew back and people's knees. Maybe it was sleep-deprived paranoia, but she felt disapproval in the stares. Or at least no gratitude for the gift of Helene's DNA, right there in their midst. The well-dressed assembly struck her as a judgmental tribe, which she chalked up to Helene's influence. Zeke's friends had always been sweet, unpretentious boys who divided things fairly and let the terrible athletes play on their teams anyway. Admittedly, she was recalling in that moment his Cub Scout days. She might not really know who Zeke had become in Boston, first as a student at Harvard Business and now striving as a young professional among some of the most famously competitive assholes on the planet.

She paced at the back of the chapel eyeing the exits, wondering whether they should seek asylum in some basement fellowship hall or head out to the street. It was raining. Funeral guests kept turning around to verify that this child was still the source of all that noise. Willa stared back, brewing some umbrage. Wouldn't it matter someday that the boy had attended his mother's funeral? Producing this perfect child had been Helene's final accomplishment and he was entitled to be there, as the only blood relative in the house. Other than Helene's parents, who'd barely arrived from London in time for the service. Aldus was the name of Helene's father, Willa had learned, but she wasn't sure that justified keeping it in circulation. She perused the front row trying to recognize

Helene's carefully tinted mother from the back. Poor woman, to have lost a daughter.

She shifted Aldus from one shoulder to the other and felt muted dismay at the amount of milk he'd brought up on the jacket. This might qualify as the worst-ever use of an Armani suit. But she had no better plans, beyond a Goodwill drop box. Maybe an email blast inviting Helene's stick-thin, judgmental friends to drop by and pick up a souvenir. Either way it felt painful to give away a fortune in designer clothing, probably the couple's largest material asset, when Zeke was taking on serious debt for this funeral.

The officiating minister, a round-faced woman in owlish glasses, was crooning her way through a one-size-fits-all prayer. It was pretty obvious this minister hadn't known Helene. Willa wondered whether Zeke had even told her it was a suicide. The Anglican church was Zeke's best guess at what Helene's parents would want, though they hadn't been present to organize or pay for any of it. He'd had to lay out credit cards in those first dizzying hours, and the cost of having Helene embalmed was mortifying. Willa drew no pleasure from the pun. The parents' one expressed wish had been to see their daughter, for closure, so he'd shouldered the cost of an open casket.

Willa had barely spoken with them, mostly to apologize for Iano's absence, emphasizing the brand-new job and disabled father, downplaying their inability to afford a quick fly-in. At a glance she read these parents as distant, and not just geographically. Helene had spent her childhood in boarding schools. They were British, so that arrangement was probably more normal than it seemed to Willa. She knew she would have to guard against stereotyping, and try not to read Helene's whole life backward as a reel of emotional injuries spooling toward suicide. Brain chemistry, Zeke kept saying, and Willa understood. At the end of her run at the magazine she'd been the science and health editor; she had a professional

grasp of disease. Helene had been a whole person like anyone else—
the woman with whom Zeke had fallen in love—except when her
brain salts began to precipitate their potent horrors. There but for
the grace of serotonin go the rest of us.

Aldus finally crash-landed into sleep and went still in her arms,
hiccuping but otherwise relaxed. Willa stroked his crazy hair. He
had more than an infant's normal share, jet black like Helene's,
standing up from his head as if in horror at this life he'd landed
in. His translucent eyelids and pursed lips aroused protectiveness
and amplified Willa's sorrow for her tall, handsome, devastated
son, who was now walking toward the pulpit to read the eulogy.
She'd warned against this, telling him it would be hard to hold
it together in front of a crowd, harder than any presentation he'd
ever given. And that was before Zeke told her what he planned to
read: the suicide note. Willa had lost it then, there had been some
yelling for which she now felt terrible. They were exhausted. When
he'd handed it over and made Willa read it, she couldn't stop the
tears.

Zeke was right, of course. The poor girl must have labored for
months over this articulate essay, a final accounting of her gratitude for Zeke's love, their three years together, and her hopes for
their child. For eulogy purposes they'd had only to edit out the
fatal caveat: Helene's belief that her best gift to her partner and son
was the removal of her poisonous self from their lives.

⋊⋉

Willa had stopped wondering if things could get worse, and now
sat in her son's bedroom going through his girlfriend's nightstand, throwing out little bottles labeled "O Play" and "Love
Lube." She felt abstractly relieved that they'd enjoyed a sex life despite everything—pregnancy, depression, drugs with well-known
damping effects on libido. This task felt as surreal as everything

else she'd done since speeding up I-95 to Boston, with sleeping in the bed of the freshly deceased as a starting point. At whatever early-morning hour she'd arrived, Zeke had given Willa the bed and slept on the couch by the bassinet. With daylight gaining traction around her she'd lain awake on the very spot where Helene had ended her life, until she finally had to get up and creep to the living room like some Victorian-novel ghost, staring at the child in the bassinet and the wrecked young father on the sofa. She longed to slip with them into unconsciousness. Anything to avoid going back to that haunted bedroom. She couldn't ask which side of the bed had been Helene's but hadn't stopped wondering, either, until just now when she finished boxing up the clothes and started on the nightstands.

Postfuneral, postburial, post- whatever they called the gathering her friends had gamely organized at Helene's law firm, the suffocating truth was descending: many lives were over. Zeke and his child would persist on some utterly unplanned path, starting with eviction from this apartment Zeke couldn't afford on his own. The lease was in Helene's name, so he could walk away without legal recourse. Willa was dubious: in her experience, landlords always won. But Zeke explained it was one advantage of their being unmarried. For another, Helene's serious credit card debt would not become his problem. Also, her Mercedes and its staggering monthly payments zipped right back to the dealer.

Their marital status hadn't initially mattered to Iano and Willa, tradition-agnostic baby boomers that they were. Cohabitation was normal. But once the pregnancy seemed here to stay, Iano thought his chivalrous son would insist on marrying the mother of his child. Iano was wrong: these kids found marriage uninteresting in legal or sentimental terms. Helene was an attorney, Zeke explained, who didn't need a boilerplate contract written by the state of Massachusetts to govern her personal life. Chivalry wasn't dead, it's just that men didn't own all the horses anymore, and women of Helene's ilk didn't need that kind of rescue. Here in Zeke's private sphere, Willa was getting the picture.

She felt at a loss to console him as he waded through his swamp of grief, hour by hour, while she watched from the outside. But she wouldn't be anywhere else, and couldn't remember the last time they'd spent more than an hour together, just the two of them. On family visits the sibling bickering and Iano's ebullience used up all the oxygen. These quiet days in his apartment were different. Willa could not have borne the admission that she preferred her son to her daughter, but there was no question which one she'd found easier to love. Easily born, easily reared, he'd grown into a temperament so similar to hers, Willa lost track of the boundaries between them. People remarked on his resemblance to his father, and superficially it was true: he had the height and shoulders, the trustworthy wide-set eyes. "Molded in the image of his papa," the Greek relatives gushed each time they saw Zeke, and Willa wouldn't argue—she loved the mold. The shape of her husband in a doorway could still bump her heart. But Zeke's ash-blond coloring was all Willa's, and so was everything inside: a handsome Greek mold filled with the pale Saxon stuff of a duty-bound maternal line.

Tig was the opposite, small and fine boned like Willa, the same high eyebrows and pointed chin, but with dark eyes peering out from an interior that boiled with her father's energy. They'd called her "Antsy" from infancy because Antigone fit better on a birth certificate than on an actual child—no surprise to Willa. The nickname was exactly right; the girl had ants in her pants. In high school she'd fought her way back to Antigone but her friends collapsed it to Tigger, then just Tig. No one called her Antigone now except occasionally Iano, the responsible party, still trying to make good on it.

Willa missed Iano badly but hadn't called home since the day of the funeral. There was too much to tell and Iano seemed almost willfully resistant to getting it. He was looking for some Greek-tragic vindication, still airing his thoughts about the pregnancy having been a bad idea, while here was Aldus installed in the living room, bassinet and changing table flanking the TV. Well beyond the idea stage.

She finished the nightstand and moved on without pause. The bathroom held a confounding array of skin-rejuvenating products for a beautiful girl in her twenties. Willa dumped it all into trash bags after wondering briefly if it would be awful to keep some of the expensive night creams. She tried not to read prescription bottles as she tossed those as well. Zeke was in the second bedroom where Helene had set up her study, pending the need for a nursery. It was still a study, despite the accomplished birth. Helene had done nothing to implement a transition, no pastel colors or mobiles, these happy things mothers do to lure babies into the world. In an apartment suffused with mourning, Willa found this non-nursery the most unbearable place, but only because she knew about normal motherhood. It's nearly always women who lead men into babyland, urging them to get serious about names and nursery themes. Zeke couldn't know what he'd missed.

He was in there now pulling together files to return to Helene's employer, which at least seemed less personal than razors and hairbrushes. Willa kept asking him not to take on any task that felt too hard, but really, what part of this was not too hard? He retained the instincts of the charming young man he was, moving quickly to take heavy objects from Willa, opening the car door for Helene's mother. But sleepwalking through all of it. When the baby cried, Zeke seemed relieved to wade out of the Helene morass and go meet simpler demands. The only happiness in this apartment came from direct contact with infant skin, so Willa made herself stand back and let Zeke do most of the feeding and changing. She watched her son becoming a father, cradling a tiny life in his large hands, searching the rosebud face at close range, but she couldn't guess whether he was falling in love, thunderstruck, as she'd been by her firstborn. The workings of love might be damaged, in a beginning overshadowed by despair. Zeke might end up blaming the child for his loss. The pregnancy had killed Helene; this was a fact. Willa spent hours trying not to speak of these things. It was hard enough to bring up necessary subjects such as where Zeke was going to live.

She took a break between bathroom drawers and stood in the doorway watching him move file boxes into the hall, lining them up like boxcars. He knelt beside a box of books and tucked its four cardboard flaps into one another.

"I can take care of Aldus this afternoon if you want to go look at apartments."

He glanced up with an expression that confused her. Fear, she would have said.

"Or I could go," she added quickly. "I don't know quite what you want, what part of town you can afford. But if you head me in the right direction I can do some recon."

He sat on the floor and exhaled, resting his forearms on his knees. "I can't afford an apartment, Mom. Not in any part of Boston. I was thinking I might move in with Michael and Sharon, but they just texted me. I guess a baby is kind of a game changer."

"Moving in with your *friends?*" Willa was dumbfounded. He wasn't some gap-year kid who could set up life on a buddy's couch. He was a father.

"They didn't exactly say it's because of Aldus. But I'm sure his performance at the funeral was a reality check. I knew it was a lot to ask."

Willa took a moment to process this, including her part in it, her failure to keep Aldus quiet. Were these people previously unaware

that babies cry? "Your roommate from grad school?" she asked carefully. "You were thinking of living with him again?"

"Right, the Michael I'm planning the start-up with. Of Zeke,
Mike, and Jake. Michael's married now, I told you that. They
bought a house in Southie so they've got a lot of room. Well, *an*
extra room. We've been thinking we could operate the business out
of that space until we can take on the overhead of an office."

"So you asked if he would take on the overhead of you and
Aldus."

Zeke looked miserable. Any rejection hurts, but this was beyond the pale. She hated this smug couple hoarding their childless
serenity. Also Helene, and her shortsighted doctors, and everyone
else involved in the outrageous reversal of fortune that had left her
son begging his friends for shelter. "You two need your own place,"
she said calmly. "You're a family now. We'll find something you can
afford."

"Mom, we won't. I have no income."

"You're working full time."

"Technically it's an internship."

"But you're doing so much. You're probably working harder and
getting more commissions than anybody in that office."

"Yeah, but it's still an internship. Usually if you turn out to be
golden, they'll put you on salary after six months or so."

"That sounds like peonage. You're already golden. They should
pay you *something*. A stipend for an internship isn't unheard of."

"They offered that, but it wasn't worth it. The minute I go on
payroll I have to start paying back my student loans. We just can't
afford that right now. Helene and I decided we'd be better off just
on her income, for now."

"All right, but your situation has changed. Couldn't you rene-
gotiate?"

"I still have the student loans."

Willa hadn't pressed for details on his debt and dreaded doing so now. Iano had cosigned when he was a minor, but it was a point of pride with Zeke that he'd handled his own finances since his first year at Stanford. She nodded slowly. "How much?"

He shrugged. "Over a hundred. Around a hundred and ten thousand."

"Jesus, Zeke. I didn't know it was like that. You worked all the way through."

"Yeah, for minimum wage. My income barely covered my books."

Willa couldn't imagine starting adulthood so indentured. She'd gone to state schools on scholarships. "We should never have let you take that on."

"You didn't want me to. Remember how hard you tried to talk me out of Stanford? But Dad said go for it, and I just . . . I wanted it so bad."

Willa did remember, painfully. The house divided, Achilles heel of their parenting. "I didn't want you *not* to go to Stanford. I just thought maybe in another year you could get a better ride. That you could transfer in, or something."

"I know. I could have taken the deal with Dad's tuition exchange like Tig did, and gone to some dinky hippie school."

"Ivins isn't that dinky, it's a good college. Hippie, I'll grant you. But tuition exchange was the right way to go for Tig. Given her track record on following through. You're different, you finish things. Iano says they never put students in a hole so deep they can't dig out. We didn't worry too much."

He looked at her, his eyes the indefinite blue of ocean. When she was young, Willa had told her mother everything: the amount of her first paycheck, the day of her first missed period. Was it normal now for parents to operate in the dark? She never knew what was fair to ask. Clearly, Zeke was shamed by his financial straits.

"Obviously, we should have worried."

He shrugged. "That's the fix I'm in. If they salaried me right now at entry level at Sanderson, I'd end up in the negative numbers."

"I see." She leaned on the door frame feeling physical loss as her assumptions fell through the floor. He'd done everything by the book. They all had. Willa and Iano had raised two children, the successful one and the complicated one. That was their story, for as long as she could remember. For how many years had it been untrue?

"Was there . . . Did Helene have a pension through her employer?"

"I wouldn't be entitled to it. We're not married."

"Oh, right. Not her social security either. The baby might be due some benefits."

Zeke seemed startled by the notion of his son as a legal person. Willa thought survivor benefits were probably a long shot; Helene was a resident alien, fresh out of law school. She might not have been around quite long enough to get in the game. "I'm sorry to be thinking about practical things right now, honey, but . . ."

"Yeah. I'm up shit creek. With a baby on board."

"I'm sorry. What about life insurance? You'd be her beneficiary, married or not."

His look darkened. "Suicide, Mom. Nobody pays you to do that."

"Oh. I guess I knew that. But isn't that discrimination? It seems so . . ."

"Punitive?"

"I was going to say ignorant. Helene died of depression. A medical condition caused by pregnancy and an OB-GYN who cared more about the baby than the mother."

"You could argue that, but I'm sure the insurance company has a nice team of lawyers to back them up."

Willa was floored. "What are you going to do?"

He looked away from her, and in that turn of his head she saw every defeat in his life: the barely missed first place at all-state track; that blond girl who reneged on their prom date. The AP exam he bombed because he had a vomiting flu. His defeats were so rare she could just about count them, or at least the ones she knew about. He took them hard, for lack of practice. Zeke was very good at everything except disappointment.

"Do you have day care lined up, at least? I assume she was going back to work."

Zeke gave Willa a strange pleading look she couldn't understand. Then he stood and walked down the hallway into the kitchen. She closed up another one of the boxes, counted to ten because she could think of absolutely nothing else to do, and then followed him. He was staring into the open refrigerator.

"I know this is hard to talk about. I can stay here awhile to help. I'll go with you to the pediatrician's appointment next week. But at some point we have to make a plan."

"I'm not asking you to do this for me, Mom."

"I know. Nevertheless."

He slammed the refrigerator. "I must have said that a hundred times. To Helene. 'We have to make a plan.' I guess I sounded like you do now. So this is how *she* felt."

"It wasn't an outlandish request to have made. When one is having a baby."

"I suggested we go look at places. Day cares. I asked her to look into maternity leave if that's what she wanted to do. But she had to want *something*."

Willa recognized the same anger she'd been harboring for days, toward Helene. They would have to take turns keeping the lid on that. The child would need to love his mother, and it was all on them, forever. "She wasn't thinking right. We know that now."

"What we know now is that she was planning this all along."

"That can't be. She loved you. Stop blaming yourself, you did everything right."

"You keep saying that, Mom. Sometimes doing everything right gets you a big fucking nothing! Did that ever occur to you?"

His raised voice caused her to lower her own. "I keep saying it because it's true. She loved you, Zeke. You were good to her. She wouldn't have plotted something like this. I mean yes, her death I guess, but not the fallout. She didn't do it to wreck your life."

"Nevertheless," he said.

The repetition of Willa's word could have been Zeke mocking her, but probably not. The two of them often opened their mouths and spoke the same words, even at the same moment. "Here's a proposal," she said. "You could come live with us for a while so we can help out. Just until you get things figured out."

Zeke made a face. "In Jersey."

"I know, you're thinking it's some gigantic tacky suburb of Manhattan. I thought that too, I was ready to—" She stopped herself from saying "kill myself," two words now excised from the family vocabulary. "I couldn't stand the thought, when the job for Dad came up at Chancel. But Vineland isn't what I expected. It's more like Virginia, really."

"And what is that like, Mom?"

"We lived there almost eight years, the longest we've been anyplace since you were born. How can you not know?"

"Because, let me think, I was in college in California and grad school in Boston?"

"But you were home for summers, a couple of them. One, I guess. And holidays. You were there almost every Christmas that I recall."

"Yes, Virginia, there is a Santa Claus. And Christmas trees, I certainly remember those. Virginia has blue ridges. It's for lovers!"

She tried to smile. "You're saying your family lived in Virginia and all you got was this lousy bumper sticker?"

"No. I'm saying it's not my frame of reference. I'm an adult, and my life experience is separate from yours."

Willa understood there was no real point to this argument except that she was standing here, and his beloved was not. He looked so tired. The sun through the window washed his face in an unmerciful light that rendered him old. Or worn, like old clothes. Not young enough to be her son.

A howl from the bassinet startled them both. The baby came to wakefulness with alarm, every time. Light, life, hunger, it all must feel like violation in the beginning. Willa let her son go to the baby. Opened a kitchen cabinet to start dinner or make a bottle or pack up dishes, she really had no idea. She watched Zeke pick up the tiny body with its dangling bowed legs and big saggy diaper. A new parent should be joyful. Not widowed, deserted, bankrupt, bereft of every comfort he'd carefully built for himself. For months to come, waking up would feel as violent for Zeke as for a newborn. Maybe for years.

"Shhhh, take it easy, buddy," he crooned as he laid his child on the changing table and nervously kept one palm on the baby's torso as the little limbs jerked and flailed. With his free hand Zeke pulled a diaper from the package, tucked it under his chin, and unfolded it. Willa remembered in her gut how it felt to be the parent of a newborn: the excruciating love and terror of breakage.

"I'm lousy at this, buddy. You have to bear with me. I'm a rank beginner here."

"You're not lousy," Willa said quietly. "We're all beginners."

2

Beginners

The walk from the builder's office to Plum Street spanned four blocks and felt like an Atlantic passage. Thatcher dragged his anchor of bad news across the threshold of his house, closed the door quietly, set his hat on the hall table, and looked into the parlor. The drapes were drawn against the heat and Rose stood with her back to the door. Alone, he was relieved to see. Not with her mother on the sofa parsing threads of gossip, both ready to drop their needlework and turn up their eyes with bottomless female expectation.

She was holding herself oddly, very close to the west window. Rose was *peering*. She held the drape aside with one hand and pressed her face into the slim vertical bar of daylight, so absorbed in some furtive observation she must not have heard him come in. He moved quietly across the room to stand behind her and set his hand on her waist, causing her to jump.

"Thatcher! You're home from the builders." She spoke without turning around.

He laid his folder of calculations on the side table so he could set both hands parenthetically on her little center and his chin on the top of her head. Unbustled and unbonneted like this, Rose was a gravitational body that drew his front against her back, his bearded jaw against her tidy zenith. Their perfect fit sent a whiskey thrill through his veins. After six months of marriage he was still in thrall of his wife's physical properties, and wondered whether this made him a lucky man or a doomed one. In the weeks since they'd moved to Vineland he'd settled on lucky. The town was slim on other inebriants.

"What do you see out there?" With his mandible against her skull he had to lift his upper jaw a little when he spoke. He felt married. A thing so unexpected.

She didn't answer. He adjusted his head to her angle of view and looked between the beech and oak saplings that framed the parlor window, into the neighboring territory of Dr. and Mrs. Treat. The doctor of that house had recently vanished, according to Rose, though no foul play was accused. Well, not quite true: rumor had him off to New York under the influence of a glamorous suffragette who was known to be a champion of free love. Thatcher didn't begrudge the doctor his freedom, but did cast an envious look at the Treats' intact roof. Scanning down the gutters, his eyes settled on something or someone in the grass, partially obscured by the yew hedge.

It was Mrs. Treat in a dark blue dress lying facedown on the ground.

"Good Lord. Is she well?"

"Yes," Rose whispered. "Now and again, she moves."

"What is she doing?"

"Counting ants. Or spiders!"

Breathless intrigue. His wife sounded like a schoolgirl inventing scandal against a rival. But Mrs. Treat in her dismal indigo and advanced years was certainly no rival. And the charge might be valid. Thatcher had heard from more reliable sources than Rose that this woman held strange entertainments. He tilted his head for a clearer look through one of the little panes, wondering what architect had dreamed up these hateful windows: multiple interlaced lenses of leaded glass as intricate as the hide of a fish. The house had a thousand of these panes rattling loose in their nettings. When any door slammed, they tinkled like a world of shattered goblets. And in this domestic nest, doors did slam.

It struck him now: the architect would have been Rose's father, in league with a covey of amateurs who'd convinced him of his competence. The builder Thatcher had visited that morning told him what everyone in this tittle-tattle village surely knew already, that the house was built on a dead man's pacts with poker-game comrades who fancied themselves craftsmen. All would know it except Rose and her mother. The news would fall on them cruelly, for in the absence of the man they had only his construction to love. Over Rose's shoulder Thatcher looked down at her neat chest, the dear rise and fall.

As for the woman outside, no movement was detectable. "Love thy neighbor, little rabbit. Mrs. Treat deserves our charity."

"She could be prostrate with grief," Rose speculated. "Over Dr. Treat."

"I think not. Unless the good doctor has seen fit to come back from New York and take up residence with her again."

"That isn't charitable at all! Everyone says Dr. Treat is tedious, but surely she would rather have him at home than no husband at all."

Thatcher grinned. "Couldn't a dull husband be cause for a wife's grieving?"

Rose dropped the drape and turned to face him, a pivot on her own marvelous axis. Smiling. "You are a beast."

"It isn't my fault. You've put me at cross-purposes, expecting me to defend Dr. Treat. You're taking advantage of my position."

"What is your position, Thatcher?"

"Husband, with the duty of taking up for all husbands. Isn't that the rule? As wives must bear the crosses of all other wives?"

Rose appeared to be thinking this over. "Mrs. Treat is a wife," she said finally. "And I won't take up for her. She is a spectacle."

"And not overly concerned with being a wife, as far as I can see. You are acquitted."

Rose tilted her chin up and he bent to kiss her, moved by the simplest physics.

They stepped apart, startled by a commotion in the hallway. That would be Polly. No other creature could make such an abruption of leaving and entering a house: Polly bashing the door shut, mewling to the dogs, tossing something with a clatter onto the hall table. She burst into the parlor, arresting Rose and Thatcher.

"Oh good, you're both here. I have the most awful news to tell you!"

"What is it?" Rose's hand flew to the ribbon tied at her throat, as if it might be holding her together. Thatcher welcomed the reprieve from delivering his own news.

"A runaway barouche! On Landis Avenue. I saw everything."

Polly dropped onto the settee and flung out her legs as if thrown from a horse herself. She was twelve, a decade younger and already several hands taller than her sister, with a surplus of leg, chin, and forehead equal to her temperament. It wouldn't occur to Polly to apologize for any of it. "No one was killed, and that is the miracle according to Mother. It was Pardon Crandall's barouche but he wasn't in it. He'd left it standing and gone to meet someone on the nine-five from Philadelphia. The train whistle set the horses off running and they went straight into a tree in front of the post office."

"That maple?" Thatcher cared for trees, more than for some people if he had to say. He kept a private habit of assigning botanical character to his familiars: Polly was a hollyhock, cheerful, forthright, tallest bloom in the garden. Rose of course was a rose.

"The maple is all right," Polly assured him, "but the crash knocked the rear wheels off the barouche. Both wheels!"

Rose's hand now went to her cheek. "You were with Mother? That must have given her a shock. She adores Mrs. Crandall."

"Mother," Polly announced, "has gone upstairs to take some Dr. Garvin's and pray about the accident."

"Well, it sounds as if the outcome is already decided," Thatcher said. "But a dose of Dr. Garvin's won't hurt."

"But you haven't heard the rest! After the barouche lost its wheels, the horses dragged it all the way down Landis Avenue on just the little front ones. It looked like a Roman chariot race. If only Mr. Crandall had stayed on, he could have been a study for 'The Charioteer.'"

The Charioteer! Thatcher was impressed that Polly had extended her curriculum to the province of naked Greek men. He glanced at Rose, who seemed to have missed it.

Polly untied her straw bonnet, an old flat boater of a kind favored by boys, absent the ribbons, and exasperating to elder sisters. She flung the hat on the settee with a thrilled little shudder that spilled her hair into a dark, careless coil on her shoulders. "The axles or something underneath left a gouge down the street. It made the horriblest scraping sound. You could hear it for miles."

"Well, we didn't," Rose stated, as if that would end the story.

"It must have just happened," Thatcher said. "I was walking on Landis Avenue not more than fifteen minutes ago."

"Yes, it was just this very minute!" Polly looked up at him with round blue eyes, exactly like her sister's and yet entirely different. Searching for truth, not rescue. "Mother couldn't watch, but I saw all of it. The horses crashed into the stand in front of the tobacconist's. And that *still* wasn't the end of the chase."

Thatcher put his hands over his eyes, grinning. "Not the tobacconist's."

"Yes! One of the horses tried to go into Finn's shop! He smashed the window and put glass everywhere. He must have wanted a cigar very desperately."

"After so much excitement, you can understand it," Thatcher said.

"All right, Polly. Go upstairs and see about Mother. And straighten yourself up, please. Look at your shoes."

Polly gave Rose an exhausted look, swiped up her hat by its ribbons, and stood to leave. Thatcher felt his soul touched by light. He hadn't known the pleasure of younger siblings and counted this one as a very good wedding gift, although that was one of several secrets he kept from his wife.

"And your hair will need a brush before you come down to luncheon."

Polly stopped and turned back in the doorway, suddenly bright eyed with more to tell. "I nearly forgot. President Grant is coming."

"What, here?" Rose blinked with pretty surprise.

"Yes. For the dedication, in a few weeks. September I think. When the school building opens. Thatcher, you will get to shake hands with His Majesty the President and sit on the stage and everything. Professor Cutler will try to be in charge, but he'll have to share some of his glory with the new science teacher because Cutler is a humid old windbag and everyone knows it. And you are handsome and mysterious."

"Mysterious," Thatcher repeated.

"Well, because of being new, and no one properly knowing about you yet."

"Oh, well. That is the lowest order of mysterious."

"But the whole town will see you with President Grant! And then we shall be famous." She strode out with the boater swinging in an arc like an o'possum caught by its tail, a sight Thatcher actually knew from his brutish boyhood. One more tale that could not be told in this house, as much as it would have thrilled Polly.

"Get Gracie to help with your hair!" Rose called after her.

"Gracie is busy consoling Mother. I'll ask Mrs. Brindle!" Polly crowed as she tramped up the stairs.

"You will not ask the cook to fix your hair!"

Rose's translucent skin flushed with the unusual effort of raising her voice. The rosy blush and intoxicating fragrance, all the exquisite agreements of Rose in name and spirit, had been the origin of his attraction. Rarely did people wear their floral identities so frankly. Aside from himself: Greenwood, the sapling. Too easily bent.

Rose brushed the skin of her bare arms as if physically shedding her vexation. "Charioteers and horses with cigars! What a creature she is, to enjoy a story like that."

Thatcher, a similar creature, knew to camouflage himself under something resembling forbearance. "Will I have to keep the reins over a dozen Pollies at a time when the school term begins? I'm not sure I'm a man for the task."

"There is only one Polly, dear. In Vineland or anywhere. We would have done better to keep her in Boston until she finished at Mrs. Marberry's. I know you disagree."

He saw Rose glance at his leather folder on the table. "Polly, left behind in Boston? That would have distressed her beyond repair."

"Or in some other school *like* Mrs. Marberry's. They must exist here, despite all the free thinking. Even spiritualists and transcendentalists must sometimes turn out daughters who need that kind of medicine."

Thatcher was only beginning to learn what spiritualists and transcendentalists required. Before meeting Rose he'd scarcely heard of Vineland, and imagined men debating philosophy under clouds of expensive tobacco smoke. He'd applied for the post at the high school because Rose and her mother, Aurelia, longed to return to this place.

"I think Mrs. Marberry is well enough left behind," he said. "Polly had no more use for her than she has for my employer. What did she call him? A humid windbag?"

Rose smiled slightly.

"High marks for poetry and accuracy. Your sister's gifts are comprehensive."

"Mrs. Marberry would have triumphed eventually."

"I couldn't call it a triumph. An active mind should be fed the meat of the world."

"Goodness, Thatcher, the meat of the world. What sort of carnivory is that?"

"Mathematical tables. Botanical names . . ."

"The *vegetables* of the world, then," she corrected patiently.

"I only mean wonderments, of any kind that compel her. Things that are real."

"Do you really see Polly improved by botany? I can only think of the further infliction on her shoes."

"What I see is that she shouldn't be punished with ladies' novels and the correct execution of curtsies. She told me they spent weeks at Mrs. Marberry's memorizing the timetables for replacing organza with crepe in the mourning period for this or that degree relative on the mother's or father's side."

"How soon men would become beasts. You have no family to lose, Thatcher, but have pity on the rest of us, please. Do you see no value in following respectful custom?"

"I do. And I expect it's all written somewhere. In case I should suddenly discover a second-degree relative on my dead mother's side, and then lose him again, I could go to a library and learn my duty in the way of armbands and cravats."

"There is virtue in training one's mind to these matters, even if they are not used."

"Precisely. Let us then apply Polly to the square of the hypotenuse."

"You'll have your chance. In a few years' time."

Thatcher would teach the natural and physical sciences, not mathematics, he might have reminded her, but Rose could hardly be bothered with the difference. She picked up his portfolio and opened it, a broad wingspan of leather in her petal hands. She wouldn't understand the menace in those drawings. And contrary to all he had just insisted, he would give anything to hide it from his household of women.

"What did the builders say?" she asked, laying down the portfolio.

"I'm afraid it's not good." He felt his heart beating at the knife edge of his collar. Rose looked up at him without the slightest change in her weather.

"Can it really cost so much to repair a roof?"

He took her hands in his, rubbing his thumbs over the plump little knuckles, and was struck with the memory of a foetal pig he'd dissected in his first year at university. Despite what he'd already seen in war and the many cadavers afterward in his years as a doctor's assistant, he still had paused at the moment of cutting into that pink curve of flesh. Then and there, in the company of scholars in a laboratory, Thatcher saw himself as a man who would open this piglet to study its organs. Most would want only to sweeten the flesh with cider and see it braised for supper. Every education brings a point of reckoning, and this was his: seeing the world divided in two camps, the investigators and the sweeteners.

But here in hand was Rose, clearly on the side of sweetness, who still had consented to marry him. The divide must sometimes yield. "If it were only the roof, we wouldn't be in for much trouble. But I'm afraid the whole house is at odds with itself."

She laughed. "You sound like poor Mr. Lincoln. Apart from the slavery question, what would divide a house against itself?"

"A mistake of construction. I'm sorry, Rose, I'm afraid it's very serious. They said it will eventually pull itself apart down the middle."

She took her hands quickly from his. "What a terrible thing to say."

"It was a terrible thing to learn, I promise you."

"But it can't be true. My father had every faith in this house." She walked quick steps away from him, pacing the length of the parlor and stopping by the cold hearth. With her back to Thatcher she began rearranging the tiny glass and porcelain dogs on the mantelpiece. This menagerie of china pets had survived being moved twice: once for the precipitous relocation to Boston when her father's death left a widow and two young daughters without means. And now back here, under Thatcher's keeping, to the very marble slab where the glass pups had spent their formative years.

"I hate to upset you, dear. It isn't a judgment against your father."

"Those horrible men! They gave me a headache tramping up and down the stairs."

"They wanted to be thorough. This is not what any of us expected. It isn't the best news for the builders either, if you consider it. I'm impressed with the man's honesty. He admitted we would be wasting our funds if we hired him to repair one crack at a time."

Rose said nothing, devoting herself to her small porcelain friends.

"Darling. It's only a house. Vineland has fine houses on every street, and many are for sale. Or we could build something new to suit us. If the *Weekly* can be believed, Captain Landis is still giving away building lots for the price of a bushel of strawberries."

She turned to face him with every feature sharpened. "Build with what money, Thatcher? If this one can't be sold or salvaged, what do we have?"

Finally the change in her weather was here. Rose's calms were sweetly obdurate, but when they gave way to the storm, it was cruel.

"I have a good situation. We're young. We care for one another. We can find our way to a new home, I'm sure." He hated the pleading tone in his voice. "For all of us, of course. Your mother and Polly as well. Is it so terrible to think of beginning again?"

"How can you even ask? Poor Mother has been thrown from rack to rails in all this. *Boston* was beginning again! You don't know how it was for her, losing Father and having to pick us all up and go there."

"I'm sure it was devastating."

"Yes! At a time when a woman should be settling in for the rest of life with the comfort of friends and grocers and . . . and dressmakers! Forced to grope her way around strange, filthy streets, with Polly hardly more than a baby, dragged into a stranger's home. Look what your new beginnings did for *her*. Polly is wild and uncultured."

"Boston can hardly be called uncivilized, Rose. It's true I didn't see your troubles then. But your aunt was not a stranger. Taking in a sister and nieces in your circumstances was an ordinary kindness."

"We were an imposition. Uncle Fred never let Mother feel welcome entirely, he complained over everything. Even the expense of our mourning clothes."

Could Rose really have grown into womanhood feeling humiliated in her aunt's household? It hadn't been apparent when he met her, with admirers panting after her like hounds. He knew of the embarrassing debts, of course. Rose's father had died suddenly and left them worse than destitute. It wasn't a subject they opened. "You never mentioned it before," he said.

"You never threatened to reduce us to all that again!"

He took a breath, disoriented. He was often overwhelmed by how right Rose seemed, even in a wholly foolish position, when so convinced of her own righteousness.

"I can't think what your father's death has cost you all. Especially Polly, who had so little time with him. But those were separate troubles from this. This house."

"I will never think of this house and my father as separate. We were happy under his roof. And would be happy still, had we never been forced to leave it."

Thatcher met her bitter gaze and had to look away. Something precious he'd possessed when he entered this room was now lost. He turned to the window, pulled aside the curtain, and pretended to look out, though he saw nothing—or worse, a nothing magnified by a hundred prismatic edges on leaded panes. The glaze of daylight blinded him. How could a man tell the truth and be reviled for it? Old wounds of a father's lickings made his ears roar with primordial dread. A wandering boy without shelter.

Rose's temper had stung him before, but the renunciation of Boston was new. He hadn't been glad to leave that city and come here, even if the position was a good one, and fortuitous, given his engagement. Their return was a social triumph for Rose's mother after having been cast out of the Garden. But for Thatcher, Boston was everything: emancipation from rural childhood drudgery, his apprenticeship and education, the world of ideas, his heartiest friendships. All his best days were lived in Boston. Happiest of all were those when he'd courted and married Rose, a woman who would not have given him a glance had her fortunes in Vineland remained intact. A woman now standing on the hearth she wished she had never left. She'd said this. Her contempt for Boston included him. She'd reduced him to a child, and the whole of it appalled him, her part in this and his own. As if he were still a beginner, begging for love and purpose.

His eyes accommodated to the shapes outside, one by one: a passing carriage, the neighbors' good brick house and dark yew hedges, their expansive lot occupying the corner of Sixth and Plum. The two saplings in his own yard that framed their view. Those trees had been planted by Rose's father to honor his daughters, the beech for Rose, the oak for Polly. Not a rose and a hollyhock but trees that now reached for the sky, years after his death. No wonder they worshipped this sentimental man, exactly the type to be lured here by Landis's elysian visions. The tale of two trees was a household favorite, and Thatcher always tolerated the words "planted by Father" without comment. He'd dug many holes in his early life, irrigation ditches, even graves; he knew how it was done and by whom. Rose's father would have stood on the grass in a clean frock coat, his pink hand pointing, directing the labor of others—a platoon of Italian boys probably, like those he'd seen this morning trenching earthworks along the rail line. If it came to pass that Thatcher should shake hands with President Grant, as Polly predicted, he would still be a man who viewed life from the bottom of the ditch, not the top. He had managed to rise a little and Rose to fall, arriving accidentally on a plane that accommodated their marriage. But the weight of their separate histories held the plane in uneasy balance.

Beyond the trees and the carriage house he could now make out the slim, recumbent shape of Mrs. Treat, still prone, her chin resting on her hands. She seemed to be watching some minuscule state of affairs playing out in the grass, as fully absorbed in that as Rose was now with her damned china dogs. Thatcher wondered if Dr. Treat had fled to New York in baffled isolation, shut out from his wife's fascinations.

And as before, Thatcher's loyalties slid straight away from Dr. Treat toward his enigmatic other half. Here was mystery of the highest order: Mrs. Treat peering into the grass. Thatcher wanted to know what was holding her at attention on a hot August day. This woman belonged to his flank of humanity, those who would pick up the scalpel and cut open the pig. Investigators.

3

⌒⌒

Investigators

The view from Willa's window turned out to be a maddening distraction. The article she was trying to write on health insurance exchanges was interesting in principle, and if she could submit and invoice the thing this week she would feel less like a deadbeat in the garret. But her concentration was kaput, constricted to death between a screaming baby downstairs and the steady pounding overhead.

She'd been away in Boston only two weeks. How was that long enough for a hostile takeover at home? Iano and his new friend Pete Petrofaccio had cooked up a scheme of stopgap repairs to preserve what was left of their home's integrity. Replacing the whole roof was pointless given the state of things, and wildly beyond their means, so they'd settled on a banged-together tin patch to close the widening rift.

Banged-together plans were Iano's forte. The surprise was the role he and Pete had devised for Willa: she would secure the funds to underwrite a full repair that involved jacking up the addition and pouring a new cement foundation. Pete claimed this was possible, a very big job, but he'd seen it work. The two men had hashed it out at their first meeting and Willa, in absentia, was their star player. Pete had told Iano about the government grants she'd brought to his attention, available for this kind of historic preservation. Iano had assured Pete his wife was an ace investigator and would get her hands on all such monies to be had.

Willa explained to Iano that she had only *asked* about preservation grants, and accepted Pete's guess that Vineland's pockets were empty. But Iano's faith in her ability to save the day was preternatural. Occasionally in the course of their marriage his confidence had infected Willa. When her mother was diagnosed with cancer he'd been so sure Willa could find the right doctors to work a cure, she'd started believing it too. She was still reeling from that brief romance with delusion. It wouldn't happen again. She had no expectation of finding the right bureaucrats to save their structure. Once while walking Dixie she'd discovered the Vineland Historical Society but felt no desire to step inside and ask if her flawed house had a good backstory. Why torture herself?

For lack of other options she'd accepted the stopgap tin patch, and that decision alone might drive her to the streets. A maddening rhythm made the hammers impossible to tune out: *BANG bang BANG bang*, pause. *BANG bang BANG bang,* pause. Did a roofing nail require four strikes exactly? Or were there two men, BIG BANGER and little banger, working side by side? Did each pause represent a new nail set in position? Were her ears staying alert for some eventual misstep, the rare and calamitous fifth bang?

She got up from her desk and pawed through a cardboard box for her noise-canceling headphones. She found tissue-wrapped framed photos of the kids, coffee mugs jammed full of half-dead pens and emery boards, and no headphones. Of course. This box was labeled "desk stuff." When she'd packed it, her desk was in a house in a tiny college town that probably had never in its history produced any noise worth canceling.

Back at the window, she peered down through the branches into the neighboring yard. This time she didn't even bother rolling over in her desk chair, pretending to take a break. She stood like a sentry. Today for the first time in many weeks, she'd declared to herself and the family that she was still a journalist, with deadlines pending. She was withdrawing from diaper duty *to her office, for the whole afternoon.* And her new job turned out to be this, keeping watch over the feet sticking out from under the cars in the neighbors' yard. Two sets wore plastic shower shoes. It was the third pair that held interest: red Converse sneakers, adult size 5-ish or boy's 12. She wasn't going to believe this until she viewed the body. The idea of her daughter over there underneath a car was improbable for many reasons. When did Tig befriend those young men? What did she know how to do to the chassis of a Ford? And wasn't she supposed to be at work?

Actually Willa had little idea of Tig's schedule or whereabouts most of the time, and had to surmise that was a normal relation-ship with a twenty-six-year-old. "Normal" fell outside Willa's experience. She'd had a first child who resigned himself to adult worries around the time he entered kindergarten, and a second who seemed likely to carry the terrible twos into old age. With both now living under her roof, Willa needed some rules for life with the oxymoronic adult child.

Tig's latest defiance was her refusal to own a cell phone, one of several extreme habits she'd brought back from her stint in Cuba along with the dreads that still startled her family. Willa hadn't envisioned dreadlocks as an option for white girls, although Tig's kinked, unruly mane was deemed "bad" even by the swarthier Greek relatives. Willa could only guess that Cubans with their spicy history of racial mélange must have every ethnic variety of hair, and time on their hands for developing its potential.

She watched as Tig and the two young mechanics finally wriggled out from under the vehicles bringing some commotion with them into the daylight. The guys brushed off their legs and Tig did an odd little stomping hand-waving dance, animating some story that made her audience double over laughing. The two tall, heavily inked young men in low-slung gym shorts were enchanted by the wild-haired, Spanish-fluent pixie next door, and Willa couldn't call it a surprise. Tig's life always brimmed with comrades and boyfriends, and her parents invariably guessed wrong about which would rise to first place. It could be anyone. Tig was a unique element with all valences open.

Willa's mother had always promised Tig would "settle out," but she hadn't survived to see it, and now Willa wondered who among them would live long enough to stop being flabbergasted by the girl. Her return from Cuba was a complete surprise: Willa opened the door and there stood Tig, after no update on her whereabouts for nearly a year, nor any indication she meant to come back at all. Iano suspected visa problems but Willa was pretty sure Tig's status there was wholly illegal; her hunch was a breakup with the man Tig had been living with. Probably they would never know. She'd shown up in Virginia two days before the bomb fell, news of the college closure that arrived without warning and reached them, crushingly, the same day it reached distant friends via national news. What with all the calamity and humiliation, they never found the right moment to sit down and extract the Cuba story.

Iano and Willa had been destroyed overnight, losing not just his tenured job and pension but also their home. Through a contract with the college they'd owned their house, not the land underneath it. The arrangement looked feudal in retrospect, but nearly all the tenured faculty had been in the same boat. These houses on college property were the town's elite housing, taken by families with most seniority. When anyone moved away, an endless stream of young faculty families had always lined up to buy the vacant house. If rumors about the college's solvency had circulated, they were muted by the 165-year history touted on linen-bond letterhead. A scenario in which the college was shuttered, jobs evaporated, and homes had zero market value was beyond imagining. They would sooner have believed in the Rapture.

By April they were desperate. The job offer from Chancel materialized in May and the move to New Jersey became a foregone conclusion, with Nick in tow, and Dixie on antianxiety meds, but a tagalong daughter had been no part of the plan. Iano ordered her back to Ivins to finish her degree in biology. Willa wondered when he would notice Tig was immune to his directives. Tig informed her parents she refused to take out bank loans, with tuition exchange no longer an option, and anyway she'd already learned more than she wanted to know about a ravaged biosphere.

The latter was no news to Willa, who'd seen how the girl always took the truth of human selfishness harder than any of her friends, even the history majors. Through semesters of oceanography and forest ecology she'd grown increasingly distraught until, one and a half semesters shy of graduation, Tig had slung a backpack over her shoulder and set off to Occupy Wall Street. A sizable chunk of Ivins's class of 2012 went with her, leaving behind dorm rooms Willa imagined looking like a collegiate Pompeii: the dirty clothes tangled on the floor, the ramen noodles still in the hot pot. When the makeshift shelters and demands for a new world order were eventually drummed out of Zuccotti Park, Tig drifted to an organizing project in Colorado where her years of college Spanish were useful in helping farm workers secure better living conditions. Willa thought the migrant labor force would thin out in winter, but no, there were Christmas tree farms. The family had seen little of Tig in recent years, even before she left for Cuba.

Willa now found herself listening hard to make out threads of conversation, her forehead pressed against the window, and shame sent her back to her computer. She sat listlessly, changing a word here, there, hitting Undo, then Redo, stuck in dawdle mode. She cocked an ear for the baby and didn't hear him now. *Aldus.* They'd all been calling him "Buddy" and "Little Man," finding his name untouchable, not just due to the Helene implications. Baby names typically wore in with a few weeks of use, but "Aldus" continued to call up the image of an old man in tweeds. Willa wasn't about to overrule a dead mother, but she had been relieved yesterday to hear Zeke call him Dusty. That might be workable, even with its ashes-to-ashes connotation.

She turned to the pile of bills burgeoning like fungus on her desk: the moving-in utility double jeopardy, the harrowing new family-size insurance policy. The pediatric visit they'd had to schedule before the new policy kicked in. Some of these bills could wait until Iano's paycheck went into the bank, some could not. Property taxes were low here, especially on a house with a terminal diagnosis, but it was hard to call *that* good news. The roof repair wasn't even in the mix yet, and she was pretty sure applying for coverage through their homeowners' insurance would result in its cancellation. For the thousandth time in a year she made an unthinking movement toward her phone to call her mother. The dead one. Willa believed in no ethereal realm but still put her face on her desk, thought of her mother, and asked quietly, "What's going to happen to us?"

Nothing presented.

One underemployed breadwinner, five dependents. Iano was making what adjuncts made, barely $25,000, and given the state of academia, probably looking toward nothing better ahead. Willa recorded her freelance income in an Excel file, but was too embarrassed to hit the sigma function and learn her year-to-date total. In her college days she'd waitressed; theoretically she could follow Tig's lead into one of the restaurants on Landis where she'd seen

Help Wanted signs. But two minimum wages weren't noticeably better than one. She'd probably written lines like that in her better-paid journalist days, believing herself savvy to working-class woes. In some sheltered life she could barely see from this one. Ticking down the list, her father-in-law was a liability, not an asset. Stunningly, her Harvard-educated son fell into the same category. It made no sense but there it was. Zeke had mind-blowing debts and an infant in his care. If forced to leave this rent-free house, they would disperse to various refuges she could not make herself think about. And yet. How were they not just a normal family?

When she got up and looked out the window again, Tig and friends had migrated from the car graveyard over to the deep shade between their two giant trees—beech and oak, according to Tig—that flanked the view from the kitchen window and elbowed the gutters on their reach for the sky. Willa rested her forehead on the glass for a better look at things down there. In exaggerated slow motion the three of them were moving through some kind of tai chi exercise. Tig led, circling an arm back, lifting a crane-like leg. The boys replicated her every move.

"What is it, Willa? Birdwatching?"

Willa jumped, feeling Iano's hands around her waist.

"Something like that." She rolled her head back against his chest, blushing. When the kids were little she'd sometimes spied on them and their friends for the normal sentimental reasons, and even then she'd hated getting caught. Iano had no such reservations. Greek parenting seemed to involve walking into a kid's life and doing whatever—crashing the tea party, superintending the love life, *doing* the homework instead of tediously coaching it—and expecting gratitude for the all of it.

Willa could feel the shift in his body when he spotted Tig down below with the two fellows. He sighed quietly. "*Ela, Antigonaki mou. What is she doing?*"

Despite his red-blooded American life, Iano sustained a charming first-generation exoticism. Maybe deliberately, though Willa thought not. He'd grown up speaking Greek at home, among sisters and cousins named after gods.

"I think it's tai chi," she offered.

"No, I mean . . ."

"I know. With those boys."

"Those boys, those clothes, that hairdo. She looks like a Charlie Chaplin movie."

The Little Tramp, did he mean? No, probably one of the homeless waifs with the dark circles under the eyes. Iano took Tig's tiny stature as a permanent rebuke. He shared his family's view that all children should eat more, period.

Iano folded his arms across Willa's waist and settled his chin on the top of her head, enclosing her like an envelope. His beard bristled deliciously against her scalp. They could stand all day like this. Maybe should have tried that, in lieu of procreation.

"Want to know what she was doing ten minutes ago?"

He made a noise, technically indecipherable, somewhere on the pain register.

"It's probably not what you think. She was under one of those cars over there. I swear to God. Helping the guys out with a lube job or something."

"She can fix cars now? Jesus, can we rent her out?"

"Let me remind you she can also knit socks." Could and did, thanks to her grandma Knox, who'd long ago tried to teach Willa and failed; her nascent feminist consciousness had required Willa to scorn the domestic arts. But that equation had flipped in a generation: modern girls reared by working moms were all over Etsy and Pinterest now, clanning together in knitting groups named like revolutionary brigades.

Willa let herself be still with Iano in a beautiful silence: the roof pounders had gone home to their wives, and the baby, unaccountably mute. They watched Tig and the two boys slowly push some invisible substance away from their bodies, then pull it back.

"I came up to tell you Zeke texted."

"Texted?" From what room, she wondered. In nearly two weeks there, Zeke hadn't left the house. He'd been a blank-faced ghost in pajama pants warming bottles in the microwave and eating things from containers while standing before the open fridge. *Suicide is murder*, Willa could not stop herself thinking as she watched him. A life had been brutally stolen from their family. A mother, a beloved.

"Listen," Iano interrupted himself, "those back stairs. Are we going to use them or just lock the door? Because just now I almost fell through one of the—what do you call it?—the tread. The wood is completely rotten."

"I think that's what we call a servants' staircase. Shall we acquire some?"

"Maybe the kind that can grade exams?"

"Please. That's what graduate students are for. They're cheaper than servants."

They stood watching Tig, this girl they'd somehow made. In slow motion she lunged to one side while lifting one hand, lowering the other, shifting her weight and turning as though being held in the arms of an invisible, slothful dance partner. The two boys likewise turned, lovingly taking the air into their embrace. Tears welled in Willa's eyes. These beautiful children seemed capable of generating contentment out of thin air.

"We have to stay in this house," she said. "You understand that, right?"

"What are you saying?"

"I'm saying this house is our only sure thing. Even if parts of it are caving in. If it comes to it, we'll put up yellow caution tape and avoid the collapsed areas. We'll huddle in whatever is left. Sorry if I sound crazy. But we don't have anywhere else to go."

"There is always someplace to go." He tightened his arms around her, and Willa pretended to believe him. His confidence was enviable and maddening. Most of the time she didn't want him to solve or contradict her worries, she just needed him to listen and agree with her on the awfulness at hand. This was a principle of marriage she'd explained many times. Today was different. She needed to be wrong.

"Zeke texted?" she asked.

"He found a Greek restaurant over in Millville."

"Millville, outside of this house? Did he go out in his car?" Her heart lurched. "Iano, you're here, I'm here. Tig is there. Who's got the baby?"

"Zeke has him, I guess. He wanted to know if he should pick up dinner."

Iano had not been stuck in this house watching every appalling minute of Zeke's zombie dance with a baby crying on endless loop. Greek takeout would strike Iano as normal.

"We should cook," she said. "This family is eating money."

"You write, *moro*. Make us rich with your article for the AARP magazine."

Iano detached from her and vanished. Willa held her vigil over Tig, the child she'd lately forgotten to worry about. For all the years her daughter had been bouncing like a molecule through an unstable universe, anxiety was Willa's steady state. Iano loved her too, of course, but fatherhood apparently subscribed to different bylaws. A mother can be only as happy as her unhappiest child. Willa believed in the power of worry to keep another human from flying out of orbit. Whatever was holding Tig here with her family, even in a falling house, might actually be the safest bet for now.

Willa knew she spent too much worry on Tig, as people did.

Physicians ran tests, parents of normal-size children offered patronizing advice, the in-laws produced evil-eye amulets, teachers scheduled conferences. Tiny stature provoked protectiveness. Willa was slightly built too, but Tig at eightysome pounds was a true featherweight. She'd stopped growing in fourth grade and no pediatrician could find anything really wrong. Standing at four feet ten, smack on the bottom line of normal, Tig was callously declared a midget by her big brother but unqualified for treatment by the medical establishment. Small was her destiny. And despite that, or because of it, she'd grown up with the furies in her sails, honing her confidence in verbal and physical combat with a brother who quickly doubled her in size. She had the temperament of the fire-eyed little shih tzu at the dog park that takes on the rottweilers with zero sense of disadvantage.

Willa forgot this scrappiness when Tig was far away, then wore out on it fast when she was around. But their new household arrangement was working out in some ways. Tig, who generally took no prisoners, had an inexplicable tolerance for her grandfather. She took his barked commands with a smile, let him cheat at backgammon, and helped with his insulin shots while ignoring his effluent of foul language. Willa was relieved of her hardest familial duties and had finally begun sleeping better, with no idea she was gathering strength for the next collapse: a new unhappiest child.

><

"Keep stirring," Tig ordered when Willa complained the white sauce wasn't thickening up. "Béchamel doesn't get done just because you want it done."

Willa kept stirring. She watched Tig select a knife, inspect the blade, give it a few zinging rasps with the sharpening steel, then slice into an eggplant with harrowing speed. The ovals fanned out on the cutting board in a manner that struck Willa as magical.

"Did you already add the cinnamon and pepper?" Tig asked without looking up.

Willa added cinnamon and pepper. Tig's restaurant-acquired kitchen skills were undeniably useful at home, where Willa had never earned more than passing grades as a cook. But the condescension grated. Throwing Wall Street to the dogs was one thing, but demoting your mother to sous chef went against the natural order.

"Those are some gorgeous eggplants. Are they from the grocery?"

"Nope."

Earlier, when Willa overruled Greek takeout, Tig had come upstairs to propose the undertaking of moussaka, a labor-intensive family favorite that frankly daunted Willa. She'd argued they didn't have the ingredients, but Tig proved her wrong. Eggs and eggplant had appeared in the kitchen without Willa's knowledge. Tig often came home from her restaurant shifts with loaded grocery bags.

"You brought them from work, then."

"Yep."

"And I have to assume your employers know about this."

The knife stopped midair. "You're asking, do I steal from Yari and Leonardo?"

"That's not what I said."

"It's normal restaurant procedure to give workers food at the end of a shift."

"Maybe leftover *meals* that would be thrown away. I can understand not wanting to be wasteful."

"Really. I wouldn't have guessed."

Willa sighed, wondering what she'd thrown away lately that invoked this censure. This guessing game she never won. "If you'd let me finish a sentence, I was saying I can see why a restaurant would give away food that's been cooked. But not fresh produce and whole cartons of eggs. Those seem like assets the business could still use."

"And this comes from your expertise in the field of restaurant management."

Willa let it go. Tig's employers seemed to treat her like family, and it was unimaginable she would rip off their struggling little business. Willa's offspring had strict honor codes, applied in opposite directions: Zeke strived to be Man of the Hour, while Tig devoted herself to Sticking It to the Man, if that phrase still signified. With that thought it dawned on Willa that she'd probably arranged to be paid in barter, keeping herself off their tax ledgers. Jeopardizing her future retirement, possibly putting all of them at legal risk, *that* would be consistent with what she knew of her daughter's nature. Not wanting to be complicit, Willa wouldn't ask, because Tig would just tell her. The girl was compulsively honest. In earlier years, Willa's every attempt to teach her the artful evasion known as "tact" would get shot down with "Mom, that's *lying!*" And Tig remained the child who announced when opening gifts at birthday parties, "Thanks, Grandma, I have one of these already and I don't really like it."

They heard Zeke come in. Willa defiantly abandoned her béchamel post to go greet the one of her children less likely to bait her into a knife fight.

She was happy to see Zeke looking fairly human, and the baby comatose. This child seemed to have the opposite of conventional colic, screaming all day and going out like a light at six. His little head flopped sideways in the fancy car seat, which they could detach from its base and carry around by the handle like a bucket.

Zeke had gone out with him for a four-hour drive, hence the sudden quiet that had alarmed Willa. "Did it get him to stop crying?" she asked.

"No. But I blasted Nicki Minaj and felt like I was pulling off an escape."

Aldus was still out cold in his baby bucket a half-hour later when dinner was on, so Willa set him on a chair at the head of the table where his grateful family could admire the performance. They were all weary of this mind-shattering child, even if they shared some version of the love that clanged in Willa's chest. But they pitied Zeke too much to complain. The exception would be Nick, who was not a man to let compassion stand in his way. But Nick had the advantage of deafness.

The escape had been a tonic; Zeke was nearly conversant. Willa wouldn't mention the cost of the gas or ask him about a job search. She'd offered to help with babysitting if Zeke wanted to look for work, but so far he seemed unable to look beyond the next hour. This was a mother's torture, watching bruise-colored shadows spread beneath his beautiful eyes. Watching him stare at space while life chirped around him.

"What did you find out there?" She was aiming hard for nonchalance.

"Farms. Pine trees. Little one-horse towns, strip malls." Zeke filled his plate as he spoke, showing signs of a former appetite. "On the edge of Vineland there's this huge hospital or something. It looks like an asylum, these long yellow buildings with little barred windows. Something from another era."

"Training School for the Developmentally Disabled," Tig said. "It's like over a hundred years old. It used to be called Vineland School for the Feebleminded. They did experiments on the kids."

"How did you come to know about that?" Iano asked.

Tig shrugged, talking with her mouth full. "Jorge and José Luis told me. They have a cousin that went there. Obviously not a hundred years ago. He's still there, in fact."

"We'd like to hear more about your new friends," Iano said.

"Sounds like you really wouldn't."

"What friends are we not talking about?" Zeke asked.

"Our next-door neighbors," Tig said. "Jorge works at the restaurant. Line cook. He invited me to hang out after work."

Nick stopped eating and turned to stare at Tig, pivoting his bulk. "You running around with the Puerto Rican hoods next door?"

"They're Vinelanders, Papu. Born here. The house is their mother's. She doesn't live here now but they said she used to be friends with Aunt Dreama."

"What, she was Dreama's maid?"

"Friends is what they said, Papu."

"How many people live in that house anyways? Ten, twelve?"

"Maybe you should go ask them yourself."

The old man turned back to his food. Willa had wondered the same. They all seemed roughly the same generation, the brothers and two slightly older women in their twenties or early thirties, with babies and young kids among them.

"And I assume everything going on over there is aboveboard?" Iano asked.

"*As I said*," Tig pronounced the words with equal weight, "Jorge and José Luis were born in the US. Their sisters live over there too, and their kids. The sisters were born in San Juan but they're all citizens because Puerto Rico is some kind of US minion state where they pay Social Security but don't get to vote. Are we done with the inquisition?"

The table went quiet except for the thrumming hiss of Nick's oxygen, while everyone devoured the remarkable moussaka.

"Antigone," Iano continued, undaunted. He never took her quite seriously enough to be cowed as Willa was. "Where did you learn tai chi?"

"Occupy. A bunch of us did it every morning. It helped keep the energy focused."

Willa saw Zeke rouse, his lip tighten into a smirk. In a heart where little else could be stirred to life, sibling scorn survived. Willa steered the conversation away from Wall Street. "You've been hiding your talents, Tig. If I'd known you were an auto mechanic you could have saved us some money this summer."

"Auto mechanic," Zeke repeated.

"Your sister spent her afternoon under a car."

"Oh yeah? Doing what?"

Tig spoke without glancing up, as if Zeke were the younger sibling unworthy of much bother. "Resealing one of the U-joints on the driveshaft of a Ford Fairlane. And fighting off ants. There's like an ant invasion going down over there."

"Since when are you a grease monkey?"

"Since I lived in a country that's kept the same fleet of Fords and Chevys running since 1959 without any replacement parts."

"Oh right, Cuba. World capital of obsolete cars."

"That's one way to put it. *Or*, half a century of the blockade has made Cubans the smartest recyclers in the world. It's not just cars. Agriculture, manufacturing, name it."

"Right," Zeke said. "Ask Raúl if he'd like the embargo lifted tomorrow."

"What do you mean by 'ant invasion'?" Willa asked, considering new categories of assault on their household. One if by land, two if by sea.

But Tig and Zeke were locked in. "I'm not saying they wanted the blockade. I'm saying in the last fifty years we had the most massive global consumption and waste in human history, and Cubans got through it without cheap gas or throwaway crap from China." She aimed the tines of her fork at her brother. "You don't know what resourceful means till you've been to Cuba."

"Poor me," Zeke said, appearing devoid of self-pity for the first time in weeks. Willa was stunned to see him restored, at least to some truculent version of himself.

"Do kids your age resent the blockade more than their parents? Don't they want the newest tech toys?" Iano leaned on his forearms, easing into his classroom persona.

"And pass up the chance to be so crafty?" Zeke said. "Look, they've even figured out how to manufacture dreadlocks out of Caucasian hair."

"Who knew our ancestors came from the Caucasus Mountains? Is it true, Papu?"

"What?"

Tig upped her decibels. "Papu, do we come from the Caucasus Mountains?"

"Hell no, mountains of Crete. Voukolies. One hundred generations."

Zeke lifted his eyes in mock reverence. "Since the first Voukolian virgin was impregnated by Zeus."

"It wasn't a human female," Tig said. "I'm pretty sure it was a swan. Look at your nose. That honker is proof, we are descended from swans."

Willa was floored. Tig had mostly left Zeke alone since Helene's death, but now at the first sign of life she was nipping at his heels. "What about my genes?" Willa asked. "A Greek last name doesn't erase your other half."

"Mom! Did our Knox ancestors come from the Caucasus Mountains?" Tig asked.

"No. Just the usual boring Anglo-Saxon stuff. As you know."

"Okay, we're not Caucasians."

"You know what I meant," Zeke said. "White."

"White is not an origin. It's a mental construct of privilege."

Willa had watched this fight forever: the Eagle Scout and the Maverick, separate but equal in self-righteousness. Through their teenage years she'd hoped college and distance might one day let them relax and find common ground, even miss each other. Maybe that had happened. But here under one roof again their child selves showed intent to rule. She could see it in their posture: Zeke stubbornly planted forward on his elbows, Tig gaining height on him by standing on her knees in her chair.

"You're saying there are no categories of relatedness among humans?"

"Nope. I'm clueing you that the term 'Caucasian' was invented in the seventeen hundreds by German philosophers who said God put the colored folks on all their subpar continents and the beautiful whiteys in the mountains of eastern Europe."

"Thank you, Wikipedia."

"I'm not Wikipedia, I just have a good memory."

"Why memorize a stupid factoid like that when you can look it up on your phone? Oh, excuse me I forgot, you don't own one."

"Holding and synthesizing information in your brain creates your personality. You're surrendering your personality to an electronic device in your pocket."

"Yep. Just one more of those boring drones that finishes his education."

"At least I have a job. I'm contributing to the household."

"Okay, that's not fair," Willa cut in. "Zeke is caring for a newborn and recovering from trauma. Grief takes energy. I still feel like I'm hiking uphill after losing Mama."

Both kids glanced at her oddly.

"I'm not saying it's the same. My mother got to live a pretty long life, she got to see me grow up." Willa stopped, avoiding her children's stares. She should be over this, in their opinion. They all observed an uncomfortable moment of silence.

"I'm going to start working from home," Zeke then announced.

"Really. Your start-up?" Iano looked thrilled.

"Our investing firm. I talked with Jake and Michael today. That's actually the reason I went out for the drive. They've been after me to talk stuff over, so we finally had this crazy Bluetooth conference call in the car, with Little Big Mouth raging in the background. But it worked out. The name of our firm is Good Money."

Wow, thought Willa. *Grief compartmentalized.*

"As in throwing good money after bad," Tig offered.

"As in the fastest-growing sector of personal finance management. Microloans, fossil fuel–free bundles. Socially responsible investments."

"Keep telling yourself that. Helping rich people get richer is socially responsible."

"Look, money's an engine and it's out there running day and night, whether you like it or not. For bad or for good. The global move to divest from South Africa is what finally brought down the apartheid regime. You can't dispute that."

Willa felt her daughter could dispute God on the scheduling of Judgment Day, or whatever the pagan equivalent might be, so she was surprised to see her clam up and reach across Nick for the salad bowl.

"So if gas and oil guys are the evildoers now, my company will help people get their retirement funds into companies that build solar cells. Or women's cooperatives in India, if that's their thing. We're disrupting the conventional models. Lots of our clients will be middle-class investors. It's just about increasing the bottom line, wherever you are."

Tig rolled her eyes. "Humans have outgrown the carrying capacity of the planet. The responsible thing would be to *shrink* our bottom line."

"Hey, gee, we tried that! For five centuries before the Industrial Revolution. It was called the Dark Ages."

"That's true," Iano said. "You can't really have civilization without growth. It would be a zero-sum economy: I have needs, everyone has needs, and the only way I could gain something is to take it away from you."

"Dope scenario, Dad," Tig said, "only the world *is* zero sum. When you take stuff out of the land and ocean, that's taking. You're just pretending there's always going to be more, which there isn't."

"When you plot low-growth periods in history," Iano said, "you see Hitler and you see Genghis Khan."

"Plot it any way you want. I'm not choosing this. I just lucked into the moment of history when your folklore about permanent expansion goes down the toilet."

Willa wondered how many tuition dollars they'd invested in this conversation, and whether she could get a refund; she wished they would all shut up and eat. Zeke was gasoline to Tig's fiery temper, even when he used the kind of stockbroker language that in Willa's experience numbed people's skulls: "Growth every quarter is the only success that matters to investors. The drive to expand is the engine of the economy. That's just how it is."

"Anyway," Iano said, "people will figure this out. Capitalism is going green."

"*God*, you guys! There's this thing called biocapacity, plant and animal biomass the earth produces, total. It's a measurable quantity. Know how much of it we're using?"

"Less than one hundred percent, I assume."

"No. More! By twenty-five percent a year. How the *fuck* long do you think that can last?"

The defiant blue note roused Nick, who'd been drooping into a nap. "Young lady, you don't know how lucky you are to have shoes on your feet and a roof over your head."

"Look, Papu, I'm barefoot." She showed him her feet.

The roof over their heads was also in question, Willa could have pointed out. But Nick was launched. "What I saw in the Greek

Civil War. Brother against brother. The communists took what they wanted and if they didn't want it, they burned it. You want to go back to that? Be my guest. Your *yaya* and me were lucky to get out with the skin on our backs, so your father and his sisters could get born in America. No father for you, your *yaya* and me starving to death: that's what the communists wanted."

The family had heard Nick's brother-against-brother rant too many times to care anymore, even if escaping the Greek Civil War was the defining event of Nick's life. And of Iano's too, Willa suspected. He was born more than a decade after Nick and Roula settled in Phoenix, and disagreed with his father on nearly everything, but he'd grown up on those stories. The communists were his Big Bad Wolf.

Iano was in full professor mode now: open face, open palms, the image of a good listener. His students were always smitten, not just because of his hot-chili-pepper ranking on ratemyprofessor.com. The charisma had probably inflamed his tenure problems, provoking rumors of student liaisons that his jealous peers were too eager to believe. "That's Europe," he was saying to Zeke, on some conversational train Willa had missed, while Tig quietly helped herself to seconds. "I agree you've got demographics working against you. But the developing countries have young populations, and most of their growth still ahead of them. And then there's China, driving everything."

"Actually, Dad, the renminbi is tanking. Rail freight volumes there are down, Shanghai equity is down."

"As of when?"

"Over a year. You didn't know this?"

"I'm a political scientist, son, not an economist."

"Everybody has their theory, but it looks like China's economy has peaked."

His or her theory, Willa did not say, swallowing the powerful impulse toward correction that made for first-rate editors and insufferable human beings. "Look at you two guys. The most optimistic people I know, shaking down the subject of doom."

"Not doom, Mom," Zeke said. "Crisis is opportunity."

It felt surreal, watching her family bicker about abstract catastrophe under an actual collapsing roof, but it was a relief to see her son animated again. Zeke embodied the contradiction of his generation: jaded about the fate of the world, idealistic about personal prospects. A house built on youth's easy courage. And Tig in her way was also brave, dissecting the world as she saw it, believing her strategies mattered. In a world of people who either let things happen or *made* them happen, these kids were instigators. Willa felt obsolete. The need to shelter her family never lifted its weight from her shoulders, but in practical terms she was useful to no one there but the dog and the baby. She sat watching her motherless grandchild, whose eyes darted under closed lids while his face worked through a range of pouty, knit-eyebrowed emotions like an acting-class warm up. At his last checkup the pediatrician had observed the howling red face and trembling limbs, and said that infants process grief as trauma. Then suggested they try a different formula.

"Per capita GDP in the US has been pretty stagnant, Dad. You know that, right? Income used to be tied to productivity of the economy but that hasn't been true since 1978. Actually it's gone the other way since then. There's different ways to chart it against inflation, but the median paycheck is definitely in decline."

"*That's* what I keep wondering about," Willa said, startling Iano and Zeke as well as herself. Both men turned to her.

"It just seems like . . . I don't know. There's less money in the world than there used to be. I don't know how else to put it. Like something's broken."

Her husband's and son's polite smiles were spookily identical.

"Obviously I don't know how it works. Supply and demand." Willa hated how naive she sounded. "I just know people have always assumed their kids would grow up better off than the generation before. You know what I'm saying. Like Nick and Roula." She glanced at Nick, drifting off, spent from his outburst. An unlikely ally in any case. The rest of the family observed Willa as if she'd blown some unexpected fuse.

"They knew they could go somewhere and make a better life. That's all I'm saying. It goes back forever, to Odysseus, or Moses and the Israelites. My serf ancestors eating rocks on the Shrewesbury plain. The one thing you can trust is your kids will have more, not less. And now . . ." Willa gestured at air. What part of *shambles* could they not see?

Iano switched on his chili-pepper smile. "Supply and demand. That's it, exactly. We're in a new era of supply right now. Productivity is exploding, and sometimes that takes new forms. Computer technology replaces jobs, for example. So you see a boom on the take side, but fewer working hours on the other. The market eventually adjusts."

"Zeke just said it's been stuck since, what, the seventies? Didn't you? That's a whole generation. More like two."

"But Dad's right," Zeke said. "New technologies have a transformative impact on economic output, and eventually that will rebound. Supply and demand is a law, like physics. If you go too fast, your car overheats and you slow down."

Or your car drives into a tree, Willa thought, *and bursts into flames.*

Iano turned back to Zeke. "So look, you have these oil-rich countries like Venezuela and Nigeria. They've still got a lot of GDP growth in their future."

"Not without a superpower to throw money into their production sector. They'll stay undeveloped, just like Cuba did. A cold global economy is like a de facto embargo. Plus, nobody's ever going to pay a hundred dollars a barrel for oil again."

Tig glanced up on the Cuba cue. "They'll wish they could when it's gone. And anyway, gross domestic product is a stupid way to measure a country's success."

Zeke laughed in his old appealing way, all white teeth and cute laugh lines. "Stop it! That's like saying gravity is a stupid way to predict downward force."

"So how do you stimulate the economy in the twenty-first century?" Iano asked.

"Now *that's* a good question," Zeke said.

Willa opened her mouth. Didn't she just ask this, in a more self-centered way?

Tig stood up and began collecting empty plates. "For starters," she said, "you acknowledge that *stimulate* is a synonym for stealing from the future."

"You're wrong, Dad's right," Zeke said. "The minute you shut down growth, you start living with scarcity. Simple math. You end up between a rock and a hard place."

"Scylla and Charybdis," Nick erupted, startling them all. *Skeela* and *Hareev-thees* he pronounced them, in Homer's own Greek. If her father-in-law had actually read *The Odyssey* and could apply it metaphorically, Willa was going to have to recalculate.

"The six-headed monster and the whirlpool that swallows ships whole," she clarified. "That's actually a thing, a Homer reference. Odysseus had to sail between two impossible dangers to get to safety. As a reader, you're sure he's going to die."

In tandem her son and daughter shifted their stares from Nick to Willa.

"Thanks, Mom, but we know it's a thing," Zeke said. "We did AP English."

"Okay, I wasn't sure you remembered."

"Exactly," Iano concurred. "You start pushing for a no-growth agenda and we all end up between the devil and the deep blue sea."

Willa studied Nick: his eyelids drooped, his chins folded themselves on his chest. Was this the stopped-clock situation, proverbially getting it right twice a day?

"Scylla," she repeated. "And Charybdis."

4

∞

Scylla and Charybdis

Thatcher returned from his meeting to find Polly inconsolable.

He'd walked home from the schoolhouse in foul temper himself, fists in his pockets, recalling days when he and his brothers ran from the old man into the forest and howled like wolves. He would howl this minute, if the world still held one person with whom he could bare his soul.

And now here was Polly with her braying. The dogs, she shrieked, missing for hours. Kidnapped. She had evidence!

Thatcher took off his hat and prepared to tread cautiously. These two hounds had come with the house, an unexpected gift waiting when the family moved back to Vineland. Rose's mother despised them, Rose ignored them, and Thatcher was sufficiently indifferent that he could not distinguish one from the other. It was Polly who knew their hearts. She'd spent the summer training them to useful tasks in the line of *speak*, *beg*, and *climb* (onto the divan). She'd discovered different temperaments in her pupils: Charybdis was Congregationalist while Scylla was Baptist. (He liked water.)

Thatcher thought their spiritual inclinations probably followed those of their former master, Mr. Nailbourne, the gentleman who'd rented the property during the years when Aurelia and her daughters lived in Boston. Mr. Nailbourne was a one-legged war veteran, unmarried, a music teacher and the owner of the town's first piano, qualities that combined to make him famous. (Also a reader of the classics, Thatcher guessed from his well-named dogs.) With his rental cheques sent to Boston he'd often enclosed clippings from the *Vineland Weekly* describing his pupils' recitals and accomplishments. Nowhere in any article had these canines appeared. The family learned of Scylla and Charybdis only from their renter's final letter, wherein he disclosed his plan to move to Kansas and bring the refinements of music to the brutish Western Soul. His two well-trained Gascon hounds were too attached to Vineland to make that venture, he said, so it seemed best to leave them behind. The woman next door would look after them until the ladies were reinstalled in their home, undoubtedly gratified to find it so well protected.

Mr. Nailbourne also left behind a reputation in town suggesting his attraction to the Western Soul's greater leniency toward alcohol. Thatcher never mentioned this at home. If Aurelia knew the dogs' history with an inebriate musician she might turn them out to the streets, where Polly might follow them.

As it was, poor Polly was exasperated with the dogs' obvious preference for the house next door. They ran away regularly to Mrs. Treat's front step, where they lay flanking the door like sphinxes. Day after day Polly fetched them back and scolded them for disloyalty. She had never kept an animal before. Thatcher explained they were honoring a duty to the woman who'd fed them after their master's abandonment. The poor creatures must have been bewildered. "They are learning to love you now," he counseled. "Give them time. A dog never fails to acknowledge devotion."

But today's crisis surpassed the ordinary. The dogs were not in their usual spot on the neighbor's stoop. They'd gone missing *for hours and hours* according to Polly, who was sure they were being held captive by Mrs. Treat.

"By Mrs. Treat," he repeated, still holding his hat in his hand. Polly hadn't let him ten paces into the house before collapsing at his feet, the bell of her striped skirt wilting around her. "The lady doesn't strike me as treacherous."

"Charybdis and Scylla visit her every morning because she *lures* them. She gives them titbits."

"So you see. Not the behavior of a villain."

"But it isn't fair! Mother won't let me feed them anything special at all."

Through the open parlor door Thatcher could see the corseted bulwark of his mother-in-law laboring at her writing desk, the shoulders grandiosely hunched in the muttonchopped sleeves of a florid dress. Aurelia was a cattleya orchid: immoderately showy. Epiphytic by nature, rising above the common dirt. Her hobby was to write letters to the newspaper decrying the corruptions on their town: Youthful disrespect for officers of the law. Spirits flowing in the Italian quarter. Thatcher now lowered his voice.

"Let's be grateful for the dogs' sake, then. Think of her as a granny that spoils them. Granny Treat!"

"You aren't listening to me, Thatcher," Polly declared. "She's *stolen* them. All the other days they stay for a quarter hour in her house and then she lets them out the back, and then they run around and around especially if there is a cat. I think Mrs. Treat encourages them to chase the cats. And then they come back here, or else they lie on her front step and wait for me to fetch them. But today it's been hours already. Please, please, Thatcher, go and rescue them before it's too late."

He watched Aurelia shove herself back in her chair. The great coiffed head tilted slightly, not toward them directly, but she was listening. Aurelia would be glad for the dogs to remain at large, and only happier if the neighbors' home removed itself to a different street. She had written one of her letters, so far unprinted, about Mrs. Treat's untoward behaviors. Thatcher undertook now to whisper.

"Are you positive the dogs are inside her house, Polly? It will be too embarrassing if I'm bringing a false charge."

Polly adjusted herself also to a whisper, but an urgent one. "They are! I swear it's true, I saw them go in the front and never come out the back. I've been waiting on the swing by the carriage house since after breakfast."

Reluctantly he went, hat in hand, apologies rehearsed. His morning had already been deeply unhappy, as he was learning not only his house but also his employment rested on precarious foundations. He cast his habitual covetous look over the Treat compound, perfectly kept, even to the little carriage house between their properties with its copper weather vane aligned to true north. Between Rose's beech and Polly's oak he strode, around the yew hedge to the Treat front door. He knocked, made himself wait a decent interval, and then knocked again. Stood in the sun's heat, listening to the insect whine that signaled summer's end. Watched a suspendered gang of working boys come down Sixth Street swinging their lunch buckets, picks on their shoulders, pausing at the corner of Plum for a loaded wagon to pass. Worn at the edges already, these boys, and so young. Thatcher wondered what manner of child in this town would be at leisure to attend high school. He gave the door a final rap, poised to abandon his mission and frankly disappointed to hear a faint voice encouraging him to enter.

He stepped inside, let his eyes adjust to the dim foyer, and heard the voice again from the interior. Abashed and unescorted he wandered into the parlor where Mrs. Treat sat at a desk near the window with a book lying open before her. The drapes were open and the room bright with daylight, but he sensed he was intruding on some private ceremony. Mrs. Treat seemed in proper order, dressed in a brown day frock, hatless, hair pinned in place. A trim contrast to Aurelia at her war post in his own parlor. Oddly, Mrs. Treat did not get up. Her eyes darted toward him but she held herself perfectly still.

"Forgive me, I'm Thatcher Greenwood." Hat in both hands, held to his chest like a shield. He lowered it. "I live next door."

"Of course you do. I am Mary Treat."

"I'm sorry my wife and I haven't called in on you and Dr. Treat. Settling into a house should not be a turmoil and yet we seem to turn over a new one every day. This morning my sister-in-law has commanded me to come inquiring about our hounds. Oh, and here they are!"

They lay under the desk at her feet, so still that Thatcher hadn't immediately spotted them. One of the two, Scylla or Charybdis, lifted a cocked head at him briefly, then dropped his chin to the floor again with a sigh.

"Please sit," Mrs. Treat urged, sounding deeply unhappy to offer the invitation.

"I don't need to trouble you. If I could just relieve you of—"

"No, please do stay a few minutes. I need the diversion, more desperately than you can imagine." Apart from an odd little laugh, her stiff countenance was at odds with her appeal for his company. Even the disdainful dogs seemed more welcoming than the mistress of the house. But her words were so extreme, it seemed wrong to refuse.

He looked around at the room, nicely wallpapered, comfortably used. The upholstered parlor set was neither shabby nor very fine. A sewing bird was clamped to one arm of the settee. A pair of very muddy women's shoes stood on the hearth drying out from some misfortune, though the parlor stove was of course unlit. Bookcases lined one wall, filled with what he presumed to be artifacts of the doctor's education. His wife must be missing him terribly to have shut herself into this parlor, harboring dogs and now begging for the company of a stray neighbor.

Thatcher physically resisted the urge to walk over and read the books' titles, a magnetism that had controlled him since the day in late childhood when he'd first set eyes on a book. Instead he put himself down on the settee facing Mrs. Treat at her desk. Half a dozen large glass candy jars, unconventionally provisioned, crowded the side table near his elbow. He leaned over for a closer look. Each jar was half filled with soil and planted with a miniature garden of mosses, wildflowers, and ferns. The breath of these small green worlds moistened the inner curve of the jars' glass shoulders. More of the jars occupied a curiosity table near the bay window and another sat on the desk along with small potted plants amidst jumbled books and papers. Mrs. Treat remained rigidly in place there, not even moving the hand that lay across her open book, holding her place with a finger until this interruption ended.

"These are unusual," he said, indicating the jars. "Would you call them terraria?"

She gave him a long study. Her eyes were an uncommonly dark brown, deep as wells. "You are the science teacher, or will be when the high school opens. Is that right?"

"Yes. I was just there now, meeting with Professor Cutler to prepare for opening of the term." *Preparation* was a mild word for Cutler's tyrannical bluster, though Thatcher couldn't speak of it. This town was a nest of acolytes and patrons.

"Then I will make a confession." Mrs. Treat's face slipped into a slight grin, the first sign of a thaw. "The ferns and flowers in those candy jars are a ruse. I put them in so my nervous lady friends can admire the little gardens without being shocked. Which they would be, if they knew the true purpose of these 'terraria,' as you call them."

"Would I be shocked, if I knew it?"

"We're about to see. Each of these jars is the home of a large spider."

Thatcher took care with his tone of voice. "A spider?"

"Yes. Tower-building spiders of the genus *Tarantula*. They make more interesting pets than even your excellent hounds, Mr. Greenwood."

"I wouldn't doubt it. And I gather you had more choice than I did, about their coming to live with you."

"I did. I capture them out in the garden."

"I see. With persuasion or stealth?" Vividly she rose in his memory, the lady facedown in the grass. Rose had guessed spiders, not spider *husbandry*.

"It isn't very difficult," she said. "I find the nests and dig them out of the ground with a trowel, and settle them into these candy jars. The spiders don't seem to mind the relocation. Certainly they notice it, but eventually they go on about their business."

Thatcher felt his day had taken a turn for the better. "And what is their business?"

"House building. Can you see?"

He peered into the jar. He thought himself a good observer, but had missed his own dogs lying under the desk. At length his eye found a construction that must be the tarantula house, exposed by clear design in the midst of randomness: a neat octagonal turret made of sticks as fine as string. The complete domicile would have fit in his hand.

"What an absolute marvel."

In the blink of an eye Mrs. Treat became a new person. She twinkled.

"Isn't it? The little builder would agree with you. She is terribly house proud. Once she builds her home she will never leave it. Her favorite position is sitting on the top of her tower with her legs folded under her. Can you see her there?"

Thatcher envied the little creature's instincts for joinery: if her home were dashed down on her head, she could scuttle over the grass and finish a whole new construction before her children's bedtime. How dire was the descent of a man's life, Thatcher mused, that he should now be stricken with spider jealousy. He got up and inspected every jar on the table, taking his time, eventually finding in each one the perfect little turret. But not a single landlady.

"I confess I can't," he said. "They don't seem to be at their posts."

"That's normal. Any unusual noise sends them scurrying indoors. I'm afraid your entrance has frightened them all. You might not see one today."

Thatcher turned around and studied Mrs. Treat for some sign that she was having him on. She looked earnest, her dark eyes vivid. She was younger than he'd presumed her to be from a distance, misled by the plainness of her dress. Not Granny Treat at all. Past his own age but in the same decade. Or forty perhaps, at the outside.

"Will they come out again, after I leave?"

"Oh, yes. They're completely accustomed to *me*, especially that one nearest the armrest there. She allows me to move her jar from one table to another without leaving her post. Just this week she's begun taking food from my fingers. But if a stranger comes in the room she always seems to know it."

"Are they all females?" He sat down again, setting his bowler on his knees.

"Yes. If I offer them husbands, it doesn't end well."

"Alas. I apologize for intruding on your sorority."

"Amply forgiven. One must not become too isolated from human society."

Indeed, he thought.

"I would offer you tea, only my girl Selma has taken the day off to look after her mother. I'm afraid I didn't plan very well."

"You couldn't know I was coming."

"No, but . . ." She shifted very slightly in her chair. "I mean for my experiment. I did not think ahead, and I've accidentally shut the dogs in for hours, and now you are here and I can't offer you a proper tea."

Thatcher turned his hat in his hands, a little alarmed, mostly curious. "Your experiment."

"Did you not see? I'm allowing this *Dionaea* to have a bite of me."

"This what?"

"*Dionaea muscipula.* The Venus flytrap. Please come have a look, it's a good specimen. They thrive in the marshes near here in the Pine Barrens. It's a wonderland for carnivorous plants, Mr. Greenwood. Have you visited the Pine Barrens?"

"No. Not yet."

"You will, I'm sure. It will be an inspiring place to take your pupils. I've collected five species of pitcher plants and several *Utricularia*. I'm beginning to think there is something about the poor soil in those swamps that encourages the flora to adapt themselves to carnivory."

He cautiously approached Mrs. Treat and leaned in for a look, astonished to have missed the most important activity in the room. She was not sitting idly at a desk holding her place in an open book. She was allowing the tip of her finger to be digested by a carnivorous plant.

"Gracious," he said. "Does it hurt?"

She laughed. "I was asking myself that question when you came in. It may be a problem for the psychologist. Is it knowledge of captivity that causes the pain? I resolved this morning to be a voluntary prisoner for five hours at least. I pulled up my comfortable easy chair here, as you see, and let my arm rest on the table so it isn't a strain. I gathered plenty of reading matter within arm's length. Normally I can be happy to sit reading from dawn until dark. What could hinder me from keeping my resolve? But in less than fifteen minutes I found I couldn't concentrate on this book for the pressure on my finger."

"How long have you and this plant been locked in combat, Mrs. Treat?"

"Since ten o'clock on the nail. For the first hour the pressure seemed to increase, and then my arm began to pain me almost unbearably. But surely I've sat still much longer, without any discomfort at all. I feel ashamed that I cannot control my nerves."

Thatcher could not stop himself smiling. No need to contrive a botanical nature to meld with this human one. Mrs. Treat was doing the melding herself. "Perhaps *I* could bring *you* a cup of tea. If you would allow a man to paw about in your kitchen."

"Oh Mr. Greenwood, I'm too much in your debt already. You've extended my resolve for an extra quarter hour. We needn't enslave more than one victim here."

"But it would be my pleasure. In the interest of science. What outcome do you anticipate? Surely you don't mean to sacrifice a digit?"

"That would be a feast to go down in the *Dionaea* history books, wouldn't it? But I don't think my little friend is up to the task. I only wanted to see whether the same digestive secretions would ooze from the surface of the trap, which has happened, as you see. If I could keep the position longer, I presume it would be more copious."

Together they took a silent moment to regard the little plant acquiring its species' first taste of human flesh. From jars throughout the room, tarantula matrons might have joined the pair, peering with their many eyes over their thresholds at the historic tableau.

Suddenly the dogs broke the peace, bounding up to lunge at the bay window and bark at a squirrel that had crept down a limb into view. Outside the window the squirrel clung to its limb and chided the dogs, mechanically flicking its tail.

"Goodness, at least let me rid you of these two wild beasts. I'll let them out the door and then fetch you some tea." Before she could object, Thatcher removed himself to the Treat kitchen, opening the front door en route and shooing his canines homeward. With little trouble he located kettle and cups, found the stove still warm from breakfast, and shortly returned with a tray of tea and biscuits. He laid it all out on the desk and pulled up a chair to join her. Mrs. Treat seemed greatly heartened.

"It must seem a ridiculous undertaking," she said. "To a man of science."

"Not at all. Curiosity can be dangerous but never ridiculous. You wanted to test the capacity of the plant. To know it better."

"I become attached, you see. After so many months with these plants, observing them intimately, I begin to feel as if we are of the same world."

"But you *are* of the same world, of course. What have you learned?"

"Well, it is a story. Mr. Darwin is also very interested in the plant carnivores, and how their unusual habits serve their survival. With this species he was curious to know whether one leaf can catch many flies successively. In his observations, once a leaf has caught a good-size insect it seems to be done in. But his specimens are cultivated in his glasshouse. I have access to a native population. It seemed an opportunity to be useful."

"To Mr. Darwin."

"Yes," she said, taking a long draught of tea with her unimprisoned hand. "Our little natives are more vigorous. I've informed him it is quite normal for a leaf to take a second insect. Many leaves will even take a third fly, but most aren't able to digest it.

I've recorded observations of five leaves that digested three flies each and opened again afterward, ready for another meal from the looks of it. But then they died after closing over the fourth fly." She helped herself to a biscuit.

Thatcher took his tea in silence. He saw that the potted plants on her desk were all the same species, the Venus flytrap. Mrs. Treat swallowed and continued. "On the other hand, some leaves aren't able to digest a single fly."

"Do you suppose they get indigestion?" he asked.

She laughed, revealing a charming set of dimples. "They do have preferences. I fret over them like children, wondering what will suit them best. I've fed them beetles and spiders, sometimes millepeds. They don't care for ants. The most curious thing is that their tastes change with the season. Only late in the summer have they begun showing any interest in the spider that people call grand-daddy-long-legs. Do you know it?"

"I'm afraid I've been called on to dispatch quite a few. They cause great upheaval in my household of women. Now I know where I should bring them for disposal."

"Oh please do, they are fascinating to watch with the flytraps. They court death by dropping their bodies into the trap with their long legs hanging out, as if they're trying the trap on for size. And then they are sorry, of course. The legs can go on wriggling for twenty-four hours after the victim is taken in. Sometimes longer."

"I hate to say it, but two of the three ladies of my household would pay a fee of admission to watch that awful writhing. Their vendetta against spiders is absolute."

"I know the loathing you mean," she said. "Hence my ruse of the flowers in the tarantula jars, for my lady friends. But do you feel, if girls could have their eyes trained to nature from an early age, they would not be burdened with this exhausting vendetta, as you call it?"

"I hold out some hope for our Polly, who might yet weep for the dying spider."

Mrs. Treat offered a sad little smile. "It is a hard business, the feeding web. I try to refrain from sentiment once the prey is in place. But it can be difficult."

"What would happen if you had second thoughts? Let's say, if you liberated the prisoner after a few hours of incarceration?"

Now Mrs. Treat grinned like a child who has inveigled an adult into a favorite game. "I expect he would look about, astonished, and then speed away as fast as he could. But only in the first hours. By the second day there is no reprieve."

"And then what, it dissolves?"

"Not quickly. On the average it takes a leaf seven days to digest soft-bodied spiders, flies, and small larvae. Hard-shelled beetles take longer."

Thatcher shot a worried glance at Mrs. Treat's fingertip, held determinedly in place. She seemed to have forgotten all anguish for the moment. "I wonder how you came to have such particular interest in these plants?"

"I can't say how it began, exactly. All plants interest me, but the carnivorous ones have become one of my special projects with Mr. Darwin."

She was either the most interesting person Thatcher had ever met, or she was mad. He had spent the better part of an hour trying to decide. "So you mentioned. Would that be Mr. Charles Darwin, in England?"

"At Down House in Kent, yes," she said, her warmth suddenly retreating. "There must be other Mr. Darwins but only the one with whom I have a correspondence."

"You have a correspondence."

"That's one of the latest I've had from him, just there on the top of that file. I can't reach it but you're welcome to look."

Thatcher felt reluctant but commanded. He reached for the letter and felt an instant jolt through his body. He had never seen Charles Darwin's handwriting, of course, but somehow felt he recognized the angular pencil strokes. "My Dear Mrs. Treat," it said below the Down House letterhead, Beckenham, Kent, and the date, June 1874. Thatcher's eye scanned down the page past the sundry thanks and good wishes.

My observations on cultivated plants of Dionaea muscipula are now complete, and I shall publish them in six or nine months, though they will be of little value compared with yours, made on the plant in its own country. I should very much like to hear about one point . . .

Glancing up, Thatcher caught the dark gaze leveled at him, and he blushed. She could see his masculine presumptions. His shame amplified as he cataloged them: The scientist's solitude he'd mistaken for an abandoned wife's loneliness. The wall of books assigned without hesitation to Dr. Treat. Those were her books, and her Mr. Darwin was the one at Down House, Kent. Thatcher laid the letter down feeling chastened.

"I envy you, Mrs. Treat. He must be the most interesting correspondent."

"I could discuss *Dionaea muscipula* all morning, and move on in the afternoon to *Utricularia*," she said. "But I know from experience, some would find it tedious."

This mild scolding, if it was that, made him keen for her favor. "I hope you will come to consider me a colleague, but I won't pretend I'm your peer. I have nothing to offer Mr. Darwin but my reverence. I stayed awake six nights running when I discovered *On the Origin of Species*, and I did the same last year when *The Descent of Man* came available in the Boston library. These books have turned the city on its head. The whole world, I suppose. But for me they bring a comfort I can hardly explain."

She seemed to relax a little. "How is that?"

He considered the question. "It's the solace of hearing a truth one has suspected a very long time. I've not had the luxury of buying many books, but those two volumes were my first purchases. This is what they have meant to me."

"Then you support his theory of descent through modification."

"It's remarkable the subject would come up. I spent this morning in a difficult meeting with my employer. When he offered me a teaching position in Vineland, I believed I was coming to an oasis of enlightenment. Yet I find Mr. Cutler has not settled his mind about allowing me to discuss Mr. Darwin's thinking with my pupils."

"Regardless of Mr. Cutler's mind, I trust yours is settled."

Thatcher took in and released a long breath. "I wonder if *settled* is an attainable state, Mrs. Treat. I torture myself with doubts. Of course I'm completely convinced by Mr. Darwin. No man could have collected so much evidence or syllogized it more clearly. But I can also see the despair it portends."

Mrs. Treat's brow furrowed. "Which sort of despair?" she asked quietly. She seemed to accept there were many.

"Well. People believe," he began, though he hardly knew how to state an animosity as widespread as the air they breathed. "*Most* people believe life can only be worth having if the deliberate business we call life belongs to us only. To mankind."

"Distinguished by God from the base existence of mosses and tadpoles. *That* sort of trouble," she said, sounding spectacularly untroubled. Thatcher envied her confidence. He turned over his hat and studied the inside of its crown, fuzzed with years of wear. His wife's strongest passion of the moment was that he abandon this hat and buy a new one.

"Yes. For *that* sort of person," he said finally. "Their distress is real. If my mother-in-law believed she shared any inheritance with the grand-daddy-long-legs, she would have to pluck off her limbs and tear out her own eyes. I don't exaggerate."

"Mr. Greenwood, earlier when I told you how I'd become attached to my little plants, you said we all are of the same world. You said, 'of course.'"

"Because I believe that! Not only believe but *feel* it. I've felt it since I was a boy catching minnows in the streams of the Catskills. In truth I have a mortifying confession, Mrs. Treat. A little while ago I was admiring the competent construction of your spiders' homes and lamenting my own, without any doubt of our kindred want for shelter."

"Where is the mortification in that? Our needs are every animal's needs."

"Yes. And like every animal, our losses and gains have shaped our bodies and made us the creatures we are. I believe it completely."

She leaned toward him now with such animate energy, he worried she might forget about her hand and spoil her experiment. "To have been made the creatures we are is a marvel. If the process required millennia rather than seven days, how can it be any less sublime?" Mrs. Treat's fingertip remained in the jaws of the Venus.

"Exactly. Mr. Darwin's argument does not malign divinity. I never thought so."

"No. Nor does he. He only means to argue for the unity of Creation." She glanced toward the photographs arranged on her mantelpiece. "I've exchanged these sentiments with Dr. Gray. He worries a good deal about God."

Did she mean *Asa* Gray? Thatcher would not be more astonished if the spiders in this parlor began to sing. "I have profound respect for Dr. Gray's crusade," he said.

"Did you know him? In Boston?"

"Only from afar."

"He is a brave soldier, determined to win our continent to Mr. Darwin's side."

"Brave soldiers sometimes die in battle, Mrs. Treat. My disagreement with Cutler this morning was painful. In Mr. Darwin's defense I might have planted the seeds of my demise."

She gave him a thoughtful look, but said nothing to this. No reassuring denial of his fears.

"You and I are not like other people," he ventured. "We perceive infinite nature as a fascination, not a threat to our sovereignty. But if that sense of unity in all life is not already lodged in a person's psyche, I'm not certain it can ever be taught."

"You are a teacher of natural sciences. Are you not?"

"I am. Also an employee, and head of a family. As it happens, a family in dire need of costly home repair. I have inherited a flawed house and find myself pledged to uphold it. If I should lose my home and vocation . . ." He found it difficult to go on. Since that awful moment with Rose, the day he told her, he had resisted believing a truth he now saw plainly. Mrs. Treat waited for him to say it.

"If I lose my position here, and fail to find means for preserving our home, I'm sorry to say my wife would probably follow. I would lose her also. I can see no happy end for myself in noble crusades."

Mrs. Treat looked him directly in the eye. "Mr. Greenwood, those are qualities personal to you. They have no bearing on truth."

Such words, and yet she'd spoken them without a hint of chastisement, only as one scientist to another. Whatever else he might be, she expected him to be rational. "Of course," he said. "You observe the situation correctly."

Now she leaned toward him, guileless as a girl in her confidence. "We are given to live in a remarkable time. When the nuisance of old mythologies falls away from us, we may see with new eyes."

"Falls away, or is torn. The old mythologies are a comfort to many."

"But we are creatures like any other. Mr. Darwin's truth is inarguable."

"And because it is true, we will argue against it as creatures do. Our eyes are not new, nor are our teeth and claws. I'm afraid I foresee a great burrowing back toward our old supremacies, Mrs. Treat. No creature is easily coerced to live without its shelter."

"Without shelter, we stand in daylight."

"Without shelter, we feel ourselves likely to die."

Again she answered his dread with a thoughtful gaze, and only that. No pabulum of reassurance. Here was the rare sort of woman who could recognize an occasion when further words are useless, and still say none. Not even to an uncomfortable companion. Thatcher had the feeling she could see into his soul.

He stood and moved his chair back to its place near the étagère. "I have overstayed my welcome. Everything you say is right, of course. Now I should clear this tray and take my leave."

"No, leave the tray. The tea and nibbles will help me bear up. But I believe I am about to concede my little botanical campaign."

"I hope you can forgive my intrusion today, as much as I have profited from it."

She smiled. "Your call was heaven sent. Please intrude again soon."

"It isn't out of the question, I'm afraid. But we will try to do a better job of keeping our own hounds, Mrs. Treat. I'm sorry."

"Not at all. They are gentle company."

He thought to ask. "Do you happen to know which one is which?"

"You'll find Scylla on your left, outside the door. He likes the shade. He's dug a little wallow there under the yew hedge. Charybdis prefers the sun."

When Thatcher stepped outside he was surprised to see the potbellied clouds of a gathering storm, and the two hounds still lying on either side of the steps, as she'd said they would be. Poor Polly would be in a lather after so much time. She would think all three of them had gotten tangled in Mrs. Treat's web.

Thatcher closed the door behind him and felt like Odysseus as he stepped between the two beasts, drawing up the mantle of his worries, turning homeward, striking out.

5

⌒⌒

Striking Out

Getting Nick ready to go for a drive set a new high-water mark for Willa's patience, definitely harder than buckling two squirming toddlers into cereal-encrusted car seats. This morning she felt nostalgia for those days when her passengers might cry, vomit, kick off shoes, or whine for ice cream but never tell her to quit horse-dicking around and get the goddamn show on the road.

Step one was to carry his suitcase-size portable oxygen compressor to the car, wedge it behind the driver's seat, and plug it into the cigarette lighter. (No! The twelve-volt outlet, as Tig had lately corrected her, because seriously, Mom, you think Americans still light cigarettes inside cars?) Start the ignition, make sure the thing was hissing, and leave the car running.

Next, back in the house, she had to detach Nick from the big compressor in his bedroom that served as his mother ship. Its powerful pump pulsed oxygen through a long, flexible tube that gave him free range of the first floor, though the line was always getting pinched under chair legs, tangling underfoot, and setting off poor

Dixie's inborn snake alarm. Willa tried not to wince as she removed the yellowed plastic cannula from Nick's face. She found the
thing repellent, especially the ends that tipped into his inflamed
nostrils. She suspected a latex sensitivity but wasn't going to bring
that up. Nick classed allergies along with mental illness as symptoms of weak resolve.

It felt treacherous to switch off the main compressor, the eternal
backbeat of their household, and to hear its pulse go silent. For a
couple of rattled seconds they stared at each other. Now he was
free, or as close to that as Nick could get, briefly off the compressor
and breathing bottled oxygen. With the metal bottle hooked to
the back of his wheelchair he could be an overland scuba diver.
Unfortunately this arrangement would get him only as far as the
car, where she would hook him up to the car-charged compressor.
He'd resist another changeover, but they'd been through all this.
The bottled oxygen went too fast, he would breathe through most
of a tank in the drive to Philadelphia. The cost of refilling it was
more than a tank of gas.

Ferrying Nick to the car in his wheelchair was nearly beyond
her power. In the year he'd lived with them, Willa had somehow
managed never to do this alone. But today she'd volunteered to
drive him without thinking it through, and the family had all
gone their various ways while the doctor's appointment loomed.
She tried to recall whether he'd been out even once, all summer,
and thought not. Such a housebound soul might be expected to
marvel at the sunlight and blue sky, rather than become a crybaby
of the three hundred–pound class. He refused to help shift his
weight as she nudged him over the doorsill onto the porch and
down two disintegrating steps to the sidewalk.

She felt a stab of lost homeowner innocence: on move-in day
they'd discussed cosmetic repairs to this porch, naively planning a
facelift when they were going to need something well beyond All

the King's Horses. Whenever the Petrofaccio team banged on the roof the whole structure shuddered, widening the fissures down the walls. Willa could see daylight through some of these cracks from her bed.

"I'm afraid you're going to fall forward," she warned as she levered Nick over degenerate concrete. "I need you to put some of your weight on your feet."

He grunted a negative.

"I'm serious, Nick. I'm not strong enough to do this without your help."

He waved a hand in the air. *"Ston poutso mou louloudia kai giro giro melises."* Meaning, "My penis has flowers and bees buzzing around it." The Greek tongue stopped at nothing to express the depth of a feeling: in this case, of not giving a damn.

"Really. Not even a little?"

"I'm a cripple. You think this chair is for giving my balls a joyride?"

What Willa thought, as she muscled him toward the driveway, was that he still managed to get himself toileted and dressed without help, so this transfer could be easier. So much of life with infirmity came down to dignity and will. Nick wanted to go to the bathroom alone, but not to the doctor at all. Willa also thought, after she'd barreled him into the car, hooked him up to his automotive compressor, and headed down Landis Avenue, that they were probably not far from the day he would require help with his intimate daily tasks. She wouldn't want Iano doing that for his father. But on their income, any request for live-in help might as well be sent to the tooth fairy.

Since Iano's mother died, Nick had made the rounds of the three older sisters who'd stayed close by in Arizona. Starting with Athena, the eldest, he'd lasted a year or so before getting passed on to Lita, then Irini. Their mother, it was now understood, had been a saint. Each sister thought she could take him, then watched Nick's afflictions grow more ruthless along with his disposition, and finally declared: Now Pop is *really* losing it, suggesting no previous warden quite knew the trouble she'd seen. Still, each transfer was accepted as a filial failure. Iano, the only son, was the end of the line.

From Landis Avenue Willa turned onto the four-lane that ran north from Vineland into flat, sparsely wooded country. Through the roadside trees she caught glimpses of one industrial park after another strung out between fallow fields and pine woods, with the odd deciduous tree laboring to turn itself red. Summer had surrendered to autumn in the last week, arriving around the same time as in Virginia but less gracefully, Willa thought. She was homesick for the blue mountains and veiled horizons of their lost college town, and with an older ache, for the steep hills of her childhood, even if they'd mostly been turned into coal-tipped wasteland now. South Jersey's table-flat terrain and white sandy soil struck her as foreign, and so did the road signs: ENTERING TWP OF PITTS-GROVE. What did that even mean? WAWA OPEN 24 HOURS.

She shot cryptic glances at Nick, who was giving the scenery some attention. Surely he must feel a tiny bit happy to be catapulting through a totally new environment, secured to his aqualung. An intrepid whale striking out to conquer New Jersey.

The whale spoke up. "What did you do with my cigarettes?"

Dying of COPD, drowning in his own wrecked, soupy lungs, Nick still smoked. She and Iano banned it from the rest of the house but Nick was allowed to roll himself out onto a little sun porch attached to his bedroom, open the windows, and puff away.

"Sorry, you can't," she said.

"What?"

The engine noise must have drowned what little hearing he had left. This would be a journey of raised voices. "Can't," she said loudly. "Sorry. Not here in the car."

"*Gamo tin panageia sou.*" Meaning, "I fuck your Virgin Mary."

"Like she would let you," Willa said. Iano's family claimed Greek swearing wasn't really what it sounded like to foreign ears, and that even *this* was a garden-variety curse used by decent people. Willa felt that sixty years in a new country might be long enough to reset the obscenity dial.

"You can't handle a little smoke?" he persisted. "Gotta be such a yuppie health freak you won't let an old man have his pleasure?"

Yuppies, Willa thought. What decade was that, in which millennium? She pulled into the right lane to let a tailgating pickup pass her. "You're breathing one hundred percent oxygen. If you lit up in here we'd probably blow up like the *Hindenburg.*"

"I smoke at the house."

"Yep. In a big, drafty house beside an open window." She tried to enunciate without sounding bossy, which was pretty impossible to do. "In this car I'm pretty sure we're an oxygen-enriched environment. It leaks out of your cannula."

He grunted.

"Iano doesn't let you smoke in the car. Your daughters never did. Am I right?"

No response.

"Why would it be different now, just because it's me driving?"

He blew through his lips a long, beleaguered expiration that let Willa know how he felt about rules like this. *Ha!* she thought, Tig was wrong. *Nick* was the American who would still light a cigarette inside a car. Risk of self-immolation notwithstanding.

"It was hydrogen," he finally said.

She glanced over at him. He was pouting, staring straight ahead with his double chins tucked down so his face melted into his neck and then his shirt collar, to dreadful effect. Jabba the Hutt. It astounded her that this man had spawned her husband. She could find no point of intersection, physical or otherwise.

"What was hydrogen?" she asked.

"That zeppelin that blew to hell and killed all the fancy-pants passengers. The *Hindenburg*."

His tone made clear the passengers had deserved their horrific destiny for some reason. The fanciness of their pants. That's how it worked in Nick World. What scared Willa was how well she could predict the bizarre parameters of that place.

"I'm sure you're right," she said. "It was hydrogen. Oxygen might be slightly less explosive. Sometime if you'd like to test your hypothesis please be my guest. As long as it's somebody else's car, and no member of my family is in it."

She heard the castigation in *my family* and felt some remorse, but this man didn't belong to her. Her own parents had given her every kind of succor their lives allowed. The person she should now be driving to a doctor's appointment was her mother. Willa had pleaded with Darcie to move in with them during her final years but her sweet mother resisted to the end, unwilling to be a burden. Instead, Willa got Nick.

They passed an exit to a town called Glassboro. "Jersey is supposed to be the Garden State," she said. "I always figured that was somebody's idea of a joke."

"Glassboro," Nick commented. "Used to make a shitload of glass in Jersey. Back before the war that was a big thing, the Jersey glass factories."

Willa found that "shitload of glass" lit up an unfortunate mental image. She tried to erase it by pondering which war he meant, and whether this could be true. Reviewing what she knew of the origins of glass, she came up with roughly nothing. An island outside Venice where she and Iano once watched artists blowing fiery bubbles, making preposterously expensive vases. They'd had wine at lunch and were struck giddy with a fear of busting up the artisan glass gallery. Their honeymoon had started with Greek relatives in airless houses and ended with sex on lots of beaches.

"Seriously?" she asked. "Glass? Why here?"

"Silica. All that white sand there is silica. That's your main ingredient for making glass. And the trees. Wood, for firing the furnaces. That's all you need."

For most of his working life Nick had been a welder, with a functional knowledge of heat and chemistry. He barely had a sixth-grade education, given the turbulent backstory of rural island life, war, and narrow escape. But the man knew his materials.

North of Glassboro the land remained empty but exits grew more frequent: *TWP* meant "township." Township of Washington, Township of Deptford. Still, it was hard to imagine a city the size of Philadelphia popping up out of those trees anytime soon.

"Put on the radio," he commanded.

"Well," she said, "that's a problem. We would have to agree on a station."

"Talk show," he said, and mumbled some call letters she didn't try to recognize. He leaned forward to study the buttons and displays on the dash. They'd had this car nearly ten years but Nick hated digital controls. He was a self-proclaimed analog man.

"Your talk radio is not going to be my cup of tea," she said. She knew what he wanted: jocular, obscenely confident commentators who disparaged any kind of progressive thinking, egged on by callers who were angry about even the most basic modern social arrangements. Gay marriage aside, some of these people seemed incensed that their kids had to attend racially integrated schools. They were offended to distraction by the idea of a nonwhite man at the helm of their great nation. Probably they weren't completely sold on female suffrage. These callers were clinging to a century-old vision of America, and Willa preferred to forget such people existed.

Nick located the FM button and skimmed through some static, then turned the volume to a level probably audible to other drivers on the highway. The self-possessed talking head came booming in with the topic of the day, a crazy presidential candidate who would surely burn out by the end of the month. The Bullhorn. He was offensive to everyone else Willa knew or could imagine, so it stood to reason Nick would admire him.

"No way," Willa said loudly. "Music or nothing. That's our deal."

Suddenly they were plunged into the outskirts of Philly. Out of the sand flats they rose into a confluence of highways and abruptly over water, the Walt Whitman Bridge.

Willa punched the radio off and Nick went slack. She knew he was scheming. He would sit there obsessed, focusing all his energy on waiting until the time was right to creep forward and get his station back on. Tig had been just like that as a toddler, possessed of a superhuman, intransigent patience. Maybe that was the genetic intersection. Nick's stubbornness had passed down to a son too cheerful to accept it, then found purchase in a granddaughter. Everything else about Iano had to come from Roula. Willa hadn't known her mother-in-law very well, so her admiration of the woman could safely flourish.

The city skyline lay ahead to the right, the stadium on their left, and signage informed Willa she would have to pay a five-dollar toll to exit the bridge.

"Damn it," she said. "Can you reach my purse?" It was in the backseat. She might as well ask him to run a 10K for charity. She eased into the far right lane, where the traffic was blessedly backed up, giving her time to unbuckle her seat belt, turn around, and grab her purse. She extracted a five-dollar bill from her wallet. Sure enough, Nick nabbed that opportunity to lean up and turn on the radio again. The jokey talk-show guys were still discussing the candidate, whether lampooning or lauding him Willa couldn't even tell. He sounded like a parody of poor statesmanship anytime he opened his mouth. She punched off the radio.

"I wasn't kidding," she said. "I'm not going to listen to those guys. I'm not asking, I'm telling, and let me remind you I have some power here. When we get off this bridge I could pull the car over and turn off the ignition."

Was she threatening his oxygen supply? Willa would not suffocate a fellow human, regardless of creed. She couldn't stand the person she sounded like right now. "I'm sorry, Nick. I'm not going to shut you off. We've been family a long time. Let's just get ourselves through one more day."

Nick grunted a beleaguered assent. Traffic had ground to a standstill as three lanes of inbound traffic merged into one. Amid a gaggle of orange cones and the filthy carcasses of heavy equipment, the bridge was undergoing some major repair.

"What you said the other night at dinner? That was right."

Willa turned to stare. "Wow. Mark the date."

"What?"

"I said, thank you, Nick. Please tell me what I was right about."

"We all just want better for our own. Tough times for you and Iano right now, with the kids and all. Everything so fucked up. I hate that for you."

"Thanks." She stared out the window at a ponytailed guy with Mr. Universe arms wielding a jackhammer, shattering pavement like broken glass. The noise was surreal. She could feel it vibrating her teeth in her jawbones. She envied Nick's deafness.

"The thing is," Nick said, "you know what the cause of it is? Why we got nothing to pass on after working hard all our lives?"

"I hate to ask. What's the cause of it?"

"The wetbacks."

Willa nodded. Of course. Please let this traffic move forward.

"The plant where I worked all those years? You should see it now. Nothing but wetbacks. Back in my time we had a union looking after us. Then the Mexicans come in and take everything out from under our asses."

"I see. Illegal Mexican immigrants invaded your plant, wrestled the white guys to the ground, escorted them out, and then told the company, 'Sure boss, we don't need any union wages.' That's how it went down?"

"Not exactly."

"The laws changed so plant owners could break strikes and bust up the unions, back in the eighties. I know that for a fact, I was covering labor news at the time. The pay scale collapsed. You know this, Nick. Weren't you forced to take early retirement?"

Nick didn't answer. She knew the layoff had injured his pride. Willa felt a pang, not of sympathy with her fellow redundant but excitement at the memory of that beat and its thrilling polemics. Older reporters had laughed at her for coming to work in sneakers, keen to get assigned to some showdown on a picket line, but they didn't laugh at the stories she got. She'd been so green then, still struggling to master a professional journalist's cool, and the ban on viewing her subjects emotionally. Even if they were getting teargassed.

"If it's all Mexican workers in that plant now," she felt compelled to explain to deaf ears, "it's because nobody else will do such dangerous work for lousy pay."

"Yeah, they changed the law. Now it says they gotta hire everybody but the whites. Girls too, they got *girls* in there now. It's not natural."

Brake lights on the car ahead flickered, hinting at forward motion, but nothing came of it. Willa considered turning off the ignition to save gas, but then remembered the matter of oxygen pump and asphyxiation. She took a deep breath.

"You're thinking of fair-hiring laws. They require companies to hire applicants if they're qualified, that's all. Regardless of race or gender. Not *because* of it." The jackhammer now seemed to be operating directly on her skull. So this is how it turns out, she thought. Hell is the Walt Whitman Bridge. *I hear America singing! Singing with open mouths their strong melodious songs!*

"Thing is, if there's girls and Mexicans in a factory, there's not going to be enough jobs for the men. That's what I'm saying."

"So we gals should stay home and let our husbands bring home the bacon. That's your proposal for economic recovery?" She tapped the gas lightly, edging almost to the bumper of the car ahead. "Well, hot dog. You're looking at a housewife with no job. Give me a medal, I'm doing my part for God and country."

"You don't have to go all pissy on me." He leaned forward and turned the radio back on. Miraculously, at the same moment, the traffic began to move.

"One paycheck doesn't feed a family anymore, Nick. Seems like you'd notice a thing like that." All three of his daughters were employed. One was divorced from a deadbeat, with four kids she had to raise on her own. Willa marveled at his capacity to live a life undisturbed by actual evidence. Nick concentrated on scanning across radio static, resting briefly on a rap song, moving on, finding more. Philadelphia stations seemed tuned to the hip-hop demographic.

He turned it off and heaved himself back against the seat. "Goddamn monkey music. Goddamn—"

"Just don't," Willa interrupted in a singsong command. "Don't say that word. You have to know how offensive that is."

"Offensive to you."

"Yes!" she hissed, easing up to the tollbooth finally, opening the window, and holding out a five-dollar bill to a beautiful young man with long cornrows and heartbreaking, curly eyelashes. He nodded at her in a rhythmic way that led her to see the twin jewels of his red earbuds. She smiled back, rolled up the window, and drove on. "Offensive to that young man and to me and most other people alive in the twenty-first century. Regardless of our own color. Sometimes, Nick. *Jesus*." She bit her lip.

"Well, I'm a sick old man. I'm not gonna be around that much longer."

Willa neither confirmed nor denied this prediction. She concentrated on finding her way toward the university medical complex. Her phone's navigator voice was in the middle of a disapproving recalculation. During her chat with Nick she had somehow missed an important cue, exiting the northbound from Vineland too soon and taking the wrong bridge. Who even knew there were two bridges into Philadelphia? The whole Walt Whitman experience had been a gratuitous wrong turn. Now they seemed to be following the edge of the waterfront. She could see no water at all, only the strange vision of gigantic ships moving along beside them, looming above buildings and trees. An industrial smokestack belched fire. The air in the car suddenly smelled of Delaware Bay and swampland.

"If Roula was here she would treat me decent," Nick said. "Roulaki, there was a woman knew how to take care of a man."

"I'm sorry she isn't here. I wish she were."

"Ha. I bet. So you wouldn't have to."

Willa would have to pace herself to get through this day. Nick was probably exhausting even to himself. It couldn't be easy to keep track of individual grudges against so many disparate objects, people, and doctrines. Surely it would be simpler to have some unifying theory of hatred that covered everything at once. Instead, they'd just have to keep feeding all Nick's fires with the extra oxygen.

✂

In the doctor's office Willa longed to lie down on one of the nice upholstered sofas under the large abstract paintings and take a nap. She couldn't get past the first page of the medical history forms. Nick refused to fill them out himself, claiming the writing was too blurry for him to read. It might have been true, vision could have been one more casualty of his uncontrollable blood sugar. She would add that to the list of boxes she'd already checked: arthritis, arrhythmia, bursitis, cardiovascular disease, deafness, emphysema, fluid retention—this drear alphabet was long. Among other diabetic swindles, Nick's extremities had initiated a horrific process of melting off his body. He'd hidden the open wounds on his legs, nobody knew for how long. Willa hadn't asked about the masses of bloody Kleenex that repulsed her when she emptied his trash, but eventually Tig noticed the bleeding through his socks. The condition must be excruciating. Objectively Willa knew that Nick Tavoularis was no place to be, a supersized house of pain besieged by aggressive fear or pride that made him resist medical attention. He believed all doctors were in cahoots, and that the intertwined snakes on their caduceus represented the twin ambitions of getting rich and killing their patients.

From their names she guessed both physicians in this practice were from India. She saw no way of preparing anyone for the bigoted outburst likely to greet the doctor's hello and extended hand. She considered writing *Tourette's* on the intake form, but she knew it was wrong to associate Nick's odium with any real disease. At least these doctors were male. To Willa's relief, every female physician on her list had been too booked up to take him. Female practitioners in Nick's view were freakish women driven by perversion to touch male strangers' bodies. He would share his opinion freely.

She wondered if he'd noticed this whole facility was being run by nonwhite workers. In the lobby downstairs, a battery of clerks checking patients into the complex were lined up in individual glass cubicles displaying a palette of sepia hues. Both receptionists in this office were African American, one with a voluminous weave and brightly colored nails, the other a striking beauty in a short-cropped Afro who resembled a young Eartha Kitt. Two nurses—one older, one young, both Asian—came intermittently to the portal to summon the next patient from the waiting room. The patients were elderly and white, without exception. From what Willa had seen of the City of Brotherly Love, this stratification of service workers and the served seemed to hold throughout.

She returned to the list of maladies, wishing she could just check those few that did *not* apply. It took a moment for her to understand the receptionist was trying to get her attention. "Miz Tavoularis," she was repeating, pronouncing it "Tavyalerius," though Willa had certainly heard worse. And it wasn't her name, of course, she was Knox. Even back in her lovestruck youth when she'd married Iano, it had seemed rash to trade away four letters for four unpronounceable syllables. Willa walked to the desk with her clipboard of overdue homework, summoned by the receptionist with the painted nails. At close range the manicure was arresting, each long nail its own vivid little painting: flowers, peace symbols, lines, and swirls.

"I'm sorry, I'm not finished with these forms. He's complicated." Willa tried a contrite smile, but the receptionist wasn't having it. She tapped her computer screen with a talon that wore a smiley face.

"There's a problem here with your insurance."

Willa reflexively reached into her purse before realizing this gatekeeper was already in possession of her insurance cards. "I gave you my information."

"Yeah, I *know* you gave it to me, ma'am. What I'm saying is, we got a problem. We can't accept that insurance here."

I don't even want to be *here,* Willa wished to declare. *Please don't make me fight for the privilege.* "I understand you don't process Medicare here and you need supplemental insurance. Your office explained all that over the phone. That's why I gave you the other card. It's our family plan."

"We can't accept the other plan either. If he had the Medigap plan plus part A, B, and D or maybe the Medicare Advantage plan, I'm still not sure about your family HMO as his supplemental. But we might be able to work with you then."

"Yeah. I think those are all things he would have had to sign up for when he turned sixty-five, and that didn't happen. I'm truly sorry it didn't. But now he's kind of the *Titanic* of preexisting conditions, and this university employee plan is what we can get." Willa tried to show sufficient remorse for having a Medicare-delinquent father-in-law. The truth was so very far beyond "didn't happen." Nick's essential identity rested on his contempt for Pussy Welfare Crybabies, which extended to matters like the Medigap.

The receptionist seemed tired of repeating herself. "Well, your plan number doesn't come up on my screen so that means we don't take it."

"It's a new policy," Willa offered. "My husband just started working here this fall and signed us up on the faculty policy. The family plan. Mr. Tavoularis is my husband's father. They told us coverage would start after thirty days." Willa watched her many arguments having no effect. "Maybe it's not registered yet, or something? Can you try checking it again?"

In a display of her infinite patience, the receptionist shook her head very slowly. "This policy you have here is an HMO. Even if it does apply to your father, which I don't think it does, you're not authorized to see a doctor outside your own network."

"My father-in-law needs a specialist. He probably needs several of them but right now his blood sugar is out of control and that's what we're here for. I called every endocrinologist in our network, and then I called anybody else that might work with an advanced diabetic, and nobody could take him. That's why we've ended up here in the University Health Complex, with the only coverage available to us through the university, and ironically you don't take it."

"We couldn't see him anyway without authorization from the manager of your health maintenance network."

"And who would that be?"

"The phone number is on the back of your card."

"I've called that number, believe you me. I was advised that if nobody in the network could treat my father-in-law I would have to go out of network. That's why we're here. To see a doctor. Which we would like to do."

"Okay, so are you saying you will accept the charges for seeing Dr. Saberwal today out of pocket, and you don't want us to bill your insurance company?"

Willa revised her previous observation about service workers and the served. This particular operative was going to the mat to protect the nice insurance companies from any pesky entanglement with Willa's sick person. "Obviously I want you to bill my insurance company," Willa said. "That's why I pay every month for health insurance we can't afford. That's who advised me to go out of network. Can you please tell me what more I need to do to make this happen?"

Abruptly she slid the glass door shut, clicked her marvelous nails on her computer keyboard, then leaned over and had a brief conversation with Eartha. They both peered at the screen, which seemed to confirm all their worst suspicions. Nails slid open the glass.

"In order to be covered for an out-of-network we need to have written confirmation from all the specialists in your network that the patient can't be treated in-network. If you want, your primary care physician might be able to coordinate the paperwork."

Willa stared. "Those doctors don't even have time to see their paying customers. You think they're going to spend their lunch hour writing letters of recommendation?"

Nails stared back. "You'll have to ax your primary care physician about that."

Willa wanted to ax someone, not a physician. She glanced over at Nick. There would be no whining to him about this—he would just say he'd told her so. Nick *really* didn't want to be there. He appeared now to have fallen asleep in his wheelchair. He also seemed blue-gray in color, although that might just have been the fluorescent lighting and zealous air-conditioning. The waiting room was freezing, and every waiting patient bore the same gray pall. Several different oxygen machines gave off small, syncopated hisses. Willa's imagination made the very short leap from there to being trapped in a morgue.

She turned back to the receptionist. "I know this probably changes nothing, but can I just tell you my father-in-law is oozing blood and fluid from most of his lower body? His pain has to be off the charts. I've been trying for two months to find a doctor who'll see him, we waited three weeks for this appointment, and today it took more hassle than you want to hear about to get him here. And the best you can do is send him home to fill up his shoes with blood? I think what you're saying is, the man needs to die."

The receptionist held Willa's gaze without any visible emotion. She probably heard pathetic pleas like this five times a day. "If you'd like to see Dr. Saberwal today, I can give you the payment forms."

"In which I give you my credit card information and a lien on my house and promise to pay all charges out of pocket. Thanks but no thanks." Actually, she thought, Dr. Saberwal could have the house. She took her cards and started to walk away.

"Ma'am?"

She turned around to see Eartha leaning out the opened glass cubicle, beckoning her back. Was this going to be a good cop, bad cop routine? Willa returned to the window. The receptionist spoke quietly.

"We've had a lot of problems with that HMO. Are you and your husband both university employees?"

"No, just my husband."

"It's not really my place to advise you, but what a lot of people are doing is taking out a separate policy for the nonemployee members of the family."

"A separate policy?"

"Yes. If you don't have your own coverage through an employer you can qualify for coverage and even get his Medigap through the ACA. You'll probably find it saves you money over the other family plan, and you'll get better coverage."

Willa tilted her head toward Nick. "I appreciate your advice, but my father-in-law would do surgery on himself before he'd sign up for Obamacare. I'm not even kidding."

The receptionist smiled. "We see a lot of that. You wouldn't have to tell him."

The window slid shut and Willa crossed the waiting room to rouse Nick from the gray caul of his slumber. He wasn't going to see the doctor after all. What an adventure: from his position, victorious.

⬥

Rather than take the day as a total loss, Willa texted Iano to ask if he could meet them for lunch. He texted back immediately: he was tied to office hours but they should come over and visit. Willa hadn't seen his office, or set foot on campus, before this day.

"Trouble will be parking." Iano added a sad face emoticon.

She shot back, "No worries! We have Magic Pass!" Double smiley faces.

Nick's handicapped parking placard was the only perk of the Nick arrangement, and Willa took it as her righteous due. Directed by Siri's know-it-all voice, she backed out of their ideal parking spot at the medical complex and headed across campus to a matching one she was sure she would find directly in front of Iano's building. Willa's dark mood reversed at the prospect of poaching on Iano's office hours. Was it ridiculous to be excited about seeing your husband in the middle of the day, after the passage of marital decades? Most of her girlfriends over the years had thought so, and were always a little too glad to advise Willa of her husband's weak points.

These friends didn't get it. Flaws included, the marriage was a miracle. Willa had *conjured* Iano, long before she met him, starting around the year she copied out the lyrics of "Tea for the Tillerman" and "Into White" in her poetry journal and argued with her eighth-grade English teacher that Cat Stevens was a modern-day Lord Byron. She taped a horizontal cordon of album covers across her bedroom wall, portrait-side out, and spent a preponderance of her adolescence gazing at the soulful black eyes and sensitive mouth framed by that close-trimmed beard and curly mane. She composed letters to Mr. Stevens at the restrained rate of one per month, sent care of A&M Records. It didn't matter at all that he never wrote back.

What mattered was that in her freshman year in college, well after she'd stopped writing fan letters, Iano Tavoularis materialized in the doorway of her dorm room (by mistake; he was looking for a girl named Kendra, same room, different floor) and didn't leave for the rest of the weekend. At the moment of apotheosis, "Moonshadow" was playing on her stereo. To Willa he was physically indistinguishable from the pop star she loved, though a decade younger, which didn't hurt, and he knew all the lyrics to "Tea for the Tillerman," plus "Wild World" and "Hard Headed

Woman." She couldn't believe her luck. He was not technically a musician, and Willa didn't care. He was funny and gorgeous and spoke Greek and found Willa amazing, both intellectually and in bed. She might have been the lone female fan who didn't wring her hands when the actual Mr. Stevens converted to Islam and quit singing, or even when he made some ill-chosen remarks about the fatwa against Salman Rushdie. Her affections by then had been fully transferred. Willa didn't need a singer, it turned out. The singer was the warm-up act.

Now she rejoiced, approaching Iano's building, to find the predicted bank of empty wheelchair-designated parking spots less than fifty feet from the door. Even that short distance was more than Nick cared to cross to go visit his son, it turned out. He was fed up with the whole wheelchair-and-oxygen-machine switcheroo. This was fine with Willa, who agreed to leave him in the car, ignition running, air-con blasting, and windows rolled down partway for safety's sake. Ecstatic to be free of her charge, she set aside the morality of using that parking spot when the designee wasn't technically going anywhere.

She cut across a small lawn where dozens of halter-topped girls and shirtless young men had parked themselves on the grass. They seemed too disorganized to be a class, but too numerous to be random sun lovers out catching the year's last rays. She would ask Iano if it was some kind of sit-in. He would know. College activists swirled around Iano like bees, eagerly mistaking his kindness for approval: the Campus Greens, the divestment committees, even the antiestablishment hard core could get Dr. Tavoularis to sign on as faculty adviser. Willa couldn't imagine this had helped his career of tenure battles, even though his credentials as a radical were in fact lousy. Arriving too late in college to protest Vietnam or burn down any ROTC buildings, and much too early to occupy anything like Wall Street, they were *that* generation. In his

Intro to Political Philosophy classes Iano always spent too many lectures on Aristotle and ended up slighting Karl Marx. But he had a certain twinkle that encouraged renegades and unsettled administrators.

And was catnip to coeds, Willa was now reminded, finding six of them lined up outside his closed door. They sat on the floor with long, tanned legs extended straight in front of them like Rockettes in cutoffs and Toms. Willa felt a twinge of intimidation but laid a benevolent smile across the lot of them anyway, and tapped on the closed door.

"He's in *conference*," one of them hissed, just as Iano called *"Moraki mou? Ela!"*

She opened the door and Iano waved her in with a big, happy gesture. Willa answered to some frankly awful pet names: *moraki* was a diminutive of *moro*, literally meaning "infant," same root as *moron*. And not one of those Rockettes needed to know. Greek was the clandestine language of Willa's marriage. In very public places Iano could and did torture her by proposing vivid sexual acts.

"Gino, this is Willa, my wife. Gino is doing an undergraduate thesis on modern instruments of foreign policy. Where's Pop?"

"Tuckered out. He didn't feel like getting out of the car. We've had quite a day. Should I wait outside till you two finish tuning your instruments?"

Gino laughed. He seemed lovely. "We're done, I was just taking off actually. Gotta rock the revolution out there at three." Gino flipped his long hair sideways, picked up his backpack, shook hands with Iano in an adult manner, and scooted out. Once the door had closed, Iano fell backward with some drama into his chair.

She lifted an eyebrow. "You've still got the cheerleader squad out there, Dr. T."

He gave Willa a helpless, pleading look. "Save me? Maybe Pop is having a heart attack or something and I have to dash away?"

"Would that he were."

Willa absorbed Iano's smile in all its facets: mischievous, grateful, weary, content. So much of their contract passed without words in five-second pauses like this.

"Sorry I can't steal you off to lunch. I should have brought you a sandwich."

"Already had one. Did you and Pop eat?"

"Didn't have time. So I have to ask. What revolution are we rocking at three?"

"A campaign speech. Well, it's not really a speech, it's a live feed in the parking lot. A van comes in with a big screen and they watch a talk that's happening somewhere else. A socialist running for president, who'd have guessed? These kids are going nuts. Kick the billionaires' asses, raise minimum wage, make college free. *That* revolution."

"Yikes, I'm in that parking lot. Will I be able to get out?"

Iano checked his watch. "You've still got half an hour."

So that was it, with the gathering tribes. Free college, clothing optional.

Iano sat up, suddenly reanimated. "Hey, did Zeke call you with his good news?"

"I haven't checked my phone. It's been . . ." She exhaled. "You won't believe this. Nick didn't get in to see a doctor. They wouldn't take our insurance."

"That's impossible."

"Possible."

"I swear I filed the paperwork. The very first week."

She had let him handle the insurance because he wanted badly to shoulder some of the burden of Nick, even though Iano was terrible at such things. Iano tried to look after his father's health and ended up buying him cigarettes. He'd probably assumed the HMO would cover Nick because they really needed that to happen. Willa sank into a chair so she and her husband would be on the same plane.

"Sweetheart, it's not your fault. I know you signed up. You did everything you were supposed to do, and it should have been enough. And still we totally and completely struck out. I'm not sure we have any options for Nick."

She watched him registering this: his father dying in their house without the kindness of medical backup. He cursed quietly.

"What *is* this, Iano? It's like the rules don't apply anymore. Or we learned one set, and then somebody switched them out. Oh, get this, the receptionist advised me to put him on Obamacare."

Iano's shoulders shook in a long, silent laugh. "It would be efficient, from an actuarial perspective. The day we signed him on, that would finish him off."

"Tempting."

Iano made a noble but unconvincing effort to smile. He was absorbing the genuine horror of this next phase in their sequence of family disasters. It took a lot to pull Iano off the happy train. His unexpected sobriety made Willa feel less alone, but also maybe terrified. What if Iano's joy was the tentpole of her sanity?

"So what's Zeke's good news?" she asked.

Iano lit up. "His investment start-up. They're getting their hands on something like ten million dollars."

"Christ. How on earth?"

"One of their Harvard connections. I'm sure we'll hear all about it tonight. Something to do with the fund he helped manage when he was a grad student. Now the college is farming out some of their accounts to private investment managers and one of his old advisers put it together. There's still some question about FINRA and internal approvals, I don't know the details, but Zeke is positive it's going to work. Good Money is off and running."

"Wow. Just like that."

"I guess that's why people go into debt at Ivy League schools. For the connections."

Willa found herself getting angry. "But really? Does this not strike you as crazy, that a kid who literally can't afford to rent a home for himself and his child is going to be managing somebody's ten million dollars?"

"He'll get commissions."

"Let us pray."

Willa knew he would. Zeke was more practical than his father about taking care of business. But unlike Iano, she just couldn't see this jackpot as some normal next step. Different as they were in temperament, father and son shared an unrealistic faith in good financial fortune. They *expected* it. In Iano's first-generation immigrant family, they might as well have had a cross-stitched sampler on the wall saying "God Bless Our Capitalist Home." Something in his bones promised Iano he was going to get into the club, and he'd passed that on. Willa's bones told her with equal conviction that the roof over their heads would not outlast the winter.

"Did the hedge fund baron mention whether he'll be home this afternoon? There's no way I can get Nick back into the house by myself."

"He's there now. He said Tig and her friend took the baby for a picnic in the graveyard or some damn thing, but he's purposely staying on hand so you'll have a landing crew when you get there."

"That was thoughtful of him."

"That's your son."

Willa was relieved to hear it, but still didn't want to go back to the car and drive home. Why do that, when she could sit here looking at her husband backlit from a window like some Raphaelite angel? Going gray at the temples, and wearing a button-down shirt, but still. In the looks department she would always believe she had married up, despite three decades of his testimonials. The

Greek tongue has an excess of words for *blue* and *ocean*, famously, but also for *love* and *pussy*, and these she knew. The turn-on for Iano was her delicacy, the fine-boned wrists and ankles he could encircle with his hands. Her little nose and cheekbones, slim hips and taut belly, corn-silk hair: all these were exotic in the swarthy tribe to which he'd been born. He adored the package.

"I'd better go. Your public is waiting."

Iano stood up and leaned across his desk to give her a kiss. "Sure you don't have time for me to eat up your *mouní* on my big industrial desk?"

Willa quaked. "Have mercy. Those girls out there would troll me."

※

Outside the building, the crowd had burgeoned into the hundreds. Unlike the tanning-bed groupies inside, this assembly was multi-colored, wildly groomed, and ready to rock, though nothing official seemed to be happening yet. The kids stood in clusters taking selfies: the insurrection on Instagram. Some wore official Rock the Revolution T-shirts but most just sported an allied shade of blue, proving team loyalty in the mode of a football game. Willa declined the offer of a bumper sticker and hoofed it to the parking lot, where she hoped she hadn't gotten herself logjammed in the new world order. The official van had arrived. Workers milled around it toting cables and setting up a gigantic screen on scaffolding.

At the edge of the parking lot she stopped, confused. Her car was gone. No, not gone, obscured. A clump of students had absorbed the spot where she'd parked. She couldn't see her vehicle, only a wall of shirtless backs, backpacks, neck tattoos, ponytails, everyone facing inward, crowding like feeding sharks around her aged Toyota. She skirted the group, starting to panic about what could be attracting all the attention. Maybe Nick really was having a heart attack. She made a complete circuit, finding no point of entry, getting angry at their vulgar curiosity. She had to get in there but would be damned if she'd push herself into that sweaty human broil. She'd reached her limit today on rescuing Nick. "Excuse me," she tried. "That's my car."

Faces turned toward her, all angry eyes and theatrically clamped lips. Not sharks, more like clams, of the very mad kind. They were *demonstrating*. Oh Christ, she thought. He'd taunted them. That would be Nick, yelling something to identify himself as anti–revolution rocker. And in a Gandhiesque method they'd learned in some peacekeeper training session, these kids were silently making a pearl of the grain of sand. Her car.

From deep inside the crowd she could hear a thread of belligerence. "*. . . and I tell you what, the dream is going to wake up. I know so many people in the energy business, great people, they want to do things for this country but you know what? They can't. People! We need leaders!*" Tinny applause roared up. The radio.

"Oh shit," Willa said aloud. He had it cranked up to max, finally getting the fix he'd been craving all day. She reached in her purse for keys but of course she'd left the car unlocked, engine running, windows down.

"*. . . and I'm going to tell you something, we're going to make this dream wake up for us, not the criminals and illegals that are taking over America right now . . .*"

Willa started pushing herself between uncooperative shoulders. "I'm sorry, this isn't . . . look, I can't stand that guy," she tried explaining to the flinty-faced kids, who weren't yielding. Reaching and groping between bodies made her queasy, but with some effort she found the door handle. Flung it open, burrowed her way into the car, and slammed herself in.

Immediately the seat belt warning started to ding. Nick sat with eyes closed in a coma of satisfaction. The monstrous man wouldn't even turn and look at her, while his hero railed on. "*You know something? We don't want them. Disgusting! We're not going to take the crap of the world anymore, we are getting this country back!"*

Willa buckled up before the *ding-ding-ding* dispersed the last of her marbles. Her hands shook so hard it took a few tries to jab the right knob and turn off the radio.

"Jesus Christ, Nick. Holy shit!" She punched the toggle that rolled up all the windows, and without really thinking about it, the one that locked all the doors. "*Jesus*," she said again. "What the *hell* were you thinking? What did you say to those kids?"

His eyes opened but he said nothing, looking straight ahead.

"Great. I can't even leave you for ten goddamned minutes without a babysitter?"

He still didn't face her, but finally spoke. "Nothing. Swear to God, I said nothing. They just came running over here."

She divined his misery, suddenly. Terror, regret, embarrassment: emotions that visited Nick so rarely she hardly recognized them, but his watery eyes would not meet hers and his hands clung together childishly in his lap. He would have had no idea his radio had been audible to the other end of the parking lot. Maybe he'd been too stubborn to turn it off, but more likely he never realized it was the problem. Or the weird demonstration had paralyzed him with fear. Or he just couldn't find the right button.

The offensive seemed to be regrouping but hadn't reached a new consensus. Quite a few bodies still jammed against the windshield, presenting as crumpled fabric, flattened flesh, a notable navel piercing, and many disembodied hands. A couple of grotesquely squashed faces. This revolution meant business.

Willa stared out through her glass bubble, dumb as a goldfish. Here was her inheritance, the job of protecting this poor old man, with exhausting labors and every dime her family could scrape together. She was trapped with her strange companion.

6

∞

Strange Companions

Polly was disappointed in the president. "He looked so *humble.*"
She chewed as she spoke. The long wait for supper had brought her
near to self-declared extinction.

"Humility is a virtue, dear."

"Not in a president, Mother. He looked as if he'd rather be riding his horse or reading a book than being a leader of men. *And* his
eyes didn't match."

"Cut your chop from the bone with the knife, do not gnaw
it," Aurelia directed. "You make the impression of being a hungry
animal."

"I *am* a hungry animal," Polly said, sawing away with her knife,
and Thatcher thought: Dear girl, she is. *Of the same world,* as Mrs.
Treat put it. With the dogs, if not yet the spiders.

Polly's forecast for today had been partly correct: President
Grant attended the school dedication and did shake Thatcher's
hand, but in a hallway after the ceremony, witnessed only by Professor Cutler and a few fellow teachers. The public events barely

outlasted the Reverend Pittinger's opening prayer, in which he blessed all things in Vineland, then on the earth, and was moving to the outer planets when a rain shower blew out of the elms and scattered the attendees from the lawn. The interruption was gratefully received. Afterward Thatcher was allowed to show the president his classroom (an opened door, a reflective nod) but to Polly's distress, finished the day with his veil of mystery intact.

"What on earth do you mean, his eyes didn't match?" asked Rose, gazing at the candle flames in their silver sconce while idly touching her throat. Her fingertips drew Thatcher's eyes to her collarbone. A wide ribbon outlined the low, square cut of her bodice and the rise of her breasts, and if men were not meant to stare at such, he wondered why women trimmed themselves out like advertising circulars.

"One of his eyes *drooped*. You saw, didn't you, Thatcher? He looked so sad."

Rose seemed suddenly startled into the present. "As you would, if you'd seen as many men dead under your command." She looked to Thatcher for agreement.

He hated speaking of the war. He'd managed to slip his father's noose and move with a regiment into Boston as a runner first, then as a medical assistant. The doctor who taught him to stanch wounds and bandage amputations took Thatcher into his home, put him to work, and eventually sponsored his education. War had wrecked the Union but worked the opposite for Thatcher, improving his life immeasurably. Leaving him with a moral debt no man could pay.

"I still think Professor Hook-Hand should have let Thatcher sit on the stage with him and Captain Landis. Even if no one but old Pittinger was allowed to speak."

Rose set down her fork. "Polly. A lady does not form opinions on the deficiencies of her elders. Especially not in the case of a missing hand."

A short laugh escaped Thatcher, pulling all the blue eyes his way. "I'm sorry. You've made him sound like a sensation novel."

"The case of the missing hand!" Polly cried.

"I'm sure I don't understand what you mean," said Aurelia.

"He means detective stories!" Polly clarified, unfortunately.

"Don't worry, Mother. Polly is not reading Wilkie Collins or Edgar Poe," Rose promised, widening her eyes at Thatcher. Mr. Collins and Mr. Poe had been passing by stealth all summer between Polly's bedside and her sister's, concealed in stacks of folded petticoats with the maid Gracie as accomplice and fellow reader. One of the two scoundrels was lodged in the parlor at this moment, Thatcher happened to know, on the settee, hidden under a wad of Polly's haphazard embroidery.

Thatcher relished his wife's small seditions, trusting that any distance from her mother would bring Rose closer to him by degrees. He assumed it was normal in a new marriage to feel one has joined forces with a stranger. Especially one so young. At barely past twenty, Rose was ten years his junior, though he'd watched her claim a poise beyond her years. Tonight he marveled at the bravery of her calm disposition. For weeks there had been a baby, an animate secret stirring between her divine flesh and his own, and then this morning abruptly, no baby. With a few tears hastily dismissed, she'd gathered up the bedclothes and declared this to be Thatcher's day. Exquisitely encased in her smart red day dress, Rose took his arm and went to the dedication, moving him to prideful anguish when she lowered her lashes and curtsied to the president. No mere teacher deserved this grace at his side.

Autumn darkness had already blinded the dining room windows, an effect that dispirited him, no matter how many autumns he lived or how predictably the light receded. Surely this year he might leave his birthright of sadness behind. He was a man, a husband and head of a household if not yet a father, comfortably marooned with his own family in the candelabra's glow. Smooth planes of female features reflected the centered light, each face an orbiting moon. The cook had served the chops before the soup at Thatcher's request, astonishing the women as if this were a clever invention and not simple good sense, with the soup not yet made when they arrived home, and Polly loudly perishing.

And now here came Mrs. Brindle, intent as a midwife at delivery, cradling the soup terrine that she set down at Thatcher's right hand. He ladled the soup into four bowls while the cook scurried to whisk away the chop plates. Thatcher had no image of the mother who'd died after his birth, and now his attempts to conjure her could invoke only Mrs. Brindle, a woman in motion. She circled the table stacking plates with their scattered bones and gristle, the effort of service coloring her stout cheeks. Her apron ruffle dusted the floor around her brogues.

"How did he lose it?" Polly pressed. "Thatcher! The professor's hand."

"We have never discussed that in a school meeting." Today for the ceremony Cutler had worn a hand carved of wood, realistically painted down to the nails, less functional but more decorous than the hook. Thatcher could not help wondering where such things were made and procured. Thanks to a war waged largely by gangrene, the need had burgeoned. "I believe it was a shooting accident when he lived in the West."

"People are always shooting one another out in the West. It isn't fair."

He tasted the soup, leek and potato, very good. "That we don't have our share of shootings in Vineland?"

"Well, I don't suppose we need them really. But it would be interesting."

"I don't think Professor Cutler was injured in a duel. I've heard it was a hunting accident, probably self-inflicted." Thatcher envisioned himself and his employer back-to-back with pistols on Landis Avenue, pacing off: may the best man win. He saw no other way to gain control of his curriculum and teach truth instead of mythology. The impending presidential visit had only given the principal further excuse for his tyrannies.

"Do you think our Mr. Nailbourne has a gun, now he's living in the West?"

"Mr. Nailbourne is not *ours*," Rose said. "The house is ours. He only used it."

"Without Scylla and Charybdis to guard him, he might need one," Thatcher said.

"I have decided it speaks well of the man," Aurelia declared, "that he gave them Biblical names. If only the beasts could absorb the lesson of it."

Thatcher and Rose exchanged another glance, but said nothing. Aurelia might take to bed if she knew her daughters had strayed past Edgar Allan Poe into the swamps of the pagan Homer. Or that Polly had borrowed *The Odyssey* from her brother-in-law.

"Only I have tried to find the reference and cannot. Do you recall the chapter and verse, Rose? Of the parable of Scylla and Charybdis?"

"I believe it's one of the Psalms, Mother," Rose said, her spoon tracking a faultless path from china bowl to rosebud lips. Thatcher felt unnerved watching his wife lie so easily. Even prettily.

"I saw Mrs. Tillotson today at the dedication," Polly said. "In a regular old dress. I thought I might get to see one of the bloomer costumes she and Mrs. Merton Stevens wore at the Dress Reform Convention."

"Polly dear, you are slurping. Our soup spoons sail away from us like ships going out to sea."

Thatcher knew he bore deficits from a childhood without mothering, but he felt Rose and Polly suffered from too much of it. Aurelia was incapable of understatement in any endeavor: her cap had lace ornaments dangling from its lace. The floral fabric of her dress could have been a seed advertisement: *Every one shall germinate!*

"How can you possibly know about that, Polly?" Rose asked.

"About what?" Aurelia asked.

"It's nothing important, Mother. Women wearing trousers," Rose said.

"It *is* important! The Dress Reform Convention had a whole column in the *Weekly*. 'Mrs. Tillotson in her doeskin pants led the grand march to perdition!'" Polly recited triumphantly. "I'm allowed to read Captain Landis's newspaper, Rose. Aren't I, Mother? You can't say I'm not. He is king of us all and Mother writes him letters."

"Not a *king*," Rose said.

"But Captain Landis did look handsome today, did he not? In his velvet waistcoat?"

"Mother, behave, you're besotted," Rose scolded. "He has a wife, you know."

Aurelia's hand rested on her crinkled throat. "The poor thing."

Thatcher gathered from the gesture that Mrs. Landis was ill. Though the *poor thing* might have caught her husband with the cook, for all he knew. This captain had grasping hands: not only was he Vineland's mayor and sole land agent but also its postmaster, acting police chief, hotelier, owner of many businesses, and autocratic editor of the *Weekly*. His governance had a habit of elevating his own enterprises and ruining competitors.

"May-I-read-the-*Week-ly*-Mo-ther!" Polly demanded again, giving each syllable equal weight as if banging on a door.

"Only the social and advertising pages. The agricultural reports if you must, but not the accidents and crimes. Those are damaging for a child of your age."

"And not the other one at all," Rose said. "Not *The Independent*. That man is very unfair to Captain Landis."

Aurelia looked around herself, momentarily overcome by revelation. "Vineland does not need a second newspaper! Can you see any reason for it, Thatcher? It causes confusion about everything, and encourages shadows of doubt."

"Some would consider that a reason," Thatcher said.

"But he is deliberately breaking the peace! And he is a foreigner."

"Is there no such thing as a peace that deserves to be broken?"

Soup spoons clicked quietly against bone china. From whom he expected an answer to his question, Thatcher wondered. The overfed dogs asleep on his shoes? He'd met the editor of the rival newspaper at a school meeting. Carruth was his name. He'd come not as a journalist but a citizen, he said, to speak up for Italian and freedmen's children in his neighborhood who could not attend school because of long work days. Their families had been lured to Vineland by promises from Landis—fields of milk and honey, land for almost nothing—and found themselves indentured to the man. Professor Cutler was irate at the charge. Landis had hired him to revolutionize Vineland's schools in the freethinking mold and this he had done, he said, by opening the doors to all races. Carruth shot back: There are many ways to close a door.

Thatcher was impressed enough to pick up Carruth's newspaper and get his eyes opened. *The Independent* exposed the extent of Landis's control, and its insidious underbelly. That despite his temperance laws, for example, Landis kept a private bar in his hotel because money could be made and more land sold by getting visitors inebriated.

"Did you try the Turkish Balm on your hair, dear?" Aurelia asked Rose.

"I did, some days ago. If you need to ask, it may not have done much good. It smelt terribly of tar but the package said it contains nothing injurious. Oh, and I spoke with the dressmaker yesterday. Polly, you're to go in for a fitting this week after school. You'll have two new day dresses."

"I don't need new day dresses," Polly said. "The old ones are working all right."

"There's the girl," Thatcher said.

"Thatcher, don't be a drudge. You will be earning three hundred dollars a year."

"Divided by more than three hundred days, it isn't a lot of dresses. Let alone beef and molasses."

"But you see, Thatcher," Aurelia spoke up, "at the end of one year there will be another, and so another three hundred dollars!" His mother-in-law laid down her spoon, exhausted from her foray into mathematics.

Let us pray, he added silently. The principal contracted his teachers for only one school year at a time. It was one of his so-called innovations, to make his staff stay or leave depending on how they took to his Plan of Modern Education. Thatcher so far wasn't taking. Cutler gave tedious lectures about shaping young minds, but would never grant Thatcher leave to take his subjects out of the classroom for a look at the living world. The request so provoked his employer that Thatcher would have dropped it, but he found himself haunted by Mrs. Treat's question: If trained to nature from an early age, could a mind be freed from its vendetta against the world's creatures? Cutler viewed field study as truant and unscholarly. Had ridiculed Thatcher's proposal in front of other teachers.

"I've been waiting for Mother to bring this up," Rose said suddenly, "but she hasn't. With the strain of moving we have overlooked Polly's coming of age." She turned to her mother significantly.

Aurelia looked troubled. "Did we? How do you mean?"

"I mean it is past time for Polly to think about corsets and bustles. I spoke of it with the dressmaker."

Thatcher met Polly's eyes, seeing a drowning look there, knowing he could not save her. The women of his family would become one with the earth's creatures only by pressing the bones of whales against their rib cages until breathless.

"It's an exciting time, dear," Rose said briskly. "You mustn't dread it. You will enjoy society. We aren't speaking of young men yet, only you have to become known. I'll take you with me to lectures and meetings."

"Mrs. Treat has begun a botanical society," Thatcher offered. "They meet Wednesdays."

"Well and good for her, but I am thinking of my sister's education," Rose informed him agreeably. "We're fortunate to have so many philosophical men in Vineland. Mr. Charles Campbell is giving one of his lectures on spiritualism at Plum Hall on Friday. His talks are always packed to the rafters. And Friday next is Reverend Pittinger on science and the Bible. When you go to meetings regularly you won't want to be seen in the same dress time and again, Polly. You'll see. And there's no need to fuss over money, Thatcher. Mrs. Clark knows you are situated and has been kind about extending credit."

"Kindly allowing us to go into debt," Thatcher said. "In the vein of important subjects overlooked, I would like to discuss the house."

Aurelia turned away from the table, signaling to Mrs. Brindle for the coffee. Rose said nothing. Later she would punish him for this. None of it could be helped.

"Mr. Martini has proposed a possible scheme of repairs. I'm

afraid the cost is more than my salary, this year or any year. But this work of salvage has fallen to me, and it can't wait any longer. If we postpone it, the damage will grow worse very quickly and this house will have to be abandoned in a few years' time."

"If he wants so much for the work, he must be dishonest," Aurelia said. "My husband did not like Mr. Martini."

Thatcher paused to collect his words. "Yes. Mr. Martini told me your husband disagreed with his advice on the building plan before they began construction. I know he was dismissed from the project. I'm sorry to have to tell you Mr. Martini's predictions about the load-bearing beams have turned out to be correct."

Neither Rose nor Aurelia looked at him, only Polly. He felt a sensation under his breastbone that surpassed pain, verging on anger. He addressed Aurelia now, staring at her face while she scrutinized her lace cuff. "You can see broken lintels and window frames from where you sit, in a structure that's hardly a dozen years old. You've said yourself, the staircase is frightening. I did not invent this problem. I am only addressing things that have already happened. The mistake was in joining the new construction to the original stipulation house."

Aurelia didn't look up.

"It was a clever suggestion from some of your husband's colleagues. I'll grant that. I understand the appeal of retaining an old structure rather than paying to tear it down before rebuilding. It might have seemed sensible to annex the upstairs bedchambers directly over the older lintels and beams. We are often persuaded that what is convenient is also right. But these associates were not architects. Their idea was unsound."

Mrs. Brindle brought the coffee. Aurelia poured, no one spoke. Rose took a sip, looked deeply into her cup, and set it down.

"Mrs. Clark has gotten in the new *Godey's Lady's Book*, Mother. You'll want to go and see. There are so many sweet bonnets. And

you won't believe it but she has new designs from Madame Demor-
est. She went to her shop in Philadelphia and memorized the styles
so she could copy them out for us. Our Mrs. Clark is cunning."

"We're lucky to have her," Aurelia agreed.

"And Thatcher, the piano should be tuned. Will you see to it?
Polly needs to resume her lessons. Mrs. Marberry or not."

Silence settled on the dining room. The candle flames flinched
in unison as an exterior door was opened and closed. Thatcher listened to a household driven by its endless preoccupations: china
teacups vexing their saucers, the pump handle creaking out in the
yard where Mrs. Brindle pumped water for washing up after their
meal. The lifting and closing of the wooden lid of the toilet stool
upstairs, where Gracie would find the stains of a secret bereave-
ment as she cleaned the bedchambers. The quiet refrains of his
disintegrating home.

⋊⋉

"I have here a substance in a bottle," Thatcher said, holding up his
stoppered vial. The students squinted doubtfully at its emptiness.
Science was a bewilderment they approached with fixed expressions
of disbelief, the young ladies adding to this a sulkiness owned by
their gender, peering up at teacher from under an eave of curled
fringe. Thatcher adored the lot of them.

"Don't worry, your eyes aren't failing. You can't see what is in
the bottle because it is not a solid or a liquid. It is a gas. We generally can't see gas, can we?"

"No sir, but we smell it sure. When my pa passes one you'll know
it in the next room. Specially if he's been at the liver and onions."

This wisdom came from Willis Chester, who looked startled
when his classmates burst into laughter. An earnest boy was Willis, smaller than both of his male classmates and most of the females. His family might have allowed him the two extra years'

schooling in hopes he might grow before getting thrown to hard labor. Thatcher had come to this post expecting to meet the offspring of historians and philosophers, but if those elderly men reproduced at all, they were adding only droplets to Vineland's ocean of toilers. Nearly all these pupils came from farm or factory stock, sprouts like poor Willis who seemed to be waiting for the first full meal of his life. Thatcher was tempted to smuggle him crusts from home.

"Willis, you are absolutely correct. We often know a gas from its smell, and that is the basis of our experiment today. I am going to open the cap of this bottle, and we will all sit very still and see what happens. When you believe you can identify our gas, please don't name it aloud. I only want you to raise your hand."

At the very instant he pulled out the cotton stopper a hand shot up at the back of the room: Icyphenia Bottom, of the frayed orange plaits and yellow gingham worn every day of her life, inherited from one or more older sisters. Icyphenia wanted fiercely to please; through trial and error Thatcher had learned the kindness of letting her fill all the inkwells each morning, and otherwise overlooking her. The other pupils, paired at their desks, now sat with eyes wide and nostrils flared, wary but keen for enlightenment. The lamps flickered overhead, no one spoke. After a moment, a confident hand rose from the front row: Giovanna Persichetti. Round faced, bookish, and quiet, Giovanna knew every answer he ever had called her to recite aloud, and probably all those he hadn't. Giovanna's deskmate followed, then more hands, all in the vicinity of Giovanna. As slowly as movement in a dream, the wave of olfaction lifted hands from the front to the back of the room. After some five minutes, only a few outliers were left with direly knit brows, still struggling either to smell or to identify.

"Very good. Now you may answer aloud, what is it?"

"Ammonia," cried the class, a motley chorus in which Thatcher also heard "alkie air" and a few other variations, along with "chicken house."

"Ammonia is correct. Otherwise called alkaline air. You've all used it at home as a disinfectant. I heard some of you say 'hart's horn.' That name comes from a manufacturing process that uses the hooves and horns of deer and other animals. Later on we will talk about that chemical process. Now I want you to think about what we just observed. How this ammonia came to your noses. Did it reach everyone, all at once?"

The heads wagged a confident negative. Thatcher reached forward to set down the flask on his desk. Then on second thought, tucked it into a drawer.

"No. It reached the front row first, and the last row last. The gas moved, just as a swarm of bees might move through the air." A few girls shuddered dramatically at this notion, so he amended his analogy. "A flock of pigeons, then. Or a school of fish moving through water. And that is because the gas is made of particles, exactly as a flock is made of birds. The particles are called molecules."

He turned and wrote the word *molecule* on the slate wall behind him, noting as always how dubious a word may appear when written large, inches from one's nose. He turned back to his choir. "And like birds or fish, which tend to move at a particular rate of speed, so do molecules. In the case of ammonia, with a velocity of nearly a third of a mile per second, as it happens. Which is very fast, isn't it?"

All the boys and Icyphenia nodded heartily.

"Now, if that is the case, why should it take the molecules such a long time to travel to the back of this room?"

He felt an odd dislocation as all their attention went suddenly to the door behind him, to his left. He glanced surreptitiously, though he didn't have to. It would be Cutler, lurking. As long as the man didn't speak, Thatcher could feign ignorance and decline to invite him in. Sometimes he went away.

"They moved more slowly because something stood in their path. This room was already filled with another gas, which we call air."

Blank gazes. He could tell Cutler was still at the door. He struggled to keep an appearance of relaxed composure that had been genuine, just moments before. "A mixture of gases, really. If you doubt that it's here, just take a deep breath and feel it expand your lungs."

Thatcher watched the power of suggestion enlarge a dozen chests. While they rose and fell, he wrote the formula NH3 on the slate, then gripped the back of his chair to steady his train of thought. "The molecules of one gas strike those of another as they travel, sometimes bouncing backward. Going every which way, really. Please pardon me, young ladies, but the molecules really behave just like a swarm of bees, with every insect darting about furiously while the entire hive moves rather regally through the air. You have all seen this sight, have you not?"

Some heads nodded. All still visibly preoccupied with the doorway. Damn the man.

"When one gas diffuses through another, the progress is like that hive. Inevitable but slow. If we could close the door to this room," he said pointedly, "and seal the windows, and wait a day or so, these molecules would become uniformly mixed throughout the air of the room. This property of gases diffusing through one another was first observed by a great scientist, the discoverer of oxygen, Mr. Joseph Priestley."

Cutler executed an imperial throat-clearing and stepped into the room. "Good afternoon, Greenwood. I see you are harrowing our children with tales of bumblebees."

"Only metaphorically, Professor Cutler. How kind of you to visit us. We're beginning our term by studying the basic properties of matter. We were discussing the diffusion of molecules."

"I keep hearing this word, *molecule*. And yet I do not find it in Johnson's dictionary."

Thatcher would be hard pressed to avoid insulting this silly man. Could he truly not know a thing so fundamental? "You're right, it is a modern word. Belonging entirely to the language of modern chemistry. We find it in Nuttall's Scientific Dictionary, which you kindly provide our students in the library. I predict the word will show up even in Johnson's, in future years." He hazarded a smile. "Since the molecules are bound to persist."

"Are we inspired, children? By the *molecules*? These modern chemists declare they are flying all about us, exactly as God created them, perfect and immutable in their number and form."

Thatcher was rattled by everything about this sudden apparition, not least by his use of the word "children," not once but twice. Without school, these students would be hammering soles to shoes or grubbing straw onto autumn berry fields. If not yet married, then soon to be. Thatcher handed over his reins to Cutler and stood watching these timid, full-grown beings poised on the cusp of their fates. Somehow they broke and mended his heart all at once. The girls were the age Thatcher's mother must have been when she began her brief, intense reproductive spate: one boy per year until the sixth one left her too weak to produce either milk or a name. As the story went, she lay gazing out the window, inspired at the last moment by the fellow sparring thatch on the roof of a neighbor's cottage. Whenever his father recounted this tale—every few years, stupidly drunk—he made it out lucky for Thatcher she hadn't spied the tin peddler instead, or some hag dumping her piss pot. Then his brothers would remember again to call him Tinker, or better, Pisspot. There was no knowing whether fondness had existed between their parents, but when the old man was in his cups he could conjure enough affection for the dead wife to blame his last runt for all present deprivations.

Cutler was going on about God and molecules, making them his own. "Thus we find when we follow the pure scientific path, we arrive at that elysian pasture where science must stop and devotion begin. Is this not correct, Professor Greenwood?"

Thatcher watched their eyes linger on the missing hand, or rather the device that stood in for it. Today it was the standard double-pincer hook, probably more useful than wooden fingers for gripping, certainly more menacing. Student lore had it that he kept a golden arm at home in a padded violin case, for high holidays. Regardless of prosthesis, he kept the wrist always hovering near his hip, probably believing it wasn't noticed there.

A long silence followed, before Thatcher realized he'd been asked a question. Eyes reluctantly parted from the absent hand, swinging expectantly to the teacher. Thatcher longed for some magical doorway through which he might lead them all away from this man. "I am not quite sure what you mean, sir?"

"Do you agree there can be no natural cause for a molecule, only a holy one?"

"What we know of natural causes, we learn from observation."

Cutler's head drew back comically, as if Thatcher had pulled a false snake from his vest. His face alone was ridiculous: rarely in his life had Thatcher seen a male so devoid of whiskers. "Can you show us a molecule?" he demanded. "We should all be delighted to see it!"

"I could, but it would require considerable patience. Before you joined us, I was about to explain to the class that Bernoulli's observations of pressure led him to suspect the existence of minute moving particles. And that the experiments of Le Sage later confirmed it. Along with Dr. Joule, who has calculated the velocity of these particles inside a cloud of hydrogen gas." Thatcher felt his confidence stabilize, as if Joule and Bernoulli were standing just behind him. "These men have shown us molecules in the same way I might show you a hurricane, for instance. Not by its visible air, but by the impression of its force against the blowing trees and damaged stable roofs. Things we can see very well. This is how we know of molecules."

Cutler made a quizzical face, unintentionally clownish. The round-cheeked face was poorly served by nakedness, a very odd choice for a man so gripped with fashion. "We know of molecules from the damage to *barn roofs*?"

Thatcher wondered what task could be more wearisome than shoring up a stupid man's confidence in his own wisdom. "Well, sir, you have caught me again in metaphorical speaking. This is how we know the strength of hurricanes, yes, and molecules we know in a similar but not identical way. In both cases we use deduction. Thank you for helping me to clarify. We study the unseen particles by observing their effects. Discovery comes from the small increments of weight and measurement we call data, providing answers to questions we have carefully framed."

"But *data* cannot enlighten us to the origin of things, you see." Cutler turned his back on Thatcher, facing the class. "The *molecules*, the planets and their orbits, all these mysteries depend on a collocation of matter. *Weight* and *measure*, children, tell us only about ourselves, for they are the products of our own aspiration. They tell us not of the universe but of man, our quest for accuracy in sight and sound, and our longing for truth. Our noblest attributes, in other words."

Thatcher stood by silently as the man ran away with himself. If Bernoulli and Joule had been at Thatcher's shoulder, they now crept off to the cloakroom. He watched Cutler's lonely right hand doing more than the work of two, chopping out the rhythm of his sentences as if conducting some half-blind orchestra. "And we may *claim* these noble attributes only because they are essential constituents of *him* who *created* us. He who in the beginning created not only birds of the air and beasts of the land. For *first*, you see, he had to create the materials of which these things are made—"

Cutler stopped abruptly, interrupting his sermon with a doleful sniff at the air. "I smell cleaning fluid." He looked about himself warily. "Has there been an accident or a spill?" He turned to scowl at Thatcher. "Not a mess from an *experiment*, I trust. We have discussed this."

"Sir, your policy is clear. I would never subject our pupils to danger." Thatcher glanced at the formula NH_3 writ large on the slate, and dared a half wink at his pupils. "A diffusion of gases, I expect. It could be a case of liver and onions."

⋊⋉

Thatcher's annoyance rarely left his mind, even at home. He pursued arguments with Cutler inside his head so often that Rose caught him in the parlor speaking aloud and asked him earnestly if he'd seen a ghost.

"Of course not." He knew to kiss her forehead and soothe her alarm. They might adore Poe and the falling house of Usher, but the women of this house would tolerate no ghosts under their own roof.

Rose retrieved some trifle from the settee and went away again, leaving him to stew in his broth. He stood where he was by the window, gazing blankly at the lawn between Mrs. Treat's house and his own. Polly had let Scylla and Charybdis out the back door. He watched them follow the ordained path of their morning constitutional: a direct line to the oak, which they sniffed and circled, then crossed to the beech where they both micturated. Rose had surely never noticed, or she would take it personally. Much happiness rested upon what Rose did not know.

Plagued by a torment he hid from his wife, he decided to speak again with Mrs. Treat about the insufferable Cutler. She had been encouraging the first time, regarding Thatcher's rectitude at least, if not entirely sympathetic to his misery. But an ally, surely. Also the leader of a botanical society attended by some of Vineland's upper matrons. Her friend Phoebe was wife of Charles Campbell, of the famed spiritualism lectures, town historian, and confidant of Landis. By way of these lateral channels, Mrs. Treat might have some influence.

* *

He waited for a new chance to rescue the dogs but they had forgotten their former savior and now swore allegiance to Polly. Left to grope for another stratagem, Thatcher decided on the excuse of borrowing or loaning a book. He took two under his arm: his treasured copy of Hooker's *Flora Novae-Zelandiae* and Gray's newly published *How Plants Behave*. The latter, written in simple language meant for young people, Thatcher had submitted for approval to use in his class. He would ask Mrs. Treat whether she thought Cutler might let it by. Thatcher was optimistic; he didn't think the man had the brain to recognize it as a primer in pure Darwinism.

He found his neighbor in distress outside her front door, poking a broom handle into the rafters of the piazza. A black cat emerged eventually and slipped like a dark spill down the ivied pillar, carrying away something feathered in its jaws.

"I despise these cats. Are they yours?"

"I'm relieved to say they are not. Only the dogs, who have finally learned to tolerate their own masters."

"You may send them back to me anytime. They were good at keeping these devils away. I hate to resort to extreme measures but I may be forced. Cats have been known in these parts to commit suicide, Mr. Greenwood."

Thatcher took a step backward, deciding his neighbor looked capable of murder. Scowling up at the rafters, wearing a stained work apron over her dress, batting irritably at threads of dark hair that escaped from the twist at her nape, she was a sight outside of the commonplace.

She smoothed the apron and seemed to return to herself. "Would you like to come in?"

"I sense it may not be the best moment."

She shook her head. "The damage is done. I was in the parlor mounting a little fern just now and heard my friends out here in distress. As any parents would be, losing their young. I'm heartsick that I heard the warning too late."

"Survival of the fittest," Thatcher consoled. "Nature red in tooth and claw."

"I'm sure you know you are quoting Tennyson, a sentimental poet. There is nothing of *nature* in these felines. They're kept by cosseting human masters, pampered to perfect health and then turned loose on the neighborhood to terrorize poor wildlings who worked so hard to make a nest and brood their young."

Her dark eyes drilled into Thatcher, who contained no adequate response.

"And then they go home at night to lap up their milk and sleep in soft cushions. It isn't a fair fight."

"I'm sure you're right."

She narrowed her eyes. "You think I'm as sentimental as Tennyson. But that pair over there shrieking in the Judas tree have already lost three nests to the cats this summer. It is too late for them to be brooding this far into autumn, just a few weeks ahead of migration. The poor birds were desperate to have one reproductive success before winter."

"I understand your misery. No one could mistake those cries for anything but despair." Thatcher gazed at the Judas tree and his own loss welled up unexpectedly: a child so briefly in his future, so permanently now in his past.

"I believe they built their last dwelling here in my piazza

thinking I would help protect it. And I failed." She held the broom under her arm now, a soldier off guard.

"Mrs. Treat. You did try."

She nodded thoughtfully. "These catbirds are particular friends. They're companionable and intelligent, and the male is the best musician of the grove. I've taken great pains to get this pair to trust me. I feed them whortleberries. Please come in."

Thatcher didn't point out that by making pets of the birds she was undermining her argument against the cosseted cats. The woman's grief was substantial. He followed her into the parlor, where she showed him a chair near her desk and went off to the kitchen. He heard her speaking quietly, giving some instructions to her girl.

He looked around at a parlor full of sunlight and potted plants, half-read books lying open, botanical drawings set among the clutter of portraits on the mantelpiece, and no embroidery to be seen. He felt at home there. Had not felt that way entirely in any room, he realized, since coming to Vineland. He had thought himself at odds in a house of women, but so was this one: a second pair of small muddy boots rested today on the hearth beside Mrs. Treat's. He stared at the four little brogues feeling a strange pair of emotions, protectiveness and envy.

A row of Venus flytraps in clay pots lined the bay windowsill awaiting their ration of flies, he hoped, and not the flesh of Mrs. Treat. He could not name her botanical essence, but it was not a flytrap. She was a tree of some kind, upward reaching and self-contained. Thatcher got up and looked in on the tower-building spiders in their candy jars. The houses remained beautifully intact but the landladies again were shy. He returned to his assigned chair. On Mrs. Treat's desk in the mess of correspondence and half-dismantled ferns he noticed a small framed photograph of a man in a bowler and tied cravat. The portrait seemed especially placed there, perhaps plucked from the clan on the mantelpiece. He leaned close for a better look: the mysterious Dr. Treat, he presumed. Aquiline nose, handsome moustache, dark, curling hair. The man was striking. A bit younger than Mrs. Treat, in this portrait at any rate. Thatcher had heard he was older.

At her appearance in the doorway he affected interest in the mounted ferns.

"Here we are," she said happily. "That's a rare little *Schizaea pusilla* I brought from the damps yesterday. Have you seen the Pine Barrens, since we spoke of them?"

"Sadly, no. I'm afraid I'm being kept very busy under the guise of gainful employment. I hope to take my students there one day, if I can extract permission from Professor Cutler."

"Of course. The high school." She sat down facing him, still in her apron, setting both hands on her knees. "How are your pupils, Mr. Greenwood? Can you yet see a light within them?"

Thatcher was unexpectedly moved by the question. No one else had asked. Rose seemed to have no curiosity about his work. "They wear pinafores, nearly all," he said. "Nine girls against a mere three boys in my advanced science class, about the same balance in my introductory. I think every day of your advice, that educating these girls can free them from a wearisome dread of nature. It's becoming my fondest hope."

"So many girls studying the sciences. How uplifting."

"So I thought, until I noticed the imbalance is general at the high school. It's mostly young ladies who are allowed to persist the extra two years in their studies. Boys of that age can hardly be spared from their labors for the sake of a mere diploma."

Mrs. Treat made an odd little smile. "Of course. Not even here in Vineland, allegedly founded on principles of vigorous health and flourishing minds."

"Did these principles influence you and Dr. Treat in your decision to move here?"

"We were influenced," she said carefully. "I saw the Barrens and forests as opportunities for studying natural history. My husband was eager to expand his studies of spiritualism. He knew men here in the Free Thinking Society who promised eager audiences for his lectures."

"What sort of lectures does he make?"

Mrs. Treat looked briefly at the ceiling, then at the door. "He has developed theories about the ethereal realm. What he calls his nebular hypothesis of the tides and planets and so forth. Gravity plays no part in it."

The man of ether, the woman of evidence: Thatcher contemplated a match possibly more precarious than his own. "I assumed he was a medical doctor."

"You are not alone. But Joseph did not study medicine. He did not make any formal studies at all. He worked as an assistant to medical men during the war."

"As I did! How surprising. But *assistant* is overstating it in my case. I was an errand boy in the Boston hospital. In retrospect I think they only let me tend to the lost causes. I'm sure my experiences weren't equal to those of Dr. Treat."

"I would not be sure of it. And yet you do not come to town calling yourself Doctor Greenwood."

The girl arrived with the teapot and Mrs. Treat rose to help her, clearing a space on the crowded desk for saucers and cake. Thatcher wondered whether he had any hope of rescuing their conversation from cat murder and magniloquent husbands. The overcast subject of Cutler would only drag her day from bad to worse.

"Mr. Greenwood, this is Selma. She is a great help in the kitchen as you see, and equally proficient with spade and plant presses. She often accompanies me on collecting expeditions."

Selma gave a prompt curtsey. A pale, fuzzy little mullein of a girl, nearly as young as Polly, he guessed, but more accustomed to work.

"Your mistress has sung such praises of the Pine Barrens," he said, "I'm impatient to see them. I hope I can join you soon as an assistant to the assistant. I am very good at carrying things and getting deplorably muddy."

Selma made a squashed little grin and glanced at Mrs. Treat.

"Thank you, dear," she said. "You may go. Please take some of the eggs to your mother, I hope she is improved."

Mrs. Treat poured the tea. Thatcher drew his chair close to the desk and accepted his cup, hoping this would bolster his neighbor's spirits.

"She seems a bright girl. Though young, to be sent to work."

"Two sisters even younger than Selma they've put out to service. The poor family. After one failed crop their berry farm has gone back to Landis. Repossessed, I assume. They are living now with no proper home."

"But she has one here," he offered. "I'm sure your influence is a great comfort."

"I try to teach Selma a bit of botany. I'm afraid she has no other hope of schooling." Mary set her cup down and gazed at it, retreating into herself. Her eyes drifted toward the photograph on the desk. The disconsolate mask returned.

"I'm sorry for the lost fledglings," he said. "Your own, I mean. The little birds."

She looked up. "Oh, dear. You saw me in high dudgeon. You'll be reporting to the neighborhood that I put out strychnine for the cats. To be honest I have thought of it, but could never do it. I am too weak hearted."

"Dear lady, in my household I've seen higher dudgeon over damages hardly visible to the eye. Yours will never be mentioned again."

She smiled, but still looked sad.

"I've come at a bad time. I only meant to discuss a book, and that can wait for another day."

"You have. Not only on account of the cats." She faltered, taking note of the books on his lap. "I've had an upset of the most agonizing kind, for which one can only blame oneself. I've made a foolish mistake." Her glance went again to the portrait on her desk. Thatcher pretended now to notice it.

"Is this your husband?"

"Oh, no. It is not. That is the state entomologist of Missouri, Mr. Charles Valentine Riley."

"Indeed." Not for the first time in this parlor he thought of Mr. Carroll's Alice and her Wonderland. Polly had been reading it to him aloud.

"He is editor of the *American Entomologist*, ever since the untimely death of Mr. Walsh. But perhaps you knew. Do you read the journal, Mr. Greenwood?"

"I haven't to now. I should happily borrow it if you have copies." Thatcher considered the prospect of a publication entirely devoted to insects, *illustrated*, gaining entry to his home. It would have to hide in the petticoats with Edgar Allan Poe. "I take it you and the editor are acquainted."

"Mr. Riley and I have exchanged letters nearly every day for years, since I began contributing to the journal. He was a wonderful help in guiding my writing style at first, and we've grown rather avid in assisting one another with identifications. I often set his little portrait here on my desk as a custom of our correspondence."

"As is natural, among friends and devoted colleagues. You must have many of both, Mrs. Treat. I understand you are widely published."

"It is my livelihood, yes. The *American Entomologist* pays good sums, rather better than the popular magazines. They pay not just for articles but also for specimens." Again she glanced at the books in Thatcher's hands. "But it may be this line of work doesn't interest an educator."

"Writing I can imagine for myself, eventually. I have done illustration work, mostly in my years of assisting medical men, before I was able to go to university. I find I greatly prefer botanicals to sketching cadavers." He could never tell Rose he'd laid eyes on a cadaver, let alone recorded countless autopsies with his pencils, but Mary took the news calmly. "It would all rest on my making a discovery worth the trouble. An educator must be an investigator first. Specimen work, I hadn't considered."

"It helps keep my coal bin filled, I don't mind telling you. And of course it is great sport to be outdoors on a mission of discovery. Today Mr. Riley has asked for living larvae and pupae of *curculionidae*, our little gall weevils."

"That doesn't sound like the making of a bad day."

"No. It isn't. He addressed something else in the letter, a professional matter. I'm pained to speak of it. But Mr. Greenwood, I am lost here. You presume I have masses of friends. But I find myself now with no proper colleague to help guide my hand."

Thatcher hesitated. "Well then. Please feel free to keep the matter private, or speak of it. Whatever best puts your mind at ease."

After the briefest pause she nodded. "I will not be at ease unless I speak of it to someone. Mr. Riley scolded me for failing to credit illustrations he made for me, in an article I published. He suggests it was an *appropriation*." She avoided Thatcher's eye. "He is so supportive, Mr. Greenwood, and I behaved as a criminal."

"Not at all. I'm sure the oversight was accidental."

"Oh, it was! And he knows." Now fully bent on her confession, she took up a letter from her desk and read: "*I know it was not your intention to fail in giving credit, but you gain nothing and lose much in not providing against the neglect. Don't get into bad habits! You are laboring hard with brain and pen, and it is only because I appreciate your work and wish to see you successful that I indulge in remarks like the above.*"

She looked to Thatcher cautiously as she lay down the letter on the desk.

"There you are," Thatcher said. "He said it himself: no harm done to your friendship. He values you as a professional colleague and begs you to see yourself in the same light." Thatcher was distracted by words he could see plainly written across the bottom of the letter: *P.S. A propos Mr. T? Is he still separated from you?*

"I wish it could be so. That I could see myself in the same light."

"Mrs. Treat, I say. You count Charles Darwin as a friend. Some of my peers in Boston would leap at that alliance over a personal correspondence with the Almighty."

She smiled, but again, so sadly. "And they would have known how to comport themselves well in either arrangement. Not indulge in stealing the work of others and getting in *bad habits*."

"You speak as if your friend has called you a common thief, but he has not. It was simple oversight and nothing more."

"Simple and dim witted. I feel like a child caught with crumbs on my face. It did not even occur to me to put his name to the illustration. And you, an illustrator yourself! You must feel the crime as one against your own."

Thatcher looked at the slender hands, ragged at the cuticles, folded on her desk as if in prayer. The hands of a worker. "Mrs. Treat, please show yourself some of the kindness you harbor for the birds in your garden. You only forgot."

"No, the truth is I did not think. Normally I submit my work with my own illustrations, or those made for me by my dear little friend Phoebe Campbell. This was my first publication assisted by a man of Charles Riley's prominence. You would have known the difference. You went to university, where you learned not only the laws of science but also these subtle rules between men. Debts and attributions."

"You haven't been to university?"

Her startled look made him wish he could swallow his tongue.

"That was a thoughtless question. I apologize. It's only that . . ." He looked around the room, at a loss to explain the clemency he found there. "In your house I've seen so many impossible things become plausible."

She blinked very slowly, as if in pain.

"And one does hear of it," he added. "I read that Mr. Darwin is helping to press the case of seven women in Edinburgh, all qualified to study medicine."

"I pray they may succeed. I am only a parson's daughter sent to a finishing school in Ohio."

Mercy of Christ. He could picture her as a girl dipping doleful curtseys before some horrid Ohioan Mrs. Marberry. "And in spite of that obstruction you've claimed renown as a scientist. I am prostrate with admiration, Mrs. Treat. It's the truth."

"I claim renown in the purgatory of a ladies' botanical society, where I am begged each Wednesday to disclose the rules of a pleasing flower arrangement."

Thatcher had a terrible urge to take both her hands into his. In this house, impossible things. "Please let me speak bluntly. The first day I sat in this chair and held in hand a letter from Charles Darwin, addressed to Mary Treat, I felt so bloated with envy I couldn't have drowned in a well. Since then I've learned you are a respected colleague not just of Darwin but many men whose presence would strike me mute. Professor Asa Gray, whom I worshipped from across Harvard yard. I'm doing my best to behave as a good neighbor and lace up my adipose envy into a corset of admiration. But I would trade my university for your finishing school if it brought me a tenth of your success."

"A *corset* of admiration, Mr. Greenwood." Finally a smile arrived with no sadness in it. A shy, elfin twinkle.

"I live in a house of women," he said. "You'll find me far too handy with a female metaphor. I can speak dress patterns in several languages, and outline the case that a new bonnet is more useful than an impermeable roof."

"That is impressive, Mr. Greenwood. I find myself handy only with plant presses and digging spades and the bailiwick of mud."

"Are we not peculiar birds?" He reached out and touched her sleeve, and that was all. But the hand that dropped back to the books in his lap was trembling.

She shook her head, not in negation but dismay. "I probably take too much pride in what I know, because I've had to teach all of it to myself. I appreciate your praise, but you overestimate. My colleagues are as remote to me as archangels. When I write Mr. Riley I set his little portrait here with the hope of feeling less alone on my beachhead."

"The desert isle of Vineland."

"Yes. How different it must be for you. I rejoice for you, Mr. Greenwood. A new school building! The president at your dedication, and a whole town standing up for you and your pinafored young scientists. They are lucky girls."

"If only you knew. I'm also stranded on a lonely beachhead. My employer Mr. Cutler is hostile to the genuine teaching of science."

She looked at him. Then drank a long draught of tea and cocked her head as if listening to his words again in her mind. Then looked at him squarely. "You mentioned hostility to Darwin, when we spoke before. Do you now mean to say the principal is hostile to science entirely? What is your evidence?"

"I submit my lesson plans and he overrules all but the most mundane exercises in rote memory. Experimentation alarms him. Modern scientific theory enrages him, discussion of Darwin particularly but not only this. The suggestion of taking pupils outdoors to study nature, he treats as blasphemy."

"Outdoors. To the Pine Barrens?"

"It would be wonderful. But to this point my proposals have been only very modest little adventures. Walking to the forest north of Park Avenue to collect seeds and nuts and bring them back for classification with taxonomic keys. Perhaps evaluate our finds for the relative abundance of species. Plant the seeds to observe life cycles. These proposals all were devoutly rejected."

"As blasphemy, you say." Mrs. Treat considered it. "If he sees this school as a sort of church, what are its doctrines?"

"Discipline and moral education, his two-headed monster. Surely you know he travels the country lecturing on his Twin Pillars of Pedagogy. Landis and his freethinkers must have been proud of the fat rabbit they snared, getting Cutler here as principal of their high school."

"Yes. Snaring the famous lecturer called up more headlines in the *Weekly* than a month of barn fires."

"I confess I was a little slow to grasp how the blood of Vineland pulses to the beat of Landis."

Mary frowned. "The man is like his hero Phineas Barnum, with the gilded offices in Manhattan Island. He only loves a circus."

"He certainly has my mother-in-law in his thrall. Even his dog shows and baby contests bring her to ecstasy."

"Your employer is a part of the dog show." Mary shook her head. "Discipline, and moral education. These are matters personal to the scholar. Discipline is a habit one brings to a study, and not the study itself. Is that not so?"

"Madam, I wish I knew. I can only tell you Cutler feels direct observation is undisciplined behavior. Discipline is found in turning the eyes inward to the soul, finding truth through God and intuition rather than reason."

"Oh, blast these transcendentalists. Your pupils are hardly more than children. What will they find inside their poor little souls but hoop-and-stick and a preoccupation with puddings?"

"One wonders. But while they wait for it, we are to keep them occupied with slavish memorization of the utopian poets."

"*Hellas* and *Arcadia*. These men think we need only declare ourselves Adam and Eve to recover all the fruits of Eden. Whereas an actual study of fruit pests does not interest them. I speak from experience." Mrs. Treat looked satisfactorily peeved. "What poems does your employer recommend to promote the study of science?"

"He concedes a shortage of these, but he is forcefully opposed to rationalists. All the worse if they are rational and foreign."

"Well, forevermore. What is science without rational observation? Where is *truth?*"

"He says it is not the place of someone in my subordinate position to decide what is true. Let alone encourage my pupils to look for it among the beetles and acorns."

"Of course the scientist's position is subordinate. Our task is to make our fussy natures invisible against the mechanisms of the universe. Truth is not ours to find within, but to search out. We study the known world in order to recognize the remarkable."

"Remarkable," Thatcher repeated, feeling a lightness he hadn't known outside Boston. Mary emptied the teapot into their cups, carefully giving herself the dregs.

"Did you happen to attend the dedication of the school?" he asked.

She waved a hand, shook her head. "I don't fare well with hub-bub."

"Would you like to know what my sister-in-law observed in President Grant?"

"A man who would prefer to be on his own farm, culling his cattle."

"Something close to that. I think she will make a scientist one day, our Polly. But you didn't see him. How did you know?"

"I read the newspapers. One recognizes a kindred disposition."

"And now he is president, poor man. Whither he goest, there will go hubbub."

She grinned. "Mr. Greenwood, twice you've crossed my threshold and twice brought a balm for failing spirits. We haven't even spoken of my little fern, or your books. Let us have a look." She took the books he handed her. "Please take pity on me and finish this egg cake. I've had it for more teas and breakfasts than I'd like to count. Egg cake is Selma's new crowning glory, and I can't bear to tell her a horse can founder on glory."

"Would you please call me Thatcher?"

She looked up from *Flora Novae-Zelandiae*.

"If I'm presuming, forgive me," he said. "I have been in the world without friends for too many months."

"Thatcher. What sorcery do you know? I've been driving the librarians to madness asking for Hooker's new *Flora*."

"Mary, I thank you. I will have the cake."

7

∞

The Cake

At the corner of Seventh and Landis, Willa forced herself to keep pushing her rubber boots through the waterlogged street. Mud was not the problem. The idea of walking in the door of the brick building she could see down the block: that was the problem, a reluctance that made no sense. As a journalist she had cold-called senators and Nobel Prize–winning scientists and the mother of an astronaut who died in a shuttle explosion. Not much could be worse.

She cut across to the other side of Seventh to avoid another windfall of tangled tree limbs on the sidewalk. The end of September had brought two giant storms, the thrashing tails of hurricanes brewed up over the Atlantic that came in oversize and early. People's idle talk of the weather had gone quiet, as if it might bring bad luck, while the TV forecasters discussed categories of storm surge and wind speeds previously unseen. Even this far inland, New Jersey was still recovering from Hurricane Sandy, which in its time, a few years back, had been called the storm of the century.

How foolish it seemed now to label anything "of the century." This one was still a teenager with an anger-management problem and a long future ahead.

Willa stopped at the wrought-iron fence to study a little wooden house in front of the Vineland Historical Society. This would be one of the stip houses, relocated to this spot; an interpretive sign declared it the first house built in Vineland. Some claim, she thought, considering all the wigwams and shelters of runaway slaves that must have melted back into the forest before the land barons got there. This little chalet looked chipper for its years, compared with Willa's house, which was melting into history on the fast track. For both the recent storms the authorities had ordered all residents to get off the streets, shutter their windows, and hole up in an interior room: shelter in place. But her home was dubious shelter. The first storm breached the roof and sent water pouring down what they'd ironically named the Servants' Staircase. Willa declared it a loss and sealed its entry doors with duct tape.

The second storm was worse. In the middle of the night they'd awakened to a crash and run upstairs to find a collapsed ceiling in shards over every inch of Willa's office: floor, desk, lampshade, books. It felt personal. She stood in tears while Iano picked dirty white chunks of plaster out of her computer keyboard and printer. They covered the desk with a plastic sheet to keep it dry until morning, when she would move her sad little stake on professionalism to a corner of her bedroom.

She'd told Iano it was unrealistic to expect someone else's money to fix their house, but today she was swallowing her pride. The plan was to root out an architectural pedigree that might lead to a loan or grant, even though she was pretty sure she was chasing down a blind alley. She was reluctant to start the chase, because after this door slammed she'd have none left.

The front door of the Vineland Historical Society had an Open sign turned out in its warbled antique-glass window, and walking across its threshold felt like time travel. Willa let that corny notion come and go as she wiped her boots on a brushy doormat and let her eyes adjust. A plate rail running around the top of the room held a bewildering assortment of vases and trinkets, and every wall was crowded with dark portraits of some town father, all of them bearded, wearing hats. No: one town mother among them, wearing a high-necked dress that looked painful and the sad-eyed face to prove it.

A gramophone with its black petunia bell sat on a table among fancy porcelain urns. It was one of *those* museums, the folkloric community hodgepodge. What to do with Grandpa's arrowhead collection when we clean out the house? The Historical Society! Here it could share a glass case with some grandmother's tarnished silver service. Through a patina of dust and filtered light her gaze jumped from one display case to another. One was filled with long, linked chains made of glass. How did glass chains make sense, unless for tying up glass dogs? Willa's head swam. The big room had a high ceiling and might have felt airy if it weren't crowded with display tables and little room-like set pieces of furniture from various decades. One corner was arranged as a nineteenth-century office with an ornate rolltop desk and a small printing press. Willa's eye caught and came back to a red-velvet-upholstered armchair constructed of what seemed to be cow horns, some weird throne of bygone vanities. She felt time collapsing around her like a falling ceiling. Her sole desire was to turn around and walk out the door.

"Hello." A man stepped out of an office. "Can I help you?"

"Hi. Yeah. I'm . . ." She struggled, distracted by his appearance. "I'm new to town, we moved here this summer. Curious about history, of course. I have a few things I've been wanting to research."

He strode forward and thrust out a tiny white hand. "Christopher Hawk. I'm here most days of the week."

"Willa Knox. I'm a journalist."

"From what publication?"

"Freelance, at the moment. I've worked for a few."

Mr. Hawk stood about five feet tall and wore a clean, extremely dated three-piece suit. His white hair was shoulder-length but tidy, his white beard neatly trimmed, and his skin so nearly transparent Willa wondered if he might have a pigment disorder.

"Knox," he repeated. "Willa like the author?"

Willa smiled. People rarely made the connection. "Yes. My mother was a Cather fan. She led kind of an Àntonia life."

His eyes narrowed slightly at these motley credentials. "Would you like the Cook's tour, or help with finding something specific? Or would you rather I just leave you to poke around?"

He sounded youthful. She gave the white hair a second look, wondering if it was deceptive. The clothes were definitely old but maybe the man wasn't, if he had albinism. His features were taut and perfectly unwrinkled, like those of a human carved of wax. She pulled her eyes off Christopher Hawk and they sailed right back to the chair made of cow horns. "Thanks, I might need some guidance."

"That chair belonged to Charles Landis. I assume you know the basics there."

"Of . . . cowboy furniture design?"

He didn't smile. "Captain Landis had exotic tastes. That was a Victorian aesthetic. The discovery of the world's frontiers reflected in the home. Primitives and oddities were the rage."

"Tell me about Landis."

He drew back in a faint wince, as if she'd said, *Remind me again about George Washington.* "Charles Landis was the founder of Vineland."

"Right, I've heard. Land developer and utopian visionary."

"Exactly."

"So he set up this place as a planned community? When was that?"

"He bought the land in 1861. Surveyed it, laid out the roads on a grid, brought in the railroad, and started a newspaper to put out the word. His dream was a self-sufficient colony of agriculture and intellectual enterprise. Fruit growers and freethinkers flourishing side by side."

Willa smiled. "How'd that work out for him?"

"Very well, in fact. We have his book, *The Founder's Own Story*. Obviously it's his version of events."

"Obviously."

"We have a deep archive here, including every copy of the *Vineland Weekly* and other local newspapers dating back to their first issues. Also artifacts and the personal papers of a lot of Vineland's prominent citizens over the years."

"Great," Willa said, trying not to betray her thinking about the curatorial technique here. Organization aside, the place was damp and dusty, probably hot and damp in summer, prone to mildew.

"The full-length portrait you see over there is Landis as a young man. In the one on the left he's twenty years older."

Willa studied the famous autocrat, with his ruddy cheeks and odd flop of hair. A little tawdry looking for a land baron, she thought, but the standards of a particular time were hard to gauge. People hadn't always bathed, for example. Mr. Hawk was still ticking through his inventory. "That landscape in the gold frame hung in his original office on Landis Avenue. The dress and shawl on the mannequin belonged to his wife. The curios on that table were collected on one of his trips overseas."

Willa understood she'd flipped a switch on the Landis gusto, and wondered what this man did in here all day when he lacked an audience. He gave off a whiff of Miss Havisham in Dickens's *Great Expectations*—the old lady still in her wedding dress fifty years after getting jilted, wafting around her cobwebby house with the caved-in remains of the nuptial banquet on the table. She fought off an image of this pale man rolling out a mummified wedding cake.

"Was Vineland so different from other towns of the time?" she asked.

"Very different. Landis believed human improvement was a cooperative venture. Everyone who purchased property agreed to certain stipulations for establishing residence within a year and improving the land according to his system of public adornment."

"The shade trees and all that jazz."

"Shade trees, setbacks, shrubbery, and so forth."

She smiled. "The happy Victorian dream. Unlimited growth that never gets out of bounds or turns ugly."

"Beauty was only the beginning," he said, pretty snippily for a docent, she thought. Though she knew she was baiting him. "He introduced a modern system of education open to all races, a hundred years before US schools were integrated."

"Really. That's impressive."

"Yes it is. He was very forward thinking. His work agreements made land accessible to poor and immigrant farmers, while he also set up progressive societies to attract some of the most prominent intellectuals and reformers of the time."

"Such as?" She couldn't decide whether to keep egging him on or back away slowly.

"It's a long list. The inventor William Daggett. Thomas Welch, inventor of unfermented grape juice. Mary Treat, one of the best-known woman scientists of the nineteenth century, who corresponded with Darwin. Quite a lot of suffragists. Susan Pearson, even Victoria Woodhull for a period of time."

"Whoa, back up. Inventor of unfermented grape juice?"

"Thomas B. Welch. The bottling plant was an important industry here in Vineland." Hawk pointed his open hand at a museum case full of grape juice artifacts. "Before Welch, nobody had ever thought of bottling unfermented wine."

"And why would they? The fermented stuff being, you know." Willa grinned. "Good enough for Jesus and all."

"Temperance was crucial to the vision," he said coolly. "Landis considered his alcohol ban a protection for families and the industrious habits of his new settlers."

"Seems like it might put a damper on the free thinking, though."

Still he refused to smile. "Within the first decade Vineland had eighteen public schools, including one of the first high schools in the country. Three private seminaries, fourteen churches, Masonic and Odd Fellows societies, a public library, and a hall built on Plum Street to host one of the country's most exciting public lecture series."

His complete humor blindness was nudging her toward the back-away option, but it wouldn't be easy now. He was launched.

"Susan Fowler and Mary Tillotson were early promoters of the Dress Reform movement. Tillotson spent time in the Vineland jail for wearing trousers. The Vineland Equal Rights Association hosted Susan B. Anthony here in 1868, which was the year the women of Vineland voted in the presidential election."

"I don't think so. That's pre–Nineteenth Amendment by around fifty years."

"They used a separate ballot box, set up next to the official one. It's over there."

Chastened by his look, and conscious of her muddy boots, she walked over to the exhibit, a slotted box covered in green velvet. An antique photo on the wall behind it showed bonneted women shouldering through a crowd of men on what appeared to be an election day of nineteenth-century vintage.

"There's no way their votes would have counted in that election. Did they know?"

"A common mistake in thinking about the past is to assume people were more childlike than we are now."

Ouch. Willa wondered how often this prickly gent mingled with the public. She conceded his point, however.

"The Vineland Women's Caucus organized the 1868 presidential vote to protest the prevailing argument of the time, that women wouldn't be interested in voting even if they were allowed. It made national news."

"Wow. Was this the first place that happened?"

"As far as we know, yes."

"That's amazing, honestly." She leaned close to study the photograph. "So this could be the first authentic image of women voting in the United States."

"Yes, we think it is."

"Are you keeping the original someplace safe? I mean, fireproof, climate controlled?"

Hawk's pale eyes grew sad and Willa saw she'd unintentionally ouched him back. "Our budget is next to nothing. We're one of the oldest historical societies in the country, dating back to the founding of Vineland. But people don't have much interest anymore and our endowments have dried up. I try, but I'm one person. The paper archives are a mess. A lot of our material is upstairs stored in beer cartons, to tell you the truth."

"Jeez. That's kind of terrible. You've got some treasures here."

Zero endowment for Vineland's crucial archives didn't bode well for Willa's gold-digging prospects. "I'm interested in all of this," she said. "I'd love to do a feature about Landis and the utopian ideal. But today I'm on an errand that's kind of specific."

Hawk rose above his despair. "I'm good at specific," he said.

"Then I'll give you a street address: 744 Plum Street. Big brick house with double chimneys, one down from the corner of Sixth. Can you tell me anything about it?"

"Such as?"

"This is fishing in the dark. I'm hoping for some kind of historic significance."

"You're interested in the possibility of historic registry, then."

"I'm interested in *grants* that might go along with historic registry. The house is loaded with antique charm but it's in bad shape. We'd love to find somebody interested in paying us to keep it from falling down."

"Well, you've come to the right place, a few decades too late. As I said, this town has gone soft on historic pride. But never say die. Let me think." He stared at Willa with odd intensity. Suddenly he was all hers.

"Come with me," he said abruptly, turning and walking toward the door from which he'd first appeared. Stunned, she followed him into a long, narrow room lined on both sides with bookshelves from floor to ceiling. Hawk went ahead of her, pulling down ledgers and slim file boxes as he talked over his shoulder.

"We don't have anything like an exhaustive listing, but we have photos of every house in town that was built before 1900. Do you think yours is that old?"

"Absolutely." Willa had no idea.

"Unfortunately that material is not well organized yet. A lot of it is in boxes. It would be tedious, but you could go through piles of photographs to see if you find your house. Assuming it's still recognizable and not wrecked by one of those savage architectural updates. Or another approach would be to go through these directories."

"Telephone directories?" Willa wondered when these had passed over from obsolete to historic. She couldn't remember when she'd last used one.

"No. Housing directories. Before telephones. We have almost every year from 1866 to the late 1870s. Landis published these annual listings giving homeowners' names, occupations, and addresses. The idea was to encourage social visits. So you could look through these to see if anybody important has ever lived in your house."

"As opposed to now," she said, but the man was really not going to smile.

"Unfortunately these listings are organized alphabetically by residents' names, not by address. You'll just have to scan pages to try and find it. What's the address again?"

"Seven forty-four East Plum."

He turned and looked at Willa.

"What?" she asked. "Is that the magic number?"

"I don't know. I don't know. I'm not making any promises but let me just look something up."

She walked around a long table and stood behind him, watching over his shoulder—she had no idea for what—as he flipped through an ancient directory. The pages were browned at the edges like a well-done sugar cookie.

"She's not here." He closed the little paper booklet and checked its cover. "Eighteen seventy-eight, she'd moved by then. I knew that. Let's go back to the early seventies."

"*Who?*"

"Mary Treat. I'm not promising anything but I know she lived on Plum, early on. Before she moved to her own place on Park. I have in my mind it was in that block between Sixth and Seventh, just down from Plum Hall."

"Mary Treat?"

"The scientist. I told you about her."

Willa racked her brain and came up with Landis, Susan B. Anthony, and the grape juice guy. "Tell me again."

"She was a scientist and writer, extremely well known in her time. One of the most outspoken American advocates of Darwin and evolutionary theory in the late nineteenth century."

"You did mention that. She was pen pals with Darwin. You're saying she lived in my house?"

"I'm saying she might have lived in your house. I'm sure we can nail down the exact address because we have all of her papers. She died without heirs, so everything was donated here."

"If you had everything," Willa pointed out, "you'd have letters from Charles Darwin."

"Oh, we do. Would you like to see?"

Willa stood gobsmacked while Christopher Hawk disappeared into upper reaches of Vineland arcana. In less than five minutes he was back with a box. He sat down at the long table and extracted a legal-size manila folder whose tiny typewritten label said: "Darwin Letters Mary Treat." Willa took a seat beside him and opened the folder.

"Ho-ly . . ."

The sight of Darwin's handwriting gave her a chill. This letter was not a copy. She must have seen reproductions of his signature because the angular letters were instantly recognizable. Original Charles Darwin correspondence archived in a beer carton. Willa looked from the pale, proud moon of Hawk's face to the letter in her hands and shivered at the Miss Havisham of it all. Here was the cake.

⋊⋉

"I swear, Iano. Charles freaking Darwin."

Iano stopped again to adjust the baby in the denim sling criss-crossing his chest. They'd spent fifteen minutes trying to figure out this infant carrier before Willa stooped to reading the instructions. It seemed unnecessarily complicated; likewise the chic diaper bag

Willa carried over her shoulder had far too many pockets labeled with icons for diapers, pacifier, and so forth. But soon they had him more or less correctly swaddled against Iano's rib cage and the baby seemed content, so long as they kept moving along the sandy trail. The air was cool and smelled of salt.

"I thought it was Robert," Iano said.

"What?"

"Charles *Robert* Darwin. Or was it Francis?"

"Damn it, you're supposed to be amazed."

"I'm amazed. I was amazed when you told me yesterday. I'm waiting for the part about Charles Darwin living in our house during his heretofore unknown New Jersey period. And the British National Trust sending over a jolly crew of workmen to make us a new roof and foundation."

"And Bob's your uncle."

"Exactly."

"I can practically taste the British cement."

"So who was this woman? The heretofore unknown New Jersey Darwin Paramour?"

"God, Iano. Can't a female be a *colleague*? Even in the nineteenth century?"

"I'm adding some human interest to your grant proposal."

"Nice try, but I don't think so. I read a pile of his letters. Not unless they had a secret love code encrypted in Latin names of plants."

"Dearest *Monomos discolos*, I long to classify your diafromia."

"Your Latin names sound kind of Greek."

Iano shrugged. "I was improvising."

Willa pitied all human beings whose spouses didn't make them laugh. Just a couple of hours yesterday with the humorless Mr. Hawk had sapped her will to live. "The British National Trust," she said. "Now there's a thought."

"I think Great Britain is about as broke as we are."

"Well of course. That would go without saying."

They stopped for another sling adjustment. "It feels like he's going to slither out the bottom," Iano said, fiddling with the straps. Willa waited, eyeing the denim contrivance and wondering what it was worth on the open market. They'd finally started mining the lode of baby paraphernalia Zeke had brought along with his move from Boston, after weeks of feeling these goods were somehow untouchable. Nearly all of it was loot from a power baby shower Helene's colleagues had thrown on her last day of work, everything still in the original boxes. Willa felt guilty about the thank-you notes unsent, though she knew that was her old-fashioned breeding. Plus ridiculous, given the full freight of Helene-related regrets.

The path led them along a weedy margin between a forest and a small, marshy lake. Willa hated not having brought Dixie along, but Dixie these days was having trouble getting herself around the block. A baby was enough for today. They were spending it at Cape May, the southernmost tip and reputed tourist highlight of South Jersey. Without any real plan they'd wound up there after packing the diaper bag and driving for the coast on impulse, at Iano's suggestion. Willa mentioned having heard of a place called the Pine Barrens, and he'd asked, *Seriously?* He steered her instead toward a happier-sounding picnic on the beach. Once there, they discovered wind plus sand equals painfully sandblasted skin, so they'd opted for this more baby-friendly hike on an inland path. It didn't really matter. Willa knew the only point was to get her out of the house. She'd been having panic attacks since the day another ceiling fell, this time in the upstairs room they'd planned to use as a nursery. Presently the baby's bassinet rotated among Zeke's, Tig's, and his grandparents' bedrooms, depending on which of them most needed an unbroken night's sleep. He still cried a lot in the daytime but mostly slept after dark now, so long as he got his nighttime bottles around midnight and four.

It was Tig who announced they were all avoiding the obvious—that Dusty needed a place of his own in this house—and marched upstairs with a screwdriver to assemble the crib that had been stored in the third-floor room since the day they'd moved in. Tig who moved the rest of the boxes and attic junk into other parts of the house, then hauled a dresser up the stairs and filled it with the clothes and toys the child had scored from his mother's well-heeled friends. She began painting a mural on the walls. Every day after her shift at the restaurant she disappeared up there for hours, the bass line of her music and a turpentine smell wafting down the stairs, until one day Willa climbed up to investigate and was stunned by her daughter's vision. It was a rainforest. Bright macaws nestled in the elbows of trees, monkeys dangled from branches, jungle cats lurked in shadows eyeing the nesting birds. Tig with green-spattered dreadlocks resembled a joyful kindergartner. Willa noticed an ominous vining of fine cracks across the ceiling plaster, but didn't mention it.

It gave way in the middle of a sunny Saturday: they heard the crash, ran upstairs, and found Tig's cosmos shattered for no good reason. There had been no wind, no storm, no cloud in the sky. Tig put away her paints and seemed to withdraw from the household after that. This weekend she was working double shifts at the restaurant, leaving Willa and Iano on the hook for babysitting. Zeke was off in Boston for a week of meetings with his partners and their new investment clients.

And Willa was falling frequently into cold sweats as she tried to stave off images of disaster. Zeke in a highway accident, the baby dead from SIDS. When these attacks came at night Iano sat up in bed holding her hand, peering at her face, asking if this was more of the menopause or something else. It was the something else, for which no words were quite enough. Unprovoked losses one after another—her mother, jobs, savings, Helene, the ceiling—had stripped Willa of the useful illusion that everything would be fine. It amazed her now to watch people walking through life with their ludicrous trust.

Iano didn't know she'd been meting out a hoard of pricey pharmaceuticals left over from the glory days of good health insurance in Virginia: Xanax, Ambien, a few tabs at the bottoms of many random bottles (months or years past expiration) that she'd hastily packed instead of throwing away as officially advised. She dreaded the end of this secret supply, had even eyed the leftover tranquilizer from Dixie's veterinarian. Happy was the day she found the untouched bottle of Valium that Iano had been prescribed to help with a tooth extraction. Valium, on *Iano*, what a waste. She'd come here today for his sake, not hers. To please their beloveds some women faked orgasm; Willa faked composure. He thought a change of scenery would help, and couldn't quite grasp that her problem wasn't the scenery or the venue, it was the whole darn show.

He stopped in the path and Willa moved close beside him, their toes nearly touching the pond's edge as they watched a pair of white swans gliding very close by on the dark, still water. The creatures looked strange in their wild setting, not ornaments in a city park but real animals with algae stains on their scarlet beaks and an unmistakable "back off" vibe. Abruptly they curled their long necks in a coordinated motion like synchronized swimmers, dropping their heads to horizontal just above the water, staring up darkly at the pair of human intruders with the strapped-on young.

"They remind me of supermodels," Iano said.

"I was thinking the same thing. Willowy and gorgeous. And they'd kill you for the chance to eat a good meal."

A couple of birdwatchers approached from down the shore, identifiable by their matching pockety vests and binoculars. Willa and

Iano had encountered many of their tribe today, some of them eager to share sightings, using a mystifying language of "neotrops" and "sharpies." Others noted the absence of binoculars and left them alone. Just by chance, Willa and Iano were there on the biggest birding weekend of the Cape May year: an enthusiastic Michigander had finally clued them in. This peninsula was the jumping-off point for most of the migratory birds from New England to upper Canada, millions of them, all headed south. Every year, but especially in this one with its two big storms, birds congregated en masse while they waited for good weather and the gumption to launch themselves out. Willa was amazed. She'd never given a thought to these little lives hurtling themselves over the dark ocean, their tiny brains still big enough to dream of a warm jungle on the far side of a god-awful journey.

The couple now approaching had no-nonsense haircuts and such similar builds that Willa couldn't distinguish the male and female of the pair until they were at pretty close range. The lavender camp shirt should have been a clue, she eventually realized. They stopped for a moment to join in the swan admiration.

"Beautiful, aren't they?" the man said.

"My wife was just saying they are her spirit animals," Iano offered. Willa subtly sucked in her cheeks and crossed her eyes at him.

"That's good news for you," the woman said. "They mate for life. They migrate together and everything, hard times and all."

"Dear lady, that is good news. You've made my day." Iano flashed his chili-pepper beam and Willa watched the poor woman melt. For years to come she would remember the handsome guy who flirted with her on the trail at Cape May.

"Cute kid," the husband said, wagging his white caterpillar eyebrows at the child in the sling. The baby had been so quiet Willa had momentarily forgotten their charge. Dear God, what if she really forgot one day and baked him in the parked car or something? He was *never* this quiet. She felt an edge of panic and tried not to think. Thinking made everything worse. "Boy or girl?" the man asked.

"A boy," Willa and Iano answered in unison.

"Oh, he's just looking all around!" the woman said. "What's his name?"

Willa and Iano exchanged a discreet grimace. Willa blurted, "George."

"Georgie porgie, pudding and pie!" The woman crooned. "You three have a wonderful day." The pair pushed on. The dear lady would always remember the handsome guy in Cape May who was *carrying a baby*. No female fantasy was ever devised to top that one.

They probably weren't fully out of earshot when Iano hooted, "George!"

"It's not too late. We could get him to answer to George, before Zeke is on to us."

"I'm game."

They turned their backs on the petulant swans and walked on, leaving the lake and entering a forest of shrubby, waxy-leaved trees. The path narrowed to one slim lane, and Iano walked behind her.

"What kind of a name is *Aldus*, anyway?" she asked.

"Saxon."

"Well, I presumed. That's not exactly what I was asking. I meant, who names a child Aldus?" She laughed. "I ask the man who named his child Antigone."

"Antigone is a good name. It fits her. One day she'll grow into it, you'll see."

"You mean our daughter will someday find the Attic tragedy life where it all makes sense? God help us. I always thought the original Antigone was a whiner, to tell you the truth. 'My brother got murdered, waah waah waah.'"

When Iano offered no defense, Willa stopped in the path and

turned around to stare at him. "Did you ever even *read Antigone*? I can't believe I've never asked."

Iano smiled evasively.

"You! Greek classics poseur."

"It's a name, *moro*. She's not the only one, that famous whiner."

"Actually, I think she probably is the only one." Willa walked on. "So *Aldus*, anyway. What the heck."

"It means 'from the old house.'"

This got a rise out of Willa that sent her into a coughing fit. "Now isn't that just perfect," she said, once she could breathe. "Only I'm sure you made it up."

"I didn't, I swear. I looked it up."

"You looked up the meaning of 'Aldus'? On what, some name-your-baby website?"

"When they first told us about the name. After the ultrasound, when they found out it was a boy. Remember?"

"I remember thinking: they have six more months, they will come to their senses."

They were quiet for a while, sobered by the memory of a living Helene and happy Zeke calling them with the news about their boy. That was the day Willa and Iano had stopped resisting and embraced it as real. *Him* as real. Their grandchild. After the phone call they'd gone to the attic together—in those days they had a house with an attic above it, solid ground underneath—to look at the beautiful antique crib they'd dragged through every move of their marriage, even after their kids had outgrown it. It was hand-made of sturdy walnut by someone in her father's West Virginia family whose only remaining scion was Willa. Against every practical instinct she'd refused to let that crib go to strangers on eBay. Now it would go to Boston, they'd said happily. To a new scion.

"Our little guy from the collapsing house," Willa said. "Well done, Helene. I'm going to have to call that foreshadowing."

"It was her father's name. We could give her the benefit of the doubt."

"I know. But still." The woodland was thinning out and Willa could hear pounding surf somewhere off to their left. "'Dusty' I can live with. It's sweet."

"The house falls and the dust settles."

"Let us pray." She thought of her mother's long-standing promise that Tig would one day *settle*. Settle down, settle out, settle the debts. Did anyone ever?

The path ahead of them divided: more forest lay ahead, and off to their right a boardwalk led over an inland swamp with a sign that offered the promising "Gossamer Meadow." Without hesitation they chose the boardwalk. Willa both loved and mistrusted the sense of walking on water, which felt like getting away with something illegal, even if the water itself was black and stagnant. The elevated path vibrated slightly with their steps. It took them into a wide-open country with a watery floor and a crop of dense, sticklike reeds where no channels looked wide enough for swan passage, although Willa heard clucking sounds. Eventually she caught sight of little duck-like creatures spiriting almost invisibly through the thickets.

They stopped to admire a shrub with giant white flowers growing straight up from the water. Iano leaned over the railing to break off a branch and present it to Willa. The droopy flowers looked like they were made of wet toilet paper, and when she touched a petal it also felt like that. Some word between *frangible* and *slimy*.

"Ick. But thank you." She wiped her hand on her jeans.

"Uh-oh," he said, looking down the boardwalk to a spot some fifty yards ahead where it ended abruptly.

They kept walking, unable to resist the precipice. "It's like we're walking the plank," Willa said, amazed by the effusive spider-webbing of yellow caution tape at the terminus they hadn't spotted earlier, now so plainly visible.

"We aren't technically obligated to follow through," he pointed out.

They arrived at a dead end festooned with so many barriers and legal warnings, a person would need some kind of death wish to get through it. Bright yellow laminated signs explained this was damage from Hurricane Sandy, that the Park Service presently had no budget for repairs, and that this portion of the reserve was now closed to visitors. Iano and Willa stood gazing past the barricade at a splintery line of vestigial boardwalk rising intermittently above the reeds. It must have gone on like that for miles.

When they turned around Willa found herself in tears. Iano put his arm around her shoulder, carefully matching her shorter stride. "*Ela, matakia*, don't be sad. Ten minutes ago we didn't even know about the Gossamer Meadow. Now you can't live without it."

Willa said nothing. *Matakia* meant "little eyes," probably a step above *moro* on the endearment chain. She tossed away the flower branch and wiped her cheeks with her shirt sleeve, and then her nose, despite the multitude of tissues and wipes in the diaper bag on her shoulder. She wondered why she'd carried all this ridiculous baggage. As if a diaper emergency unattended would be the end of the world.

"What is gossamer, anyway?" Iano asked. His instincts were good; words were Willa's most reliable distraction.

"Flimsy. Now you see it, now you don't."

"Okay, so now we don't." He stroked her cheek.

"I'm sorry. I know you hate this. But you might just have to let me be sad, okay?"

"Okay. But for what?"

She shrugged, looking away. "I don't know. Damn Hurricane Sandy and the damn Park Service budget cuts. We can't afford to stop doing the shit that's screwing up the weather, and can't afford to pick up the pieces after we do our shit."

Iano nodded. "This is what in my field we call a conundrum."

"This is what in my field we call assfucked."

"Speaking as a journalist?"

"Speaking as the unemployed."

She looked at Dusty, still wide awake, and wondered at what point in her tenure as his guardian she would have to stop saying words like *assfucked*. She'd managed it before, when Zeke and Tig were small. But her frustrations were so much smaller then.

"What if Tig is right?" she asked.

"When is Tig ever right? About what."

"That the problem is actually the world running out of the stuff we need. That capitalism can only survive on permanent expansion but the well eventually runs dry."

"Nothing is ever that simple, *moro*. First of all, *well* in the sense you're using it is just a metaphor."

Willa didn't know what else to say. Her heartbreak was for something well beyond the Gossamer Meadow. The fact that taking all the right turns had led her family to the wrong place, moneyless and a few storms away from homelessness. Also, the fact that she couldn't legitimately feel this sorry for herself while carrying a Gucci diaper bag. Probably made by Asian children more moneyless and homeless than herself. If metaphorical thinking wasn't useful here, she was rooked for other options.

They reached the spot where the path had forked and this time took the other one. In minutes they came out of the trees into bright sunshine and the view of a long lake divided from the Atlantic by a dam of white dunes. The path widened and Iano walked beside her again, heartily taking her arm in his as if they were college kids or revolutionary extras in *Les Misérables*. Willa watched Dusty's little round head bobbing gently against Iano's chest. His eyes darted up and down, taking in sky, trees, movement. Willa remembered reading that infant vision was limited to close range, but he seemed to know he was outdoors. Or at any rate, someplace a lot bigger than usual.

"We've hardly taken him outside," she said. "Actually, have we ever?"

"I don't know. Tig takes him for walks in that Rolls-Royce of a stroller. She and that neighbor kid take him to the cemetery a lot. Which is weird, if you ask me."

"True, but that probably doesn't feel like outdoors to him. That stroller is like a rolling baby pod. Also the young man has a name and it is Jorge. Apparently he's good with babies, thanks to the nieces and nephews. I've noticed his two older sisters seem to run a tight ship over there."

Iano made no reply. With Tig and romance there was no parent handbook, but she and Jorge had been spending a lot of time together. Willa wasn't sure whether Iano opposed this union or hadn't noticed it.

"He seems like a nice kid," Iano finally said without conviction.

"I've never seen the baby this happy. Look at him."

Iano looked down, pulling in his chin to regard the face pressed against his sternum. "You're right. I'm a baby happiness machine."

Willa laughed. "That's probably what he's needed all this time, to be pressed up against somebody's warm body and taken outdoors. It might not be you in particular."

Iano made an exaggerated pout.

"The pediatrician said he might cry a lot when we put him down. She said a lot of stuff about trauma and attachment issues, but I was kind of shell-shocked and it didn't really register at the time. Now that I think about it, Zeke hardly ever picks him up."

"Zeke is not any kind of a happiness machine," Iano pointed out.

"I'm not blaming Zeke. It's all of us. We have that fancy-schmancy car seat with the detachable baby bucket so you go from home to car to stroller and naps to feeding without ever touching your baby."

"Willa. Fancy-schmancy?"

"I know. That sounded exactly like Nick. You need to get me out of the house more, I'm getting infected with Nickness."

"*Gamo to.*" Meaning, "fuck it."

"*Gamo to*," she replied.

"*Putana thalassa pou se gamoun ta psaria.*" Meaning, "whore ocean where all the fish fuck each other." A family favorite. In her early days among the Tavoularises she'd actually looked that one up, refusing to believe such an expression could belong to a common parlance. Oh, youth.

Iano put an arm around her waist and pulled her close, intuiting that the mention of Nick might bring on a panic attack. They were both trying not to think about him. For several days running he had refused to get out of bed. Tig was giving him all his insulin shots now, and changing the bandages on his legs, and Willa hadn't even asked the bathroom question. This morning he'd yelled for Tig but she'd already left for work, and when Willa showed up instead he'd gotten pretty belligerent. She didn't need to fuss over him like a damn baby, et cetera. She and Iano had nearly canceled their plans, but he insisted they should take the brat and go. Leave him alone. Nick's version of kindness.

He would probably be fine. Tig was coming home and would check on him at some point midday, between her shifts. Or maybe she'd only worked through lunch and was doing something else that afternoon, Willa wasn't sure. She'd been volunteering at the school formerly known as "For the Feebleminded" on Saturday afternoons, digging up a giant garden with the kids. They were part of a big group of volunteers and inmates, including Jorge's resident cousin, who collectively called themselves the Feebleminders.

Willa wasn't mistaken, Tig had told her this. Their garden project was called Feeble Field. Who could begin to interpret these kids' moral language, with the wires of political correctness, outrage, and irony carefully crossed so as to keep out anyone too old to grasp Lady Gaga.

"Tell me about your lady scientist," Iano said. "Mary Trick."

"Treat!" She punched his shoulder. "So she's mine now?"

"If she made famous discoveries in our house, I think we can parlay that into a decent fortune."

Willa smiled. Iano was trying to walk her back from a panic attack, but in present circumstances one ledge backed up against another. She didn't want to think about grant writing or house rescue any more than she wanted to think about Nick.

"How much fortune do we need to raise, exactly?" she asked. "According to your pal Pete. Just so I know the ballpark I'm shooting for."

Iano blew out a long breath. "An acre or so of tin roofing, a ton of cement foundation, new brickwork on walls and chimneys, a lot of new framing inside, plus sheet rock, et cetera. That's not even counting labor."

"Maybe I don't want to hear the numbers." Willa had the familiar sensation of losing ground. "It doesn't seem fair. Mary wrote about it as just this cozy little abode."

"This is a new century, *moro*. For modern happiness, forty acres and a mule won't touch it. We need four hundred acres and a Triple Crown winner. And you will get us there, because you're superwoman."

"No I'm not. Sorry to crap on your Lady Scientist museum, but I'm not even a hundred percent sure Mary's house is our house."

Dusty had finally eased into sleep. He was a stunner, this child, with loads of black hair they'd attributed to Helene. She'd been the rare kind of beauty with blue eyes, creamy skin, and jet-black hair.

But Dusty was starting to get pigment, his eyes headed toward brown and the skin no longer translucent. Looking like a Tavoularis. And starting to achieve some predictability: he would wake up hungry around the time they got back to the car. Willa would open a convenient one-pack of formula and heat the bottle in the handy device that plugged into the car charger, and all would be right with Dusty's world. That much future she could handle at the moment.

They stopped in the trail, arrested by the sight of thousands of birds overhead. The flock moved like an aurora spreading across the sky, abruptly contracting into a dense oval and then flinging out again. Maybe they were unnerved by the storm clouds building in the west. Willa couldn't take her eyes from the mass of birds, a billowing scrimmage that slowly achieved the shape of a dark funnel cloud with a tail reaching toward the ground. The tail dropped lower, lower, and then touched a shrubby tree at the edge of the lake. In seconds the whole cloud seemed to get sucked into the tree. All birds vanished.

"Whoa," she said. "What just happened?"

They stared at the trembling foliage. A tree of leaves that were actually birds.

"I think they're swallows. They used to come down our chimney and my mother would get hysterical. It's some old-country curse, having birds in the house."

"Really. Don't I remember she had a parakeet?"

"Mikis, sure. Mikis was not a bird. According to my mother."

Willa nodded. "I see how she managed to live with your father."

They stood for a long time, hypnotized by the trembling bush. It must have been a bird ritual, the drumming up of collective will to take the blind leap of faith, forsaking all safety to fly across an ocean to the southern hemisphere. How could they trust something so unknown, and for how many years had they done it, Willa wondered: A thousand? Ten thousand? While humans altered everything on the face of their world, these birds kept believing in a map that never changed.

"She had a thing for birds," Willa said. "My Mary Treat. I'm reading one of her books, *Home Studies in Nature*."

"The tiny man let you bring home one of her books?"

"No, I found it online. Illustrations and all. The writing is so sweet, Iano, it just kills me. She had relationships with the birds and insects in her backyard. She's like this Disney princess scientist, talking to the creatures and letting them in the house."

Iano crossed himself. Willa smiled.

"I don't think she brought the birds in the house. But other things. Spiders, actually. Tower-building tarantulas. She kept them in big glass jars in her living room."

"Sweetheart, this is not helping our entrance fees."

"I know. I think she was a little eccentric, even for then. But she sounds so blooming happy. In her writing, I mean."

"This is when, eighteen seventies you said?"

Willa nodded. The storm in the distance was building pretty ominously. Willa could feel a change in the density of the air as they stood mesmerized by the bush of birds, waiting for something to happen. She took a few cautious steps closer, pulling Iano with her. They paused, then approached a little more. Eventually they stood close enough to see individual birds hopping all around manically inside the bush like electrons confined in their orbits. Like Jiffy Pop. It was a wonder of the bird world.

"Sounds like you're getting infatuated with your Mary."

"What's not to love? A happy naturalist in a leafy utopia founded on science and ambition and plenty of everything to go around. If I weren't infatuated, I'd be jealous. As far as I can tell, she got to make a good living writing stories about birds and spiders."

"You mean as characters?"

"No. Strike the Disney princess. She was a real scientist. But into domestic things, bird nests and spider towers. How they learned to build them, what forces affected their survival. Evolution was a new idea, so I guess nature wasn't just a cabinet of curiosities anymore. It was a machine, and everybody was keen to know what made it tick."

"She made a living from professional publications? *I'm* jealous. We have to pay the journals a page fee to publish us."

"Believe it or not, she wrote for popular magazines, *Harper's* and *The Atlantic*. Can you imagine? Submitting a story about the catbirds in my backyard to *The Atlantic*? People were so . . . precious back then. Less worldly, I guess."

"Or more interested in catbirds."

"Or more interested in catbirds."

"So all this will go into your historic preservation grant?"

She turned to look at him. "Okay, here's why I adore you. We have no idea if she lived in our house. I'm going back Monday to see what I can find. Meanwhile you've got the British National Trust putting new tin on our roof and the museum ready to open."

"And here's why I adore you—" he said, interrupted by a siren-loud blast from Willa's phone. Thousands of birds burst from their tree skyward like a house going up in smoke. Dusty woke and howled.

"Jesus!" Willa said, digging through the diaper bag for the phone. The thing must have had two dozen exterior pockets. The ringtone was ear splitting; she'd set it on max the previous night so the alarm would wake her out of her Ambien fog for the baby's feedings. She finally found her phone, in the pocket labeled with a phone icon.

"It's not a number I recognize. Should I answer it anyway?"

"No," Iano said firmly. "Probably a junk call. Who would be calling that you don't know?"

"Nobody." She turned the phone to silent and watched the connection end. Immediately it vibrated with a text coming in.

"Oh, it's Tig," she said, watching words materialize. "Using Jorge's phone, or somebody's." She went quiet, and held the phone up for Iano to read:

Mom come home. Taking Papu to ER. Bad storm, they're saying Shelter In Place.

8

∞

Shelter in Place

They took the train to Batsto and stepped down into a hive of coveralled workers coming or going from their shifts: mill, glass-works, foundry. Mary cut a straight path through gangs of men who rubbed their hands together and expelled quick frosty breaths, turning to look as she passed. Thatcher felt vaguely traitorous, to whose side he couldn't have said. He walked behind Mary, thread to her needle, seeing what they saw: the slab of wooden plant press under her arm, the folds of indigo skirt swinging below the short black coat. Little Selma trotting alongside like a spaniel.

October was not an ideal time for his first visit to the Pine Barrens, Mary had allowed, and the brown landscape of Batsto confirmed it. Rain-darkened buildings of rough-sawn lumber, mud roads sucking at boot heels, trees in their phases of loss, all he despised of autumn gathered there. But every season has partic-ular gifts! This was Mary's claim and her new idea for a series of articles, "The Pines in All Seasons." An editor at *Harper's Monthly* had returned an encouraging correspondence, and Mary took all encouragement to heart. It was a quality Thatcher noticed because he lacked it. Rose hinted at his weak ambition, but the disease was more crippling than that: he distrusted praise, and took detractors at their word. Whenever he told Mary of his troubles at the school with Cutler, as he urgently wished to do today, he knew he was provoking her support so he might cement his little barnacle of confidence on that sturdy pier.

They turned from the road and tramped down a mucky lane where one log house was like the next, all with the same rutted yards, the same narrow rectangles of turnip and kale. He thought of soldiers he'd tended. When facing life's end they always wanted to speak of where they'd begun it, a humble log shelter too kindly recalled, on some lane like this one where mud climbed a man's trousers to the knees. Thatcher felt humiliated for the dressing-down he would get from Rose. He would try to spirit these trousers directly to Gracie and Mrs. Brindle, who made teamwork of boil-ing the laundry cauldron, neither of whom would bat an eyelash at the master's muddy trousers. Where was the marital ease he'd expected in due time? His thoughts of his wife were a tangled thicket: Rose the irresistible opium and the bed of thorns, her ex-quisite scent, her not-quite-trustworthy graces. She had been am-orous these mornings lately, probably thinking of another baby. And after, when he was drowsy with postcoital exhaustion, *then* Rose would grow energetic on the subject of household acquisition. Their own buggy and horse, now. For poor Aurelia, how was she to make social calls on her well-to-do friends?

Abruptly Mary halted and cried out, "Mr. Foggett, good morn-ing!"

Foggett stepped out the door of his cabin in a red flannel union suit and trousers, the suspenders dangling, the boots unlaced. Well past nine in the morning.

"Well Missus Treat. Out for a day in the drear swamps, are we?"

"We are. This is my friend Mr. Greenwood, joining our excursion. I need to go back and check on my little ferns, if you will oblige us today."

Foggett shouldered his suspenders, went indoors, and reappeared momentarily with a grimy shirt buttoned up beneath the braces. The boots' brown tongues still lolled, a pair of panting dogs. He fetched his mare from behind the cabin and hitched his phaeton.

When he had the horse ready and the buggy dusted off with a gray rag, Foggett gave a hand up to Mary and walked around to mount the front bench beside her. Without assistance Selma clambered into the footman's seat at the rear, still toting the oversize lunch bucket and small shovel she had carried on the train. Her pale eyes faced forward, the brittle hair poked like straw from every edge of her bonnet. Thatcher glimpsed the loneliness of these outings for the girl. Given Mary's absorption in her botany, Selma would likely be forgotten until something required hefting and portage. Already Mary was chatting away with Foggett about the predicted frost. Thatcher took his place with Selma on the seat behind the driver, which was not much more than a sanded plank.

Foggett clucked and off they sped, throwing Thatcher backward to grip the bench and wonder how footmen did not get flung in ditches. Selma gripped the lunch pail on her lap like a young heir. He resolved to address her today as he would his students, if they were released by Cutler to the outdoors. Likely they never would be, given the grave state of relations with his employer. Thatcher could see what lay ahead of him in too much detail: a wife's indignation, the cracks in a collapsing house. And Mary's disappointment, for the damage inflicted by Cutler on his pupils. Poor long-faced girls buttoned up in their boots, locked in a schoolroom until they could be handed over to kitchen and marriage.

Trapped, Rose had flung at him that morning. *In this suffocating house!* As a girl Rose had loved to ride. More than anything, she said. On little lanes between farms and vineyards she would fly all the way to Mays Landing, bonnet strings to the wind, sometimes with friends, often quite alone. Her father had kept a little white gelding for her in a stable out on East Avenue, consumed by the debt of its keeping after he died. How was it fair, Rose demanded, that she'd begun with so much and now had to live with so little? When she had done everything ever properly asked of her? Thatcher was mortified for all he had failed to see on her behalf. Easy enough for him to find contentment in a pair of old shoes and a half loaf of bread, she'd pointed out; *his* fortunes had taken the opposite path. It was true. He'd begun in a cramped hovel and marched out into the world, a life that felt larger by the year. A better husband would have seen how Rose's need for comfort differed from his own. A wife had greater wants, naturally, and could do nothing to help her own situation.

Mary turned around to draw Thatcher's attention to the flora. "Wax myrtle!" she shouted above the clop of the mare and shrieks of the mail spring under them. They'd left the town now for the spotted daylight of a tall pine wood. Selma seemed to know what Mary knew. Already she held one hand out to be slapped by the waxy-leaved shrubs they rushed past, whose branches bristled with white berries. She held her little palm to Thatcher's nose for a sniff of the myrtle fragrance. Ocean, lemon, candlewax.

"The early settlers used myrtle to make their candles," Mary said loudly. "It's a good wax, it doesn't melt in hot weather. Thoreau wrote about it. He made some tallow as an experiment."

So Thatcher's intuition of candles was correct. He wondered if it came up from memory, and whether some of the crones in his childhood village might be counted to this day among Mary's "early settlers." Vaguely, darkly, he recalled every kind of broth being boiled from twigs and leaves. Old women with nothing, pressing succor onto motherless boys. "Is it the berries that give the wax?"

Mary nodded, a gesture nearly lost in the lurching of her entire body. All four passengers bounced in unison as their buggy flew, a precarious little craft on choppy seas. Foggett their captain grimaced in concentration.

"You boil the berries to render it and the oil rises to the top. So says Thoreau. What use he made of his tallow, I can't tell you."

Her familiar tone might suggest scorn, admiration, or that she'd kept a personal correspondence with the late Mr. Thoreau. Thatcher knew not to rule out any possibility. He observed the passing blur of a forest unlike any he'd known. The tall pines were close spaced and even, as if planted, with a low understory that mostly obscured the forest's sandy floor. The road ran close to a river of deep red waters, an alarming color. Two men poled along in a flatboat maneuvering a net along the bank.

"Fishing?" he managed to ask.

Foggett pissed out a laugh.

"For iron," Mary said. "They're dredging up bog ore for the iron-works."

Strange territory, thought Thatcher, of bloody rivers where men fished for iron. But the chemistry he could work out well enough: the water-soluble iron, the acid peat of the bog, the anaerobic decay of plant matter. Equals limonite. During the war he'd heard men say the best iron for cannonballs came out of the swamps, and his childish imagination had the glossy spheres rolling fully formed out of the mud.

In another moment the carriage hurtled into sunlight as they passed through a section of forest cut to the ground. Splintered trunks bled sap into turpentine-scented air. Crews of men moved about ant-like, hauling pine trunks and laying them upright against great smoldering hills of logs. Making charcoal for the iron smelting, he guessed. The forest closed over them again. Mary pointed out a grassy hummock covered in what she called *Xerophyllum setifolium*, its taxonomy recently revised by Professor Watson at Harvard. Did Thatcher know Professor Watson? He did not. And here was the small shrub *Gaylussacia*, named in honor of the chemist Gay-Lussac. This tossing of names would have annoyed Thatcher had it been between men, but he believed the plants themselves were Mary's friends. Plants standing in for colleagues.

After a distance of miles, more than five, less than ten, and many more slashed clearings, a sinuous line of dense green grew visible ahead of them. He watched it as they approached, as distinct as a shoreline, much darker than the pine woodland. The blue-green reef turned out to be a wall of cedars. And their destination. Foggett let them down and negotiated with Mary the time when he would return there to collect them: three o'clock, she repeated thrice, and promised the man his payment upon their safe return, as usual. Mary wore no timepiece Thatcher could see, only her tin collecting box, dangling on its long purple ribbon like hefty jewelry. Selma shouldered the shovel and would not be separated from her lunch pail, so Thatcher insisted on taking the heavy plant press from Mary. Off they set into the dim cedar forest. Degrees cooler, instantly.

"It seems forbidding, I'll grant," Mary said cheerfully.

"The place for ghouls," Selma suggested.

"Oh that's picturesque, Selma. I will use it. The readers like to be frightened."

"Why do they, Mrs. Treat?" Selma asked. "I can fair enough get a fright up at home when Pa has had the drink. Wouldn't need to look for it in a magazine."

"Darker and darker it grows as I cautiously advance, with an oppressive dread of something which I can not define."

"Oh Mrs. Treat. Have mercy!" Selma shuddered.

Mary set an arm across the child's shoulder. "I was only testing out my prose on you. We're safe here and you very well know it."

Thatcher saw he'd been wrong to assume Mary ignored the girl. Here in the forest they were like mother and daughter.

"Where does your father come by the drink?" he asked. Both their faces snapped toward him and he reddened. "I'm only curious. Because of the temperance laws."

"Millville," Selma said. "They've got depravery and Italians."

"I'm sorry to hear it."

They continued on the carriage road, wide enough for three to walk abreast but at this point better suited for boots than wheels. The earth was damp sponge, like a trifle cake. His trousers were doomed. Mary had hitched her skirt with some sort of complicated tuck in the waistband so it did not drag in the mud, and Selma had worked a similar trick with her own. They must have done it in the carriage.

"What do you think of the Barrens so far?" Mary asked.

"That there's more industry in them than many a Boston ship-yard."

"In that section we came through, it's true," she said. "In every direction out of Batsto the saws and dredges are eating away. Five years ago I could walk from the train into untouched forest inside of ten minutes. Pine woods as deep and quiet as they stood two centuries ago. We still have tracts like that standing, of course."

"But now you have to hire Mr. Foggett to get you to them."

"Now we must prevail on Mr. Foggett, yes."

"Was Vineland a forest like this when Landis purchased it?"

"Much the same. Poor barrens. The moment they were discovered to be fertile instead of barren, their destiny was yoked to pro-creation."

"So unenthusiastic for the captain's Garden of Eden, Mary. Yours are the first shadows of doubt I've met since coming to Vineland."

"The Garden of Eden might be well and good for the farmers and grape juice bottlers. Our forests will become the greatest gardens in the Union. And then farewell to the rare floral treasures none of us can save."

"I suppose we all must eat," he said. Selma thoughtfully bumped the lunch pail against her thigh as she walked. The ground grew wetter, the cedar darkness more dense.

"Look there," Mary said, stopping suddenly. *"Helonias bullata.* Do you know it?"

Rosettes of sharp leaves poked from the ground. "I do not," he confessed. The whorled clumps spread over the forest floor in a carpet of leafy daggers.

"Swamp pinks. It only grows here in the cedars, and only in a very few spots. You can see it's rhizomatous. It spreads underground. This group extends two or three acres and then disappears. You will walk fifteen miles before you find the next clump."

He wondered if she meant to do so that day. Mary was as animated by her *Helonias* as Rose with a new *Godey's Lady's Book.* This forest was home to her.

"Think how curious, Mr. Greenwood. It is scattered through this swamp, absent for miles, then cropping up again, always along a stream. What is your diagnosis?"

He diagnosed that she did not use his Christian name in front of the girl, and he should do likewise. Otherwise, nothing came to mind. He looked hard at the plant.

"I think we deduce it does not only spread by its roots," she said in a lowered voice, revealing a secret. "I believe it also disperses its seeds through water."

"This bog water! It's acid enough to melt horseshoe nails."

"Yes, nearly." Mary's eyes sparkled. "It would require extraordinary adaptation. Dr. Gray has a theory about the chemistry of it. He says it's the lipids . . ." She faltered slightly, then pushed on. "A good example of natural selection to survival in a bog environment."

"You're surely right."

Mary knew she was right. She knelt down to pluck a spent seed stalk while Thatcher watched. The childhood wasted in curtseying lessons, the grasp of taxonomy and chemistry entirely self-taught, and still she had marched her theories to the doorstep of Asa Gray. Whereas Thatcher, when he once met the great man coming through the door of the Harvard library, had gone pale with the effort of trying to say good morning. How did a person come to be Mary Treat? He could stand all day watching energy, logic, and indifference to judgment combine with such glorious force.

Selma took over the project of winnowing seeds from the stalks and shaking them into a glassine envelope produced from her apron pocket. Mary stood and brushed off her hands. "If I find other species that have similar chemistry in their seeds, it will support my theory. I've asked Mr. Darwin's opinion and he agrees. I've sent dozens of seed samples to Dr. Gray to analyze."

"A hundred, more like," Selma offered from below.

"Not a hundred, surely. I can't make myself a burden. Dr. Gray's letters always complain of how busy he is."

The seeds were collected and a live specimen tucked into Mary's collecting box, and on they marched. She wore the tin vasculum over one shoulder so it bumped against the peplum of her jacket and Thatcher walked behind her trying not to covet it. He could not say why the little box moved him, it was not new, but very beautiful, made of pleated tin and painted leaf green. A little latched door opened on the front. He wondered if it had been a gift from her father. Or her husband, in happier times.

They marched over trailing vines of partridgeberry and shrubs of heath, and under fronds of the royal fern, *Osmunda regalis*, reaching higher than Thatcher's head. Mary paused often to show him her favorites, the carnivores, and take collections. Along with the Venus flytrap she found glossy sundews and pitcher plants. She was happier in a dank bog than any woman or man Thatcher had known, under any shining sun.

The object of their day was to check on her little fern *Schizaea pusilla*, to which nature had assigned just a few lone spots on earth, including this one, where she was the first botanist to find it. It grew in a plot scarcely a mile across. Outside that zone it was seen no more. She had looked for it in all other parts of the bog, and concluded it existed in nought but its single home. Her search had been thorough and patient, she insisted, an unnecessary defense from a woman who could sit through a morning letting a plant digest her fingertip. Mary held herself to standards outside ordinary human existence.

"In the years since I discovered it, we have dug little clumps of my fern and transported them to spots with exactly similar soils and sun exposure, miles away, where we transplant them." She patted her trusty vasculum. "We take the greatest care, I promise you. Don't we, Selma?"

"Ma'am?"

"Our little ferns. We replant them so carefully, do we not?"

"Yes ma'am. Tender as baby mice."

"We give them to the care of nature, but nature refuses to recognize any right to the change. She allows the plants to languish and die. We mark the spots and return in a few months to check their progress, but they fail to take root. Every time, they are shriveled like this."

He gazed at the spot on the forest floor, copiously marked with ribbons, where one of her small transplants had breathed its last. Brown fronds plaintively shriveled, so small they would go unseen if not for her markers dangling from surrounding trees.

"Your belief is that the ferns should go forth and multiply?" he asked.

Mary considered the question. "Belief is the concern of religion.

My observation is that they cannot. And so one has to ask, why would a species persist in only one small place? What element of a new environment impedes them?"

One has to ask. He recalled the day he first saw Mary prone on the grass.

They had traveled very far from the carriage road, following faint deer trails that netted the dense forest. How Mary knew which fork to choose, he couldn't guess. Selma took the lead from time to time, appearing at ease, a little bonneted rabbit in its warren.

At last they emerged onto the relative openness of a stream bank. The canopy was still closed overhead but their line of sight, to Thatcher's relief, extended fifty feet or more across the stream.

"Is it noon, ma'am?" Selma asked.

Mary peered up through branches at shreds of sky. "I think it must be."

Selma shed her apron in a flash and threw it on the ground, then knelt on it to set out the contents of the lunch bucket, unwrapping cheeses, salted ham, and apples. A pot of cream, another of jam, a dark loaf of bread. Egg cake!

Mary meanwhile stood motionless, staring across the carmine stream toward the opposite bank, where water had undermined a substantial section of forest. Fallen logs lay across one another in shades of deep decay.

"A person might think we had not wholly emerged from the carboniferous era," she observed, and Thatcher saw he could never name his friend with one tree because she was many. The fossil ferns, ancient cedars, and flowering plants joined at the root to the different eons of their emergence: Mary was all these at once. She was phylogeny.

Selma commenced to eating a slab of bread with butter and jam.

Mary revived from her trance, folded her apron, and sat down on it. Thatcher found an accommodating rock. Selma handed him an apple, the jam pot, most of the ham, and two-thirds of the loaf, which grew difficult to balance on his knees. "How much will the magazine pay for your series on the pines?" he asked. He'd found Mary forthcoming about financial particulars; she volunteered them. Perhaps in her effort to inhabit the world of men.

"Eighty-five dollars per article." Mary inspected the butter pot closely and picked out a luckless insect. "With illustrations, six or eight to each installment I should think, which I will draw myself." She glanced at him. "Or else I will properly attribute them."

"I would never doubt it."

Eighty-five dollars. Even if it took her the full year to produce four illustrated articles, she would earn more than his three hundred from Cutler. And of course it wouldn't fully occupy her year. Mary found time for dozens of projects on a given day. (Or a hundred, if Selma were asked.) It crossed his mind to offer his services as an illustrator, but it might seem he was begging a favor. Certainly Thatcher didn't begrudge his friend's fortunes, but he sank now in the grave of his own. He had forgotten his financial miseries for the span of a morning, and wished for more mornings like it.

"One would think it easier to write for a popular magazine than a scientific one," Mary mused, "but I never find it the case. They'll want the proper telling of the thing to be slathered on all sides with froth, like a charlotte russe. 'In the death-like stillness a mysterious awe steals over my senses,' that sort of business. 'I am transported back through the ages to a time when nymphs presided over the wood, punishing those who shortened the lives of the trees.'"

"It's only Heavenly Father that can rule over us," Selma protested through a mouthful of bread.

"And I will make that plain, dear. Otherwise your mother will not let you come to me anymore."

"And charlotte russe has the jelly on the inside, not the outside."

"Well then, a Victoria sponge." Mary laughed. "Have mercy on me, Selma. You know what sort of a cook I am."

"Yes ma'am." Again, the squashed little grin.

"Why bother with writing sponge-cake prose, then?" Thatcher asked. "You've said the professional journals pay more. You have so many questions of science to pursue. With Charles Darwin and Asa Gray as colleagues."

Mary frowned into the cedars. "It has to be done," she said at last. "Most people look at a forest and say, 'Here are trees, and there is dirt.' They will see nothing of interest unless someone takes them by the hand. I am astonished at how little most people can manage to see."

"I admire you, then." Thatcher felt a few degrees elevated by a vocation he shared with Mary Treat. How could it not be noble work, to rouse a disaffected humanity and press the world's physical truths into its palms? Even the magazine readers, even the pinafored girls. Mr. Darwin was preoccupied. And Dr. Gray was too busy.

Abruptly Selma remembered something, pawed through her bucket, and produced a bottle of cold coffee. She flipped the wire bale and poured coffee into battered metal cups, passing one to Thatcher.

"Have you always known yourself to be a scientist?" Mary asked him.

He felt self-conscious under the watch of Mary and Selma, who seemed eager for him to eat quantities of bread and ham. Witness the exotic appetite of the male. "I never seem to know anything about myself at all. Except that I am curious, and put more faith in what I witness than what I am told."

"Then yes, a scientist born," Mary pronounced. "My curse as well. So my husband called it. He described himself a swimmer in philosophies, free to speculate on tides and spheres while I stood on shore seeking proof of the liquid nature of water."

Thatcher took note of the past tense. "One might envy the swimmer's freedom."

"But how muddly-puddly!" Mary said, clearly not envious. "To believe, without hindrance of actual evidence."

Thatcher had never heard so creative a damnation as *muddly-puddly*. "When did you and your husband come to Vineland?"

"In the eighth year of the settlement. We met a man in Troy who invited Joseph to speak at Plum Hall, and he was thrilled to oblige. That was in the autumn of sixty-eight."

"What was the subject of Dr. Treat's lecture?"

"'The Future of Vineland.' Extolling Captain Landis's wholesome ideals of fresh air and the agrarian conquest. Joseph had good instincts in those days for a topic to stir an audience. He even thought to mention women's suffrage. It was a week before the election, and everyone knew of the scheme for women going to the polls in Vineland."

That scheme was news to Thatcher, though Polly might know of it. She tormented her mother by following the adventures of Mistresses Fowler and Tillotson, of the Grand March to Perdition in Doeskin Trousers. "I take it Dr. Treat's homily was a success."

"Oh yes. Mr. Campbell invited us to return in December as his guests. We learned Vineland's fruit trees had suffered a crisis of pestilence the previous summer, so I helped Joseph prepare a lecture on the extirpation of pests by interrupting the larval cycle. I had studied insects in my father's orchards since long before I married."

"Had you?" Thatcher could picture that girl in the orchards. A species of Polly, with less leg and longer discipline. "With the intention of scientific discovery?"

"With no proper intention at all, I suppose." Mary looked thoughtful. "But my investigations found purpose in Vineland. He gave the lecture in January and published a tract called *Insect Extin-*

guisher that sold more than a thousand copies in a month. Dr. Treat became an instant success and we never returned to New York. We leased the house on Plum and had our things shipped from Troy."

"It was *your* success. Your work entirely. The lecture and pamphlet."

She smiled. "It was."

Wives assisted their husbands, naturally, but Thatcher saw how she would have come to confusions about proper attribution of another's work. He also noted Selma's disappointment in his progress on her victuals; he set himself to an apple. Mary was contemplative.

"Vineland was different in those days. Freethinking was purpose and endeavor. Not entirely, of course. The spiritualists and such had their following as well. Landis has never understood any of the philosophies. He only cares that he is emperor of the realm."

"Captain Landis has more of a practical bent, you believe?"

"A practical man who has learned from his past failures. In Vineland he created an Eden he could rule by strict regulation, and made himself powerful by attending to his subjects' longings. Whatever they might need, he claims this place to be."

Thatcher had scarcely conversed with the man, but Mary's account squared with Aurelia's devotion. His newspaper tormented her with the dangers of drunken foreigners and rowdy youth, women in trousers, the wolf at the doorstep, and then on the next page soothed her with impossible reassurances. After all the losses in her life, Aurelia had great need of a man with such talents.

"In the early days people were more rational," Mary said. "There was interest in my work on the gall moths. A thousand copies of our tract sold in a month! Think of it."

Thatcher did think of it, wondering at the price per issue.

"And then I found this place, my pilgrim's rest." She lifted a hand toward the bog.

"While Dr. Treat found his contentment in astronomy."

"He called it astronomy."

"His lectures on it in the Plum Hall were famous to put folks to sleep," Selma offered, causing Thatcher nearly to choke on his apple. But Mary seemed unperturbed. The two of them began packing up the remains of lunch.

"He lost his instincts for stirring an audience," Mary said simply.

"My pa says the doctor is full of his own beans."

Mary sealed the lid of the lunch bucket. "Selma, do you remember where we transplanted our June experiment with the ferns?"

"Yes ma'am. Near to the fork of this crick and Maple Branch."

"You'll follow this creek until Maple Branch. Then what?"

"Twenty paces up the bank to the big chestnut. Way before the Penn Gap. If you get to Penn Gap it's too far. We marked the plants with lemon-color ribbons."

"Lemon? I thought white."

"No ma'am. The white was the April batch."

"I could consult my notes, but I'm sure you're right. Off you go, dear. If you find so much as one leaf alive, come tell us and we will go take a measurement. And if anything else, collect it." Gravely Mary hung the tin vasculum on its ribbon around Selma's neck as if it were a medal for valor.

"Yes ma'am." Selma happily dashed off into the tunnel of cedars, more than ever rabbit-like.

Mary looked sad. "She'll find them as dead as all the ones that went before."

"*Ubi sunt,*" he offered.

Mary seemed about to get up, but remained in her spot. Thatcher tried to imagine his pretty wife so comfortably seated on the ground, but could not. Beauty had its price. On days other than this one, he'd felt lucky to pay it.

"I think this will be our last trial of transplanting the ferns," she said. "Dr. Gray encourages me but I hate to take more lives, even for the good of science."

"I'm very sorry about all that," Thatcher said.

"No warrant for it. My conclusions are clear, it is time to publish. And I've always been careful not to distress the original population."

"I mean I am sorry about Dr. Treat. For your sake, Mary. If news of his soured reputation has reached Selma's father, the humiliation must have been extensive."

"In case the news had not yet reached every toad in every pond, Joseph finished the business with his vendetta in the newspaper against Reverend Pittinger. I suppose you missed all that. It happened last autumn."

"Oh. Did . . . does Dr. Treat stand opposed to the Christian faith?"

"It's more preposterous than that." Mary exhaled. "Reverend Pittinger, of all people, took it on himself to press the case for empirical science. Gravity and Newtonian physics, the measurable effects of the moon on the tides. This poor man of the cloth gripped his pen week after week in defense of weight and measurement. It's Joseph's opinion that calculable laws are not real. He held forth and would not yield an inch."

Thatcher had no idea what to say to that.

"I believe he is losing his reason," she said quietly. "He grew so agitated he stopped sleeping. All last winter he sat at the desk writing strange little figures on every bit of paper he could find. Not proper mathematics but something he invented, the forcing of nonmathematical things into calculations. I would find his rants written on the margins of my own correspondence: 'Fact! The perfect difference between men and animals equals the reduction of Darwin to less than zero quantity.'"

"Oh, Mary. He disparaged Darwin?"

"My friend did not bear the brunt alone, I assure you. Plato and Copernicus were not spared. Joseph drew up long, nonsensical treatises against science and had them published as pamphlets. With illustrations."

"How awful for you. But surely other people noticed his affliction."

"To the extent of making him a town entertainment, as you heard from Selma. She feels she is coming to my defense."

"That is ghastly."

"It's difficult to sympathize with someone so full of himself. He insisted I enclose his tracts when I wrote to my colleagues. Charles Riley got several, and so did Dr. Gray. I confess I only pretended to send one to Mr. Darwin. I left the envelope unsealed and slipped it out on my way to the post office."

Thatcher was thunderstruck. "He was jealous of your correspondences."

She looked startled. "Why do you say so?"

"Because he is mortal. A proud man, greedy for praise, calling himself doctor without earning it. Quietly surpassed in intelligence and accomplishment by his generous, diligent wife."

"Oh. I see. Then it is thanks to me he became a disciple of free love and went to New York with Victoria Woodhull."

So it was true. "No, Mary. A man can be a beast on his own initiative. So I've been informed by my wife. But for your sake I can't feel very sorry he's gone."

"This is what Charles Riley said. He told me he'd met Joseph once in Troy and found him so idiosyncratic as to be half out of his mind. He said I should not much miss Joseph's support, but greatly welcome the peace in which to work."

"And is it so?"

"Very much so. I was thinking of it on the day you and I first met, when you came in the parlor while I was trapped with my *Dionaea*. It occurred to me as I sat so still in that place: it was *my* desk now, *my* study. My spiders in the jars. I never could organize experiments properly with Joseph around. It is in his absence I prosper."

Thatcher was moved by the confession. They both went quiet watching a heron stalk through reeds at the creek's margin. With each stilted step the long head slid forward on a smooth horizontal axis. Thatcher knew the danger in that serpentine head and neck, the forceful thrust of the knifelike beak. He had a childhood memory of floating in shallow water near a heron with his eyes just at the surface, his belly skimming mud, trying to draw close, mesmerized by the graceful locomotion. He was near enough to touch it when the head suddenly reared like a dagger drawn to strike and the boy leaped up from the shallows, startling the bird and himself, heart pounding, reckoning how near he'd just come to losing an eye. It never came naturally to Thatcher to see any life as enemy to his own. Even in that place where anything not human was apt to be claimed as food. No place for a boy who longed to know a heron.

Thatcher felt drawn to reciprocal confession. "It had been on my mind to meet you since the first day I saw you out my window. You were lying in the grass. I wanted very much to know what you studied. Now I know. The tower-building spiders."

Mrs. Treat looked at him oddly, and he felt abashed. He and Rose had been spying. "I'm sorry, it isn't worth the mention. A long time ago, it seems now."

Her narrow-eyed gaze held. "Which day was it?"

The day his house began to fall. "The day of Pardon Crandall's famous carriage accident on Landis Avenue. I recall because my wife and I were speaking in the parlor and Polly came in directly from the calamity, quite thrilled with the damage."

Her face rearranged. "Oh! The Crandalls' runaway carriage. That day was a different business, nothing to do with spiders. I was watching ants. It happened to be a remarkable day for the *Polyergus*. Do you know *Polyergus breviceps*, Thatcher?"

With Mary, conversation itself was a runaway horse. "I know they are ants, abundant in our neighborhood. And that every member of my household devoutly wishes their whole tribe dead. Polly and myself excepted. I suppose we are agnostic."

"Oh, well, you must prepare for conversion. There is no more interesting hymenopterid in the kingdom. Did you know *Polyergus* is a social parasite?"

"I did not."

"*Polyergus* has lost the ability to rear its own young. They can't forage, feed their queen, or clean the nest. They raid the nests of other ants to steal their pupae, and when these hatch they become workers of the *Polyergus* nest. The mutualistic relationship can persist a very long time. I'm writing an article on it." She looked perfectly happy again, the wonder of ant parasitism supplanting any residue of the wretched Dr. Treat. How odd was her simplicity, Thatcher thought, how admirable and sometimes maddening.

"How is your wife?" she asked then, rather abruptly, as if she had just recalled an instruction to do so.

"She is well, thank you." He sighed involuntarily. In the physical sense Rose was hale. A single fruit in a bushel with the unfair advantage of ripeness. On Rose an ordinary dress looked extravagant, causing women to ask about seamstresses in a vain hope of duplicating the impression. And her effect on men was the opposite; they tended to go silent and awkward about the eyes, as if guilty of seeing more than they deserved.

"I'm sorry I haven't called in," Mary said. "It was my place to do so, when your family moved to Vineland. But I happened to meet your mother-in-law at the post office one morning and she behaved rather strangely. I suppose I felt discouraged."

"Please don't take too much offense at Aurelia. She is a woman of powerful preferences, and was very fond of the neighbors who lived in your house before. The Newcombs, I believe they were called."

"Yes. Mr. Newcomb still owns the house, but has relocated his law practice to Philadelphia. We let the house from him."

"Ah. This, Aurelia would hold against you. That the esteemed Mr. and Mrs. Newcomb are her neighbors no more. She was forced to live away from Vineland for ten years, and many things changed without her approval. She feels disoriented. And cheated by time, I suspect. She left as a mother and returned a dowager."

"I see. It was during the war that she left?"

"Near the end of it. The cause of departure was personal. Her husband died suddenly and she needed the support of her sister in Boston. You can imagine her distress. Rose was still a girl, not yet introduced. And little Polly scarcely weaned."

"The world has grown many shades darker in that time. Not only Vineland. The wounds of this ruptured nation lie open and ugly."

"I'm sure you are right," he said, mildly surprised that her sympathy fell to the nation's misfortunes rather than Aurelia's. Mary seemed oddly uncurious about Thatcher's personal life. He had waited all day for even this small exchange. Aurelia's snub in the post office had dealt its blow, no doubt. But on previous occasions when he raised his predicaments, Mary had seemed sympathetic.

"I would like to impose on you for advice, Mary. Not on the subject of my mother-in-law, but something else. And I worry that Selma might be upset by the topic. How soon will she return?"

"In another quarter hour, I think. It must be about cakes, or the Heavenly Father. The girl is fearlessly open minded on all topics but those."

"It is the latter. My employer wants him to preside over my science class."

"As he should. As he does over all our endeavors. Do you not think so?"

"Of course. I have no objection to the Lord's Prayer we recite at assembly. My complaint is with some of the Lord's more extravagant prophets. Namely Sir Thomas Browne and the *Religio Medici*, as interpreted by Professor Cutler."

"Oh, blast. I suppose it does no good to tell you Cutler was an ally of Joseph's, at least for a time. They had long chats in our parlor about this porridge-minded Thomas Browne. I always excused myself to scour the stove grate."

Thatcher was thrilled by a glimpse of fire behind Mary's decorum. "I wish I could do the same. He comes into my class uninvited to lecture on mysteries imperfectly answered in the scripture. To which we are to find answers with the help of Thomas Browne and himself."

"How did all creatures disperse from Noah's ark, when time is but five days elder than ourselves? That business?"

"That business exactly. How can we have creatures here that are not found in Europe and Asia, given that all began their progress from the Mountains of Ararat? With the help of bridges made by archangels, he says. We need only look to the great Professor Cutler to answer all questions, using scripture bent back on itself like a fish hook."

"And he knows nothing of modern thinking on the age of the earth? Has he not even read Charles Lyell?"

"He reads next to nothing. It might interfere with his knowledge of the universe."

"And he inflicts this nonsense on your pupils. How disgraceful." Mary's disgust was gratifying.

"We are his trial audience. He says these difficult times in our shattered country call for a return to fundamentals. I suspect he is growing restless in Vineland and wants to return to his former eminence on the lecture circuit."

She offered a sly grin. "If he leaves, you will not much miss his support, but greatly welcome the peace in which to work."

"I wish it were so. Cutler won't leave Vineland permanently. The school is too valuable as a platform. He will keep the reins over us here while he launches his magnum opus, explaining every scientific paradox unanswered by the Bible."

"While adhering to its want of scientific logic. Well forevermore. This is an affront on the good book, do you not think?"

"I do. I can find consolation in the Psalms when no amount of earthly reckoning will satisfy my heart. Precisely because those verses are not an earthly reckoning. They ease us from ourselves."

Mary nodded. "That is so. Science directs us to study our maker's creation, but his thoughts on its purpose are only his to reveal." She looked at him, alarmed. "Does Cutler see himself as a prophet, then? Does he mean to write a new book of scripture?"

"I think he does. Reconciling the problems of our modern century with the Bible."

"I see. And your campaign of teaching scientific method is at odds with his ambitions."

"He wants to be rid of me. He shuts down anything I propose. Field outings, experiments in the classroom, every reading I submit for his approval. Cutler is offended by the clear logic of Darwin."

"The offense is widespread, I'm afraid. Dr. Gray writes me that the dread of Darwin is rising to hysteria, even among his learned colleagues. It was not long ago people blamed Darwin's *Origin* for encouraging the abolitionists and the war. But now even abolitionists and transcendentalists have turned against him."

"How are people so irrational?" he asked, but he knew. Even the abolitionists had no wish to be placed inside creation, subject to its laws. They wished to rule over it from the head of God's table.

"People may be persuaded of small things," Mary said, looking away from Thatcher, speaking in the direction of the forest. "But most refuse to be moved on larger ones. An earth millions of years old appalls them, when they always have seen it otherwise.

A humanity derived from the plain stuff of earth frightens them even more. Rather than look at evidence they would shut themselves up in a pumpkin shell like Peter Piper's wife." Her head nodded very slightly as she spoke, continuously and almost imperceptibly, like a grass touched by breeze. "Presumptions of a lifetime are perilous things to overturn. Presumptions of many lifetimes, in this case."

Of all lifetimes ever lived, in this case. Every person in history must have placed himself at the head of a Creator's table. To see that table overturned, cutlery and china dashed to the floor, one's very place lost, was to witness the sky falling. Thatcher hadn't fully considered Darwin in such threatening light. But still, the old constructions no longer squared with the evidence. A pumpkin shell offered poor shelter. Could not men see the uselessness of clinging to their outmoded philosophies? And if not, why were he and Mary different?

"No breach in this world seems to heal," he said. "We try to reason with one another, but only manage to tear ourselves apart."

She gazed at the running creek. Thatcher brushed bread crumbs from his trousers. He picked up a pebble and tossed it at the rust-colored water. "Life should be simpler than this," he said. "I only want to do my work. Truth is objective. A man should be respected for telling it, not threatened."

"Mr. Darwin and Dr. Gray must sometimes feel even God is against them, for the abuse they've had to bear," she agreed. "Mr. Agassiz goes all around the country declaring them monsters."

"I've *seen* Agassiz. He says anything to please a crowd, exaggerates, and oversimplifies. His need for acclaim has compromised his science. Agassiz was a good geologist in his time but now he behaves as a showman who only cares for the size of crowd he can draw. First he won Europe, now he'll have the Americans."

"Mr. Darwin is dismayed by the violent attacks." Mary seemed physically pained by the misery of her friend at Down House. "He doesn't truly feel he invented his theory. Others were on the same trail, he was only first to turn over enough stones to find it out and set it credibly in writing. Why should a man be blamed for his diligence?"

"Mr. Darwin blamed for the finding, and Dr. Gray for standing as its champion on our side of the Atlantic. And for bringing it to Vineland, I am threatened by my employer."

"And still your pupils depend on it, Thatcher. Their little families have come here looking for safety, but they will go on laboring under old authorities until their heaven collapses. Your charge is to lead them out of doors. Teach them to see evidence for themselves, and not to fear it."

"To stand in the clear light of day, you once said. Unsheltered."

She looked at him with such warm regard, Thatcher felt light-headed. He had little experience with admiration. "Your school must have other beneficent men who support the same endeavor," she offered hopefully.

If the alleged beneficents were his fellow teachers, they excelled at camouflage. "I wonder what service is possible, Mary. When half the world, with no understanding of Darwin at all, will rally around whoever calls him a criminal and wants him hanged."

She said nothing to this. But it was no exaggeration, he'd witnessed this very thing in a market square in Boston: the crude effigy dangling from a noose, the monkey's tail pinned to the stuffed trousers, the murderous crowd chanting *Lock him up!* The provocateur was an itinerant preacher in a threadbare rabat and pieces of an infantryman's uniform, boots, and greatcoat he must have pulled from a dead soldier. Thatcher had stood astonished, watching violence in its own bloody birth canal.

The heron now patrolled the bank of the creek very near where they sat. Thatcher and Mary watched it snake through the tall reeds seeking its prey. Watched the red creek flow, blood of this forest dissolving its earth.

"I suppose it is in our nature," she said finally. "When men fear the loss of what they know, they will follow any tyrant who promises to restore the old order."

"If that is our nature, then nature is madness. These are more dangerous times than we ever have known."

>*<

Thatcher found his household in high dudgeon. The women were dressed to extremes and already exasperated with Thatcher even before his train returned to Vineland. They would be late to the performance at the Merchant's Hall. If Thatcher had any previous knowledge of this engagement, he had forgotten it. The performer was General Tom Thumb.

"And his wife!" Polly all but screamed.

"A wife! Does she tower over her spouse?"

"No, no, no, she is just like him. The most gracious lady you ever could meet, and no taller than a butter churn."

She must have memorized the handbill. Poor Polly, admiring the dimensions of a butter churn, destined herself for the tall, lank frame of the Jersey cow. Rose fretted over every inch of new growth for the further limits imposed on her sister's prospects. She was already taller than half the town's well-heeled scions. She didn't care now but would soon enough, Rose warned. And so the female tragedy would commence, for Polly as with all the rest.

"As you can see, we're already dressed for the performance," Rose said, pulling on dove-colored gloves that looked unfamiliar to Thatcher, and expensive. Scylla and Charybdis had slunk to a far corner of the parlor, sensing the winds of war. They stared at Thatcher from under the settee.

"And as you can see," Polly announced, "Mother is trying to asphyxiate me."

"Ah. Filicide. It happens in the best of families."

"It isn't humorous, Thatcher. It's horrible!"

He gave Polly a second look. "You've changed something, haven't you? You look older. Is it your hair?"

"No, it's a corset!" she wailed, and Thatcher saw the female tragedy had already commenced. How sad, in Polly's case. So much energy squandered in the unwinnable war waged by woman against the life-form she is.

Rose assessed the day's work on his trousers. "And you are fit for mucking a stable. Oh, Thatcher. What have you done? How disappointing. Come upstairs."

"Mrs. Brindle will come to the rescue on Wednesday," he said, following her up the stairs at a trot. He thought of Mary piloting through the Batsto men with himself in her wake. A follower.

"You cannot always count on the rescue of women. You must learn to look after yourself. But how could you get so filthy?" Rose ushered him into the bedroom and closed the door behind them. Instantly her tone shifted from burdened matron to wronged wife. "It's beyond understanding, why you would want to spend the whole day with Mrs. Treat and leave your own family."

"Dearest. I spent the day in scientific endeavors. A man must work. And the few who are lucky as I am get to come home at day's end to a beautiful wife."

"A man must work! Your position is in the school, not the barnyard. Everyone says Batsto is horrid with mills and liquor. I can't think what you and that woman could find to do there all day."

"I was with Mrs. Treat and her associate, and we weren't in Batsto, we were in the forest. Studying the adaptations of plants to a bog environment."

"There, you see!" Rose wheeled and flung her open hand at him as if he had testified against himself. Then pulled off her gloves and turned her attack on the bureau, opening drawers with unnecessary vigor, retrieving clean stockings and trousers while he removed his offending attire. "Thatcher, you can't go on neglecting us. The paper is peeling from the wall in Mother's room. With all these rains the plaster has grown damp inside. You must call a man at once. But you're never here, how would you know what we need in this house?" She turned and narrowed her eyes at his throat. "The shirt will pass, I suppose. With a fresh collar."

"I needn't go. I can live without seeing a man the size of a butter churn."

"You're confusing him with his wife. The general is thirty-nine inches tall."

"All the same. Men I have seen, some large. This one is small."

"Thatcher! Are you exhausting on purpose, or just simple? General Thumb is *famous*. One of the most famous men in the country, here in Vineland for only the one engagement. You are shockingly ungrateful to Captain Landis. Your attitude is very distressing to Mother."

"Ungrateful to *Landis?*"

"Yes! For how he looks after us in Vineland, bringing these enlightenments."

"I'm sure you are right. Wretch that I am, I will be content to stay home from the enlightenment. With a plate of cold ham and a book."

"And leave the three of us defenseless, without an escort."

"Honestly, Rose. Pouting doesn't suit you."

"Oh, well. I assume Mrs. Treat never pouts."

"Will you stop." The runaway calamities of marriage could never be explained to a single man. Shouldn't be, for the good of the species. "Please just quiet down."

She stood with eyes ablaze and mouth clamped in a fierce pantomime of subjugation. *Quiet* did not sit well on the fair shoulders of Rose.

"Darling," he coaxed. "You are my only wife, to whom I've pledged eternal devotion. Comparison is absurd. I think of you every minute while I spend my days with colleagues. When I must be with Mrs. Treat we speak of science, and that is all."

"I suppose I'm a useless companion if I can't discuss the palpitations of a bog."

He looked down, buttoning his braces, hiding a smile. "You are the fairest of all companions. Look how bewitching you are in your yellow frock. Of course I will go, for the pleasure of having you on my arm and the envy of every male who has eyes."

He saw her shoulders soften slightly as she pretended to rearrange the drawer, unready yet to surrender the advantage of indignation. She was hardly past girlhood, and working so hard to be mistress of this house. She needed a child badly, Thatcher thought, so she could rule it. Please, Heavenly Father, let it be soon.

"You grieve, don't you? For our child," he risked saying, and she wheeled, seeming angry, though her pale eyes brimmed.

"And you don't!"

"Of course I do, Rosie. Only it must be different for men. I never felt the babe was real, as you must have."

For a long moment she didn't move. Then sat herself on the bed, a simple lowering of herself that collapsed her skirts like a bellows. She covered her face. He sat next to her, but felt some current from her body that made him hesitate to touch her. Instead he folded his hands between his thighs.

The storm passed, abrupt as a spring shower. She lowered her hands from her face but looked straight ahead. "I found Mother weeping today. In the pantry."

"In the pantry." He could no more imagine his mother-in-law

in the pantry than in a shoe factory. Aurelia did not labor, she deployed.

"She went looking for the bottle of Dr. Garvin's tonic, and saw the biscuit tin with the sweet picture of the little boy and the pup. Mrs. Brindle must have put it away there so we wouldn't see it."

"Mrs. Brindle cannot know we've lost a baby."

Rose looked at him with such wordless astonishment, he could see himself as she did: as an outsider to a house of female confidences. As he ever would be.

"I'm sorry, Rose. We're bereft, all of us. But babies arrive in houses every day." In wombs, he meant, but couldn't make himself say it, even if he had rested his head on her belly and stroked the soft yellow grass of her pubic hillock, as many times as he cared to remember. "I love you," he said. "Where there is love, there will be children."

He took one little hand into his. Rose looked down at it in his lap, seeming to study the composition like an artist preparing to draw it.

"You make it sound simple, and it isn't. Mother is old. She is nearly fifty, Thatcher. She fears she might not live to see our children."

"I believe she will, Rose. She has nothing to dread, where our mutual intentions are concerned. I will tell her so, if you like."

Rose nodded, withdrew her hand, and then the moment was over.

"We will be late," she said.

He stood up, put on his good coat, and opened the bedroom door, taking some pains to lead and not follow his wife down the staircase. She set up a fresh scolding from the rear flank as if nothing at all had just passed between them, and he wondered what part of his married life was real, what was performance. She quickly drew in her recruits, who waited at the bottom of the stair in their capes and bonnets.

"He says he shall be the envy of all the men at the Merchant's Hall! Isn't it a pity we've taken so much trouble to dress but won't be seen? Thatcher has made us so late, the hall will be filled and we will be left standing at the back."

"Oh, dear," Aurelia whimpered. "Shall we have to? The man is so small. We might not be able to see him."

"We *will* see General Thumb," Polly insisted. "People are always too timid to take the chairs at the front. I'm right, aren't I, Rose? The whole first row goes empty. And I am not timid so I can dash right ahead and claim the best ones."

"Very well done," Rose said to Thatcher. "We shall be the talk of the town: the Greenwood family who arrive late, and push to the front of the line."

9

∞

The Front of the Line

It was barely light outside when she let the girl in. Willa had been
zoning out on the sofa giving Dusty his morning bottle, in such a
deep trance it had taken a minute for the steady noise to register
as someone pecking on the kitchen screen door. It was not another
piece of this house torn loose in the last big storm and banging in
the wind, and not the throbbing of Willa's sleep-deprived head.
Instead of taking ibuprofen, she needed to set Dusty into his baby
bucket and go answer the door.

And now this fuchsia hair and pierced flesh. Some associate of
Tig's, maybe from the restaurant. The constellation of facial studs
seemed unsuited to food service, but Willa was no expert, as she'd
been told.

"I saw the light was on in here," she announced, and from there
prattled on bewilderingly before Willa had quite understood she
was coming inside. "So my brother says it's just the battery, right?
But wrong, it's totally the ignition." She'd said her name, it came
and went. Gwendolyn?

"Sorry, do you need to use the phone?"

"Um, no?"

Willa heard her own idiocy. Come into a house to use a phone, what a thought. This one had no landline. "Sorry, you're not here to see me. Have a seat." She pointed at the dining table. "Not sure who's up yet."

A glance at the clock surprised her, almost eight and still so dark. She was not going to love winter in Jersey. Dusty was screaming now, with sufficient grounds: *bottle interruptus*. Willa dived into the kitchen to put on coffee before she retrieved him and sat down at the table across from the girl, making a brave stab at sociability. She hadn't made coffee earlier, in the vain hope this bottle might just be *night interruptus* for Willa and Dusty, and then they'd both go back to bed. She rocked him against her shoulder trying to calm him down enough to resume his breakfast. Dixie in her deafness had slept through the initial invasion but now raised her head to study the intruder. It took a moment but she discerned no threat, sighed, and dropped her chin back to the floor.

"Okay," Willa tried, once Dusty was happily nestled in the crook of her arm with the bottle plugged in. "Do you know each other from work?"

"He even here?" The visitor looked around, her focus eventually lighting on Willa's armful. "Jesus. A *baby*?"

"How about we try that again as a complete sentence?"

Willa had spent regrettable decades correcting her kids' friends' grammar, with nothing to show for it. This one declined the assignment, but continued to watch the baby chugging the bottle as if it were the first meal of his life, making rhythmic gasping-swallowing noises while gazing into Willa's eyes. Every feeding was like this, arousing a lusty joy otherwise absent from his micropersona. Genetic memory, Iano claimed. All those starving ancestors in the Greek Civil War.

"Okay, well, I'm Tig's mom. Willa. Good morning."

The girl stared now at Willa as if doubting her story. Willa returned the gaze, assessing. Tig hadn't hung out much with the goth kids even in high school, back when they were officially a crowd. This one was probably a blonde underneath all the war paint, heart-shaped face, milky complexion, nice figure packed into a tiny red dress. Black leather boots and jacket, both with a surplus of metal rings, like her face. A pretty girl except for something alt-human about the visage. It took a second look to get past the kohl and see there were no real eyebrows. All plucked out, painted back on. Hair galore though, pulled up in a pair of vivid Minnie Mouse poufs, so it wasn't chemo. So much energy these girls burned through, just trying not to look like their own lovely selves.

"I didn't know there was like a *baby*," she said finally.

Willa resisted pointing out it wasn't *like* a baby, it was the actual article. This was not much of a friend, if Tig hadn't mentioned the baby bomb dropped on the family.

"I mean, that you guys were still, you know, parents. It's *little*."

With some effort Willa worked out the girl's mistake, and nearly laughed. She could have been flattered but knew better; fifty-five and thirty-five look just alike to the more self-absorbed of the younger set. They don't see themselves reaching either of those ages, so it doesn't matter. And it wasn't a compliment: braless in her sleep T-shirt and sweatpants, Willa was the picture of worst-case motherhood. And in no mood for chitchat about the family tragedy, frankly. She opted to stick with small talk until she could be dismissed.

The girl cocked her colorful head, eyeing the baby and beginning to melt a little in the inevitable way of young girls, however steel studded. "Boy or girl?"

"Boy."

"What does he do?"

Now Willa did laugh; this girl seemed incomprehensible as a point of pride. "You mean, professionally? Not much. Eats every three or four hours around the clock and fills up his diapers with bright yellow shit. It's a surreal color. I think it must be from some vitamin they put in the formula."

The girl blinked and something shifted in her steely gaze, seeming to suggest that Willa needed to get a grip. This couldn't be ruled out. Even before the crisis with Nick she'd felt herself skating at the edge of some notable mental stumble, beyond panic attacks, hopefully short of psychosis. Exhaustion was a lot of it, now that she was on baby duty most days and nights. Yesterday when she'd needed to buckle in Dusty and drive to the grocery she'd experienced the bold confusion of a drunk driver. For sure, she recalled pulling up to a green light and stopping to wait till it turned red. Luckily Vineland traffic was always dead.

She heard the coffee machine heaving through the last asthmatic gurgles of its cycle and her heart raced; Willa needed coffee right then with the full-blown craving of a heroin addict. "Here, take him for just a sec," she said, handing off Dusty to the stupefied goth girl and scurrying to the kitchen, not unmindful of addict mothers who jeopardized their children for the sake of a fix. "You want coffee?" she yelled. "Black okay?"

Willa didn't quite make out the answer but brought back two mugs, quickly taking back Dusty before any eventualities with scalding liquid ensued. She put him on her shoulder to keep him out of harm's way while she poured coffee down her throat.

The girl stared at her own mug as if she'd never seen one of those either, then drank without a mumble of thanks. She began chewing the cuticles around her black-lacquered fingernails with deep intention. Willa noticed a Deathly Hallows wrist tattoo creeping out from under the leather cuff. Iano always said these inked kids would regret the pop-culture references when they reached middle age, but Willa thought not. Her generation was defined by the rebel music they'd shared, and now they'd be damned if they regretted David Bowie. Millennials had their million personal playlists but no one universal soundtrack for youth, so their brash common ground would have to be shored up by something else when the time came. Corny tattoos on wilting flesh, why not?

"Okay, let me just go tell Tig you're here."

"Who?" The eyes lifted to Willa's, registering a blank.

"*Tig.* Your friend."

The Minnie Mouse head shook slowly. Bafflement was complete.

A wave of comprehension crashed over Willa: Oh, no, *this*. Not again. She braced herself for what this cat had dragged in, the inevitable dance around withheld details. The undeclared major standing in for the undeclared crush on Doctor T.

The girl seemed unaware of the sea change in her host's mood. She continued to gnaw on her cuticles, evidently unable to make the first move. Willa wondered if she was supposed to run this meeting. Really, there was no good starting point.

"You must be one of my husband's students."

"Well *yeah*." The girl drew her head back sharply, suggesting she rarely dealt with individuals quite this slow on the uptake.

"I'm sorry. Doctor Tavoularis is in the hospital."

"Shit, *what*?" the girl cried, spilling coffee as she half leaped from her chair and then sank back to it in a gratifying little explosion. Suspicions confirmed.

"He's over there most of the time, when he's not in class. Ever since his father had the stroke." Willa reached across to mop up the spill with the dish towel she'd been using as a burp cloth, then finished her coffee with a long drag. "It's been pretty rough on the family. My father-in-law is in critical condition. About to have one or both legs amputated, if he lives long enough."

The girl glared with such indignation Willa briefly wondered which one of them was behaving rudely here. Decided she was in the clear. Her home turf was being invaded, for Christ's sake, in a shocking attack of youthful entitlement. Not for the first time or probably the last. Willa was delighted she'd let the girl believe Iano had fathered this baby with his duly wedded wife.

The visitor seemed to be coming down with a cold. She wiped her runny nose, then fiddled with the steel eyebrow ring, then wiped her nose again, all of which made Willa wince. Even if she'd had doubts about Iano—and she wasn't entirely new to that game—it was not going to be this one. Iano was a stickler for hygiene.

"How did you find out where we live? How did you even *get* here? From Philly, at eight in the morning? Most people your age don't qualify as alive at this hour."

"I walked. I live here, in Vineland," came the flat reply.

"Oh. So, you're *not* one of my husband's students?"

"Yeah, I just don't live on campus. I can't afford it. I have Dr. T for poli-sci."

"I see. And can you tell me why you're in my house?"

"I told you, I saw the light was on."

Willa absorbed the stalker overtones and snapped into focus. "And you thought you'd catch him here first thing. Before office hours."

The black-lidded eyes remained fixed on something behind Willa. "So I missed a lot of class because I've been having this stupid thing with my car, and if I don't keep my grades up I lose my scholarship. I talked to Dr. T about it and he was so just, you know, nice and everything. It just like *came up* that we both live here."

"I see."

"He said I could catch a lift with him sometime if I needed to."

"Oh, right. You've been carpooling." Willa faked a smile, making some internal adjustments on the fly. "I don't remember if he mentioned that."

"No, not . . . so far. I was just thinking I would ask."

"Maybe it would get you to class on time. For a change, evidently."

At this the girl retreated to some inner room of her armored persona. All sniffing and fiddling ceased.

"I don't know what this is about," Willa said, now fully certain she did, and finally feeling a good caffeine-and-outrage buzz. "But if you're thinking carpool equals romance, you're overestimating your potential."

"*Romance*," the girl spat, suitably rattled, instantly defensive. "Like that's even a thing. Do you know how screwed up guys are? If you're not into the prep cokehead scumbags or the little boys on their Nintendos wanting you to do their laundry—"

"That's not a conversation you and I need to have," Willa snapped. The girl could go condescend to her own damn mother. Willa's left arm was going numb from the weight on her shoulder. Dusty had dropped off to sleep after his bottle and Willa resented having been robbed of the chance to do the same. She could see no safe exit from this conversation, but was ready to risk pretty much anything to get to the next cup of coffee.

"Why don't you just tell me what you're up to. Because I don't think you came here just looking for a lift to class."

The raccoon eyes finally betrayed dread. "I did though. My car died, and I don't know. I'm not like—"

"And Dr. T is so *nice*," Willa interrupted. "He probably takes in strays. That's your story?"

"Look, whatever. I don't have any story."

Willa, given the home court advantage, decided to wait this out. It took all of ten seconds.

"Okay, I came here for a ride. That's it. And yeah, Dr. T is really nice, so don't get all salty with *me* about it. He's the one making all those girls think they're in love with him or something." The eyes widened to punctuate *in love*, an irony emoji. She wiped her nose with her wrist.

"He *makes* them. They have no agency. Where's the feminism in that?"

She shrugged.

"So you were thinking you'd be the one to take matters in hand?"

Again, she took the Fifth. Willa watched the chapped fingers shredding a Kleenex that was already pretty far gone when she'd pulled it out of her backpack. Presuming some premeditated emotion here, couldn't she have packed some fresh tissues?

"It might not have happened to you before, but grown men and women often ride together in cars without having sex. I hope someday you'll get to have that experience."

The girl rolled her eyes, and Willa caught sight of some anguish inside the carefully curated ennui. The poor thing did seem fed up beyond her years. Willa would need to guard against pity, which never helped. "All the guys your age are still acting like little boys, so your only good alternative is married professors. That's your thinking?"

The girl's eyes widened briefly, a tiny spasm of confession before she went narrow eyed again.

"Hey," Tig said. Willa turned to see her daughter padding down the stairs in pink plaid pajamas and heavy wool socks, hair standing on end, as was perfectly usual. Tig stared at the girl briefly, en route to the kitchen. Then came back to the table and sat down with a cup of coffee. "What's up?"

"This is . . . I'm sorry. I've forgotten your name."

"Gwen."

"Gwen. She's a student at Chancel, in poli-sci. We were just having a chat."

"What about?"

Willa looked to Gwen, inviting her to produce some fascinating fib or make a break for it, but she seemed incapable of speech.

"To tell you the truth," Willa said, "we were discussing men. How a lot of the guys your age are still acting like little boys. Seems like Gwen is more attracted to maturity."

Over the rim of her mug as she drank, Tig's round eyes looked from one of them to the other. "Oh," she said, setting down the cup. "She's got the wide-on for Dad."

The guest looked electrocuted. Here was a coffee klatch for the books. Willa thought of the day she'd disposed of her son's dead girlfriend's sexual aids, which in retrospect was a piece of cake. No conversation required.

"Should I leave now?" Tig asked.

"Not on my account," Willa said, going on blind impulse. Maybe if sufficiently mortified, this girl would take it back to the rest of the coed colony, like that special poison you gave to ants. "Gwen, this is our daughter Antigone. Tavoularis."

The girl studied Tig cautiously, deciding whether to creep back out of hiding or remain shut down. Willa had watched this routine so many times, kids testing out the safety zones with each other. "Oh," the girl said finally. "So the baby's *yours*."

"Oh, no, Dusty? He's my brother's kid. Absentee Dad. Mom and I got left holding the backpack on that one."

"*Right?* My brother too!" she yelped, with the relief of an exile finding a fellow traveler. To Willa's eye, these two birds belonged to separate species: the Steel-Studded Furious, the Fuzzy-Headed Feral.

Tig got up and lifted Dusty from Willa's arms without waking him. To carry him back upstairs to his crib, Willa assumed, but instead Tig sat back down at the end of the table and settled the baby on her lap. Willa had rashly called dibs on authority here, and no one was letting her off the hook. She tried to take

heart from the little things, like the tingle of circulation returning to her left arm.

"So would you agree?" she asked Tig. "About the dating scene
with guys your age?"

Tig cocked her head, considering. "Depends on what you're looking for. I kind of like athletic. Not *antwack*. I mean. My *dad*?" Tig
offered her compatriot a spectacular grimace. "But you can't settle
for taking their crap, that's the thing. Older guys in general might
be more, I don't know. Over themselves. I could definitely see that."

"But what you're seeing isn't just age," Willa pointed out.
"With a married guy, for example. You're looking at the result of a
partnership. Somebody helped those men grow up, maybe worked
to put them through grad school, and vice versa. Put in the time,
helped raise the kids. You with me here?"

The pink-haired girl shrugged infinitesimally, a perfect nonver-
bal *whatever*.

"So," Willa continued, "it's like a marathon. You see the runners crossing the finish line with sweaty faces and all that ecstasy.
Everybody wants some of that. But do you really think if you jump
up and cross the finish line at the last minute, you'll get it?"

"No," she said almost inaudibly, as if this whole conversation
were beneath her.

"No. You won't. Those runners are high on the whole day they
just put in, and the years of training before that."

The wad of tissue dropped and both palms went to the table,
defending one corner of this triangle. "You don't know me, okay?
Neither one of you. I'm not a cheating person. I had a 4.0 in high
school. I have a work-study in the poli-sci department."

"An honorable woman," Willa said. "I salute you."

Tig wore an expression of careful neutrality that might be as
close as she'd get to high-fiving her mother. All three women took
a moment to study the white tissue crumbs strewn across the table.

Tig could be counted on to wield truth like a blunt object, but she probably had no idea she'd rescued Willa by showing up. A scene that was threatening to pull her into tawdry territoriality had instead tipped over and drowned this girl in embarrassment. Now Willa just felt sorry for her. One part wife, two parts mom, she really couldn't help it.

"You're not the first person to make this mistake. My husband is a really, really nice guy, and that's rare. Believe me, I get it. Don't beat yourself up too much, okay?"

Now came the tears, full-throttle makeup blowout. Willa's kindness had landed harder than cruelty on this poor girl, puncturing the facade, letting vulnerability bleed out in arterial spurts. Maybe her story was mostly true: car problems, imperiled work-study, the honor society kid from Vineland High, shining light of her working-class family fighting her way into college. Probably she needed all that armor just to show up every day and endure the scrutiny of privilege. Guessing that the tissue supply was extinct, Willa handed over her kitchen towel, regretting the kohl damage in advance.

Gwen scrubbed at her face briefly, then made an effort to gather her mess. And still she didn't get up to leave. She flipped the steel ring in her eyebrow up, down, up, down. Willa traded a worried glance with Tig.

"It's not just me," she finally squeaked out, struggling for dignity. "Half the girls I know are trying to make it with their professors. Not just for the grades. It might be true what you said, but older men seem so, just, safe, you know? Like they already know all the stuff you're trying to figure out."

Willa smiled. "Oh honey, they don't. You have to start where you are and learn what's going to work for the world you're getting into. The only stuff people my age have figured out is what was going to work for us."

Out of kindness, or maybe to save face, Willa didn't tell either of them the rest of the story: that it hadn't.

⋊⋉

Vineland could have been anytown, of any industrial era. Christopher the historian liked to say these old houses with their ornate trim and bay windows were holding the confidences of centuries. If so, Willa felt they were giving in to the modern custom of blurting out all secrets: satellite dishes perched conspicuously on the Victorian gables and banks of gas meters clamped on exterior walls betrayed internal divisions where many different families now lived on separate checks. A handwritten sign in a yard advertised diabetes supplies cheap, leading Willa to wonder how *that* worked: Had the patient died, leaving the family an inheritance of insulin and needles? Did people now use underground markets to trade around leftover prescription drugs, and if so, could she tap in?

On Landis she passed Lulu's All You Can Eat, Martini Shoes, the brutalist architecture of the welfare office (on the very spot where Charles Landis's office once stood, according to Christopher), and the tumble-jumble storefronts of shops selling secondhand clothes. A hand-painted arch advised her to Keep Vineland Beautiful. Most of these businesses had people living above them, judging from the laundry and other signs of domesticity hanging from the second stories. A lot of those apartments had an oddly tilted-out window she recognized as a cheap enclosure of the balcony space, the simplest replacement for ornate bay windows long gone. She was learning to see Vineland's architecture through the lens of her new friend Chris Hawk, in which certain historical rules held sway. One was that complexity gives way to the simple.

Willa could see how this law applied to life in general. In the last three weeks she'd been forced to replace any oversize personal or professional ambitions with a few simple ones: First, to take care of Dusty. Since Nick's stroke, coincidentally the same day she fig-ured out how to use the infant carrier, the infant had hardly been out of it, and he was turning by degrees into a happier baby. At this moment he nestled against Willa's chest wearing a brown hat with ears, knitted by Tig, designed to make him resemble a bear cub. Willa's next worry was to get a medical release in case of a baby emergency, since Zeke had been called back to Boston by prospec-tive clients. It was just for a few weeks—Tig's charge of absentee dad was predictably overstated—but they probably did need to get something on paper. The words *in loco parentis* kept ringing in Willa's ears, emphasis on the *loco*. She'd left Zeke a voice mail and was waiting to hear back.

Her other new goal, which she couldn't quite talk about yet, was to get the family on Medicaid. She'd learned of this possibility from the hospital social worker who talked her down from a panic attack. The bills from Nick's hospitalization were staggering: after surgery and rehab, in the same ballpark as Zeke's student loans. The social worker, Clara Petrofaccio—not Pete's daughter but some kind of cousin, third or fourth—had handed Willa tissues while she cried and tried to breathe. Then asked her some polite personal questions, and written down the link to a website.

Willa was approaching the historical society building when Zeke rang her back. She turned and walked the other direction so she could have this conversation in the privacy of open air among passing strangers.

"Hi Mom, sorry, I've been in meetings all morning. What's up?"

"Nothing big, just the home team checking in. It must be hard to be in Boston, seeing all your old friends, without Helene. A lot of reminders."

"Not really. I mean yes, seeing friends. But it's not harder here than being there. I don't think there's anyplace in the world I'm going to feel good in, to be honest."

"I know. I'm sorry. It feels like you keep waking up in the wrong life."

"Yep."

"It will get better. I promise."

He was quiet.

"What helps? When do you feel a little bit okay?"

"When I'm doing something. Not thinking but, like, accomplishing."

"Well then, it's good for you to be in Boston. Accomplish money. Send checks home to your ma and pa. Save the farm!"

Zeke laughed. But she wasn't exactly kidding.

"So is it going well? You're bringing down the evildoers?"

"You have to be in charge of some actual money first, before you can divest it."

"So, when apartheid fell in South Africa, you were in elementary school."

"Yeah. And?"

"I was just thinking about it. You were arguing with Tig one time about how international economic boycotts helped end that regime. How do you even know things like that?"

"Mom, seriously. How do you know who won the Civil War?"

"Well okay. But the history of investment activism is a bit more obscure."

"Not to me. I did a whole presentation on it in Model UN."

In seventh grade, the boy was underpinning *Cry, the Beloved Country* with a cost-benefit analysis. He really did need to be where he was, there among the movers and shakers of the money trees. "So it's looking good? With your would-be clients?"

"I think so. Hard to tell with these guys. In meetings they're all game, talking basketball teams, bullshitting like you've sealed the deal and they're your boys. Then an hour later the secretary calls to tell you they're going with Merrill Lynch."

"Oh. That's disappointing."

"It's the business. Rome wasn't built in a day."

"Well, okay. Mainly I called because I had a question about Dusty."

"Yeah? He okay?"

"He's fine." Willa could not help feeling he should have asked sooner. A parent worries, that is the rule: seeing her name in his missed calls, Zeke's heart should have lurched a little. "He's still not much of a napper, but he's been crying less in the daytime since we started carrying him all the time. I think he needed more physical contact."

"Okay. That all sounds good."

"So it's kind of important. Do you have another minute to talk about this?"

He hesitated. "Sure."

"Okay, we're dealing with all this hospital stuff for Nick and I realized we also might need paperwork that would allow me to make medical decisions for Dusty, if that came up. I know it's hard to talk about. I don't want to scare you. It could just be an ear infection, some little thing. But I'm not sure I'm authorized to take him to the doctor."

"Sure, that makes sense." Zeke was not finding this hard to talk about. "I'll ask my lawyer friends what route we should go. Medical power of attorney, or some kind of shared guardianship thing."

"Thanks. I'm kind of gifted at imagining emergency scenarios. As you know."

He laughed. "You're the mom."

"I've had some practice, you're right about that."

"So is that it?"

"It is. Your little fellow's good. We're doing okay here."

"Thanks, Mom. You're a true American hero. Super Grandma."

"Don't sell the movie rights. I'm just muddling through. Tig is actually a huge help, she's got the knack somehow."

"Great. She'll teach him all the useful skills. Weed smoking, Dumpster diving."

"We're a few years out from those hazards. And your sister has grown up a lot since high school. You haven't been around to see it."

"So was that it?"

"You've got to go. Go build Rome."

"Will do."

Willa was surprised to find she'd traveled many blocks from her destination, and now turned back toward the historical society. The mélange of personal artifacts there no longer oppressed but now consoled her, proof of many eccentric individualities surviving against the long odds of being erased by time. She was determined to get to the bottom of the Mary Treat question; namely, whether the famous scientist had lived in their house. If so, possibilities might arise. Meantime, Iano had to knock it off about the grant.

She'd come to depend on Christopher Hawk, who had taken Willa under his wing with the zeal of a man who'd spent years without very much to do. Now he sifted through boxes of un-labeled photos and reams of spotty public records, and had even come by to check out the house so he'd know what he was looking for. He texted Willa updates with the attentiveness of a new boy-friend. Iano, in fact, called him "your new boyfriend."

But the object of her desire was Mary Treat. Willa was work-ing her way through every word written by or about this woman, admittedly one of the more eccentric individualities in the collec-tion. Reading between some lines, Willa wondered if maybe Mary was on the spectrum. But so lovable! Not a Disney princess but a kind of natural-history savant, seemingly able to forget human cravings and immerse herself in the nonhuman lives around her. Willa remained alert for clues about street address whenever these immersions occurred in or around Mary's house, as they often did. Might the yew shrubs mentioned be those scraggly old evergreens in Willa's backyard? Was the so-called piazza their dilapidated porch? Could the ants colonizing Mary's yard be ancestors of the ones presently driving Jorge and José Luis mad when they worked on their cars?

She called it research, but was dipping a whole lot farther than necessary into the Mary Treat well. Willa had spent decades making short work of researching articles, priding herself on how efficiently she could skim primary resources or get in and out of an interview. "Take only pictures, and for God's sake don't leave footprints" summed up her lifelong relationship to her material, as an officer of the press. And now she found herself breaking and entering, pulling open closets, trying on Mary Treat's clothes and wishing she could sleep over. Willa had no explanation for why she felt herself so eager to inhabit another woman's life. This was not exactly her own bucket list—tramping through the Pine Barrens In All Seasons, or comparing notes on pond creatures with Charlie Darwin—but it sure as hell beat fighting with the insurance company. Mary had been free to examine the world as she saw it. Willa burrowed into that freedom as if reading a trashy romance, and it made her happy for hours at a stretch. It wasn't fiction, it was real. If Willa was living in Mary's house—if that shelter had stood while the world fell apart and reassembled in its crazy ways—then her family could be sheltered there too. If this didn't all make perfect sense, it was working for now, to the extent that Willa had stopped obsessing about her last two Xanax.

Today she would get only a couple of hours at the historical society, and she already felt wistful about it. Too much of this morning had gone to the drop-in caller from Gothland, and Willa had to be at the hospital by noon to take over the vigil from Iano. He would drive straight to Philly and teach class, no doubt looking sexy and rumpled in the clothes he'd worn all night. Since Nick had been moved out of ICU he'd needed a family member on hand to negotiate his care while the medical people seemed to be running in place. Hours could pass with no one coming to check on him while urine bags filled, pain meds wore off, and orders got mixed up, so the family was trying to keep up the daily vigil. Sometimes Nick became violent and hard to manage, in which case Iano would reward his bad behavior ("just saying," Willa just said) by staying overnight. Willa was grateful to have Dusty duty to keep her mostly out of the fray.

But Iano had classes to teach, Zeke was away now, and Tig had been socked with double shifts at work because a coworker (not Jorge) broke his pelvis in a motorcycle accident. Willa felt like a soldier ant in the complex colony of her family and village; they were still working out who would take the larva this afternoon. She would try to get Dusty past the nurses' station into Nick's room, and if not, would pass him off to Iano at the changing of the guard. Iano could strap him on and take him to class, and wouldn't that just about finish off the besotted lasses.

Willa wouldn't mention the carpool hopeful when she and Iano switched off at the hospital: not the time or the place. But the longer she waited, the more she would think about it, and this was not a happy prospect. Iano's record wasn't perfect. There had been plenty of these coed dramas, all smoke and no fire, which Willa bore with the patience of the chosen, but there had also been affairs. One anyway, shortly after Tig was born. Iano was a postdoc doing what postdocs do, trying to please everybody, awfully young and guileless, and a spiky-haired go-getter anthropology professor had bowled him over with her go-getting, from the sound of it. Willa was in babyland just then, wandering around bleary-eyed in blouses all stiff and stinky-sweet with dried milk, having not quite rallied to the joy of sex for an unspecified little while. She was shaken of course, but Iano's remorse was out of all proportion to the crime. He wept, Willa forgave, and that was that, except for her outraged friends, who accused Willa of lacking the newly discovered resource of the era known as self-esteem.

Willa knew her deficit. It was the several hundred consecutive days without delta sleep. She and Iano had started their family as grad students, when other academics were dutifully postponing family for career, so Willa and Iano were ahead of their crowd. Her girlfriends had no inkling of life with two kids in diapers: that on a good day Willa got to take a shower; once a week she might get as far as socks *and* shoes. To leave a husband, it stood to reason, one would need the whole outfit plus combed hair. And then what? You're doing this to yourself, said her friends, and they were right. How typical, they said, that a man would stray *right then* while she was up to her ears in his babies, and they were right about that too, she gathered. They were living a mammalian cliché. She forgave Iano because he was so sincerely sorry. She adored him and the genes they'd combined in their tedious, utterly charming babies. With all said and done, she still felt happier than she ever remembered being, though of course her memory was shot.

Those days had been wafting back to Willa lately as she found herself again daydreaming about REM sleep. Things like showers and focused lovemaking had taken a backseat while she relearned how to organize life around the all-consuming nothingness and everythingness of an infant. Maybe Iano was reliving those days too, neglect and all. Just a thought.

※

In order to study the character of Polyergus, I captured several and made them prisoners. I gave them every necessary accommodation, and placed an abundance of food before them. But they seemed to scorn the idea of labor, and would not even feed themselves. I kept them in this condition three days, until I was satisfied they would all die without their slaves, so I put a few in the prison with them. These faithful creatures manifested joy on meeting their half-famished masters. They stroked and licked them, removing all dust from their bodies, and prepared food and fed them; finally they excavated a room for them, and took them from my sight.

They were reading in bed. Or Iano was. Willa was waiting for the right time; this would have to be the place. Suddenly she realized his paper had drifted down to his chest and she might have missed her window. But he wasn't asleep. He was staring at her.

"What?"

"You look so happy."

"Do I?"

Was she? Admittedly she'd become engrossed, to the extent of forgetting she was reading, and actually hearing Mary's earnest, levelheaded voice.

"People don't get that blissed out reading anything but the Bible. Or porn."

She laughed, tipping her tablet toward him so he could see for himself, no God or penises. "Mary Treat. My new Bible."

"Your new porn."

"Not that sexy. But interesting. She's describing these creepy ants that can't do anything for themselves, so they have to steal babies from other ants and raise them as slaves. It's like a parable of the One Percent, as told by ants."

He smiled and went back to his paper-clipped pages of student essay. A demoralizing pile of these loomed on his nightstand.

"Thanks for going back over there tonight, Iano. You're a good son. Better than he deserves. You know that, right?"

He didn't look up from his reading. "I know that. And if he dies alone tonight, I'll still feel like a piece of shit."

She rested her tablet on her chest and lay watching this beautiful, patient man in reading glasses surrender himself to an endless river of badly constructed sentences on what have you. American Federalism. Teaching struck Willa as a saintly calling, especially given the pay. But even saints shouldn't be stuck with intro classes forever.

"I'm sorry I couldn't stay longer with Nick this afternoon," she said.

"It's really okay." Still reading.

"I had the best-laid plans, but Dusty ran through all the fuel I brought with me in half the time expected. He's turned into an eating machine."

"That's good, right?"

"It is. But it would be nice to stretch out the feedings, especially at night." She powered off her device, set it on the bedside table, bit a hangnail on her thumb, and then stopped, thinking of the goth girl. Few were the moments that day when she had not. "It seems early to start him on solids. But I might try mixing a little cereal into his formula."

Iano raised his eyebrows. "Cheerios?"

She laughed. "Baby cereal. You remember this stage. Rice cereal or grits, the porridgey things that aren't quite food yet."

He seemed to think about that. Did he remember the porridge stage? "Grits are corn, right?"

"Yep."

"Do we say 'grits *are*' or 'grits *is*'?"

"I have no idea. I've been out of West Virginia too long, and it's all your fault."

Iano lowered his glasses, turned to her, and made an extremely exaggerated sad face that made Willa laugh. Like those big-eye kids.

"Screw Paris, preppie. Paris and music and all that stuff you think you stole from me." She tried to flare her nostrils like a dying

Ali McGraw in *Love Story*, but never had that knack. "And thank you for caring, by the way. About the grammar of grits."

He blew out an exasperated sigh. "These kids are poisoning my brain. If you read one of these papers your head would explode."

"So flunk them all."

"I can't. I'm supposed to have a sense of mission. Did you know Chancel started in a church basement, as a study group for the disadvantaged?"

"This is not PC, but are all these kids really destined for college? Is it reasonable for society to pressure them into poli-sci 114 instead of a hostess job at Red Lobster? So shoot me. But where has all our education gotten *us*?"

Without looking up from his reading, Iano lodged a finger just above her ear and pulled the trigger. "On average, college graduates still make more money."

"And have those big, sharp student loans. The better to eat your juicy paycheck. Somebody at a *bank* is getting rich from their college careers, that much I'm on to."

"Mine is not to question why, *moro*. Mine is just to poli-sci."

"I always hated the sound of that. Polly Sigh. It sounds like mass hysteria in a sorority house."

"Or one of those inflatable sex dolls." Still he read.

"And you've got the sighing Pollies to prove it." She rolled over on her belly and put her face close to his. He looked up, the essay still folded back in one hand, reading glasses on his nose, as if he expected his wife to go away at any moment. Bless his heart.

"So what's the story on Gwendolyn?"

"Gwendolyn?"

"She came to the house this morning."

He stared at Willa, frowning, then at the ceiling, frowning. Then something hit him visibly. "Guenevere? With the purple hair? *She* came here?"

Willa felt rising hysteria, of the silly kind. "*Guenevere?* You can't be serious. Are women *trying* to give their children ridiculous names?"

Iano seemed at a loss. He of the family of Athenas, et cetera, wrong question.

"So which are you?" she asked. "The Lancelot or the King Arthur?"

"What?"

"Lancelot was the seducer, King Arthur was the sad older man. Guenevere, as usual, the victim of circumstance."

He wasn't even a little amused. "She came here, *today?* Jesus. What did she say?"

"Like, I guess I knew he was like married and all? But I didn't know there was like a *baby* . . ."

"Willa. Why did she come here?"

She rolled onto her back and looked at the ceiling. She would never tell him how off the wall it had been with Tig there. Willa still felt hysterical, along comic rather than tragic lines, which was the wrong track. Iano was beside himself. She probably should be too.

"So I guess it's over. Is it over?"

"Over? My God! Nothing ever started."

"No?"

"*No.* She has a work-study in our department and apparently her duties include lurking around the copy machine so she can stare into my office. I keep closing my door. I hate to damage her record, but I'm thinking of getting her assigned someplace else."

So Willa wasn't wrong, the girl was infatuated. At moments throughout the day her outrage had alternated with remorse, for maybe humiliating an innocent student in a fit of groundless paranoia.

Willa raised herself up to look in his eyes. "Really. No sin with Guenevere?"

"*Moro.* Are you asking, seriously? That eyebrow thing is off-putting, to be frank."

She stared at his deep brown irises and saw what was in there: No Guenevere. Not even impure thoughts. "But without the piercings, you'd consider it?"

He closed his eyes, genuinely miserable. "Willa. This isn't fair."

"Sorry. I believe you."

He opened his eyes and she saw his fear. A thing she hadn't considered.

"Oh God, Iano. I'm really sorry." She plummeted from hysteria to anguish. "She didn't say you were having an affair, don't punish her for that. Technically she said you were having a *carpool*. I was just reading between the lines. Sorry. I guess I just thought I'd run it by you."

"Christ, Willa. You scared the hell out of me. I had this *Fatal Attraction* thing running in my head, a crazy girl telling lies about me, going to the dean."

"Sorry," Willa said again, the word that could never be said enough in the space of one marriage. Ali McGraw in *Love Story* notwithstanding.

"I'm sorry too, *moro*. This bullshit you have to put up with. It was crazy for her to come here bothering you. She lives in Vineland, this girl. I don't know how she found out we're here, but early in the semester she asked me if she could get a ride. I'd forgotten that. She was having car trouble and blah blah. I don't think she's getting much support from home. I gave her a couple of excused absences but I certainly made no offers."

"You were probably just polite. In her age bracket that's practically a proposal."

"Right. *Boundaries*, everybody keeps saying this word and I never get it. Am I stupid? First men are pigs, and now we can't even be nice without some kind of implied sexual fallout?"

"Iano, you didn't do anything wrong. They're still children, even if they're twenty. Nobody's teaching them manners." What she really thought was that these girls had tapped into a moxie mine that was unknown to females of Willa's generation. When she was in college it took half a semester's worth of courage just to show up at office hours. *Especially* if the professor was hot.

"This kills me, Willa. That you wouldn't trust me."

"I do." She looked deeply into his eyes, trying to channel some other loving wife, less neurotic and better rested. "You wouldn't lie to me. I know that. End of subject."

This appeared to be enough for Iano. She watched him take up the essay again, and marveled at the teaspoons of reassurance that could be enough for Iano. Was he faking that? All other humans she knew, herself chief among them, seemed to ache with unfulfilled wants. He read to the end of a page, turned it back, and read on. After an indefinite interval he noticed her silence and looked up.

"*Ti, moro?*"

"It's not the girl. I'm just thinking of life in general. You're not disappointed?"

He considered this for roughly two seconds. "No. About what?"

"I don't know. You gave up so much trying to get tenure and security, we all did. And here you are back on the bottom rung, reading bad essays for crummy pay."

"I *did* get security. Unfortunately my college didn't."

"I know. I'm not blaming you. The same thing happened to both of us, we lost what we'd worked for and I feel cheated. Some days I'm still so mad, I can't stand being in my own skin. Isn't it just human, to keep wanting?"

His eyes crinkled at the corners, and here was the smile she could no more resist after thirty years than the Gueneveres could at freshman orientation. "*Se thelo,*" he said.

"I know. I want you too." She kissed him, feeling something that had been dormant awhile, a stirring of sap in the heartwood. But she pulled away before he did. Sat up and rearranged the oversize T-shirt that kept falling off her shoulder. "Okay. This has been bothering me and I need to talk about it. You're stuck below your station and I don't think we should just . . . you know. *Give up*."

"What are you saying, Willa? I'm a happy loser?"

"No! Not a loser. But maybe I'm looking for a little more fire in the belly, on your own behalf? You deserve more."

"Deserving, getting, and wanting are three different things, *moro*. Typically unrelated."

She thought this over. "Yeah. The first two are pretty static, you deserve what you deserve, you get what you get. And that last one runs away with the family silver."

He laughed. "What is it you want, Willa Knox? What do you really, really want?"

She looked at him lying back on the pillow, glasses on his nose, essay in one hand, the other arm cocked behind his head; portrait of a man relaxed. "To be as happy as you are. For all of us to be okay. For Zeke to be himself again, and Tig to be reasonable."

"I'm asking about *you*. Just for yourself. What is it you don't have, that would make you happy?"

"I don't know. I want the sexual energy of a twenty-year-old and several kinds of genius. To write like Virginia Woolf and sing like Beyoncé. And *look* like Beyoncé."

"I was discussing the material realm, not the magical."

"Okay. A roof that doesn't leak and a car that doesn't conk out. Health insurance that doesn't reject our claims."

"Those are *un*wants. You're wishing problems away. I'm asking you to come up with things you actually want."

"Oh, I could give you a list. Believe me." She ran both hands through her hair at the temples, concentrating. "I'm out of the habit. I've spent years trying not to want. Just, you know, as an endeavor, like quitting smoking. Let me think. I want to fill the grocery cart without keeping a running tally in my head. To be able to buy a nice bottle of wine sometimes and drink it, just because we feel like it." She gazed at the peeling wallpaper over the chest of drawers and unfocused her eyes, loosening the reflexes of parsimony. "I used to want Limoges. Nice china. I know that sounds stupidly materialistic. It was in my twenties, I didn't know we'd be moving every few years and breaking everything except the cast iron and the plastic sippy cups." She exhaled. "I wish we had a life that didn't have to leave behind a trail of broken pieces."

She paused for comment. Iano offered none. She knew she was failing the assignment: he was giving her permission to be stupidly materialistic. "Okay. Eight dining room chairs that match, with no wobbly legs. A classy leather jacket. Maybe a nice pair of boots. Which would be a waste because I never go anywhere. Okay, I want to go somewhere. Is that materialistic enough?"

"That depends. Where do you want to go?"

"A week at a beach house. Or I don't know, England, the British Museum. Or your parents' village on Crete. What's the name of that beach with the pink sand?"

"Elafonisi."

"Elafonisi. And those amazing cream-of-wheat pastries we ate in bed with our coffee every morning. What are those called?"

"Bougatsa."

"God, yes. I want bougatsa." She could probably get herself sexually aroused on the memory of those breakfasts. "Okay, wild card. I want a hot tub in our backyard where we could lie around naked and look up at the stars."

"You would have to cut down those mother trees."

"We couldn't do *that*." She shot him a glance, then closed her eyes again. "Don't mess with me, I'm on a roll here."

"You're wishing for a different life."

"Not completely. I want *this* life, with *this* husband, maybe a slightly revised house and kids. Except in this version we drink our coffee and kiss each other goodbye and go to *work*. Both of us. Instead of one of us going stir-crazy on lockdown with an old man and a baby, while her former wit ferments into bitter broth. I'm bored to tears, Iano. Am I allowed to say that? I want a job. With a good magazine that still has a print edition, and smart colleagues. Is that a magical want?"

"A paycheck is material."

"I want a biweekly paycheck."

"When you had a biweekly paycheck, you kept wishing you could quit the magazine and write freelance full time."

"You're right. I did."

"Really you wanted to write a book."

"I did."

"And if you did, you would want it to sell a hundred thousand copies."

She thought about this. "It's true. I'm not a happy-on-the-midlist kind of gal."

He shook his head, smiling. Like the loving parent of an impossible child.

"What? You think I'm unusual? That's human nature. In terms of the available options, it's inevitable to want *all* the goods. Isn't it?"

This question he considered at length. "Not inevitable," he said finally. "If that were true, people would never marry. But we do. We choose to be monogamous. Maybe wanting less than everything translates to quality over quantity."

She looked at him, feeling suddenly as if she might come undone. From plenty of middle-aged men that choice would be an empty compliment, but from Iano it wasn't. If today had taught her anything.

"We've been good, haven't we?" she said, lying down again, staring up at the cracks that mapped their ceiling. "Except for a couple of lapses, monogamous and happy. So much for my theory of bottomless human voracity."

"Not *lapses*." He looked stung. "Only one *lapse*. A hundred years ago when I had shit for brains."

She rolled over to face him, and despite all her best efforts, thought of the tattooed magenta visitor. Wondering what girls like that wore to bed: probably *something*, given the penchant for costume. Not ancient pajama bottoms and an oversize Steely Dan T-shirt. "Two, counting the swimming coach. That redhead."

Iano assessed her smile the way Willa would study a bank statement. "We've been through this. I did not go to bed with her. And she wasn't a redhead."

Willa moved her face very close to his. "Not in a bed? In a chair, then? Your office chair, that big squeaky one?" She ran a finger over his lips. "Or did you do it in her little Honda? Working around the stick shift, steaming up the windows?"

He groaned. "Holy mother. No, my love, we did not. And furthermore it hurts my back thinking about the stick shift."

He set his readers aside, threw the essay on the floor, and slowly rolled on top of her, keeping his weight on his elbows, clasping both her wrists and pressing them into a hands-up pose of surrender on either side of her head. "Thank God we're old. You see, *moro*, this is the beautiful thing. We don't have to make love in cars ever again." He kissed her for a very long time.

She lifted her pelvis against his erection, opening up and moving to fit herself exquisitely against him. He took her lower lip between his teeth and gently began humping her through the veil of her pajamas and his silk boxers, a move charged with the illicit, explosive eroticism of youth. She was stunned by how quickly she aroused toward orgasm as images broke on her brain like fireworks, herself and not herself, dorm rooms, backseats, times when you couldn't get naked, people with whom you didn't dare. She couldn't help how much this was exciting them both. Was it a crime to cop a turn-on from the adrenaline rush of stolen goods and ancient infidelities? Was she allowed at this point to say *fuck it*?

He released her wrist in order to adjust things below, then slipped inside her so easily Willa gasped. She held her breath, tensed exactly the right muscles, and tilted herself to fine-tune the friction of his thrusts. Threaded her hand through the wilderness of his hair, pulled his face against hers to feel sandpaper jaw and his breath on her neck. Everything about his body could strike a current in hers that zinged through the present haze straight back to the days when sex was the best thing they had, constant and ferocious, two bodies hungry to learn each other by heart. The dangerous allure of novelty might have sparked this torment, but in the eye of the storm they held on hard to the world they knew.

><

Willa felt the lightness of having forgotten something as she walked down the hallway of HealthVine with no baby strapped on. He'd surprised her by taking an afternoon nap. Iano was at home all day grading papers, and had promised to keep an ear out for when he woke up. Willa couldn't recall the last time she'd been this far from Dusty. Even the nurses noticed when she passed by the spaceship curve of their station.

"Where's our little man today?" the short one asked, looking up from the computer where she was logging in patient notes at the speed of light. Delyse, Jamaican, Willa's favorite, though who among this overworked angel band did she not adore? A multicolored bouquet of child and grandchild photos bloomed amid the medication orders on the bulletin board behind them. It turned out babies were welcome in rehab wards, where contagious diseases weren't the problem and everyone needed to lay eyes on a positive prognosis.

"Today it's my turn to look in on the *big* baby. How's he behaving?"

Both nurses rolled their eyes, almost identically: the look reserved for very special patients like Nick. Willa put her hands together in a little *namaste* of thanks. Christmas decorations had gone up since she'd been there last, she noticed: weary tinsel garlands and a tiny silver tree on the meds station. It was barely November. In a place like this, she supposed, the best thing to do with the calendar was get it behind you.

Usually she could hear Nick's TV from the nurses' station, blasting down the hall, probably in violation of the rules. Nick had given up parts of both feet and the use of his right side, but in exchange he'd bullied his caretakers' pity into the freedom to keep his conservative station on full time, full volume. Right now Willa didn't hear it, though, even as she approached the open door of his room. Iano had mentioned the late-night arrival of a roommate. Some compromise must have been required.

She paused at the doorway and looked in at the white-sheeted mountain range of Nick. He was no longer critical, and unlikely to lose both legs; under duress she'd exaggerated. But the stroke had been a close call on a stormy evening of downed power lines and everyone ordered to stay indoors. While Iano and Willa sped back from Cape May, Tig and Jorge had braved flooded streets to get him to an ER. Since that night they'd all been shuffling through the wreckage of Nick, looking for what valuables might be left within the gray-faced man propped on pillows. His bulk was laced with white cables like the ones people used to plug in their phones, as if Nick were getting charged up to some functional percentage. It wasn't clear he'd get there.

Tig was sitting at his bedside with her back to the door. Her dreads were swept up in a red bandana tied in front like Rosie the Riveter, and in that can-do spirit she was spooning green Jell-O into Nick, one slow bite at a time. The stroke had affected his ability to swallow, among a hundred other things. The curtain beyond him was closed, concealing the new roommate, if any. Willa saw the TV was on but muted, on closed caption. It was Nick's news station, of course, showcasing his new idol the Bullhorn, who else. The interviewer was that pretty, steely blonde who seemed smart enough to know better, in Willa's opinion. The amount of airtime devoted to that man was far out of proportion to any actual ideas he seemed to represent. Not that Willa was an expert, but there were things you couldn't manage to *not* know, and this guy was it. Everyone talked about him. Tig and Nick, from the sound of it, were talking about him.

"Good deal is I win, you lose."

"So let's say he did get to be president. Our country would win, and who loses?"

"Terrorists. Muslim, Chinks. Okay? Or he bombs their asses."

Willa stood in the doorway remembering precisely, inside her rib cage, how it felt to watch Tig when she was three years old feeding her doll babies. When Tig was Antsy. Before she discovered the trick of tying her doll babies on tow ropes and dragging them behind her trike.

"You sure you want us to get in that war, Papu? They probably have the big bombs too, you know. The Iranians and North Koreans."

Willa couldn't see her face but knew Tig's mouth would open unconsciously each time she spooned a bite into Nick's.

"Yeah, ours work. Better. Americans know to build stuff."

His speech was recovering slowly, but he still struggled to get his lips around words and sometimes they were disordered. And Nick being Nick, it hardly mattered.

"You're always saying we have the worst everything, Papu. You told the nurse this hospital was a shit hole."

He grunted. "Damn Nazi nurses."

"It's called physical therapy. Don't you want to get better and come home?"

Nick waved off the Jell-O and Tig put down the little cup. "You want to try something else? We've got mashed potatoes and . . . something." She leaned over to peer closely at the tray. "Mystery meat. Should we give it a try?"

He nodded. She gave him a tiny bite and waited for him to swallow. Then another. Nick said something Willa couldn't hear.

"Not really," Tig said. "American schoolkids always come in last, in the smartness tests."

Nick grunted and pushed the spoon away. "Criminals, other countries. Dumb it down."

"You were an immigrant, Papu."

"Came to work. Not this gimme gimme."

"Jorge and his brother and sisters all work. He has a full-time job, plus fixes cars."

Willa wondered if this had been their starting point. Jorge and Tig were definitely now an item. On the night of the stroke, Jorge's heroic efforts on the family's behalf had either clarified the attachment or cemented it. Tig tended to draw this level of devotion from her friends, pushing everyone to the limits, herself included. But somehow she always managed to be cherished. It defied the rules Willa knew. She herself had been bullied a good deal, even as a polite and decently normal-looking child, for her country ways and bland homemade clothes. But really for the shyness that left her defenseless. Willa-Vanilla.

Nick had accepted a few more bites but now waved off the spoon emphatically.

"All done?" Tig asked, and he nodded, closing his eyes. "Okay." She moved the rolling shelf-table away from the bed and tucked the sheets in around him. Willa knew she should speak up, but couldn't bear to put herself in this scene. Had nothing to bring to it that measured up. Tig pulled a book out of her backpack and was sitting down on the sofa when she saw Willa and froze, as if caught in some hijinx.

"He'll be asleep in ten seconds," she whispered, touching her lips.

Willa watched, astonished, as Nick's face went slack. "Wow," she said. "What are they giving him? I need me some of that."

"They're not really sedating him that much anymore. Not in the daytime. But he still goes out like that after he eats, every time. Something to do with poor circulation."

"What time do you need to be at work?"

Tig shrugged. "I've got a few minutes."

"Then could you help me? I'm trying to plow through these government forms and it's like being back in school. I'm having test anxiety. The BAGI-based methodology under the IRC-based statute."

Tig looked puzzled, then got it. "Oh. To get on Medicaid."

Willa made a warning face, sliding her eyes toward Nick.

Tig laughed. "He's dead to the world, Mom. Say it loud, say it proud. You're a welfare mother!"

Willa helped Tig clear aside some of the clutter on the faux-leather sofa: jackets and shirts, a very long striped scarf Tig was knitting, even a pile of Iano's uncorrected essays, all evidence of her family's squatting rights. She wondered if they'd now have to start sharing with a roomie's clan. No signs of life had presented from beyond the curtain. The HealthVine rooms were touching for their attempted hominess, like little living rooms with entirely disinfectable surfaces.

Tig took off her sneakers and tucked her feet under her while Willa opened her laptop and waited for it to wake up. The TV clamped to the wall above their heads must still have been venting its outrage; she could practically feel the waves of doom.

"You're so sweet to Papu. I don't know how you do all that."

"All what?"

"Everything. Feed him, talk to him, listen to his racist diatribes without throttling him by his walrus neck."

Tig grinned almost shyly, and Willa felt guilty. Tig didn't get a lot of admiration from her family. Willa opened the Medicaid website she'd bookmarked, and scrolled through the sections she'd already tried to work through.

"So here's my problem. Eligibility is based on the MAGI, whatever the heck that is. We three kings? Gold, frankincense, and myrrh?"

"Mom. Modified adjusted gross income. It says right there."

Willa wondered if children had shamed parents thus since the dawn of time. "I see that. Okay. I don't know why I'm getting so bogged down. I guess it's a clunky website."

"You're welcome. It's not that clunky. You're just having trouble with the idea of us as a Medicaid family."

"Believe me, nothing would make me happier," Willa snipped, noting her own use of the conditional tense. The social worker had been encouraging, but the cards never fell Willa's way. Why expect these Magi to throw her a rope? "Some of us might be eligible, but I'm not sure how we fit together as a family. Would I include you and Zeke in our plan, or do you file your plans separately?"

"You mean my brother the hedge fund manager to billionaires? He gets to go on welfare with us?"

"He still owes more than he's earning. I'm not saying any of this makes sense, honey. But you see what I'm up against." Technically Willa knew even Nick might not qualify as a dependent, let alone the adult offspring, and some paperwork needed to be settled for Dusty. But her impulse was to drag all bodies onto the lifeboat.

"Here," Tig said, reaching forward to toggle through some

screens. "Zeke and I have to apply for ourselves, it looks like. Over age twenty-six. Yippee, I'm a grown-up."

A choking gasp suddenly came out of Nick. They watched several different monitors discreetly signaling something, probably nearness of death. He appeared to have stopped breathing. After a few more gasps he started again.

"Apnea," Willa said. "Can't they put a positive pressure mask on him for that?"

"They tried. He goes ballistic." Tig got up, went to his bedside, and spoke in his ear. "Okay, Papu?" She pushed the button that elevated his bed almost to a sitting position. Willa wouldn't have known to do that, or how to adjust the bed.

"You're amazing, Tigger. I mean it. I watched you feeding him Jell-O and letting him rant about the evil foreigners. You're so . . . indulgent, I guess is the word."

Tig settled back on the sofa and reached across Willa to the laptop, toggling through more screens. "You have to go to your state's website to look up household income eligibility. I don't know. With Papu I mean, why I let him rant like that. I guess it's all just kind of fascinating."

"If you say so. I sure don't get it. He loves this billionaire running for president who's never lifted a finger doing anything Nick would call work. Why *that* guy?"

"Because rich white guys are *supposed* to be running the world. Papu thinks this dude must have put in the time and gamed the system to get his billions, because that's how it works in America. So it's his turn to be president. What Papu can't stand is getting pushed out of the way by people he doesn't even think should be voting, never mind getting jobs or benefits or whatever."

"Never mind the White House."

"Definitely that. He thinks they're cutting into the line ahead of him. How can black and brown people get to have nice stuff and be in charge of things? Or women, God forbid. When Papu didn't get his turn yet?" Tig was studying the laptop screen as she spoke, with a wide-eyed, eyebrows-up concentration face that Iano claimed was exactly like Willa's. She couldn't see it, but of course you never really saw yourself.

"This particular brand of tyrant, though. Yikes," Willa said. "I can't take him seriously. He's going to burn out before the first primary."

"Don't count on it. There's a lot of white folks out there hanging on to their God-given right to look down on some other class of people. They feel it slipping away and they're scared. This guy says he's bringing back yesterday, even if he has to use brass knuckles to do it, and drag women back to the cave by their hair. He's a bully, everybody knows that. But he's *their* bully."

"I thought you didn't believe in white people."

"Right? Or Santa Claus? Total fantasy. I mean, look around, who do you see that's living la vida *white man*?" Tig focused on the computer screen, scrolling alphabetically through states to get to New Jersey. "Really it's just down to a handful of guys piling up everything they can grab and sitting on top of it. And a million poor jerks like Papu still hoping they can get into the club. How long can that last? Five or six more years?"

They both looked at Nick, who was sleeping quietly with his mouth open.

"So I can be nice to Papu. He's basically over."

Willa didn't believe the world could be as simple as Tig made it, but she admired the pursuit of a theory. It was easy to forget, among all the advanced degrees, that their barefoot rebel dropout was the family's only scientist. Willa watched Tig lean into the screen, refusing to be daunted by section 36B(d)2(A), probably not even conscious of her takeover as she pulled the computer onto her own lap.

"Here we go. Modified Adjusted Gross Income eligibility standards, New Jersey. You plug in the number of family members
applying. Policyholder and all dependents."

"Start with six," Willa said. Against all evidence, trying to keep
the fledglings in the nest.

"A family of six would be eligible for free care if the household
income is below forty-four thousand, nine hundred dollars."

This was well above their combined take. Willa felt relieved
and also disoriented. To have a name for this prolonged asphyxiation that was turning her into the walking dead: poverty. If it
still didn't quite register, she refused to accept Tig's accusation.
She was not clinging to any God-given right to look down on
families like hers.

"What about just the four of us," she asked. "Since it looks like
you and Zeke have to file separately."

"Four?"

"Dad and me, Nick and Dusty."

"How do you guys get Dusty?" Tig tilted her red-kerchiefed head
and frowned at Willa, suddenly possessive. "Wouldn't you have to
adopt him or something?"

"He's a minor relative living in our household as a dependent.
Power of attorney is in the works. We get Dusty."

Tig conceded Dusty. "Below thirty-three thousand, five hundred
dollars."

"Wow. We're a Medicaid family."

Tig grinned. "There you go. Gift of the Magi."

10

Gift of the Magi

Thatcher slipped alone into the crowded hall and stood at the back, hoping not to be seen by his pupils, whom he regularly scolded for failures of punctuality. The lecturer was droning like a bagpipe, his exposition on miracles under the micro-scope well underway. Another latecomer had just arrived, judging from the snowflakes still melting on the shoulders of the man's coat. Plum Hall was stifling. Yuletide garlands appeared to perspire in the gaslights, and an infant in the audience protested the misery of its swaddling. Thatcher removed his topcoat for the first time in weeks, save for the respite under the mountain of quilts Rose piled on their bed. Her father's house, devoutly defended through autumn, was revealing its adversity. Gracie bent herself double keeping the fires lit in rooms that inhaled winter through wheezing walls and windows. Polly had worn a fur hat to supper that evening and declared her Christmas wish was to grow wool like a sheep. But the women would not move out. Thatcher was expected to shore up the failing edifice, if not with money then his own hands.

He saw his students encamped across the front row. Requiring them to attend this lecture had been Cutler's idea, and Thatcher hadn't objected on principle. A glimpse of minute pond creatures would relieve the long spate of chemistry. Thatcher felt no passion for the physical sciences, a truth he worked to conceal. Botany and zoology were the sugarplums that danced in his head, and would likewise dance—he felt sure—in these nascent minds once they were properly introduced to the natural sciences. The postponement was a torment, but he still awaited permission to speak of the unities that made the whole living world comprehensible: the origin of species by natural selection. He'd submitted his materials, argued for their legitimacy, and over Cutler's objections argued again. Now came patience. Where dangerous opponents were concerned, Thatcher's habit was to keep his head low and wait; in his experience, bluster was a sign of poor stamina. Cutler would lose interest in the daily particulars of Thatcher's classroom. By springtime he might consent to field trips. Meanwhile, this lecture. But Thatcher had requested a waiver of their fifteen-cent admission.

Cutler had declared that was out of his hands! (Daring Thatcher to blink at the plural.) The price of a Plum Hall lecture had been decreed by Landis from the very first days of Vineland, along with the precise distance a house must be set back from the street, and the species of trees set before it. Like all stipulations, the fifteen-cent rule stood unquestioned. Thatcher was continually astonished that his townsmen submitted to Landis like a modern-day King Herod. For many of his pupils' parents, fifteen cents was a full day of ironing shirts or digging drainages—a difficult trade for an hour in a lecture hall. The principal could hardly believe any of his scholars derived from ditch-digging stock, but eventually was persuaded to "put it in the captain's ear," a favored repository for Cutler's words, evidently. The fee was waived.

And even gratis, Thatcher now saw the price was too high for the goods. Professor Bowman hit every word at the same high pitch with a curious absence of emphasis, leaving anyone to guess where one sentence ended and the next began. This purported Unique Lecture, called "God's Drops of Water," had been delivered so many times the professor himself seemed to find it soporific.

". . . And thus to begin, I bring before your eyes tonight . . ."

Good Lord, *to begin*? Thatcher had hoped a significant portion of this sentence might already have been served. He eased out his pocket watch and perceived a quiet sigh from the latecomer standing near him. The man was tall and broad, still wearing his rough topcoat with the beaver collar turned up, though the snow on its shoulders had perished. Thatcher considered making his way to a seat but didn't like to be noticed. He watched his captive students from the rear: already restless. He'd tried to cajole Polly into coming with him that night but Aurelia had other plans for her daughters, a séance at the Crandall home. Aurelia had taken up conversation with her dead husband via some charlatan, and was eager for Polly to greet her father. Thatcher was horrified. But now glad he'd conceded. Whatever sport Polly might make of a medium with a lace curtain on her head, her intolerance for professorial windbags was well known.

Bowman seemed to rouse slightly, for now after the long uphill drag of preamble he was ready to reveal the first of his Illustrative Crayon Drawings.

". . . to wit, I bring before you the most curious menagerie that the micro-scope reveals . . ." The professor engaged in lugubrious battle with his oversize sketching book, its weight threatening to tip the flimsy easel. ". . . Some of which creatures you will find . . ."

The easel tipped and the book fell, slapping the floor with a startling report. The professor squatted, red faced and resolute in his frock coat, and recommended the struggle of righting the tablet and turning back the enormous page to reveal the first illustration. ". . . Some of which creatures my dear ladies and gentlemen . . . shall astonishingly reveal themselves to you . . . in form . . . to be more highly organized than the horse or the elephant . . . *to wit* . . ."

Thatcher could see very little from where he stood, though the professor's regrettable voice reached every part of the hall and likely the belfry, where somnolent bats might be dropping from their roosts. He scanned the audience for his employer. Found him sitting with Landis to the right of the stage, their chairs angled for a view of audience and lecturer. With a plunging heart Thatcher realized the captain would be expecting some public ingratiation from his pupils for the privilege of free attendance. He should have foreseen this, had them write a card of thanks. Oh, blast. In these trifles of etiquette Thatcher was a dunderhead. No mother had schooled him, so the burden fell unfairly to Rose. He adored her for accepting a defective husband, generally with grace. And again wondered idly, from weeks of habit, what he could possibly conjure as a Christmas gift. Any item within his means would displease Rose categorically. She wanted a horse.

He watched his pupils. Female heads were tilting together in conspiratorial pairs, the hair bows trembling. How well he knew the symptoms of their inattention. The end of term was approaching and they strained for release to the pressing engagements of advent and nativity, what with geese to be cooked and church pageants to be rehearsed. These strapping lads and lasses had aged beyond the silent roles—the thunderstruck holy parents, wise men, and shepherds—into the serious thespian business of Roman despots and harking angels. Thatcher felt himself in daily contest with the baby Jesus as he tried to hold their attention to the so-called imponderables of physics: light, heat, magnetism, conservation of energy. He was losing, to the more ponderable Virgin birth. His fellow teachers advised against trying. They scheduled end-of-term examinations in January, after the holiday, by which time Thatcher knew he would have lost the battle to entropy.

At some point between *the astonishing Hydra with tentacles like the head of Medusa* and *the mystifying Euglena which is half-plant, half-animal as if the Lord were indeed undecided about the day of its creation—why, perhaps he made it at the stroke of midnight* (the pause here for audience laughter proved gratuitous), Professor Bowman began to wax theological. His highest pursuit, *indeed* the only justification of the modern apparatus called the micro-scope, he declared, *to wit*, was to reveal God's hand. But no scientist could dare guess the Lord's divine purpose for creating these life-forms.

Thatcher noted his employer's beaming approval and sighed, perhaps audibly, for the tall man in the overcoat turned to him with a face of comic dismay. Thatcher returned it, appreciative but unsettled. Did this man know him? Thatcher recognized the face, dark as a Turk's, with a full beard and haunted eyes. But what face in this village had he not laid eyes on at some time or other? In the boot shop, the tobacconist's, in school assemblies attended by parents. But still he felt he knew something of this man. Racked his brain through the entire deposition on the Enigmatic Amoeba, ignoring the enigmas.

Then he remembered: the newspaper man. Carruth. He'd come to a teachers' meeting to raise concerns over child labor and its detriment to schooling. The man's ardor had moved Thatcher to pick up the *other* newspaper, the one that so distressed his mother-in-law, and now he read it weekly, finding its bluntness bracing. The *Independent*'s challenges to Landis orthodoxy relieved his impression of Vineland as a hill of slave ants. Most amusing were the ironic editorial pieces and a series of caricatures called "Lamentations" in which a poor, bent farmer lodges his weekly inquiry, and Landis replies in the spirit of Marie Antoinette. "What shall I do for bread?" asks the wretch. "And the Prince replied, Pine cones and acorns shall be thy food, the waters of Parvin's branch thy drink, and as to raiment thou shalt wear a *gunny bag*." Thatcher surmised it was nearly a one-man operation, Carruth and a few hands turning their press in an office on Landis Avenue, brazenly located directly next door to the *Weekly*. The *Independent*'s masthead declared in twelve-point type: "The Liberty of the Press Is the Safeguard of a Free People." Thatcher wondered that the man had not yet been overrun by a wagon.

Professor Bowman seemed to be inching toward his climax: the vision of science as no more or less than the study of God's creation. "Perfect, congruous, and governed by his laws. Our Creator has stocked our planet with its wondrous creatures, neglecting not to fill even the minuscule drop of water, *to wit*, as a farmer chooses the livestock for each paddock of his farm. To study this menagerie is the naturalist's noble calling, for in this study we may find revealed to us the mind of God. To borrow the words of the great Agassiz . . ." Here he fumbled through his notes, fearing to misquote the great Agassiz. "Ah. 'We may find revealed the free conception of the *almighty intellect*, matured in his thought before it was manifested in tangible external forms.'"

The professor paused and the audience inhaled, sensing deliverance, but into that half-second silence before the applause Bowman injected his next "*to wit*." Hands fell to laps; the lecture inconceivably bore on. "We see all species distributed according to the divine logic . . ."

Thatcher knew his duty was to stay, greet his pupils, shepherd them into a proper herd, and drive them to Landis for the formal grovel. Suddenly that prospect brought bile to his throat. Invocation of the glory-hound Agassiz was the coup de grâce. He glanced about for a covert route of exit, and again this man Carruth seemed to read his mind: he tilted his head, eyebrow raised, and subtly hitched his thumb toward the rear entrance. Hardly troubling the air around him, he slipped away. Mesmerized, Thatcher followed.

≫≪

"How do you know me?"

"You are better known than you think."

The coffeehouse at the corner of East and Landis was Thatcher's favored refuge from the petty disputes and frigid temperatures of his household. But tonight his companion walked quickly between the tables and led him into one of the wooden booths at the back. A serving girl followed with the coffee urn. These dark, boxed-in seats were uncharted territory for Thatcher, who assumed men would need them only for brokering unseemly contracts. The man who sat down across from him now pulled a small tin flagon from his vest and poured an amber drop into Thatcher's cup, then his own.

"You overstate my notoriety. But you are editor of *The Independent*. You came to a school meeting, early in the term."

"Carruth." The hand protruded like a giant paw from the bearish coat. "Uri Carruth. Pleased to make the acquaintance." The voice matched the hand, and the coat.

"Thatcher Greenwood. As you know, evidently."

Some would think the acquainting to be prerequisite for sharing contraband whiskey, not a postscript. But Thatcher was no expert. He lifted his cup and experienced the exquisite combination of coffee scald and whiskey blaze in his gullet. He'd not tasted alcohol since the day of his wedding. A lifetime before this one.

"You come from Russia, I've heard it said?"

"From Wisconsin. My father emigrated there from Russia. Whence come all breeds of agitators and bandicoots, you've heard it said."

Thatcher smiled carefully. "And you moved to Vineland for its healthful climate."

"Something like that." Carruth grinned, drained his cup, set it back in its saucer. He had the extremely deep-set eyes of a man accustomed to going hungry, an impression much at odds with the hearty countenance. He might be a cabbage, Thatcher thought. Or a barrel cactus, whose round, bristling form he had seen only in drawings. But no, more fauna than flora was this one: a bear. "I put myself to that contemptible sermon tonight," the bear declared, "because I thought I might find you. I wanted to meet the man who brought the walls of Jericho tumbling down."

"Ah. You have the wrong man. No vanquisher of walls here." Thatcher thought of his house: on the first Sunday of advent the broken parlor lintel sagged abruptly, an ominous few inches. And Aurelia's bedchamber was now uninhabitable from dampness in its walls, forcing her to share Polly's. Neither was pleased with the arrangement.

"I'm referring to Landis and his fifteen cents. *Lex loci.*"

"The law of the land." Thatcher held his cup in both hands, absorbing heat. "But not the battle of Jericho. Cutler saddled my students with the obligation of attending that sermon. Bowman is an old friend of his. I only brought to his attention the problem of these pupils' and their families' destitution. He was quite surprised, I assure you."

Carruth squinted and shook his head slowly, as if spying a trap he was clever enough to avoid. "The problem of their *destitution*, good sir, is the Bastille. You've stormed it."

"I'm sure I told Cutler nothing he didn't already know."

Carruth laughed at that, a full-bellied growl. Thatcher, at a loss, looked out the door of the booth. Across the room, the girl who had served them now stood behind the counter, wiping cups. She was the owner's daughter, a child of Polly's age doing a woman's job, in a pink lace cap and an apron pinned to her unfilled bosom. On the wall behind her, many rows of polished silver coffee urns aligned on shelves, coyly catching the lamplight. It seemed an excess of coffee urns. He was thinking of the painter Vermeer, an exhibition he'd seen in Boston, when the girl glanced up, startling him.

He hadn't meant to summon her, but now Carruth made a signal with both hands and she hurried across the room to refill their cups and set down a plate of oysters. Despite her youth she bore the patient air of a wife, carefully hanging both their hats on pegs on the wall of the booth before hurrying off to attend other tables. Suddenly the room had begun to fill with patrons. Plum Hall must have liberated them at last.

Carruth only now thought to shoulder out of the overcoat he'd kept on through the full suffocation of the lecture. Possibly to hide the sack coat underneath, which was separating at the shoulder seam and several years out of date. If Thatcher could think so, then probably a decade out of date. Rose would be traumatized by this coat: her strongest argument yet against reading *The Independent*. The editor leaned forward, sucked an oyster from its pearly shelf, dropped the shell in the dish, and fell back against the booth. "Man, do you not read that tabloid Landis churns out every week?"

Thatcher drank his coffee, now without benefit of spirit rectification. "You might ask, do you not drink the water of Vineland?"

"Then you know. There is no *destitution* in Eden." Something in Carruth resurrected as he spoke. "Every acre of Vineland is green as the banks of the Nile. Every bushel spills over with harvest! Every farmer is solvent and all the bricklayers well paid. Half these men believe it themselves, and wonder why they're still going hungry."

Thatcher, hungry himself, began devouring his share of the oysters in measured succession. This was another abstention since his wedding. Rose and Aurelia detested oysters because they were cheap, resembled snails, reminded them of Boston, and bore carnal associations: thus defining the perfect gulf between these women's tastes and his own. (Although on the last point, Rose held considerable private dissent.)

"I read Landis's self-promoting rag," Thatcher offered between oysters. "My neighbor compares the man to Phineas Barnum."

"Your neighbor is wise. I'm sure Landis would agree with Barnum's famous statement that advertising is to the genuine article what manure is to the land."

Thatcher smiled. "That it largely increases the product."

"Our town has been well buried in the stuff."

"I'm aware of Landis's deceptions because I read about them in *The Independent*. If any man is accused of blowing Gabriel's horn, I should name Mr. Carruth."

The bearish head shook mournfully. "If it could be so."

"You've grown extremely bold in your critiques of Landis, these last months. 'The Prince Travels Abroad, Hoping to Eclipse Her Royal Majesty.' Even the captain's wife is not spared. I have to say I'm impressed."

"The loudest horn does nothing to move deaf ears."

"You're being modest. Your paper has its subscribers, I trust."

"A fair number, it would please me to say. And also its detractors."

"Naturally."

"*Not* naturally. It doesn't always go along lines you expect. The peasants don't like hearing how they've been used, paying for land that will go back to Landis the day they lose their first crop. They refuse to believe they're getting tricked into building wealth for the masters of this town."

"No man wants to hear he has been a fool."

"But they hear it, and still they persist. Landis passes around his bill of sale, this *egalitarian* Vineland where every man stands an equal chance, and they lap it up like cats at the dish. They are all for the great captain, while he indentures them and eats their souls and property. Somehow he gets them to side against their own."

"They are happier to think of themselves as soon to be rich, than irreversibly poor." In that moment Thatcher was thinking of his wife.

Carruth nodded thoughtfully. "A delicate business, telling the truth. So long as Landis writes a happier falsehood for these men to tell themselves, they can believe in opportunity. They are the nearly rich, as you say. Waiting for what is theirs. The Lord is good, the trees will bear fruit, and the Plum Hall lecture will always cost fifteen cents. Because no man or child ever lived in this town without fifteen cents to spare . . ."

Carruth paused there to finish off the oysters. The endeavor was passionate.

". . . and then comes this man Greenwood who changes the rule. I am deeply curious about the source of his influence."

"I have none. In this moment I am not quite sure of you as friend or foe, Mr. Carruth. But I am sure you are wrong about my influence."

Carruth leaned across the table to swat a paw against Thatcher's shoulder, twice. Evidence of friendship, presumably. "You can be sure of me. As sure as we know our common enemies."

"Ah, enemies. I try not to make them. It strikes me sometimes as my life's work."

At this Carruth laughed hard, shoulders shaking. Everything about the man was without restraint or artifice. In other circumstances, Thatcher imagined this might be endearing. "I come from the Badger State," he declared, wiping the mirth from his eyes. "It was the miners that started calling it that. The first industrious fellows to settle there. In winters they had to burrow into the hills like badgers to survive." Carruth leaned forward on his elbows. "I'm the youngest of three brothers. Or was. The eldest was crushed under a pallet of logs, working for a boss who would brook no complaining about the risks of the operation. The second brother, killed by a lightning strike, ten minutes short of the end of his shift at the rail yard. This is what I've learned about being a badger, Mr. Greenwood. As to the *career* of avoiding making enemies. You can't dig any burrow deep enough. Might as well stand and look them in the eye."

"I expect I should go home to my wife, Mr. Carruth."

"And I to mine. Do you have children? I have five. Three girls, two boys, all scoundrels. But not an anarchist in the brood. I've failed completely."

"Would I know them? I have no Carruth among my pupils."

"No, not yet. The eldest you'll have next year, twins, and then their sister. They're a coven, those three. All at once, papa is an embarrassment. They'd rather toady up to their prosperous associates with the smart crinolines and the shiny boots." He leaned forward in painful confidence. "They want to go *riding*. With the wealthy girls."

Thatcher smiled sympathetically, for this refrain he heard daily from his wife. Then he felt the physical shock of an inspiration: something he might arrange for Rose. Not gold or frankincense, but potentially more useful. And within his means. "Are the associates cooperative?"

Carruth shook his head. "Disastrously not, to date. Though my little hens keep trying. They have revolutionary fortitude, if nothing else. But the smart crinolines seem to be the price of admission."

Smart crinolines Rose had in abundance, not to mention a rare faculty for making her company coveted—a talent the Carruth daughters probably lacked. Thatcher could picture these unfortunate hens, saddled with the large-boned inheritance of their father's frame and reputation. But yes, for his beautiful Rose, a pair of riding boots it would be. Wrapped and beribboned, with dates and riding companions arranged. He had two female colleagues with stable-owning fathers: the dance instructor Miss Dunwiddie, and Miss Hirstberger, who taught French and called herself Made-

moiselle. Both asked shamelessly after his wife's habits and wardrobe. He could set Rose up with the right clothes and friends, and
the horse would come about on its own, with someone else paying
for its keeping. Thatcher's heart filled with some substance lighter
than blood or air.

"And you? Got a brood yourself?" Carruth was asking.

"None yet. I am a beginner at marriage. Sharing my home with
a mother-in-law who still seems to hope her daughter might marry
better than she did. And a little scoundrel of a sister-in-law who
thinks her sister stole the prize. If I were Jacob, I think I should
labor the extra seven years and marry her as well."

"Quite a confession, from a man whose life's work is avoiding
enemies. Leah and Rachel were always at one another's necks, as I
recollect." Carruth smiled. "Ah. But they never blamed Jacob, did
they? Bartered mandrakes for the right to sleep with him."

Thatcher said no more, thinking it best to end this interview
quickly. He watched his companion take out the flask again and
with solemn regard, top up their cups.

"I sought you out this evening for a reason. I have something
important to tell you. It involves Cutler."

"*Cutler?*"

"Your employer."

"As I know."

"With whom you have had some difficulties."

Thatcher felt his limbs grow cold. He was no more eager than
any Vineland peasant to hear Carruth's summary of his plight.

"I regret to say your feud has reached beyond the walls of the
school. I overheard Cutler discussing it with Landis. In a meeting
of the town council, Thursday last."

"With *Landis.*"

"Cutler described your campaign to drag the heresies of Darwin
into his academy. Do you think I am inventing this?"

"No." Thirty seconds earlier, Thatcher could have stood and left this place.

"Do you have support at the school?"

"Support? I hardly know. My pupils come to class. The other teachers are looking out for themselves, currying favor where they can. We are hired only from one year to the next. A system guaranteed to turn colleagues into a den of knaves."

Carruth suddenly seemed deeply concerned. "Cutler sought Landis for advice. He claimed this feud was demoralizing the entire school."

"A *feud* requires two active parties. I petitioned, and I was refused. There it ends."

"Not for a man of Cutler's breed. Any disagreement is an affront to his power. He won't rest until he has remedied the so-called insurrection. Landis advised him."

"You *overheard* this?"

"A talent of my vocation. Even an ox like myself can become invisible." Carruth waved a hand in the air, as if erasing himself. "Especially among men who loom that large in their own eyes."

Thatcher's eyes closed involuntarily. "What did Landis advise?"

"The way to catch a rat is to lure it into the open."

Carruth reached across the table to pat his forearm, as if waking him. "Sorry. The man is loathsome. Better to know than not know, eh?"

Thatcher did not think so. "What poisoned bait is to be used, to lure this rat?"

Carruth looked around, perhaps for eavesdroppers, or to summon the girl for more coffee. He leaned forward on his elbows. "A colloquium."

"A colloquium?"

"Assembly of some kind. Before the whole school."

"Ah. That. One of Cutler's pet practices. Every teacher is required to present his expertise to a school assembly. Not just to pupils but staff as well, and they do protest. They would enjoy the hour at leisure from their charges, but Cutler insists we all attend. Learn from one another, the bee and the pollen and all that."

"And your day is coming. To be the bee."

Thatcher shrugged. "I plan to summarize the great practical achievements of our enlightenment. Joseph Lister sterilizing wounds, Louis Pasteur and the bacteria. No man dislikes science when it is sparing him from death and putrefaction."

"You're free to decide the text of your lecture?"

"Yes. Well, in theory not. Cutler represents it as a conversation. He sits on stage with the presenter and asks prodding questions from time to time. 'Please explain, sir. Do go on.' He sleeps through these talks, along with the staff and pupils."

"So Cutler will be there to ask questions."

"Yes, but he would . . . I cannot imagine *he* would bring up the unspeakable Charles Darwin. That is unfathomable."

Carruth's strange, hooded eyes met Thatcher's. "My friend. Fathom it."

>≪

Mary drew aside a curtain of suspended ivy and pulled open the door of the carriage house. It was oddly quiet within. The dry silt floor silenced their steps. The framing was of rough timbers but the diffuse light through dust-covered windows made Thatcher think of a chapel. Ants boiled darkly from small volcanoes in one corner.

"My *Polyergus* friends," she said. "And there is my collecting box. Selma must have put it here." She stepped quickly to retrieve the vasculum from a table piled with her plant presses. Bathed in the window's white light, she looked like a girl, or a sylph. Happy in this place. Thatcher guessed her husband must never have come here.

"No, he didn't," she confided. "After Mr. Newcomb took his carriage away, I don't believe Joseph gave another thought to this place. It was my refuge in dismal times. I did my experiments here." She looked up brightly. "Now my investigations make scandalous onslaughts on the parlor, do they not?"

"A happy scandal, for the spiders and flytraps. They would not care for this cold."

"Oh, dear. Is it too cold for you here? I could bring you a stone bottle." Her brightness fell away, and Thatcher cursed himself. Another man to burden her.

"Mary, please don't. You've given me too much already." He put his hands lightly on her shoulders to prove himself earnest, but the sight of his own house through the window troubled him with how they would seem to someone looking in: like lovers. Or simply two friends in overcoats, a tall man and little sylph, sharing a conspiracy. He took back his hands and turned from the window. "This is all I need. The frigid air will brace me for my enemy while I practice."

He had found it impossible to write or rehearse his speech at home, with every room full of women and complaints. Gracie had not lit the stoves properly; a new patch of wallpaper was peeling in the dining room; Polly needed to come fetch the dogs this instant or Rose would have them sent away. This refuge of Mary's suited him well. He noticed a ladder leading through a hatch door to the upstairs. Also a narrow cot in the back corner, opposite the anthills, with a blanket neatly folded on it.

"Mary, did you have to escape here entirely in the dismal times? Forgive me, it's forward to ask. I find myself angry with a man I've never met."

"No need. Joseph has made enemies enough to last his life. The little bed is for Selma. She sleeps here when her father gets in his drink and she fears going home. They have had to move into a rooming house that sounds appalling. She also comes here to pray."

"I might do the same. I confess I am terrified."

"Of addressing a room full of children?"

"Not a room. An auditorium."

"But this you do every day. The difference is only one of degree. I am entitled to be a nervy mouse when I give the rare botany lecture. But you are not."

He could hardly think of Mary as a mouse, having seen her so queenly in her bog, or with her sorority of tower-building spiders. So fearlessly rapt when in conversation with another alert mind, whether that of Charles Darwin or the wagoner Mr. Foggett. He had seldom seen her in ordinary society, where her shyness must have surpassed even his own.

"This is not a thing I do every day," he insisted. "My pupils may ignore me, but they do so without malice. Cutler is crafty. However I try to make my case for science and rational thought, he will trick me into speaking of Darwin."

"Well forevermore. Speak of Darwin."

"I will, eventually. With pupils who might listen. But in this so-called lyceum, one mention of the name will give Cutler the right to end my lecture and open his own. So he believes. He truly knows nothing of Darwin, Mary. But he hates to discuss even the methods of scientific inquiry. His brand of science is an edifice built of scriptures and saints."

"A strange science that must be."

"Strange and fearsome. He needs no evidence to convict me as a witch. With my pupils watching, he will build his pyre and burn me before their eyes."

"You describe the behavior of a frightened man. Half the world fears Darwin, of course, and the rest have yet to hear of him. But Cutler most especially seems to fear *you*, Thatcher. Why should he?"

Thatcher regarded his friend's face: the open, trusting innocence and unexamined courage. "I know you feel isolated in your
work, Mary. But isolation is a far kinder place than the wolf den of
ambitious men where I have to make my way."

Again her look shifted to one of pain. He had belittled her.
What an odd business it was, to speak of men's concerns with a
woman. "I'm sorry, I've made a thoughtless presumption. You work
with colleagues, as I do. So you know how men are, afraid of anyone
who would expose them as fools. They protect themselves by doing
it to others."

"I suppose they might." She was unconvinced.

She had spent her life among untypical men, he realized. For
better and worse: cursed in marriage, blessed in scientific pursuits.
"You have had good fortune," he offered carefully. "This is not
presumption but observation. Men like Darwin and Gray are earnest investigators at the frontier of a new world. I wonder how you
found them."

She blinked, seeming surprised. "I wrote to them. For exactly
that reason."

"So you did. I'm afraid I am stuck with the rear guard. Cutler is an old authority. Men like him dread new views, for fear
they'll have to set aside their hard-earned credentials and begin
their climb again at the bottom rung."

"But you haven't asked Cutler to be anything he is not. Why
should you not be allowed to give tools of understanding to those
coming up behind him?"

"Because his explanations are convoluted and fanciful, and he
knows it. Darwin explains geographic distribution with beautiful simplicity, compared with the buttresses and gargoyles of Cutler's angel bridges. His strange science is a falling house. If I train
young eyes to be observant, they will see cracks in his construction
of the universe."

"I think his lecture circuit will not last long. If he accepts nothing new at all."

"He speaks to those who want nothing new."

"And that is most people nowadays, I suppose."

"That is most people nowadays. They hunger for any crumb of explanation that sustains their old philosophies." Thatcher thought of the riot he'd seen in the Boston square, the scarecrow Darwin hanging from a lamppost, the crowd terrified witless at the prospect of shedding comfortable beliefs and accepting new ones. If people were thus, Thatcher wondered why the shedding came so easily to himself and his friend. Perhaps they both had a tactical advantage: Mary, reared in her finishing school to behave as an empty vessel, and Thatcher, who began life in a grimy, unsheltering family with no proper philosophies at all, or a book to its name.

"I suppose it is the nature of our times," Mary said. "Dangerous, as I've heard you say. We are a nation of the bereaved, half burned to the ground. People want comfort."

"They do," he agreed. "To be shut up tight in their pumpkin shells."

"While the shocking Mr. Greenwood attempts to pull Creation from under their boot soles," she said, with a marvelous twinkle.

"Abetted by the scandalous Mrs. Treat."

"I will leave you to your labors." She did, and he missed her instantly.

⚹

The view from his perch was harrowing: a crowd of human faces and no other species. How could anyone get a sensible bearing on life from the stage of an auditorium, or make any useful statements from that position? Thatcher had never addressed an audience larger than the ramshackle dozen in a classroom. As Mary had said, this was only a multiple of that same ramshackle, along with a sprinkling of teachers firmly committed to ignoring his every word. The appraisal did nothing to calm his nerves.

At least this audience seemed captivated less with Thatcher than the plump, empty armchair to his right. He joined them in gazing at the chair, mate to the one on which he sat, green-and-white-striped chintz with ghosts of tea stains on the voluptuous arms. The chairs had been brought out from Cutler's office, which he furnished like a Bouguereau brothel. It was predictable that Cutler would keep himself elsewhere until the last minute while Thatcher sat on display like some What-Is-It? of P. T. Barnum's, with the consequence of traumatizing Thatcher and proving Cutler's superior importance. Thatcher prayed this might be the day when grandiosity finally sublimated the man from solid to gas, leaving Thatcher here below to conduct an interview with himself.

But now here he came, striding down the aisle like a fighter to the ring. Thatcher applied himself to maintaining control of his bodily functions.

"Greetings! Greetings all! Pupils, esteemed instructors, I thank you . . ." Once on the stage he bowed a little from the waist with hand(s) held stiffly at his thighs, a move calculated to draw applause. All those present obliged. In just one term he had managed to tune this body of pupils like an instrument. "I ask for your full attention this afternoon in our *lyceum* presented by our science teacher Mr. Greenwood. Now as you know, the lyceum was the location of the Peripatetic school of Aristotle . . ."

Thatcher could ill afford to lose concentration this early in the match, but Cutler's rambling introductions were always the same. Tensely he awaited his cue, which eventually arrived: "and without further ado I present to you Mr. Greenwood."

Thatcher stood to accept a handshake and they took their seats, knees angled slightly toward one another as was the custom in these pony shows. Thatcher loosed one button of his coat, fixed his eyes on the sturdy lintel of the door at the back of the hall, and issued the opening sentence of the lecture he'd spent one day writing and four days memorizing in Mary's carriage house. His plan for this lyceum was to plow like a mule through the history of practical science from Kepler's laws of motion to the modern breakthroughs of Lister and Pasteur, thus evading all questions about Darwin's theory. Failing that, he would meticulously avoid the word *evolution* by calling the process "descent with modification." Both Darwin and Asa Gray used the same trick.

For several minutes Thatcher engaged a dizzying fantasy of speaking without breath or pause for the full allotted time, then exiting the hall with his fists in the air. Deprived of oxygen though it was, his brain seemed to lift from his shoulders like a hot air balloon. As he billowed toward the eighteenth century he sensed from his peripheral vision the impatient twitch, the upper body leaning forward. The sharpening of the knife.

"Now Mr. Greenwood . . ." Cutler interrupted, rudely speaking over Thatcher, who had given him no other option.

"Professor Cutler?"

"Let us clarify. You described Mr. Hooke's discovery of the cell in 1665."

"I did."

"And you briefly mentioned his contemporary who disproved the theory of spontaneous generation. Please tell us more about this Mr. Redi, or should I say, *Signor* Redi. I presume the man was an Italian?"

"You are absolutely correct. Francesco Redi was Italian, like so many great innovators, and also some of my pupils, as they have pointed out to me." Thatcher took a moment to smile at the audience, ingratiating himself to every Persichetti and Petrofaccio in the house. Then turned back to Cutler. "I don't claim to be an expert on Redi's work, but my professors at Harvard respected him as a father of our field, founder of experimental biology." Harvard was a deliberate stab; Cutler had attended no university.

"And please enlighten us, how did he do that?"

Thatcher took a calculated risk. "With maggots, sir."

The stir of laughter in the hall coincided perfectly with Cutler's look of dismay. Thatcher relaxed by another inch. Cutler might have tuned this instrument, but Thatcher's ken of its range was beyond his opponent's.

Cutler found no erudition to offer on the subject of maggots. "Well, sir. Indeed. For the sake of our young ladies, I hope you have no plans to repeat this experiment."

"I find the young ladies in my classes are entirely as clever and curious as their counterparts, Professor Cutler. And that is our good fortune because they outnumber us three to one." Again came the appreciative stir from the audience. "But no, we have no plans to replicate Redi's famous experiment. I would be glad to describe it for the audience, though. Since you asked?"

Cutler did not respond.

"Very well then. In earlier times, people believed living things could derive from nonliving matter. They thought fish sprang from mud, for example, and mice from corn cribs. That maggots came spontaneously to life out of rotting meat. They believed they saw these things every day, but they weren't looking very closely. It was Redi who first devised a truly scientific experiment to test this hypothesis. He placed fresh meat in two jars; one he left open to the air, the other he covered with a cloth. Within a few days the meat in the open jar was crawling with . . ."

Thatcher paused here and made a deferential bow to his commander.

". . . with living things, shall we say. Larvae. But the meat in the covered jar had no such creatures at all. Redi did find them crawling on the outside of the cloth. Where flies had laid their eggs in frustration, you see, not being able to get inside. He proved that life comes only from life. It does not spring up spontaneously from dead and disparate matter. Thus he disproved the long-held theory of spontaneous generation."

Cutler nodded thoughtfully, but the affect was a ruse; the fangs were bared. The serpent would strike. "Then how would you, or would *Signor Redi* if you prefer, how do you men of science explain the generation of the original life on our earth?"

"Well, sir, that is very simple. We do not. What we admire about Redi's experiment is the simplicity of its design. The hypothesis was that maggots derived directly from meat, without intervention of the fly and the egg. Remove the fly and egg from the meat, and the hypothesis is disproved by observed results."

"I see. You concern yourselves with simple little questions, and satisfy yourselves with simple little answers."

"Simple answers, bit by bit, lead to large truths. In this case, hundreds of scientists performed similar experiments on other kinds of matter, over many years, finding not one instance of life spontaneously generated from nonlife. Leading us to the modern scientist Louis Pasteur, who has worked with variously constructed bottles to exclude—"

"Did any of these scientists prove—"

Thatcher wriggled past the interruption. "—who devises bottles that can maintain a sterile environment, excluding contamination of life-forms from the outside air."

"Did any of these scientists *prove*," Cutler demanded, for Cutler would not be wriggled past, "that God did not create all forms of life on earth by fiat, out of chaos?"

Thatcher looked at him. "Sir. No one could make such a big bottle as that."

At this the audience burst into its own spontaneous life. Even Mademoiselle Hirstberger might have laid aside her magazine.

Cutler was feigning composure but Thatcher recognized the extra pomp in his cadence that signaled outrage.

"I suppose you find the Scripture an *amusement*, Mr. Greenwood, but I do not, and it is my duty as an educator to impress upon my pupils the same respect." He turned to the audience, and Thatcher's heart fell. Cutler had traveled the nation for years as a professional orator. He would not lose this contest.

"Children, do not become confused by what you hear on this stage today, because we have proof of God's plan for our wondrous sphere. Of course we do. It is our holy Bible. And this truth is credited by all men. No scrupulous scientist would try to steal from us God's promises to man. And what are these promises?"

Cutler turned unexpectedly to Thatcher then, seeming to invite the continuation of his march toward modern enlightenment.

"I'm sorry, I'm not sure which promises you mean. Shall I . . . should I continue with Louis Pasteur?"

Cutler shook his head sadly, sharing with the audience his deep sorrow for Thatcher. "The contract our Almighty has made with man. How could any of us forget his promises to us? Man's supremacy over the earth. Man's power of articulate speech, man's gift of reason, his free will, his fall and his redemption. How could we forget the incarnation of the Eternal Son, and the indwelling of the Eternal Spirit? These gifts cannot be reconciled with any story of our creation except the divine. Children, do not let yourselves be degraded. You were created in the image of our redeemer."

Cutler turned back to Thatcher and swept the air with his single hand as if ushering his companion through a doorway. "Now we have set a few things straight, I pray you. Go on with your presentation."

Thatcher touched his fingertips together and felt his pulse pounding as he struggled to swim from this wreck. He started from the beginning with his mnemonic: Pack a bag, lad. Ptolemy

Avicenna Copernicus Kepler Boyle and Galileo Lavoisier Avoga-
dro Doppler. But what had become of Occam and Newton? He'd
covered Redi, obviously, more than adequately, but there was another trick for the moderns that escaped him now completely. Pasteur, Leeuwenhoek, something, and Priestley. Where did that leave
Joule and Kelvin? And Bacon! The pioneer empiricist Bacon, completely left behind. *Damnation.* Thatcher despaired to hear a faint
whimper escape his own throat. There was no saving himself now,
he'd got his centuries crossed. He had lost his place.

⨯

Only the odium of winter at her solstice could conceive this demon
hybrid of wind, snow, and frozen rain that was stinging his face.
He pulled his hat low and hurried to get from the school building
as fast and far as possible. The term was ended and the holidays
begun, with *that* humiliation. If he'd thought to wish his pupils
a happy Christmas before dismissing them, he had no memory of
it now. His bowels were in knots, his face burned, his shoes were
inadequate to this weather, and suddenly out of nowhere, someone
was walking beside him. A bear in a coat.

"Well done, man! The walls of Jericho are a-trembling, I feel it."

"Carruth. You've picked a ghastly day for a walk. I told you I'm
not your man."

"Not my man? For standing up to the tyrants? What did I just
witness, then?"

"Damn it!" Thatcher now felt he might be sick on the foot of
one of Landis's blasted maples. "Do *not* tell me you just witnessed
that disgrace. Do not!"

Carruth obliged.

"Do you poke your nose into everything that happens in this
village? Why waste your time on a trifling school assembly?"

"You think I would have missed it?"

"I wish you had. I wish we both had. Now I suppose you'll write it up for your paper. Did you enjoy the spectacle of the rat getting lured from his hole?"

Carruth's laugh was jollier than necessary. "Man, the rat wasn't lured. That barmy zealot crawled down the hole with his pistols blazing. He would have chased you right to the core of the earth, he was that determined."

"He was that determined."

Thatcher felt he now understood the suffering of saints who'd had the skin peeled from their bodies. But Carruth was clapping him on the back in a congratulatory way. "And still you came out of it alive! I've seen men less injured by cannon shot than you were in there, and here you still stand. Revolutionary fortitude, my friend."

"Is that what you think? That I'm still standing."

Thatcher in fact was walking east on Plum at a gait bordering on a canter, driven by a craving to get himself from this place. The problem was, to where? Going home to Polly and Rose and their festival mood would be unbearable. At this moment he could face no human companions, who would require him to fabricate a palatable version of today's events, nor could he face being alone without such a story, anywhere. Every place on the earth was the wrong place for Thatcher Greenwood.

"You held your own," Carruth insisted.

"I came apart completely. After Cutler called in the horsemen of the apocalypse to trample the Enlightenment."

"You had a scramble there in the middle, before you got your sea legs back. But I only saw it because I have a fear of crowds myself. I know the symptoms."

"*You?*" This ox of a man, intimidated, was beyond imagining.

"You stuck it through, Greenwood. Didn't you hear your pupils cheering for you? They saw their master in good form facing down old Captain Ahab, fending him off with the saber of rational thought. And maggots!"

"You're mixing your dramatis personae. Captain Ahab's enemy was a maniacal whale. And Ahab had a peg leg. Not a hook for a hand."

"You empiricists. Can't a man have a little poetic license?"

"Save it for your newspaper, Carruth."

Finally his venom had punctured the thick hide. Carruth went quiet. Thatcher regretted striking out at this man, who only wished him well. A friend, as he'd said, who knew their common enemies.

"I'm sorry. You and your weekly are a rare breath of honesty in this town."

Carruth shrugged.

"You should leave me. Go home to your bandicoots, Carruth. They'll be wanting their happy Christmas. I am fit company for no one right now, not even my wife and family."

Carruth cuffed his shoulder. "Women are good for the spirits. It's only a bad day, friend. After worse ones than this, the sun still rises."

"No. An *impossible* day, at the end of an impossible year, in this impossible town where even the trees are bullied into conformity. Where just now I would give everything I own for a shot of whiskey."

"Come with me, then. You may want several. They'll cost you less than you think."

"What, here in this saloonless town, in the broad light of afternoon?"

"Here and now. I have excellent inside sources."

Carruth hooked his arm into Thatcher's, just long enough to steer him south, then released him. With hands in their pockets and heads ducked against the gale, the two men crossed the decorous expanse of Landis Avenue and headed into an unadorned alley behind the steam and flour mill.

"You're a font of surprises, Carruth."

"Those are my line of business, as I reckon." He threw Thatcher an odd glance: his face, just visible between hat and upturned collar, was creased in a jolly grimace. "We like to call them revelations."

11

∞

Revelations

When her phone buzzed, Willa was lying on a mattress on the floor with Dusty for the naptime coercion. He was gaining on civility but still resisted afternoon naps more fiercely than seemed possible for a five-month-old. He would get so tired his head drooped on its stalk, but even with the afternoon bottle he refused to drift off like a normal baby. He sucked at the formula with a furrowed brow until his lunch turned from liquid to squeaky air, then howled at life's injustices. Willa had tried offering a second bottle to follow the first. Everyone had tried something, rocking, strollering him around, even leaving him to "cry it out" as experts now recommended, but this kid could wail for hours. His grip on wakefulness must have been powered by a fear of loss. In his world, the minute you closed your eyes, a mother could vanish.

It was Tig, with her uncanny patience, who discovered the cure was physical reassurance on a near-superhuman scale. Thus the afternoon ritual of lying with him for as long as it took, rubbing his tummy in circles and singing until words and tune petered out into mindless, rhythmic shooshing sounds. Slowly the gaze would rise to the ceiling, the lids would blink and finally close. That was the exact moment Willa's phone woke up on the arm of the sofa, silenced, luckily, but well out of reach. She let it go. The call vibrated itself out and went still within thirty seconds.

She lay with her chin on her forearms admiring the baby's wren-feather eyelashes and delicate nostrils, the bottom lip tucked into the infant overbite. The melon of belly expanding, contracting. Nowadays babies were always put to sleep on their backs; in face-down position they would succumb to SIDS, if the pediatricians were to be believed. This "back-is-best" propaganda was news to Willa, whose kids were born in the decade when babies *always* had to be put to sleep on their tummies, lest they die of SIDS. The absolutism of these Cheshire-cat dogmas seemed funny, or maybe valiant. Probably nobody knew why little lives sometimes evaporated like smoke, but all guardians wanted to be given the amulet of prevention. And they didn't want "maybe."

Willa's phone went off again and she watched it buzz like a big square beetle, inching itself with each vibration toward a leap off the arm of the sofa. Even Dixie noticed it, from the position she'd recently secured at the foot of the mattress, and she watched Willa expectantly. Humans responded to such cues. The caller's persistence was piquing Willa's curiosity, but she stayed put. Dusty wouldn't have grown roots into this sleep yet, and she knew getting up would trigger the salvos. If she could keep him asleep awhile they would be rewarded with an evening of reasonable temper, and no phone call was worth risking that. Besides, Willa was not the average phone owner who felt at every ring the tug of some potentially fantastic news. Some other phone *that* would be.

This mattress on the living room floor was now Willa and Iano's bedroom, wedged between the sofa and the nonfunctional fireplace. The sofa was their nightstand. The horrid paisley print she'd wanted to reupholster forever was now hidden under a drift of contact lens cases, books, and uncorrected papers, and so there was one problem solved, anyway. To a visitor's eye their home might have the air of a disaster shelter, but Willa had no plans for entertaining. She'd made no new friends in Vineland, settling for electronic exchange with her many old ones, mostly to complain about Vineland. This living room was the normalization of their present shambles. They were cold, all the time. For the first time since the kids were around ten and enjoyed the nearness of dirt, they were all using sleeping bags. From the camping gear they'd also pulled out the old green propane stove to use in the kitchen after a ruptured gas line forced them to shut off the main. (With Nick's oxygen in the house they'd be crazy to take chances, said Mr. Petrofaccio, who had seen a thing or two in the arena of household explosions.) Willa purchased a whopping electric space heater she set up on the ground floor, knowing it would sap their future via credit card payments and electric bills, but seeing no better option. It kept the house a few degrees above the jeopardy zone for plumbing and human life. Sometimes after dinner the whole family went to the coffee shop on the corner to stoke up on warmth before the long night. When Willa dressed Dusty in his one-piece footed flannel pajamas, she seriously wished they made these in her size. To stanch the icy drafts blowing down the chimney they'd stuffed the fireplace with garbage bags full of the leaves that fell from the two giant yard trees.

Their only nice furniture was the antique walnut crib that had launched Willa and her Knox forebears. Now it stood beside the TV, but they seldom used it for naps due to the awkwardness of standing over Dusty to massage him to sleep. This mattress on the floor had become a family bed—an odd arrangement for their kind of people but common enough worldwide, Willa knew, in countries with closer-knit families and meaner economies. She and

Iano had dragged it downstairs at the first sign of snow through the cracks in their walls. Dixie had crept in guiltily to curl up close to their sleeping bags for warmth—Dixie who never in her long life had been allowed on furniture, but who now had a palsy in her hind legs and other signs of being not long for this world. Next to arrive was Tig, who'd tried stuffing the breaches in her room with socks, but gave up as the temperatures fell. She spent most nights at Jorge's but sometimes ended up there with her bumpy little spine pressed against Willa and her thin arms woven around the baby. The first time Willa woke up in this fragrant jumble of dog-daughter-husband-baby she lay in the dark feeling tears crawl down her cheekbones. She hadn't been this close to Tig since a fifth-grade softball concussion put them on a week of night watch.

Not everyone shared the family bed, of course. Nick had been moved home for the holidays in a Cadillac of a hospital bed, allegedly covered by Medicaid, that plugged into the wall. Zeke was expected on Christmas day, but had absented himself to Boston for the month with the report that Good Money was starting to get somewhere. Willa was happy for Zeke on principle, and stopped asking his intentions regarding Dusty.

Unbelievably, her phone rang again. Curiosity now congealed into dread. She eased her weight off the mattress and crept across the carpet like a soldier under fire.

"Willa! I've been trying and trying to reach you."

Chris Hawk. Not a death in the family. She lay on her back letting her heartbeat slow to normal. "I just got the baby to sleep," she whispered. "Let me call you back." A novel thought struck her then: this could be *good* news. It happened. "Wait. It's about Mary, right? This is her house. Please say yes."

Silence. So, there went that.

"Okay," she hissed, "your big emergency is to tell me I'm dead in the water."

"It's not that simple. Can you come over?"

"I've got a baby and an old man here who both need tending, so no. It is that simple. If it isn't yes, it's no."

"Or something else you didn't expect. Just call me back, okay?"

It wasn't entirely true that she'd made no new friends. Christopher Hawk was dedicated to her cause, and Willa spent more time with him than with most members of her family. She still couldn't get him to laugh, but they'd exchanged some confidences and found common interests. He'd done a double master's in linguistics and history with a specialty in period slang. His thesis on Victorian obscenity made him a professional collector, and Willa took hypocritical pleasure in passing along some of Nick's most egregious curses. But Christopher was not a guy you had over for dinner. He had peculiar aversions, allergies galore, and according to himself, no life outside the historical society. Willa enjoyed the friendship partly because it made her own life seem normal.

She waited another five minutes to be sure Dusty was securely down, then called him back from the kitchen, keeping her voice close to a whisper. In the odd way that conversational volume is contagious, so did Chris.

"Sorry, you don't have Mary's house. The news there is bad. Her house is gone."

"What do you mean, gone? What's your source?" Dixie had gotten up from the mattress and plodded into the kitchen to keep an eye on Willa. She lay down in the doorway, an audible drop of bones.

"I found a stash of envelopes with the address that were separated from Mary's correspondence, stuffed in a throwaway file. What moron did that, I can't say. I mean, I *know*, but I can't say. She's on my board of directors. She volunteers one day a week and I spend the next two cleaning up after her."

"Chris. The facts, please."

"Okay, all these letters from Charles Valentine Riley are addressed to her house at 640 East Plum, between 1870 and 1875. The numbering system has changed since then, but I cracked the code on that a long time ago. We have the old and new addresses of several public buildings and we can extrapolate. It's mostly a matter of dropping every block number by three hundred, but in that section of town it's only by one hundred. Now, Charles Riley, you remember who he is?"

"The insect guy. Let's come back to Mary's house being gone." Willa looked out the kitchen window at a balmy day like no December she'd ever seen, and with her free hand moved dishes into the sink, harnessing her impatience. To converse with Chris was to wander in a maze of extraneous details. Maybe all historians were compulsive about the particulars, but Willa got the picture on why this one didn't have a lot of friends.

"The address puts Mary's house one door down from yours. On the corner lot."

"Oh. Over there. So it's *gone*." Willa saw the story of her life, already written: one house away from hallelujah.

"It must have come down mid-to-late twentieth century. Ironically, the stipulation house is still standing on the back of the lot, but they tore down the main house. To make way for that reprehensible hovel with the vinyl siding."

"Right." Willa felt defensive on behalf of Jorge's family. It's not as if they tore down Mary Treat's house with their bare hands. She cast an envious eye at the little ivy-covered garage that had stood the test of time. Tig and Jorge had been cleaning it out, for no reason Willa was allowed to know. "And you rang my phone off the hook to tell me this bad news. Sorry, am I repeating myself?"

"My dear. History is not good news or bad news, it's just one big story unreeling. There are no small parts, only small actors."

"And small paychecks. I get the part of Mary Treat's neighbor. Thank you."

"Listen. A person of interest lived in your house."

"Oh yeah? Tell me."

"He was a schoolteacher. Hired as part of the original staff of Vineland High School, we have records of that. He would have been living in your house the year they opened the school and President Grant came to town."

"And you figured all this out how?"

"From Mary Treat's correspondence. This guy comes up in her letters to Riley. She's listing his qualifications, maybe trying to help her neighbor find a new job."

"What are you saying, *her* letters? You told me you only have correspondence that people sent to her. The letters that were in her possession when she died."

"I told you I've been trying to track her letters down, in every collection where I know they have to be. Asa Gray's papers at Harvard, Darwin's at the British Museum. The Smithsonian. These archivists keep emailing me back saying, 'Mary *who?*' She's not a wife or mistress so she falls through the cracks. Probably they see a woman's name on the letter and catalog it under 'personal,' not 'colleague.'"

Willa said nothing, recalling Iano had made the same assumption. Dixie was starting to make a high-pitched whine they'd learned not to ignore. Her bladder no longer lasted beyond the edge of the yard, if even that. Willa let her out the kitchen door.

"So I kept telling them to go back through the personal files and try to find her. I finally got some cooperation from the National Agricultural Library. They sent copies of almost a hundred letters Mary wrote to Charles Valentine Riley."

"What?" Willa nearly dropped a plate. *"When?"*

"They came Tuesday but I only got into them this morning, after I got rid of Madame Historical Board."

For three whole days Chris had been sitting on a lode of Mary Treat letters. He was territorial, Willa knew this, and tried to give him some grace. He'd been the master of his dusty little universe over there for a long, long time before Willa showed up. She framed a courteous request. "I would like very much to read those letters."

"That's *why* I've been trying to *call* you."

"Oh."

"So, I wasn't really looking for him but the schoolteacher neighbor keeps popping up. I think Mary had an important relationship with this guy."

"Really. You mean, *relationship* relationship? Because that husband of hers was a narcissistic cheating asshole. I keep hoping she had a boy toy tucked away somewhere."

Chris made a huff of disapproval. Through the window Willa watched Dixie pace through her routine: first she circled the big oak, then walked across to the beech and peed on its foot, then returned to the house. Always the same, as if some director had blocked this on her script.

"Sorry, you think I'm being prurient." She opened the door to let Dixie back in.

"I think you're letting your emotions influence your reading of history."

"My *emotions* are why we're here. I have a passionate attachment to the money I might get for saving my house."

"That's different. That's motivation. For us to do accurate research."

Willa tried again for contrition. "Please tell me more about the schoolteacher. Can we spin him as a Vineland hero?"

"More of an antihero, actually. He was in the middle of a major controversy and he might have gotten run out of town. Mary was definitely on his side."

"What kind of controversy?"

"Over teaching evolution. He got in trouble with the principal and then the town fathers. He was reprimanded, they put on this big debate in Plum Hall to try to shut him down, and from there it gets ugly. This thing was in letters to the editor for years."

"Wow. You mean like the Scopes trial?" But this would have been many decades earlier, she realized. How tenacious, the minions of history, clinging to their flat earth.

"Something like the Scopes trial, but more *prurient*. You're going to love this part, Willa. This town had an infamous murder. Looks like your guy was involved."

"What?"

"I told you it was good."

"Holy cow."

Good was not how it struck her at all. From her window Willa had a perfect view between the two big trees, across the yard to the cluttered emptiness where Mary Treat had lived and left no trace. In a house that had taken on absolute dimensions for Willa, where spiders lived in jars, birds built nests in the eaves, and everything was put to the page at a desk in a cozy parlor. Not here, but over there. Now nowhere at all. Willa felt despair, not just for her own lost prospects.

And Chris was insisting she should shift her loyalties to the controversial bit player. *His* house had stood for a century and a half, and that was something. Apparently while the ground shifted perilously under his feet.

"So my guy—*our* guy, I mean. The neighbor. Does he have a name?"

"A name out of a novel. Thatcher Greenwood."

❊

Here was a giant snowman made of twinkling white lights on a chicken wire frame, with garbage can lids for vest buttons and an orange traffic cone for a nose. Here were plywood sleighs with reindeer, and low-rider cars with reindeer, tricked out in Christmas lights. A provocative display under a COEXIST banner had all the Disney princesses dancing with the wrong mates: Snow White in the arms of Aladdin, the Little Mermaid with the Beast. A tableau of mannequins showed Ralphie's friend from *A Christmas Story* licking the frozen flagpole. Nativity scenes abounded, some on the quirky side but mostly earnest. This neighborhood was still called Little Italy but now housed working-class families of many derivations, none of them eager to mess with the born-in-a-manger premise. And all on board with this over-the-top festival of Christmas decoration. Overhead, Willa noticed, even the leafless maples and oaks were looped with strings of lights, suggesting some municipal investment in the way of bucket trucks.

They'd come here at Jorge's suggestion on a weirdly balmy Christmas night. The week had been unseasonably warm, by no means normal according to longtime New Jerseyans, but any potential relief in Willa's household was damped by melting snow on their leaky roof and the impossibility of feeling Christmas spirit while wearing sunglasses. They'd had their Christougena feast on the picnic table in the yard but finished too early, leaving the family restless for some holiday-themed entertainment that was baby friendly and free. Little Italy in Lights wasn't an instant sell, even though Jorge insisted it was a very big deal in Vineland. He was meeting up with his boys over there as soon as it got dark because their ladies were adamant. Tig was agreeable, Zeke thought it sounded lame, Willa was on the fence, Nick and the baby were hostages to the collective will. Iano broke the tie as usual in favor of what-the-hell.

And Jorge was right, all Vineland was there. The neighborhood's streets were blocked off and given over to herds of people who roamed the dusk hailing friends and pushing strollers from house to house admiring the lit-up displays. It felt exotic to be out among hundreds of people, walking, after dark. Willa couldn't shake the feeling of having stepped into some other country.

Jorge caught up to a group of friends that included both his sisters: pretty, outgoing Sondra, the in-home care nurse, and shy Lara, who took care of other people's children at her house, along with her own. Tig fist-bumped herself into the crowd, much happier there than with her own family, Willa noted with the habitual pang. A thousand times she'd asked her mother after this wildling was born, could a mother and child just have bad chemistry? She'd spent years putting careful love letters into Tig's psychic mailbox when what the girl seemed to want in there was birdsong, or a bucket of frogs.

"Heisborn," Iano said. "What is that?"

Willa studied the word made of giant plywood letters, stapled with lights, marching across the whole yard. "I have no idea. Heisborn. Is it that football trophy?"

"No, *moro*. That's Heisman."

The mystery word was planted in a garden of illuminated snowmen, elves, wise men, and shepherds, and a super-lifelike baby doll Jesus on his bed of real hay. Despite the troublesome presence of elves and snowmen in the holy blended family, a placard announced this yard had taken the prize for "Best Religious." This Christmas-light-pallooza was a juried event. Already they'd seen "Best Humorous" and "Best Creative."

Iano moved on with Zeke, who was pushing Nick's wheelchair. The elder ignored the festivities while father and son argued some obscure point about global trade. Willa paused to reposition Generation Four in the baby sling. "What are we going to do with this mess?" she asked him, pulling her fingers through a head of curls beginning to run wild, as Tig's had at that age. Willa tried to settle his weight comfortably in the sling, without success. Zeke had argued against the stroller, saying two fancy chariots would make a bit much of a parade, but he hadn't offered to carry Dusty, who had officially outgrown this carrier.

She ended up walking a little distance behind Tig and her friends, watching with a voyeur's lonely heart. Jorge's "boys" sported a lot of shaved heads and were wearing sleeveless T-shirts, which was pushing it, Willa felt; it wasn't *that* warm. But the young male engine ran on high octane. Intricate tattoos encircled their beautifully muscled upper arms. Jorge had an inked armband of barbed wire that had always struck Willa as self-punitive, but half-obscured in darkness like this, all their markings resembled some secret ancient language. Cuneiform. The ladies wore tight jeans, gold bracelets, and impractical shoes. Willa felt a new soft spot for Jorge, who'd chosen her spiky little daughter despite the obvious group preference for wide bottoms and cascades of telenovela hair. If Jorge had paid some social price, he looked perfectly content now, walking with one arm pulling Tig close. They seemed to be settling the tiff that had kept Tig from sleeping over in recent days. Willa knew only the vague outlines: José Luis had skipped town and left Jorge holding the bag in some manner Tig thought was unfair. But Jorge refused to be mad at his brother. Willa had never seen a family like theirs, a big, loyal household of parentless siblings holding it all together.

Suddenly one of the guys turned on Tig and picked her up by the waist, alarming Willa. But this was a game, they began tossing Tig around like a kid sister while the girls scolded and fluttered their painted nails. All of them laughing, Tig especially. In the end she landed on Jorge's shoulders and there she stayed, riding high as they all kept walking.

"That's weird."

Zeke had caught up to Willa, just in time to disapprove of the spectacle of his sister. She waited to see if he would look at his son cuddled against her chest. He didn't.

"Your dad always used to carry Tig on his shoulders like that in crowds. So she could see more than just people's belt buckles. Remember?"

"I remember childhood, yes. I understood it was supposed to end."

"Of course." People like Willa and Zeke never stopped being surprised when it didn't. She remembered arguing with Iano in Tig's middle school years, calling a halt to the piggybacks, insisting they not condescend because of her stature. Now Willa saw the severity of that judgment. Adult or not, in a crowd like this Tig would see nothing from the ground. Up on Jorge's shoulders she looked ecstatic, the darling champion.

"Did you leave Nick next to the recycling bins?" she asked.

Zeke laughed. "He probably thinks recycling is a communist plot."

Willa smiled. He probably did.

"Dad's got him. They were having technical difficulties."

"Uh-oh. Do we need to go?"

"No, I don't think it was urgent. Only, like, three-alarm curse words, not five."

"'My penis has flowers and bees around it'?"

"Exactly."

A woman with a small child in hand turned to give Willa a look.

"I'm *so* sorry. I didn't mean to say that in English."

The mother moved away from them into a deep crowd that had gathered before a house with an aggressive glow. From this far back Willa could see no details, only glare. The crowd flowed around them. "You should go hang out with the cheerful young people. I'm sure Jorge's cute sisters will let you into the reindeer games."

Zeke shrugged, not really wanting to be there, she could tell.

"You doing okay, honey? It's tough, the holiday scene. We haven't had much time to talk. There are some decisions about Dusty I wanted to talk over with you."

"Oh, I forgot to tell you. I brought the document from the court clerk. It's called a voluntary child custody agreement. Pretty straightforward, we just have to fill it out and sign in front of a notary."

"Oh. That's the route you want to go? I didn't mean to pressure you."

"No, you didn't."

"Okay." By *decisions* Willa meant vaccination schedule, starting solid foods. Her head swam a little. *Custody.* "You didn't seem to think much of the state of our household yesterday, when you first got here."

He'd been shocked to find his gypsy family encamped in the living room. And upset to find clothes and books he'd left upstairs badly water damaged, in a room now uninhabitable. Willa was mortified that she'd overlooked that battleground within the greater arena of their disaster. She'd let him lose a chunk of his life recorded in A+ school papers, attendance certificates, and yearbook testimonials. Zeke had been tight lipped for a few hours but had come around, pointedly telling Willa it wasn't her fault.

Now he shrugged. "You guys will sort things out. It's not like you'll have to pass a home visit from the child welfare lady."

"Well, *that's* a relief," Willa said, trying for levity, feeling overwhelmed.

"At least you own a house. You know, with a family. You're a home."

"Glad you think so."

"I'm saying I thought about this, Mom. I talked to a friend who handles this kind of stuff all the time in her practice. She said it's just paperwork, one way or another, but this is a more robust document than medical power of attorney. It gives you flexibility."

Willa had to wonder whether their particular situation was quite so run-of-the-mill, but he'd obviously spoken with a lawyer. Who else would call a document *robust*? "We shouldn't move too fast," she said. "Any therapist would advise against making huge decisions when you're recovering from a trauma." Willa was in no condition herself for a decision of this order. But Zeke didn't need her worries on top of his own.

"It's not a huge decision. It's just formalizing what we're already doing."

"You'll always be his father. That's permanent."

"Right. I mean, I want to do the right thing. When I get my act together, I will."

"I know, honey. You're my son who does the right thing, and you always will be. For now I just want you to find some peace. Are you doing that?"

"It's been okay. I'm going out, seeing people. And we're getting some really great contacts built, with the business."

"Sorry, but I don't want to hear about the damn portfolios, I'm asking about your mental state. What are you doing to help yourself feel okay?"

"What I do to feel okay is go to ground. That's just me, Mom. The damn portfolios make me feel like a better person."

"What does that even mean, 'going to ground'?"

He thought about this. "I guess, hunker down on my home turf. Find a place where I feel like a success. Sometimes that might mean moving backwards a little. I'm just trying to get back to where I was before everything bad happened."

Before Helene. Which meant before Dusty. From some storms no shelter was possible. "Enough with the mom talk," she said. "Go keep an eye on your sister. Make her introduce you to her pals. I'll wait for Dad and Nick to catch up."

He hesitated a moment, then flashed the smile that had never failed to win people over to Team Zeke. He left her and the crowd absorbed him. She wondered if "going out and seeing people" meant he was starting a whole rebooted life in Boston. He'd never been six months without a girlfriend. Willa wanted that for him again, of course, but not yet, surely. She watched him threading through the crowd, tracking Jorge's group with Tig as its visible masthead.

The crowd thinned, finally allowing Willa a gander at the overly dazzling yard display made of thousands of lights twinkling from tall triangles meant to suggest evergreen trees. Not just a few, a forest. The effect was blinding. She spotted an award placard, "A.C.E.'s Favorite," and that one she knew: Atlantic City Electric. She tried to take the joke without thinking too much of her own ACE bill, probably overdue. It surprised her that Tig could approve of all this gratuitous burning of electricity in a neighborhood that was far from affluent. Then again, Tig might be condemning it right now from her human soapbox. Willa watched Tig's group among all the dark people-shapes backlit by Atlantic City electricity. Zeke had joined them and was visibly interacting. He'd inched back from hollow-eyed despondency to his customary level of social ease: one personality gene he had to have gotten from Iano. Or maybe it just came of having been born gorgeous, for both father and son. Beautiful people liked to claim looks didn't matter, while throwing that currency around like novice bank robbers.

Dusty whimpered and she rubbed his back, regretting the low and cynical spirits she was probably shedding like a virus on the people around her. Any normal woman might feel happy and blessed by a husband's and son's good looks. But *happy* and *blessed* had been in short supply that winter as Willa looked for something to pull her out of her funk. For a while it was Mary Treat, near enough to touch, she'd wrongly believed. After that blow had landed, Willa made herself look toward Christmas when the people she loved would be together. And the day had gone well enough. Greeks did Christmas with church and food, and what Iano's generation lacked in godliness they made up for in the kitchen. The four of them had spent the whole day braising a leg of lamb, making papoutsakia and avgolemono soup and diples, all of them wearing aprons and talking over each other, remembering Christmas feasts in all the many kitchens of their family's life. The sabbatical year in Cyprus when they famously ate an octopus. The grad school apartment where they'd washed dishes in the shower, which Tig and Zeke couldn't possibly remember but swore they did. Whole lambs turned on the spit, the Christmases they'd gone back to Phoenix. Aunt Athena's lemon cake. This remembering should have made Willa happy and it nearly did. And now those dishes were in the sink.

Jorge's group had moved away from the electric forest toward the dark center of an intersection, closer to Willa. She watched Tig dramatically hammering Zeke on the head with her fist, operating like a pile driver from her superior position. Zeke played along, sinking lower with each stroke, but then suddenly he leaped up, grabbed her from Jorge's shoulders and held her in the air for several writhing, screaming seconds while their middle school years passed before Willa's eyes. Zeke had come early into his growth, which accounted for his success with high school sports and girls and probably much of what followed. Tig alone refused to succumb to his charms. When he set her down on her feet she tore into their permanent argument, loudly enough for Willa to hear her shifting between languages, *cabrón* and *pendejo* threading fluidly with "mad cool for the one percent." Willa decided to go look for Iano and Nick.

She found them several blocks behind, trying to change the tank in his portable oxygen system, stymied. Iano brightened. "Willa! Thank God, we're saved."

She was alarmed to see the dial on zero. She'd stuck an extra tank into the mesh basket on the wheelchair without expecting they'd need it. But Nick had been on his portable throughout their Christmas dinner outdoors, and now this extended outing. It was going to be a two-cartridge night—possibly the biggest splurge of their holiday. Her hands trembled as she turned the valves to swap out the cartridges. What kind of world left the critically ill in the hands of amateurs feeling their way in the dark?

"I was so afraid," Iano said. "He tried to tell me how to do it but I couldn't read anything on those little gauges. I was afraid of shutting him off."

"It's not your fault. I should have thought about it earlier."

"Pop, how about it? I almost killed you, but you're going to survive."

Willa's heart pounded, mostly for Iano, who'd been minutes from watching his father asphyxiate in the stupid glow of Christmas lights. That beautiful, buoyant soul would have carried the damage. Whereas Nick seemed indifferent to the narrow escape. Scowling, mute, with a lap blanket covering his disfigured limbs, he stared off down the dark street, pointedly not looking at Willa. Since coming home from rehab he'd hardly spoken to anyone. They could have welcomed the respite, but Nick's silence felt as eerily wrong as the warm December weather. Minus the bluster, Nick was a husk.

"What is it, *moro*? Don't worry. We would have figured it out."

"You would have," she lied.

He stared at her face. "You want me to take Dusty for a while?"

She shook her head, tight lipped, warning him off, because words might unstop the flood of emotion she'd kept pressed in her throat for hours. It was just too embarrassing to walk around sobbing at a festival of Christmas lights. Fake cheer it would have to be. She linked arms with Iano to help push Nick's wheelchair over the uneven pavement, and tried to reconstruct the brief glow she'd felt when they first arrived—the sense of having stepped into some exotic time and place where people went outside at night and walked around together enjoying the neighborhood. But the crowd was thinning out. And Iano wasn't giving her a pass on the fake cheer.

"Tell me. It's Christmas, and you've been sad all day."

"No. It was a good day."

"Don't tell me this, *moro*. You've been sad for a hundred years."

"That's not exactly kind," she said, laughing, and then her eyes and nose began pouring like a faucet, and she had no tissues. She kept such things along with car keys and wallet in the pockets of her coat, which she'd left at home that night. Using an old navy peacoat for a purse worked well for people who left the house only to go to the grocery or walk the dog. Willa's throat constricted around some noise it wanted to make.

"*Moraki mou.* What am I going to do with you?" Iano pulled her head against his shoulder, which made their progress awkward, but they kept walking.

"I don't know. Trade me in."

In their odd formation they made their way down the block surrounded by the ebb-tide energy of a party winding down. She spotted Tig and Zeke. Iano waved them over. "What happened to all your friends?"

"They ditched us," Zeke said. "We're boring."

"They didn't want to be seen with a running-dog hedge fund investor."

"Sorry for helping the economy. I guess your friends don't need jobs."

"Oh right, your richie riches are making jobs happen in Vineland."

"*Ela*," Iano said. "Enough."

"I'm asking. Do they spend their millions on things that create jobs?"

"In this country? Not really. There's only so many goods one person can buy."

Iano stopped so abruptly his silent cargo in the wheelchair pitched forward. "Will you two stop? You're giving your mother a nervous breakdown."

"That's not true," Willa protested.

"Okay, never mind. We love watching our children rip each other to pieces."

"Where *did* your friends go?" Willa asked.

"They decided to drive around. But we wanted to be with our dear darling family." Tig peered closely at Willa's face. "Are we giving you a nervous breakdown?"

"No! I'm fine."

"In this century it's known as depression," Zeke said, sounding territorial.

"Don't worry about me," Willa said, sounding pathetic even to herself.

"But we had such a perfect Christmas!" Tig insisted, sounding twelve.

"I know, honey. Maybe it's just . . . not what I pictured for us at this point in life."

"Your mother misses Virginia."

"No!" Willa looked at Iano, surprised. "That's not it. I never minded us moving around. I just thought we'd end up settled somewhere. In a house with, you know . . ."

"A roof and walls?" Zeke asked, in a jocular way, but Willa felt stung. A half hour earlier it had been home enough for his son.

"I *thought*," she said, "*eventually*, we'd get to stop worrying and retire in some kind of reasonable comfort. You two would come visit us. With grandkids. From places where you had your own houses and jobs."

"Uh-oh," Tig said. "Mom's having a visitation from the Ghost of Capitalist Fantasies Past."

Willa bristled. "I don't think I'm asking for too much."

"Nobody thinks they're asking for too much," Tig bristled back.

"Fine, then, Tig. Why are we walking around here in fantasy land? This is a travesty. A lot of poor people pretending they have money to waste on holly fucking jolly and electricity. Why is everybody pretending?"

"Good question, Mom," she said, winning in three words, as Tig did.

Willa decided she was done with motherhood for the night, if not the remainder of her allotted years. Somehow they'd made a complete circuit and were approaching the Heisborn yard again. The baby doll in the manger was such a realistic replica Willa had briefly been fooled—alarmed, actually—the first time around. Under scrutiny she saw it was handcuffed with a zip tie to its wooden bed, a precaution against thievery, she presumed. Such realism would come at a price.

"Let me just say," Zeke said, "I'm not the one still parking my ass at home with the parents."

"Let me just say, I'm not the one that abandoned my child."

"Tig, honestly," Willa said.

Tig ignored her. "You never answer me. Where does it go? All this fabulous responsible money you're investing."

"All over the world. Microloans, helping people grow their businesses, that kind of thing. And for every transaction, a little bit for Zeke, Mike, and Jake." Willa watched his discreet little victory dance and understood this was Zeke "going to ground."

"The three musketeers rape the planet. Go team."

"Grow or die, that's just the law of our economy, Tiggo. You can't get around it. It's like Darwin's law of survival of the fittest."

"Except your law is invented and natural laws aren't. What you can't get *around* is there's no more room to grow."

"Do you remember," Iano asked, "when you were little and I used to stop the car and put you both out in the grass by the side of the road?"

Willa linked arms with Iano and gently turned him away from the fight. "Remind me why we didn't drive off and leave them?"

Iano only now noticed the lifelike doll in the nativity scene. "Christ, look at that. We could have bought ourselves a couple of those."

"I suppose in AD zero," Willa mused, "the pediatricians of Bethlehem were saying back-is-best, like they are now."

Iano nodded. "Thank goodness. Think how all the crèches would look if the babies were lying ass-up in the manger."

The offspring were escalating to a decibel level that was drawing some notice. "So it's survival of whoever rips the food out of somebody else's mouth. That's one heck of a mean old world. Extra bad for midgets. That's what you want?"

"Want want *want*!" Tig shouted. "That's the only force in your equation. So you have to be a whore, licking the balls of the Wall Street bull."

Nick's shoulders heaved in a gurgling chuckle: his first sign of life in hours.

"Oh. He is born!" Willa said. It struck her as revelations often do, after no one cares anymore about solving the puzzle. HEISBORN was He Is Born, badly executed. The letters were too big to fit across the yard with proper spacing between the words.

"What the hell," Zeke said. "Mom's gone all Jesusy on us."

"Trust me, I haven't."

At last the family went quiet. Tig gave her another probing

look. "Did you see the alien invasion one, Mom?" she asked. "It's in the next block down."

"Think I missed the alien invasion."

Willa thought she must have imagined the compassion in that look, but Tig startled her by grabbing her by the hand. "Come on. It's my favorite, you have to see it before we go home." Tig seemed so young, a little girl tugging her mother toward something she needed to share. She didn't drop Willa's hand until they stood looking at the display, a busy installation of little goggle-eyed creatures and spaceships covering the lawn, like some madcap sci-fi Grandma Moses. It took Willa a moment to understand that everything was made from plastic bottles. Bleach bottles, soda bottles, all cut apart and cleverly reassembled into personae with bottle-cap eyes and bulging, jointed limbs. No two were alike. Willa spotted a one-horned, one-eyed flying purple people eater. The cultural reference suggested a creator of a certain age.

"Take me to your laundry," Tig said.

"That's pretty cool," Willa agreed. "Did it win any prize?"

"Nah. Of course it wouldn't. There aren't any lights."

Willa hadn't noticed until she pointed it out, the display had no lights. The recycled plastic visitors to planet Earth were taking advantage of recycled light, basking in the electric glow of neighbors on all sides.

><

Crying jags and sleep problems were to be expected, the pediatrician explained, as part of the grieving process. Willa recalled staring at the doctor, and was embarrassed in retrospect. He meant the baby, not her. But maybe it was that simple: in a life of loss, people tossed and turned. They cried. Dr. Patel had been patient with their long list of questions at Dusty's six-month checkup, promising Willa and Tig he was out of the worry zone: eating well, gaining weight, hitting his developmental milestones, ready to try out solid foods. They could relax. Dusty wasn't likely to die on them in the night.

Nick was.

"This is why we have families," Willa explained in the darkness of Nick's room. "So we never have to go a single day without worrying ourselves sick."

The oxygen compressor hissed and hissed, waves against a shore.

"I used to have this dream when I was little," Tig said dreamily. Tig who was still, who would always be, little. "About trying to carry water. I was supposed to get it from here to over there, or something bad would happen. You or Dad or somebody might die. I didn't have a bucket or anything, just my arms. I kept scooping up water like a bundle of sticks, and of course it would all just run out."

Willa nodded. "That's what life will feel like when you have children."

The two of them sat watching Nick sleep, propped nearly upright in his fancy bed, chin jutting forward. His body always leaned like this, reaching for something even in his sleep. The nurses had called it "air hunger." An instinct. The body remembers to survive, even when the mind signs off.

"I do," Tig said.

"You do what?"

"Have a child. Dusty."

"Of course. You'll always have Dusty. He's your nephew."

"Mom. Are you not seeing? Or just pretending, because Zeke's the golden child."

"Oh, honey. Don't do this."

Tig reached down to the floor to pick up her knitting. Since Dusty's birth she'd made him a series of jackets, larger as he grew, all based on the same pattern: a single oddly shaped piece with corners and angles. When she finished she would fold it, stitch up the shoulder seams, and voilà, a baby kimono. She'd also knitted rafts of hats and booties, but the origami jackets amazed Willa every time. This one had bold stripes, orange and blue if she remembered right. It was too dark in the room to see color.

Mother and daughter curled together in the recliner they all called the Big-Ass Chair, constructed for people of that particular make. It was an old thing, brown corduroy, beyond huge. Tig could lie in it sideways. Willa hadn't seen a piece of furniture like it before or known such things existed, but she'd seen the asses of course, so it stood to reason. The recliner had belonged to one of Sondra's clients, now in hospice, and the family wanted the furniture gone. Jorge brought it over in a friend's truck with a bevy of guys to carry it in, after learning someone had to be in there every night keeping watch over Nick. The cannula often fell off his face, or he slumped into the wrong position and lapsed into choking gasps that alerted the watcher to reposition the cannula or the patient.

Usually one person did the duty alone; usually it was Iano. But Zeke's arrival had shaken things around. To head off his awkward, unaffordable proposal of going to a hotel, Willa suggested he share the living room mattress with Iano for the few days he planned to stay. She and Tig would take the chair. It was seductively comfy, now that they'd spent enough Febreze on it to dismiss the faint scent of urine, so Willa didn't mind being there. Or hadn't, until Tig went cold on her. As she could have foreseen.

Willa tried stroking her head, and surprisingly Tig let her. She'd never explored her daughter's locs and now found their texture both softer and firmer than she expected. Each one grew from its own little square plot on Tig's scalp, within a grid of perfectly even partings. To spend a night like this, inches from her daughter's skull and everything it held inside, was a tender agony Willa could have explained to no one but her mother.

"Zeke is no more golden than you are," she tried. "You connect with your children differently but love them the same. I know you never believe me. But it's true."

"I'm too old for you to tell me stuff like that, Mom."

"Apparently you're not."

"I'm not asking you to love me. I'm saying I love Dusty and I want to keep him."

"Sweetheart. This is not a 'can we keep him' situation. He's not a puppy."

Tig turned to look at her, dark eyes glinting in darkness. Willa had an uneasy feeling she could keep no secrets from those eyes, including the papers she and Zeke would soon be taking to a notary.

"I know what you're saying about Zeke," Willa conceded. "I don't think he ever bonded properly with the baby. He was so depressed."

"He can have his reasons. I'm not trying to make this about Zeke."

"But he's coming back to himself now. He's a lot better than he was."

"And he didn't bond with his child. He wants to be in Boston and make money and hang with his friends."

"He wants to make money to help keep a roof over our heads."

"*Our* heads. Yours, mine, the baby he ditched."

"It's not abandonment, striking out for a paycheck so you can send money back to the family. Young men have been doing that since the beginning of time. He's the only one of us with very good prospects right now, so I appreciate the effort."

"*Prospects*," Tig said, making it sound like a disease.

"You two will never approve of each other. I can't help you with that."

"Mom. You're not even listening. I'm telling you what *he* would tell you if he had the guts. The life he wants doesn't have any place in it for a baby."

"I thought that too, at first. Having this baby out of the blue seemed pretty out of character for a guy who does everything by the book. I hate to say it, but I thought Helene trapped him into it. But it's not true. He really wanted the baby. He convinced me."

Tig inhaled, a show of patience. "He *wanted* the baby," she said. "Past tense. He was so gone for her, Mom. Helene was the first girlfriend of his life that he thought was actually too good for him. He was terrified of losing her. The baby was a mistake, of course. But he talked her into keeping it, thinking it would make her stick around."

Willa was stunned by this story. "You don't think Helene wanted the baby?"

"She wanted zip. Obvi."

"And Zeke thought the baby would, what, keep her attached to life?"

"He trapped *her*, Mom. If we're going to discuss entrapment."

"She could have ended the pregnancy. She certainly had a mind of her own." And a Mercedes and a closet full of Gucci that Willa didn't mention.

Tig shrugged. "Maybe she didn't exactly have her own mind at that point. And Zeke is persuasive. All I know is, he didn't think she would ever check out on a baby. And that way he'd get to keep his wonderful Helene."

"How do you know all this?"

"I have eyes and ears, and a brain."

"Thank you."

"Mom, you can't be objective about your own kids. You say that yourself, you can't see our flaws."

Willa understood Tig was being charitable in using the plural. "Helene loved Zeke. I just can't believe she didn't."

"Oh, I'm sure she thought Zeke was smoking dreamy. The ladies always do. *And* she was messed up in the head. You just said, depressed people can't bond properly. So Helene . . ." Tig shook her head. "The theater went all dark and she didn't see any reason to keep showing up to play her bit."

The explanation of suicide impressed Willa with its economy. "Zeke thought he could fix her. I'm sure you're right about that. I see more than you think. Your brother almost always gets what he wants, he's had a charmed life. Up to now. That could lead a person to believe he could fix unfixable things."

"But it all fell apart. And now he's stuck with this serious by-product of his major mistake. Why would he want to raise Dusty?"

"Because he always does the right thing? You can't argue with that, surely."

"And you would hold him to that. Make your son keep living forever in this house that's already fallen down. Even if it makes him miserable."

"I want him to be happy. That's all I want for both of you. That's why we're taking care of Dusty. We've talked it over, more than you realize, and I've told him I'm willing to do that. Until he gets situated."

"Situated. Like with a nanny? That's how this goes down?"

"Dusty is not yours to take on, honey. It's too much, at your stage in life."

"It's not too much at *your* stage in life?"

"I'm handling it, I think."

Tig held up her knitting and counted stitches with her fingers as if reading a document in Braille. She would finish this little jacket tonight. The last one had little buttons shaped like dogs, salvaged from an old sweater of Zeke's she found in a keepsake box. Willa had thought it a sweet gesture, but now she wondered if Tig had been trying to bait her brother back to his own DNA, like tossing a piece of the missing person's clothing to a bloodhound. Trying to reconnect the pieces of her shattered family.

Finally Tig spoke. "When Dusty turns twenty-one, you and Dad will be eighty."

"Not *eighty*." Christ almighty. Not quite, but close enough. "I can't really think that far ahead right now."

"You're the one always yelling at me to think ahead."

"Yelling. Really Tig?"

"Scolding. Helpfully *informing*."

"I'm sorry it feels that way. I'm just a plan-ahead type of person, I guess. A leopard can't change its spots."

Tig said nothing to that, broodily clicking her needles to the end of a row, turning the piece around, and clicking her way back across.

"I'm not mad at you, Mom," she said finally, and it sounded perfectly true. "The crazy thing is, nobody in this family but me is actually thinking ahead."

"I do think about Dusty's future. Believe me."

"Yeah, I'm sure you do. While Rome burns around you. Just like you were thinking of Zeke and me the whole time we were growing up. Sorry, but you know?"

"No, I don't. I'm Emperor Nero now?"

"No." Tig sounded reluctant to get into it.

"Seriously, I want to know the charges. How was I not thinking of you?"

Tig exhaled. "Okay. You and Dad were always just worker bees to this quest for a bigger, better-paid life. Moving from this college to that college, new town, new house, starting over in school every time I started feeling happy with my friends."

"That's completely unfair! If we were looking to be rich, forget academia. The quest was tenure. We didn't have a choice about moving. We were looking for security."

"And too bad, if everything I cared about got thrown out the windows as you drove down the road."

"We did what people in our position had to do, trying to make a good life. I guess I can't expect you to understand that. I'm sorry your childhood was so terrible."

"But at least you've finally got that wonderful life you worked so hard for." Tig turned the sweater upside down and began another row.

Willa's ears roared. How could she go on letting this child turn a knife in her heart? She needed to care a lot less, starting now. "Well, lucky for Dusty, it looks like I'm permanently unemployed. So I can't sacrifice him on my climb up the career ladder."

Tig didn't look at her. "I'm not even really talking about Dusty. I'm saying you prepped for the wrong future. It's not just you. Everybody your age is, like, crouching inside this box made out of what they already believe. You think it's a fallout shelter or something but it's a piece of shit box, Mom. It's cardboard, drowning in the rain, going all floppy. And you're saying, 'This is all there is, it will hold up fine. This box will keep me safe!'"

"I guess I don't have any idea what you mean."

"That's my point."

The three-word win. Willa pulled a sigh from her depths. Having run out of words, and apparently condemned to reside in a wet cardboard box, she watched Tig finish another row of knitting and turn it again. She thought of old-fashioned typewriters, that physical way of working one's way across a page, and envied the steady, incremental mode of accomplishment. It embarrassed her that her daughter had the practical skills of the family, in reverse of normal expectation. After Willa had bought Dusty's first baby food, Tig pointed out that those little jars cost twenty times the price of their contents, not to mention the additives, then proceeded to make batches of applesauce and mashed vegetables she froze in ice cube trays, easily thawed for his meals. Willa would be damned if she would admit it, but they needed to keep the girl around. She knew how to do all the things Willa's generation of females had skipped in favor of Having It All.

"I did try. As a parent. I put you kids first in every way I had in my power, which admittedly wasn't much. You have to give me that, or I'm kicking you out of the Big-Ass Chair." Willa was 100 percent serious.

Tig grinned. "We fight, Mom. That's just us. Sorry I was mean."

With the caution she would use to approach a fox curled in her lap, she stroked Tig's hair. Again, surprisingly, Tig let her.

"Remember those knock-down, drag-outs we used to have over getting your hair brushed out? Every morning before school. My God."

"Dad called it the Hundred Years War of Hair."

"We didn't last that long."

"No. You gave in and let me go all 'fro in middle school."

"The Brillo years. Sorry. Not your best look, you have to admit."

"Nope. That's why I locked it up. Now I'm done with the hair wars forever."

"I wasn't the right mother for hair like yours. In my family we're all fine and flaxy, so brushing was all I knew. *This* I wouldn't have thought of in a million years." Willa traced a finger over the neat square grid of partings. "How do you even do it?"

"You mean, get it started? Step one, move a thousand miles away from your mom and her jank hairbrush."

Willa laughed. "But somebody had to help you with this. Parting it into all the little sections. It's so tidy and perfect, like a little garden."

Tig didn't speak for a long time. Nick snored softly in time with his oxygen pump, the reason for their being there, but easy to forget. With his hearing aids out, no thunder on earth could wake him. The clock by his bed blinked a declaration of midnight, as it had been doing for days. When the electricity flickered off, even briefly, every clock in the house went back to an immutable starting point. Thanks to moisture in the walls and badly outdated wiring, this was happening so often they'd stopped resetting the clocks.

Suddenly Willa had the strange notion Tig was crying. She pulled her head gently to her shoulder and kept her hand there, cradling the side of her face. Feeling dampness.

"Tigger, sweetie. What is it?"

"Nothing, just. Remembering stuff."

"You've never, ever talked about Cuba. Did somebody hurt you?"

"No. The opposite. They loved me. So, so much."

"Who did?"

"Toto's family."

A thoughtful silence. "I'm going to guess that's not a family of dogs."

Willa felt the subtlest shift in Tig's facial muscles. A smile. "Aristóteles. His family calls him Toto."

"You dated an Aristotle? Jesus, that sounds like a Tavoularis fantasy."

"Yeah, I thought of that. Dad would have approved on a first-name basis. Would you believe I met other Antigones? Cubans are so literate, it's madness. Down the block from our house was the Dulcinea bakery."

"Dulcinea, as in Don Quixote."

"Yep. The manager's name was Cervantes Garcia. His daughters were Thalia, Erato, and Terpsichore. He said he was hoping for nine girls so he could get all the muses in his house."

"Wow. That's not what I picture when I think of Cuba."

"What do you picture? Cars with fins?"

Willa thought about it. "Honestly? For a few years I just thought of it as the island that ate my daughter. A black hole. I guess I was hurt that you disappeared, and then turned up again with no explanation."

"What would you like explained?"

"I don't know. Where you lived, what you did. Why you stayed."

After a long moment of quiet: "I lived in the city of Trinidad. It looked like a birthday cake."

"That sounds like the beginning of a fairy tale."

"It was. Kind of."

"Why do they read so much? Because of no TV?"

"They have TV. They can get American soap operas, the BBC news, anything. It's called 'the *paquete.*' You go down to the newsstand every week and load whatever you want onto a thumb drive. For, like, two dollars."

"Oh." Willa felt an instinctive concern for the copyright violations.

"They read because they're educated. Everybody can go to college. Farmers, mechanics, anybody, because it's totally free. All the way up to a PhD, everything's covered including room and board. Books, shampoo, tampons, the works. As long as you want to keep studying, you get to stay in school."

Willa thought of Zeke's debts and their collateral damage, the mercenary life he was pressed to live under their weight. But there had to be a catch. Cubans must pay for their free ride in other ways, no jobs after graduation, something, because fairy tales aren't real. These arguments rose to her tongue and then stopped, as Willa recalled Tig's jubilance on Jorge's shoulders that evening and the descent into hell with her brother. How this family rained on her every parade. It was no way to get the story.

"Tell me. How does a city look like a birthday cake?"

Tig considered this, clearly surprised to be asked. "More like cupcakes, actually. All in a row, blue, pink, yellow, white, all these little houses with icing-colored stucco facades and lacy grilles in the windows. Little narrow cobblestone streets, all running uphill to the Plaza Mayor and the cathedral. The city is five hundred years old and they've kept it perfect."

Willa considered her next question. She wondered what perfect meant, who decided, and how anyone kept it that way. Certainly she wondered how an oppositional temperament like Tig's fit into a society that wasn't known for tolerating dissent, but that question would have to wait. It had been a few years since Willa was this nervous about blowing an interview. "How did you meet Toto?"

"Hitchhiking. He was going to this little town called Bayamo on the eastern end of the island. I said, 'Bayamo is good, you can leave me off there.' So, I didn't know this but it's a nine-hour drive to Bayamo. We stopped for lunch. Stopped to pee in the bushes, separate bushes of course. Stopped at this secret beach, because he wanted me to see it. By the time we got to Bayamo we were . . . friends."

"He'd fallen for you. Because you are so smoking dreamy."

"Mom. In the guy universe, half of them think I'm a smart-mouthed little freak."

"Thank goodness. Because honestly, who has time for *all* the guys in the universe?"

Tig chuckled a belly-deep little stutter of a laugh that sounded just like Dusty's, and Willa registered with a small shock their shared DNA. His next-of-kin after Zeke, exactly as related as Willa.

"What was your new friend looking for at the end of this long drive?"

"He went to see his friend. A doctor. She'd just graduated from med school and the government sends you someplace to work for two years. After that you go where you want. The top kids in the class go out to run clinics in the smallest villages. It's the same kind of building wherever, the doctor lives upstairs and the clinic is downstairs, and medical stuff is all free, you probably knew that."

"Wait. The achievers get sent to the boonies? That sounds like punishment."

"No. Think about it. If you live farther from a hospital you want the best doctor in your town. Somebody that can handle diagnostics, emergencies, stuff like that."

"I can see that from the patient's point of view. But still. Wouldn't med students blow their GPA on purpose so they won't have to go to the gulag?"

Tig exhaled. "It's a huge honor. That's all I can tell you. Not all people are selfish. And not every small town is the gulag. You can believe it or not believe it."

Willa edged back from the precipice. "Tell me about Toto."

"Just, like, the sweetest person you can imagine? He has four older sisters, I think that's why. They taught him how to give compliments, to listen and not just talk. But he's also the family brain. Two degrees, medicinal chemistry and engineering."

"So he's what, a professor?"

"A lecturer, part time, like Dad. But he makes more money as a mechanic. The family runs a business repairing cars."

"And that's how you learned. They put you to work."

"They put me to work."

"You lived with the Toto family?"

"Yep. They all thought I was adorbs. His sisters, his mom and dad. So clever, so cute, *chiquita Antigoñita*. They basically adopted me."

Willa ached with jealousy. "*We* all think you're adorbs."

Tig emitted a curt, soundless laugh.

"But it sounds like you and Toto were not exactly brother and sister."

"You mean, did he administer cruel and unusual punishment? No, he didn't act like my brother."

"I guess I'm asking . . ."

"I know what you're asking. Did we have sex? Yes, Mother. Did we use protection? Yes, Mother."

"Tig, have a heart. I'm trying to ask what you meant to each other."

"I don't know. The world?"

"Okay. I get that."

"We had our own little place. It was tiny. Technically it was a shed. But we made it nice. I've lived in worse, to tell you the truth."

"Like right now?"

"Maybe. Kind of. I mean, this house is bigger and has its own plumbing but it's not exactly cozy."

"Wait. Sitting with your mom in a giant recliner isn't cozy?"

Tig went quiet. Willa tried to be patient, but nothing more seemed forthcoming.

"If you don't want to answer this, you don't have to. Why did you come back?"

Tig shrugged. "Things fell apart."

"I'm sorry, honey. I'm glad you're here, I have to say that. But I'm not glad for whatever made you leave him. It must have hurt a lot."

Tig sighed deeply, and her breath shuddered in a way Willa remembered from her childhood. Usually in the aftermath of tears.

"You don't have to talk about it. But it only keeps hurting when you don't."

"And sometimes also when you do."

"Yes. Sometimes also when you do. I assume your visa situation was complicated. Which is not your fault."

"Yeah, I wasn't legal. Don't tell Zeke or Dad. The Cuban government didn't mind me being there, the hitch is with all the US restrictions. I had to go in through Mexico, and every ninety days I had to fly back to Cancún and reenter on a tourist visa. Or I was supposed to. It got, you know, just hard. I didn't want to get the family in trouble."

"Of course. But it must have broken everybody's heart. For you to have to leave for stupid legal reasons."

Tig nodded her head slowly, for a long time. Trying to feel convinced of something, it seemed. Finally she spoke. "So, there was another reason. The friend in Bayamo he was going to see, the doctor? Was Toto's wife."

"His *wife*. Oh, honey."

"I know. Stupid, stupid me. He told me, at the time. He never lied about being married. I hung out for the weekend in Bayamo, and he invited me to ride back with him to Trinidad, and meet his family. And one thing just led to another."

"As they say."

"Don't judge me, Mom."

"I'm not. I guess I'm mad at him. And this family, everybody who led you on."

"They all liked me better than her. Than Lucia, that was her name. *Is* her name. It wasn't just Toto who regretted the marriage. All his sisters and his mom said they knew it was a mistake, Toto getting married so young. They were nineteen or something. Then university, grad school, med school. They grew up to be really different people."

"That happens. I'm sure they have such a thing as divorce in Cuba."

"Oh God, yes. Nobody gets very hung up on marriage."

"So."

"So okay. This is hard to talk about. So, why would he drive all that way to Bayamo once a month, when gas is crazy expensive and everything?"

"Because he still loved her, maybe?"

"No. To see his kids."

"Oh."

"*Two* kids. A boy and a girl."

"She had children? As a medical student?"

"That's not a problem, the day care situation in Cuba is like, utopian. The point is, Toto's their dad. I fell for a married father of small children. Can you believe it?"

"Oh, gosh. I see. When her two years were up in the little town in the boonies, he and Lucia were going to have to work things out. Probably move to the same town and make some kind of parenting arrangement."

"Yep. And I had no business putting myself in that equation. He really wanted me to stay. But given my status, I couldn't make any promises about the future. I had to be honest about that. I didn't want him to give up anything because of me."

"That was such an unselfish decision. And painful. Nobody your age does that."

She shrugged. "I'm my age. And I did it."

"You did."

Tig rubbed her nose. "Remember when that leather babe came to our house and you gave her the lecture on marriage? Like, you can't win the race without running the marathon? I guess I've always known that. From watching you and Dad."

Willa felt stunned, for more reasons than she could count. She drew Tig into her arms. "Knowing and doing are different things. You did the hardest thing in the world. I had no idea."

Tig crumpled in her embrace and wept, giving in to her grief while Willa suffered an avalanche of memories: Tig showing up on the doorstep in Virginia with the beaten look of a stray dog. Tig sitting shell-shocked in the living room while she and Iano vented their angst over the loss of all security, channeling too much of it as anger at a wayward daughter. Iano lecturing her on getting herself back to school. Speaking to a child. Willa regretted every failure while she held her daughter and stroked her hair and marveled that mothers' and daughters' hearts can be crushed so repeatedly without learning to defend themselves. She thought of times she'd fallen apart in her own mother's arms, and let herself be put back together.

When words came to Willa, she heard them in her mother's voice, and said them aloud. "Tell me something you did with Toto that made you happy."

"Mom. It's over. I'm with Jorge now."

"You are, and I guess it feels disloyal to talk about somebody you loved before. I might not be the right mother for this, either. I've only ever been in love with one person. Which is so weird. Most people are like you, leaving pieces scattered along the trail."

"But I'm happy now. With Jorge. So I don't know why I'm so *sad*."

"Maybe because this hasn't healed yet. You're trying to forget things your heart still wants to remember."

"The past is the past."

"It is. And you were really happy, so it's worth remembering. Tell me something that was wonderful. The secret beach."

Tig shook her head, the garden of locks. "No. I'll tell you the best date of my life. We went to a restaurant."

"Was it a special occasion?"

"Oh yeah. It was a fancy place, way too expensive for every day. It was Lorenzo and Natalia's fortieth anniversary. Toto's parents. They took the whole family out."

The best date of her life was a celebration of her ex-boyfriend's parents' anniversary. Willa took this personally. Her mothering had driven her daughter to seek asylum in a family of foreigners. "It must have been some restaurant."

"Oh God, was it ever. It's in an old house, hundreds of years old. The family has had it since before the revolution so a lot of the furniture is original and everything in the whole place is beautiful and old and perfect. Like the china and silver, candlesticks, hand-made lace tablecloths, napkins. We were all dressed up, and when they seated us I just sat there holding my breath, looking at the table set with those pretty china plates and silverware and sparkly crystal glasses. Every single thing on that table had to be over fifty years old, Mom. From before the embargo. Different tables had different settings, what do you call them, china patterns. Not all just alike. And none of it's broken, and all of it is twice as old as me. It was the most amazing experience."

Willa wanted to understand, but as far as she'd ever known, Tig cared less than nothing for the likes of china and flatware. "So did they feed you, or just dazzle you with the presentation?"

"Oh, the food was amazing. And the music. They had this super smooth band playing mambos and sarabandas. The singer looked all prim but then opens her mouth and out comes this killing sexy voice, and of course we all danced, between courses. *Everybody* dances in Cuba. They've perfected all the fun things that don't cost anything, like dancing and sex. But Mom, think about it. When did you ever see fifty-year-old china in a restaurant?"

She thought about this. "Never. It's always generic white plates. In fancy places, fancy generic I guess. But new. Probably it's all made in China, for restaurants."

"Exactly. I asked them here, at the restaurant, and Yari told me they have to reorder every year because it gets chipped and messed up. People are careless. If they break it there's always more. But in Cuba, whatever it is, you probably can't get more, so people take care. When you pick up a glass it's like you're raising a toast to all the people that drank from it before. All those happy anniversaries in a beautiful place, and all the future ones. It made me so happy, Mom. That night was our turn. We got to be in the treasure chest of time."

12

⁐

Treasure Chest of Time

Before we march into territory where angels fear to tread, I would like to make four statements that will offend no one in this room. May I, sir?" Thatcher made an obsequious little bow to the moderator with his hands pressed together as if in prayer—a flattery unavailable to his one-handed opponent. On this night anything was fair.

"Yes, yes, proceed." Landis was impatient. The point of this forum was to get Thatcher mired in the angel swamps. In his newspaper he'd billed the debate as a forum on Darwin versus Decency. The man knew how to fill a hall.

"Thank you, I will." But instead Thatcher paused, as advised by his able trainers. He offered a genteel nod to Cutler at his podium, pink cheeked as a pig, in a new frock coat and his best wooden hand. Then to Landis, sprawled in his chair between them. Then to the ladies and gentlemen, farmers, spiritualists, and scalawags who had paid their fifteen cents to see him hang. Polly and Mary sat in the second row: Polly bursting, Mary grave. Rose absent.

Rose had gone riding, with her new boots and companion Louise Dunwiddie, both given her by Thatcher.. They had locked up such a fast friendship he wondered why Rose never thought to initiate it herself. Pride was the answer. The well bred did not self-invite or supplicate themselves to horse-owning families.

Polly gave a secret, infinitesimal nod: now he should speak.

"First principle. Individuals within a population are variable. This is obvious, isn't it? A farmer who raises cattle knows it. Any household where a dog births her particolored litter has seen it. Tall corn and short, swift foxes and sluggish, when we study Creation we see variety among members of a kind." Thatcher turned to see Cutler alarmed: the Creation card already played, on the side of indecency! Thatcher smiled. "I will pause so Professor Cutler may refute the premise."

Landis uncrossed his long legs, turned to the audience, and pulled a face that aroused laughter. He couldn't bear boredom, or any man hogging his light. "Well Cutler, it's your go. Do you wish to refute the *premise* that a bitch can throw a ragbag of pups?"

"To spare this audience more tedium than my opponent needs to inflict, no sir."

"Thank you." Thatcher rested his hands on the podium. Pause, look, speak. "Second principle. Traits in their variation are inherited. The ragbag medley of pups all derive from their mother. A greyhound's pups may be white or black but they will not be Skye terriers. Unless the father was a Skye terrier, in which case the pups will bear some resemblance to both parents. We do not know the mechanism for this inheritance, but we cannot deny life holds some elixir for transmitting character from progenitor to offspring. Or, perhaps Professor Cutler does wish to deny it. Please, sir."

"An *elixir* for transmitting *character.*" Cutler rucked his mouth as if he'd touched his tongue to shit. "I do not like the sound of that. I do not. It makes me think of a witches' brew." He gave the ladies a moment to shudder, hat feathers to quiver. Thatcher thought of herons. "My opponent refutes himself!" Cutler boomed. "We *cannot know* the mechanism of this inheritance. Why? Because the universe is a mystery sprung from God's mind. Its order derives from the orderly mind of its creator." Cutler bore his customary stiffness, wrists hovering near the bend of his waist. "The pups of a greyhound are greyhounds because God wishes them so. And may we be thankful, lest we have squids and marmosets getting born on our kitchen floors to our four-footed friends!"

A breeze of laughter ruffled the room. Thatcher scanned faces for sympathy and found an Italian matron with a faint moustache who looked ready to clasp him to her bosom. She wore a flat little bonnet like a fried egg. He tried not to lose concentration while waiting for permission to speak. Their moderator's mind seemed to have wandered from Plum Hall, but the silence brought him back. "And to this you say what, Mr. Greenwood?"

"I did not say we *cannot* know the mechanism of inheritance, only that we don't know it yet. The Swiss doctor Johann Miescher . . ." Thatcher carefully slowed his pace. People *expect* to be bored with science, Polly had told him, so you must dole it out preciously like Turkish delights. ". . . has discovered a substance in the seepage from wounds that contains mostly nuclear matter. He believes it functions in transmitting heredity."

The mention of seeping wounds moved Cutler to theatrical disgust, while poor Captain Landis stifled a yawn. Polly's face was long. During his rehearsals in the carriage house, Mary had offered suggestions on matters of science but Polly took full charge of rhetoric. Thatcher steered back to his charted course. "Next I offer the third principle, which is death. Death stalks us all!" Polly's face brightened; the line was hers.

Cutler's naked cheeks flamed. He must have expected a repeat of the ritual drubbing at the school auditorium, not this dodging

and weaving. Thatcher stepped from his podium, displaying a confidence he could nearly imagine. His eye found the moustached
matron, who seemed ready to express maternal milk on his behalf.

"We are many more of us born to this world than will live to
an old age. It's true for men, truer for flora and fauna. Consider
the maples that line our streets, dropping their whirligig keys like
snowdrifts on our walkways. Every one is a seed. A hopeful tree."

He took a few more steps from his podium. "Imagine if each of
these grew to be a maple. There should be no room in Vineland for us
to stand between them. It's the same with mice or dandelions. Many
more seeds and pups are dropped than may prosper. Otherwise we
would be pressed like keepsakes among all the flora and fauna of this
planet. Our saving grace, ladies and gentlemen, is what?"

He watched mouths move in a silent chorus: Death.

"Yes. Our salvation is the reaper. The mouse reaps the seed,
the cat reaps the mouse. By its infinite means, death overpowers.
Into this world—this orderly model of God's mind—more lives are
born than are granted to live. What say you, Professor?"

"What say I?" Cutler was rattled, and left to fend for himself
while their moderator examined his velvet-waistcoated belly. "To
the suggestion our world is dangerous? I should call that stale
news! Our nation bleeds itself dry! One in five of our young men
died in the war and we are still riven, north against south, country-
man against immigrant, laborer against lord." Cutler seemed to be
clutching a runaway horse set off by a gunshot. "We see black men
rise up to threaten their former masters. Here in our own streets
we have seen women in trousers! Desiring to lord themselves over
men, turning against God's own domestic harmony. All sense of
order is sundered. When men are not running themselves through
the blades of threshers or falling under carriage wheels, they murder one another outright. It curdles the blood to read the morning
news."

At the mention of his newspaper Landis left off his belly gazing and drew up rather sharply. Cutler toadied. "And we are blessed to be well informed of the rancor that looms in our nation, *thankful* for the protections granted us in Vineland. Here we have order. But! We are wasting this audience's time. Has my opponent chosen this forum for the purpose of declaring the obvious, that danger stalks?"

Thatcher had hardly chosen it; he was invited as a condition of his employment. And now his only choices were to lose his case, or humiliate his employer and pay the price. He would have preferred a duel of pistols: to shoot or be shot, not both. "As I said in my opening statement—"

Cutler interrupted. "May I ask my colleague to keep to Darwin and decency?"

"You may. Here is the last of my four principles: survival is not haphazard. Creatures differ in their ability to survive, not by chance but owing to traits inherited from their progenitors. And with these four declarations of the obvious, I'm finished."

Cutler looked stupefied. "You haven't. Where is Darwin? Where is decency?"

"Both here. You took no objection to Darwin's theory of descent with modification by natural selection, which I've just explained in full."

"Liar! You never even mentioned his name."

"We could discuss the laws of motion without mentioning Sir Isaac Newton. Scientific laws are not the property of a man. They exist outside of us."

"Mr. Greenwood, you will not slink away from your heresies!"

"If I were a heretic, I'm certain I wouldn't. You are a gifted inquisitor." He risked a devilish glance at the audience. "But I wonder if my opponent has read Mr. Darwin's book?"

"Have not. Will not."

"Well of course you wouldn't have, the thing is more than a thousand pages."

"I don't have to!" Cutler cried. Thatcher had succeeded nicely in nudging him near to combustion. "I read Samuel Wilberforce's reaction to it, I have it just here . . ." He sifted through the mess of papers on his podium, located a journal, and aimed it like a firearm at Thatcher. "In the *Quarterly Review*!"

"I can explain natural selection," Thatcher continued patiently, as if nothing at all had exploded, "using an example from Darwin's book. Wolves catch their prey by fleetness and craft. In every litter, variation exists—principle one!—with some poor pups inclined to sloth and dullness. As teachers and mothers know, every litter has them—"

"Wilberforce said Darwin's views tend inevitably, and I quote, to banish from the mind most of the attributes of the almighty!"

"Now, remember the reaper. In some years the prey for our growing brood of wolves will be scarce and difficult to catch. Only the fleetest siblings will kill enough rabbits to advance themselves to breeding age. Their dull brothers, alas, will perish. But to the quick survivor, stronger, fleeter pups are born in turn. Variation will persist, but over time the fierce and the quick will come to predominate the species we call wolf."

A loud knocking brought the hall to silence. It was Cutler's wooden hand banging the podium. It went still, and Thatcher continued. "As the predator grows fleet, so does his prey. The longer-legged rabbits survive to multiply their prowess." Cutler resumed his banging but Thatcher talked over him, loudly, feeling his words drawn into the rhythm as music is pulled to a metronome. "Or imagine this. Among *speckled* rabbits in *snowy* country, *fortune* falls to *those* whose coats are *white*, like the Arctic *hare*, which *hides* well from its *enemies*. The hare did not *decide* to become white. It *benefited* from generations in which lighter color won out. This is called an adaptation. It can be a structure, like the rabbit's coat. Or a behavior." He caught a breath. The banging had stopped. "Like persistence. Thank you. I rest my case."

Roused by the sudden shift of attention, Landis alerted at the shoulders like a marionette. Both his hands flew up. "We adjourn now for a short interlude!"

This was a surprise. Thatcher felt they'd hardly begun. But Landis was a man of instinct and his gut called for an interlude. Already people were out of their seats. "I know you will not go far," Landis shouted over their noise, "as Decency will be calling you back for the second half of our forum."

Thatcher watched Landis glad-handing the better-dressed patrons in the front row. They might not reconvene until the captain had pressed every inch of lady flesh that showed itself south of a sleeve. Mrs. Landis would not be there, she never attended lectures, as she was widely said to be fragile. Thatcher wondered what was being widely said of his own wife, who also neglected lectures lately, preferring Louise Dunwiddie and Marvel, the speckled Arabian. He only hoped the association would bring Rose the standing she craved. Aurelia certainly approved of the Dunwiddies' fortune in glass manufacture. They all rode out together: Louise; her foppish brother Leverett; Orville, the widowed father; and sometimes Aurelia, not to ride but to watch the young people with poor Mr. Dunwiddie. The "poor," Thatcher gathered, was for a wealthy man still going about in the last suit his dead wife had chosen for him from fashion plates five years in the dustbins. Rose and Aurelia discussed Mr. Dunwiddie as if he were a cut of meat that needed spicing. Thatcher knew what women intended when they spoke of improving a man. He let himself imagine a new life, Aurelia moved to another house, finally married to someone whose fortune held up. What peace they all might find then, he and Rose especially. A mother's unfulfilled ambitions lie heaviest on her daughters.

Thatcher found himself invisible as people milled about greeting their neighbors. He wondered if he was expected to press the flesh of Plum Hall or stay at his post. Cutler stood fast, shuffling through papers with ominous intent. Landis now approached Polly: Thatcher watched her tip down her little bonnet, pretend to mind her step in the aisle, and deftly avoid him. Impressive. She made her way toward Thatcher looking so womanly in her bustled skirt and basque bodice, he felt sad for her lost, uncorseted youth. Mary was still caught at her seat by her friend Phoebe and the interminable Mr. Campbell, who had the historian's gift for sparing no detail of a story. Thatcher held his eye on Mary until she glanced up and returned his smile, flooding him with assurance. He had carried their banner decently through the first half. He surprised himself by wishing Rose had been there to see it. An odd thought, probably a violation of some truce between them. He'd promised Rose the debate would be tedious, to save her from having to make an excuse. And himself, from risking further humiliation in her eyes.

Suddenly he could not bear another minute in that room, breathing its depleted air. With a look of sympathy for his trapped friend, he signaled the door at the side of the stage and moved toward it. Polly caught up to him and out they slid, a pair of cats.

It opened onto the street. The cold air hit his lungs. "Strooth!" he cried.

Polly giggled. "You can say hell or damn. I won't tell Mother."

"Hell, then." They both laughed, ice needling their lungs. "Damn!"

"Thatcher, you were bricky! It was just as you said, he didn't even know you were started until you had him in the noose."

"He's not in the noose yet. We still have a second round."

"You'll take the egg. I know you will."

"I'll do my best. And I won't tell your mother you've learned to talk like a paper hanger. Is that what they teach now at the Spring Road School?"

Polly lifted her proud chin and stamped her boots to warm her feet. "We still have your pictures to show. Oh! I left the easel and drawings at my chair, all your perfect fossil creatures! They are so good, Thatcher. Mrs. Treat was very impressed to see how well you draw. Someone might want to steal them for their parlor walls."

"I shouldn't worry about that, darling girl. She will keep them safe." Thatcher smiled to think of his neighbors coveting heretic animals for their parlor walls. Polly's faith in him was a gift beyond his experience.

He felt his bones shudder from the cold, like prey in the jaws of a terrier, and wished for the wool overcoat he'd left in the hall— precisely where, he couldn't remember. He had been blind with nerves when they arrived, and everything had happened quickly. Polly had also left her mantle behind for Mary to guard. Poor Mary, who despised all hubbub but had braved it tonight for his sake. How she must be suffering in that hall. If Mr. Campbell ever finished with her, the botanical society ladies would pounce. Mary called them her Flower Mites.

"We should go back in. If I let you perish out here, your mother will make a nice new pelisse of my hide."

"I'm not cold!" Her cheeks were bright roses. But she did have the advantage of wool gloves, a bonnet, God alone knew how many crinolines and shifts.

"I think you're fibbing. If it's true, I envy women all your folde-rol. It must be horrid in summer but useful in January."

"It *is*!" She shivered, more prettily than a shudder ought to be, he thought. More like her sister by the day. "I never ever thought I would *want* to wear thirteen petticoats."

"Until you lived through winter in a house that is falling to pieces. I'm sorry."

"The worst is having to share with Mother. Oh, Thatcher. She *snores.*"

"I'm sorry. We'll get it fixed up."

"I know you will."

He'd spoken with Mr. Martini about razing and rebuilding, but an estimate of ten thousand dollars had made it a brief conversation. Thatcher felt his eyes go sticky, as if freezing to their lids. He looked up through the bare-armed trees at a sky full of stars, and even their blaze seemed ruthless. The Italian matron in the audience came to his mind, and in the round face and strong eyebrows he suddenly saw his peerless pupil Giovanna. It was Mrs. Persichetti, hoping to greet him at the interlude and hear praise of the humble family's shining daughter. Any normal man would have done it. Blast his shyness.

He blew on his fingers, feeling some sympathy for the wooden-handed man. "This weather is treacherous. I worry your sister will be frozen to her steed."

"Frozen Rose, Rose is froze! Oh, poor froze Rose, her nose and toes!"

"Goodness, you must have a heart. I'm truly worried. It seemed unwise for them to ride so far out in this weather."

Polly bit her lip, looking up at him as if stung by a bee. In his fondness for Polly he played at this secret alliance, the two of them against Rose, but it was no game for her, he saw. Too late. He had risen to the enemy's defense, and now little feathers would need smoothing. "I'm not a bit angry. I know you care for your sister. We wouldn't wish the smallest harm on her nose or toes."

"My sister would never put up with anything unpleasant. I'm sure she is all chickaleary now, drinking chocolate with Louise and stupid Leverett at their cottage."

"They have a cottage?"

"On Union Lake. Rose didn't say? I suppose she thinks you'll be jealous of old jollocks and his bags of money."

"Mr. Dunwiddie can have all the money he likes, why should I mind?"

Polly lifted her chin and said nothing. Thatcher wondered if he would regret having matched his wife with Louise Dunwiddie, who ended her dancing classes the moment she took up riding with Rose. She'd come to the school on a lark in any case, Rose reported, to rankle her father, who disapproved of female employment. His wife, prior to decease, had been seeking a mate for Louise among the Philadelphia baronets, and Mr. Dunwiddie found himself at a loss to continue the project. Aurelia was sure to interject herself—having failed so badly with her own daughter, Thatcher thought acidly.

Polly looked direly cold, but seemed unready to cede her grievance. Thatcher worried the interlude might be ending, people returning to their seats. Cutler looking for a victory by default. He needed to go back inside and forget whatever he had stepped in here. He had long known Polly's capacity for pique, but never as its victim.

"You're right of course, your sister can look after herself. Only it's a long ride back from Union Lake. I don't like to think of them being out so late in the cold and dark."

"Don't be silly. The Dunwiddies have their carriage."

"But the horses. They can't just leave them at the lake."

Polly let out a little bark. "The Dunwiddies have servants and hired men to do anything *dreadful*, Thatcher. Like bringing back the horses in the dark."

Over that little barked laugh he grieved, foreseeing the loss of Polly. Just like her mother and sister, she so easily grasped what Thatcher never could: the power of money to disperse any worry. "Of course," he said. "Silly me."

They stood watching the breath escape their mouths in frosted clouds. He thought miserably of Mary, abandoned to the Campbells and the Mites. If he succeeded tonight, the success would be Mary's as well. If he failed, she would think no less of him, but absorb his pain as her own. How like a friend she was in this way, and unlike a woman. Unlike Rose, at any rate. He had not known very many.

"You mustn't be cross, Polly," he said, in a tone he did not like. "I only wonder why Rose would have gone along with the adventure on a day like this."

"She *wanted* it to be today, Thatcher. Because of your forum."

"She had no need to contrive an excuse. I told her she needn't come."

Polly looked suddenly twice her age, shaking her head as women did when making ready to lance your heart: as if life left them no choice. "She didn't want *them* to come. Leverett saw it in the paper and was going on about it until Mother and Rose got beside themselves, afraid the precious Dunwiddies might attend and find out you are on the side of Indecency. Rose was the one who suggested they all ride out to the lake."

Nausea rose in Thatcher's craw. Had she been that certain he would make a pitiful showing? Even Polly, his loyalist, seemed to believe it. "I need to go back inside," he said, more testily than he meant.

Instantly Polly was a child again. The little eyebrows pinched together. "But we should practice. You were good at the first part because you remembered to do everything we said."

Forgiven, then. He reached out a hand to tug her bonnet string. "My excellent taskmistress, I won't forget. I shall be bricky."

※

Cutler had made use of the interlude to locate a fresh batch of confidence. "And how did the Arctic hare arrive in the Arctic? Before it underwent a putative *ee-volution?*" He strutted from his podium to Thatcher's, wheeled, walked back. Behind his bottom the lone hand clasped its wooden friend. "Did Noah sail his ark to the northern seas and fling out his pair of black hares on some desolate plain for which they were badly suited?"

The audience chortled a little, then went still. Cutler was earnest.

"Noah did no such thing!" he bellowed, snatching a Bible from his podium. "I read to you from Genesis 8:19. *'Every beast and every fowl went forth out of the ark. And Noah builded an altar unto the Lord; and took of every clean beast, and of every clean fowl, and offered burnt offerings on the altar. And the Lord smelled a sweet savour and said in his heart, I will not again curse the ground any more for man's sake; neither will I again smite any more every thing living, as I have done.'"*

Cutler offered a grand little pause, and Thatcher leaped into it. "May I ask a question, sir? About the animals burnt on the Lord's altar?"

Cutler affected surprise. "I see my opponent does not read his Bible. Well, naturally, it has so many pages."

"I do read it, and admire its capacity to stir a curious mind. For example. Noah took on his ark only one pair of every kind. Is this true?"

"At the Lord's command, yes. Even a child knows this."

"And then he burnt some of them on the Lord's altar. I have wondered for years, how did their widowed mates manage to go forth and multiply after that, all alone?"

"You will find it in here. Every answer is here." Cutler quickly turned pages, his hairless cheeks trembling. "Here we are, here we are. God blessed Noah and his sons, saying, *'Everything that lives will be food for you. Just as I gave you the green plants, I now give you everything.'* I give you everything! What could be more plain?"

"What seems plain to me is that an animal needs a mate to reproduce."

"For pity's sake, can we keep this discussion above lewd debauchery?"

Crinolines shifted audibly; female gazes dropped. Cutler's bizarre accusation of lewdness had made itself true. "We can," Thatcher conceded, mortified. "Of course."

"On God's authority!" The hand slammed down, wood upon wood. "We were not put among the creatures of this world to live with them as equals. This world is *ours*!"

Someone in the audience slowly clapped, inciting a scattering of followers, like gravel thrown at a roof. Thatcher labored to keep his head. He was prepared for this. Polly had spent weeks helping him comb the Bible for nonsensical facts. She'd done it at night so Aurelia could see her reading by candlelight in the manner of a young saint.

"I understand Noah lived to be nine hundred fifty years old. Is that also true?"

"So says Genesis. So it is true. Yes, he did."

"And here is God's advice on discipline, from the Psalms." Thatcher read from copied notes, having brought no Bible to his podium, now wishing he had. "'Happy shall he be, that taketh and dasheth thy little ones against the stones. That taketh the infants from their mothers' arms and dashes out their brains against a rock.'"

Silence seized the hall.

"Professor Cutler, do you obey God's word in our school? Our audience would want to know you follow the Bible by dashing out the brains of misbehaving pupils. Our new building has a rock foundation, I assume for this purpose?" Thatcher scanned the audience for smiles, finding none. Mrs. Persichetti looked alarmed.

"We do not murder children sir. That you should *suggest* it."

Cutler paced, he shook his head. The audience watched him march across the stage and back. "Piglets!" he finally erupted, to the sound of exhaled breath in the room. "Now I recall the verse you quote. It refers to suckling pigs being prepared for a feast. To celebrate God's glory."

It referred to the prophecy of vengeance on Babylon, Thatcher happened to know, with the Almighty in full support of the child bashers. Cutler had yanked his suckling pigs out of thin air. A fabrication that so relieved the audience, Thatcher would have to let it live.

"The idea. Bashing children's brains." Cutler shook his head. "I'm sorry the ladies had to hear it. I promise you, we keep a close eye on the likes of my opponent at Vineland High School. We are vigilant against atheists and Darwinists."

Suddenly the house was set on its edge. Several ladies gathered capes and overcoats, preparing to leave.

"Ladies, gentle neighbors, calm yourselves!" This was Landis, up out of his chair with one arm raised like a Baptist, and no surprise. The captain's home territory was fracas, and his genius was for the precise balance of terror and mollycoddling needed to keep a public suckling at his teat. They settled now under his benediction. "You fear the world's evil and are sustained by its goodness," he crooned. "We've come to sort it out. Trust in our citadel, its protections will prevail. Let the gentlemen speak." Landis did not sit down then but remained midstage near Cutler, like a soldier of the professor's bodyguard.

"Thank you," Cutler said. "I was about to explain my theory of animal distribution, to refute the story of Noah flinging black hares onto the ice—"

"Excuse me," Thatcher pressed, without result.

"—We know that all beasts left the ark on Mount Ararat, in the Near Orient. The modern scientist asks: How did the grizzly bear and elk arrive in North America, which are not on the Asian continent? Now, the Bible tells us of many perils that confronted God's chosen, particularly in the realm of waters. God parted the waters of the Red Sea. He made the River Jordan stop flowing to let his priests pass. It was his method, you see. God imagined our continent to contain elk and bear, so he parted the waters and let them pass to their home." Cutler bowed so expertly, the audience could not help applauding.

Landis joined the applause. "Well now. What can we say against that?"

Thatcher stared at both of them. "Are you suggesting God rolled back the Atlantic so bears and elk could walk across a dry ocean floor?"

"I don't suggest it. I conclude it."

"Why stop with the bears? The mammals found only on our continent are so many: bison, jackrabbit, coyote. Muskrats, raccoons. Let's not forget birds, we have prairie chickens, which can hardly fly. They would have marched across the dry coral beds with the bears and bison. It must have been a regular circus parade."

"It must have been," Cutler agreed. Landis nodded also, refusing to sit down.

"Are there any written accounts of it in our history books?" Thatcher asked.

"I don't believe so."

"How do you suppose no one noticed when the Atlantic rolled back on itself to make way for the carnival of the animals?"

"I suppose it happened at night."

Thatcher glanced at the audience and saw no amusement in this citadel, only apprehension. He tried for the tone of a sympathetic uncle. "Mr. Cutler, the Atlantic between Europe and our continent is nearly four thousand miles wide. A prairie hen on her best day might manage to walk four miles. If she struck out from Brittany in early spring, let's say, we could expect her on Cape Cod by Christmastide, not of the following year, but the year after. Quite a weary little hen."

"To be sure," Cutler agreed.

"And what of the insects? Did they join the parade? We haven't even mentioned the plants. Thousands of species grow nowhere else but here. How did this happen?"

"There is considerable evidence the seeds of plants clung to the coats of the mammals and arrived by the same route."

"Considerable evidence," Thatcher repeated, watching Landis pull from his waistcoat a fat gold watch, the equal of a year's salary for Thatcher, and fondle it with lurid affection. He was bored. The captain preferred bread and circuses. "Evidence!" Thatcher said again, loud enough to startle Landis, who put away his watch. "He pretends to lean on evidence for this wildly problematical theory, when another explanation of animal distribution sits before us in perfect simplicity. Descent with modification—"

"Simplicity?" Cutler interrupted.

"—explains how one single natural force, universally applied—"

"Is it a point of pride for you, being a simpleton?"

Thatcher made himself pause. "It's a brilliant act of imagination, Professor. This Atlantic parting. Your literary training shows itself in the grandeur of your story."

Cutler looked wary. "Thank you."

"A poet can make a story as fanciful as he likes. In science we're constrained by cause and effect. We collect data and examine it. We're allowed to use nothing outside the evidence to make our explanations. When multiple explanations confront us, we have a rule. We assume the simplest one is best."

"Ah, here he goes," Cutler said to Landis. "Defending the simple brain." A hiss of suppressed amusement escaped the audience like steam from a pot.

"The law comes from a better brain than mine," Thatcher said. "It's a principle we call Occam's razor. Natural philosophers have applied it for hundreds of years."

"A razor!" Landis said, stroking his splendid door-knocker. Cutler, with his paucity of whiskers, said nothing.

Thatcher appealed to the audience, assuming more brains out there than hereabouts. "William of Occam was a man of God, a Franciscan friar in the fourteenth century. He argued that a complex explanation, when it does not hold water, will always grow more complex as it attempts to patch its own holes. The less adorned explanation is the one more directly tested, and more plainly proven. And in science, proof is all."

Cutler put a finger in Thatcher's face, standing so close the smell of hair tonic filled his nostrils. "You cannot *prove* a thing that already happened. Waters parting, wolf pups magically growing legs, it is done. Without witnesses. There ends your science."

"No." Thatcher edged forward to hold his ground. "We can observe transmutations of species by several methods. The study of life-forms of the past is called paleontology. I have drawings to show the audience. Treasures from an ancient time."

"No, no, no!" Cutler shook his head violently.

Thatcher looked up to signal Polly, but Mary's dark eyes at full attention nearly knocked him from his rail. He turned carefully, grasping what Mary saw: his opponent was not Cutler. The manipulator of this charade was making puppets of them both. Thatcher should address himself to the king of this court. "Captain Landis. May I ask my assistant to come forward with pictures for our enlightenment?"

Landis threw both arms in the air. "Pictures! Divert us, please!"

Cutler objected but Polly was already on the move with the easel and folder of Thatcher's watercolor-tinted drawings, over which he had taken a good deal of pleasure. "The remarkable creatures I will show you are genuine beasts, preserved in rock, found embedded in the cliffs above a beach in the south of England—"

Landis moved around to have himself a look, impeding the audience's view.

"—discovered by a girl called Mary Anning, no older than my sister-in-law."

Polly curtseyed, beaming, no less a hound than Landis for getting herself admired. Thatcher hated sending her back to her seat, all that self-possession gone to waste. "The little girl loved to walk the beaches collecting fossils . . ." Thatcher took a step toward Landis in a futile hope of urging him aside. "Her hobby turned up relics that made wise men stand at attention. Here you see the ichthyosaur, a sort of alligator with flippers for feet and saucers for eyes, so large it would fill this stage."

He turned a page. Landis crowded in, while Cutler circled around to stand behind Thatcher, looming. "Here is the plesiosaur, a giant long-necked turtle. These creatures are nowhere in existence today. They help us to see time on this earth in a different light—"

"Wrong!" Cutler interrupted, so loud and close Thatcher jumped. "Captain Landis, if I may—"

The captain seemed riveted by the beast in question, or its likeness.

"God does not make mistakes!" Cutler roared. "If he created a giant long-necked turtle, it would swim in our rivers today. The Lord said, 'Never will I again smite every thing living, as I have done.' I ask you, where is God's holy promise?"

Thatcher watched all eyes in the house move to Landis, begging rescue from this quandary. Cutler was up on his horse now, but Thatcher saw Mary had judged the match correctly. Vineland's foolish emperor might be naked but his subjects did not care, they would take truth from Landis and no one else.

"What God creates is perfection," Cutler wheedled on. "He does not change his mind and strike his works from the record. Do we believe God is still in his firmament?"

Landis turned to the audience and made a great, conclusive gesture like an orchestra conductor, then applauded loudly. Only then did they follow, heads nodding, hat ribbons bobbing. God remained in his firmament.

"As I said," Cutler groused, plainly annoyed with the pilfering of his heavenly thunder. "The creatures do not now exist, so they never did."

"Perhaps they do," Landis suggested, "but have retreated to warm southern seas."

Cutler all but rolled his eyes, again edging close to combustion. "Sir. Wise men have studied these so-called fossils and declared them a hoax. The mischievous girl cobbled them from bits of stone with her father's help, for fame and money."

"Mary Anning's father died when she was a baby," Thatcher corrected.

"The mother, then!" Cutler shrieked, arriving at a state Thatcher judged approximate to hydrogen. "What does it matter, they are connivers! Urging good men to doubt the beliefs that have comforted us all from the cradle."

Again Thatcher saw the audience looking expectantly to Landis. "No good person would lead men to blasphemous illusions," their captain told them. "The child must be a she-devil."

"But surely it was God who gave us the curiosity—" Thatcher began, but Landis cut him off. After a moment's lapse, he had located his unguent and meant to use it.

"Oh, come now, Mr. Greenwood, let us finish this business. Darwin is repudiated. Professor Cutler tells me anyhow he has retired, so we'll be hearing no more of his nonsense."

"Mr. Darwin is collecting data this very day, I am sure,"

Thatcher argued, feeling pulled underwater. "He maintains active correspondence with scientists the world over. In this very audience we have—" He stopped, unwilling to cast Mary into the flood. "In Boston, one of our nation's most respected scientists, Dr. Asa Gray, is a champion of—"

"Asia Gray? Never heard of him," Landis said. "I assure you I know all the important men. If this one were of any count, I certainly would know him."

Thatcher looked to Mary to steady himself, and was rattled to see at the back of the hall another face, with bearish beard and hooded eyes glinting with merriment. He could not have come in unnoticed. It was as he'd claimed, he had a knack for invisibility. The boldness was impressive. Carruth's satires against Landis had lately been ruthless.

"Darwin is repudiated!" Cutler repeated grandly, the flea imagining itself the dog's master. "Reasonable men will not abide the notion of our universe flung to the mercy of blind chance."

Thatcher studied the audience, many faces as worn and weary as their clothes, and perhaps their patience. What could he give them that Landis had not? "None of us wishes to be at the mercy of chance," he appealed. "And we are not. Natural selection is predictable, not random. Farmers in the audience will be familiar with the actions I describe. Think of how you cull your cattle, removing weak calves to make a stronger herd."

"We do have excellent cattlemen here in Vineland!" Landis declared.

"And they should glow with pride," Cutler informed his silly guardian. "For my opponent has just compared them to God."

"No," Thatcher corrected, "I compared them with wolves. The wolf does not want to create faster deer, but his consistent culling shapes the herd toward speed, over time. His action is like the farmer's. My point is the shaping of life is not random."

Landis leaped belatedly to comprehension, or his version of it. "Now he says God is a wolf! Dear ladies and gentlemen, I hope you are praying for Mr. Greenwood's soul!"

Thatcher carefully addressed himself to Landis. "Sir, couldn't the shaping of life be God's gift to us? Adaptation is a greater marvel than rigid stasis, for it opens a path to survival. We don't change ourselves deliberately, for no leopard can change its own spots. Each of us is stuck with our birthright of traits and habits."

Landis gazed at him with some curiosity, and the audience followed, the farmers and wives. Thatcher turned and spoke to them. The mothers. "Change comes only to the offspring, as time and adversity mold them. The luckiest will inherit the gift of survival."

Cutler was all but hopping from one foot to the other, angry at being shut out, impatient to snatch his victory. "This theory outrages every Christian alive. Where is omnipotent power? If you wish to teach our youth, why dispute the miracle of a tadpole becoming a frog?"

"Because it manages the job without knees on which to request Divine help?"

A hint of laughter from Landis made Cutler fume. "He mocks the Creator!"

Thatcher again spoke pointedly to Landis. "Scientific theories can only rely on physical causes. Gravity does not ask God for help. We don't dismiss God, we only allow him to attend to other matters."

Cutler stepped directly in front of him, like a child vying for a parent's attention. "Sir, he insists on a trudging, single process for life's formation! We have our angel choir, while *he* would have us all descended from one slithering . . . ancestral . . . fish!" Cutler spat the words as if tasting slime, with visible effect on the ladies. "A belief that would lead to anarchy! The animal kingdom needs man as its ruler, just as a town needs firm governance to keep it from falling into riotous free-for-all."

Again Thatcher saw all eyes in the room pulled to the gravity of Landis. These poor reeling planets craved safety in their universe, in any false form their master might pull from his pockets. "Dear ladies and gentlemen," Landis said in a honeyed voice, "the giant alligators you heard of tonight may have roamed our inland waters once. I still hear of attacks off the shore, now as I think of it, bloody attacks. But I promise you we'll see none of these monsters hereabouts. Not in the Delaware River, not in our Union Lake. Rest safely tonight in your beds. You have no cause, *no* cause to fear these beasts."

At this the audience burst into hearty applause. Several men stood to support the program of all giant alligators banished from New Jersey waters. One of the men standing was Carruth, showing himself. From Thatcher's position behind the captain's back he perceived the precise moment when Landis spotted his enemy, the spine recurving like that of a startled mongoose. The jester grew predatory.

"The evil we must watch for," Landis simpered, "is not a beast in the river. It comes on two legs, infiltrating our towns. Bringing riot and drink, broadcasting false complaints against our order, craving the wealth that belongs to other men. Grasping it! They push themselves ahead of those who have dutifully followed the law! Some will name this the progress of our times. Some will try to make our Bible a fairy tale. We do not let them! We seal our town against the enemies of gracious authority. We do as our hearts tell us, and slam the portals."

The audience held the quiet of a graveyard. All disguise here had fallen away: no more the jocular carnival barker, their king was a vengeful despot. Thatcher had watched Carruth's face throughout the attack, in which Landis cast provocative editors and underpaid bricklayers into hell with Thatcher and Darwin. Carruth had looked unmoved. Pleased, if anything, to have rattled the man.

His friend was offering up dispassion as a gift, as he'd once prof-fered a small tin flask, and Thatcher bent his will to drinking it in. He studied the crowded hall. This place of old philosophers and doomed progenitors was nothing to him. He was a supple branch, fleet of foot, motherless, unsheltered. Every adversity to this moment had made him a survivor. He watched Carruth; the great bear actually winked. Landis saw, and followed the trail to Thatcher. His eyes blazed fire.

Thatcher met his gaze. "Scientists are not like other people, sir. We cannot slam our portals. We have to follow evidence where it leads, even if no one likes that place. Even if it suggests that all we have ever believed might be mistaken."

Landis and Cutler both gaped. What was the use for courage in times like these?

"Professor Cutler, I know you admire Sir Thomas Browne and his theological interpretation of Aristotle's Great Chain of Being."

"The universe is a stair," Cutler intoned as if some holy valve had opened in his larynx, "rising in degrees from the rocks through lower life-forms up to man, and then the angels."

"Exactly," Thatcher said agreeably. "Christians have been happy with the *Scala Naturae* for centuries. It agrees with Darwin in as-signing the ape to his spot just next to man. Why make such a fuss over it now?"

"The *Scala Naturae* assures us a species knows its place and does not climb. I will stand beside the ape, Mr. Greenwood, but I will not let him get aspirations. I will not let him wear my trousers or bed my wife!"

Landis had sheathed his fangs—though Thatcher would never again forget their existence—and now pretended to find Cutler's line of attack very jolly. "Perhaps you would want your monkey friend to be shaved first. With your Mister who's it? With the fa-mous razor? Mr. Orpheus?"

Thatcher avoided both men's eyes, lest they see disgust reflected. The truth remained intact, however bludgeoned here. Carruth would be waiting outside to congratulate him. They would walk Mary and Polly home, then find their way to a celebration. He only wished Mary could share their lark over the Grizzly Atlantic Crossing. How fine it would be if his friend were a man, free to don trousers without sundering God's domestic harmony, and raise a glass of whiskey to the Enlightenment without causing the sky to fall.

"The name you are trying to call," he said, "is Mr. Occam."

"Yes!" the naked king cried happily. "You would have the beast dressed and trimmed up trying to pass for a man. With your Mr. Occam's razor."

13

Mr. Occam's Razor

He said he could stand in the middle of Fifth Avenue and shoot somebody, and people would still vote for him. Am I dreaming this?" Willa asked.

"No."

"No. He said that. It couldn't have been more than a week ago."

"Apparently he was right."

"Iano, nobody gets away with murder. You can't behave like a madman when you're running for public office. That kind of trash talk is supposed to end careers."

Willa had avoided news for most of the day by sneaking off for a hike in the Pine Barrens, but the minute they got back to the car Iano clicked on the radio. The New Hampshire primary was all over every channel, with newscasters sounding a little too thrilled with the shock value. Like Orson Welles reporting on the alien invasion.

"No more," she begged. Iano scrolled over to a jazz station.

This trip to the barrens was Willa's sixth or seventh since getting the news that had overturned her assumptions about their house. Iano felt she was now obsessing on the Greenwood-Treat connection, poring over the records and stalking their hangouts. It might have been true, she was obsessed. But the Pine Barrens had their own appeal. It took less than an hour to drive to Batsto, a little historic village empty of tourists that time of year. Five dollars' worth of gas or a little more, round trip, but her car was usually the only one in the parking lot and no one ever turned up to charge an entry fee. She could hike out on one of the sandy paths into the woods where the solitude and darkness and dire blood-red color of the creeks all suited her mood that winter. She felt guilty for recognizing exactly none of the plants Mary had written about so fondly, and knew she ought to learn some, but couldn't muster much heart for the chase. Mary and Thatcher had lived in enviable times, when biologists were discovering new species right and left, not watching them go extinct. Willa contented herself with the personable pines. They wore their rough bark like crocodile hide and held their needles upright like tasselly hands on long, curved arms, like Dr. Seuss creatures offering some warning chorus everyone needed to hear.

She didn't expect Iano to see the charm and had warned him of that, insisting winter wasn't the best time for his first visit to the barrens. (She'd been there no other time.) But he was at loose ends, adjusting to a new semester with no Tuesday classes, and had come along for company. They'd carried in only sandwiches and water—no baby whatsoever—and walked around for hours enjoying the winter sun, charting their course on a phone app so they wouldn't get lost in the maze of trails. It was much too warm for early February but Willa wasn't complaining. Her bones felt like permafrost. She'd kept on all her layers just for the pleasure of sweating through them.

Now, in the car, she wriggled out of windbreakers and fleeces one by one. By a stroke of luck, the radio cued up an obscure Keith Jarrett piano concert she and Iano used to favor in their newlywed days. In bed, particularly. Iano reached over to put his hand between her legs. She closed her eyes.

"Wow, this. Those first four notes used to make us salivate like Pavlov's dogs."

"Who were those sex maniacs? Shouldn't they have been at work or something?"

She wondered. One more couple they'd lost touch with through the years and relocations. "When have we ever been that happy, since?"

"We cooked pasta and lentils on a hot plate and had to wash our dishes in the shower."

"And?" Pasta and lentils they were eating *now*.

"And our only furniture was junk we found on the sidewalks after the undergrads moved out of their dorms. The castaways of the castaways."

"And?"

"We didn't have children."

"*That's* it."

Objectively, Willa knew she didn't regret Tig and Zeke. No rational guidelines existed for comparing youthful freedom with the heart-enlarging earthquake of family life. "Honestly? I think we were happy with our bare-bones life in that shoebox apartment because we knew it was temporary. We had nothing to lose and everything ahead of us to gain."

"We were happy," he corrected, "because ninety percent of the time we spent in that apartment, we weren't wearing clothes."

This was inarguable. By no means was it a glamorous life— she recalled being naked around *cockroaches*—and yet they'd shared an exuberance that eventually suffocated under tenure applications and mortgages. This was not a new story. Maybe Iano still had access to that kind of joy, but she'd surrendered it as her half of the marital bargain. Willa listened to piano phrases as sensuous as breathing, and tried calling up specific memories of that apartment, a converted garage they'd rented for two hundred a month. Her mind wandered instead to the whereabouts of that album, and from there to the boxes she still needed to rescue from upstairs before they went the soggy way of Zeke's high school yearbooks.

Iano had been quiet all day and was not much chattier now. He returned his hand to the wheel and kept his eyes on the road as they passed through a monochrome landscape of leafless blueberry farms and fallow vegetable fields. Half of these farms seemed to be shuttered, probably thanks to years of storms, droughts, and a doozy of a hurricane that had brought seawater farther inland than anyone knew it could go. They passed a ramshackle farmhouse she'd noticed before with a hand-painted sign in its yard: DEAR MOTHER NATURE, PLEASE SPANK SANDY!

The sexy piano surrendered to news at the top of the hour, and today it was all about money: the US dollar falling while the Swiss franc and Japanese yen gained, sending investors to seek shelter in safer currencies amid global financial turmoil. And despite their coveted currency, Japan's ten-year yield falling below zero.

"Oh, that's bad," Iano remarked in an offhand way, as if watching a fumble by a sports team he followed only casually.

"What does that mean, yield falling below zero?"

"Investors in Japan are now paying for the privilege of lending the government money."

"Why would they do that?"

"It's a bet. Like everything else."

Taken by people with cash coming out of their ears, was Willa's bet. She thought of Zeke's billionaires swapping around ludicrous excesses that had no bearing on their actual lives. Zeke's deal through the Harvard mentor had fallen through, but the scent of blood was keeping his team on the trail. Iano defended the morality of their venture—a lot of it seemed to be about microloans, women in India getting self-determined in small businesses and such. Success wasn't out of the question, in Iano's view. But Willa noticed he wasn't organizing their family life around the coming of Zeke's lifeboat.

The financial report was interrupted by news of the primary, with exit polls suggesting a sizable lead for the man who'd insulted every minority and threatened murder on Fifth Avenue. The Bullhorn. Willa moved quickly to change the channel.

"Welcome to the Granite State," Iano said. "We have rocks in our heads!"

"I think of New Englanders as the salt of the earth. You know?"

"*White* salt."

"True. Not a lot of pepper up there."

It was the hour when news could not be escaped. On the public station, after a musical punctuation between stories, a doctor from the CDC was called in to explain the connection between global warming and the spread of mosquito-borne diseases in the United States. Zika test kits were being sent to Florida that week, while Ohio and Pennsylvania had reported their first cases.

"Those damn mosquitoes are *here* already?" Iano asked.

"Not yet. I think it's just people who've been traveling in the South."

Iano seemed entirely reassured by this, while Willa imagined taking a fun beach vacation and bringing home the souvenir of a brain-damaged baby. The expert doctor was thanked for his terrible news and the regular report resumed: The Supreme Court had put the EPA's carbon rule on hold, siding with industry groups that wanted to do as they pleased while fighting a legal battle against regulation. Shares had dropped in several solar power companies as they fell short of their installation goals.

Iano, meanwhile, faced the windshield as if it were a firing squad, and Willa waited for whatever he wasn't saying. He was driving a car with nearly 200,000 miles on it and no warranty, but that was never going to be a Iano kind of worry.

"What is it?" she finally asked. "I'm going to save our shambles, okay?"

"I know this."

"I actually didn't believe it before. I was just faking confidence to make us all feel better. But this new guy who really did live in our house is a historical celebrity."

"Mary wasn't?"

"She was, but she didn't live in our house. Her house is gone. Our house belonged to the illustrious Thatcher Greenwood. It needs to be a national monument or something."

Iano made no comment on that prospect.

"I've downloaded the registry application. Most of it is pretty straightforward. I have to track down an expert in historical construction to come and put a date on the house. Chris is helping me find the right person."

"I'm sure he will succeed."

She stared. "So what is it? You've been stewing on something all day."

He shrugged. "Nothing."

"Oh, Jesus." The catalog of possibilities ticked through her head, cancer and infidelity included.

He looked at her, a little desperate. "It's not terrible."

"Then what?"

"I've been thinking about what you said. My lack of ambition."

"Iano! That's not what I said."

"Fire in the belly, absence thereof."

"Sweetheart, if you're happy, I'm happy. I just wanted to be sure."

"So I talked to the dean yesterday. About contract renewal in the fall."

Her stomach clenched. "How's it look?"

"He said I'm good. They might even raise my course load. Not a lot, the money is pretty much what it's going to be."

"But it's going to be. For another year."

"Longer than that. The institution is no longer granting tenure, so nobody's moving up. But enrollment is pretty stable. He said the foreseeable future. I can count on staying where I am until, you know. As long as I want."

"Until Social Security kicks in and you can retire. That's really good news, Iano. You're secure."

He glanced at her, checking for sincerity, finding it in place. He smiled. "Securely anchored at the bottom. I am a barnacle."

"My beautiful barnacle," she said. It could have been a Greek endearment.

She gazed out the window at this Jersey she would never fully accept, made of a soil so sandy and pale that plowed fields looked ghostly, and unpaved roads tended toward sand traps. The flatness was stultifying. She wouldn't say this aloud because in light of other worries it seemed self-indulgent, but Willa missed mountains. Missed them *hard*, with the psychic equivalent of a toothache. She'd never known a place this flat in her whole vagabond life. She'd leaped on her scholarship from West Virginia to Colorado, then tied her fortunes to Iano's and bounced pinballwise up and down the Rocky Mountain states, then finally back to the Blue Ridge. And then the collapse.

They passed a field where two horses stood staring at their own long shadows in the dusky light, and she wondered what else they did for fun. She puzzled over a horde of dark shapes stalking in unison across a meadow, bent on getting somewhere. Wild turkeys. She thought about Dixie, who seemed every day less inclined to keep living. Dixie, who loved Willa with the force of a religion, the rescue dog she adopted the year they moved to Virginia and named to celebrate never having to move from the warm, green South again. As it turned out, they'd had to put Dixie on dog Prozac to pull off the departure, and even this struck Willa as a sign of profound loyalty. She tried to formulate some small hope for her dog that wouldn't be too selfish. Not that Dixie would outlast Nick; that seemed immoral on all counts. Though she suspected it had run through everyone's thoughts.

That Dixie would live long enough to smell green grass again. She settled on that. The radio had turned without her notice to the New Hampshire primary. She snapped awake. With most of the votes counted, the Bullhorn had blown it out of the water.

"I don't believe this," she said.

"It's only one primary."

"But still, it's surreal. That the electorate could validate such a mean, grabby, self-aggrandizing man. At any level."

"Pop will be happy, anyway. Until the guy crashes and burns. But Tig will be chewing up the furniture."

"She won't."

Iano raised his eyebrows, suggesting doubt.

"Have you talked to her, Iano? Not that she's a fan, but she totally has this guy's number. He's exactly what she expects of her elders at this historical moment. He's legitimizing personal greed as the principal religion of our country."

"Not the first prophet in that line."

"No, but this one's apparently kind of a savant, incapable of pretending there's any shame in it. He's put the pride back in avarice."

"If that's what we've led Tig to expect of her elders, we should all drive ourselves off a bridge."

She gave him a careful look, but Iano didn't have a suicidal bone in his body. "I'm just telling you. She says today's problems can't be solved by today's people, we just keep shoring up our bankruptcy with the only tools we know. Making up more and more complicated stories about how we haven't failed."

"She thinks she could do better?"

Willa blew out some air. "She thinks we're overdrawn at the bank, at the level of our species, but we don't want to hear it. So if it's not this *exact* prophet of self-indulgence we're looking to for reassurance, it will be some other liar who's good at distracting us from the truth. Because of the times we're in."

"That's preposterous."

"Tell me."

The broadcast moved on to less preposterous news: a clothing company suing a department store for copying its famous plaid. The Coca-Cola Company fighting a legal battle to register a trademark on the word *Zero*. And also, surprisingly, restructuring itself to help offset the impact of weak sales abroad.

"What, foreigners aren't buying Coke anymore?" Willa asked. "The nerve."

"Sure they are. 'Weak sales' only means the sales didn't grow in the last quarter. In the trade world, standing still means you're falling backward."

"Huh," Willa mused. "What if they've already tracked down every person in every desert and tundra on earth who wants to buy a Coke?"

"There you'll have it," he said cheerfully. "The end of the world as we know it."

≫≪

They were two blocks from home when a text came in from Jorge, relaying apologies from Tig because she hadn't had time to make dinner. They should pick up something if they were hungry. "Hands full here."

They could hear the dissonant thunder of profanity before they opened the front door. "Sundowning" this was called, according to the hospice nurse who came three times a week to bathe, debride wounds, and chart the declining vitals. Apparently it was common for people in Nick's condition to rage on a daily schedule against the dying of the light. The nurse, Jane, who came only mornings, warned that their loved one might start saying things very much out of character, which they shouldn't take personally. She didn't know anger *was* Nick's character, now present in only two versions: silent or loud.

Willa and Iano arrived at an awkward moment and lingered in the doorway to his room while Tig and Jorge finished changing Nick's adult diaper. They worked together efficiently through the steps of the procedure: unfasten the tabs and fold it down, roll the man on his side, slip out and replace the old with the new, clean, and roll him back. The nurse had taught them the rolling trick, which also worked for changing the sheet underneath him without lifting him from the bed. They'd learned how to crush morphine tablets and administer them with a dropper under the tongue to a person who couldn't fully awaken or swallow. In a lifetime of professional curiosity Willa had never thought to wonder about such things.

"Thanks, guys. I feel guilty for taking the day off," she said.

Jorge touched two fingers to his forehead. "No problem. You needed it."

"Is Dusty down for the night?"

"Hopefully." Tig gathered up soiled paper products and stuffed them into a lidded pail. "We gave him a bottle and got him down, like, half an hour ago, wouldn't you say?"

Jorge nodded. His recent shave was growing out so his head looked gorgeously upholstered in black velour. He seemed a little dressed up, wearing a colorful print shirt unbuttoned over the standard sleeveless T. She wondered if they'd made other plans that had been spoiled by the delinquent, tardy parents. They both disappeared to the bathroom to wash up and disinfect themselves postskirmish.

Iano stood leaning against the doorway. He hadn't spoken since they entered the house. Willa felt anguish for all of them: a father, son, and granddaughter trapped in this excruciating intimacy. Even worse for Jorge, the innocent bystander drafted into service. He didn't have to be there but there he was, feigning good-natured little spars as he dodged angry swats from the big, clumsy paw. During the diaper change Willa could have sworn she heard Nick call him "the goddamn spic," and Jorge looked only faintly exasperated, as if at an elder for using outmoded slang. As in fact he probably was.

"How is neither one of you at work tonight?" Willa thought to ask when they came back. Tig and Jorge rarely had an evening off together.

"Restaurant's closed, Mom."

"On Tuesday? I thought only Sunday and Monday."

"They've cut back to weekends only. Winter schedule, I told you that. From New Year's till Valentine's Day people always decide they're never going to spend money again. Or eat."

"Then they get over it," Jorge added.

"Dad, watch it! Don't sit," Tig warned. Iano picked up an open syringe from the Big-Ass Chair, where he'd been about to collapse.

"Sorry for that," Jorge said, taking the needle from Iano and working it point-first into a clear plastic waste container that was bristling already with needles inside. "Tig just gave him his insulin right before the . . ." He tilted his head toward the bed, tactfully not naming the other procedure. Jorge had a permanently well-groomed look Willa attributed to the smooth hairline above the heavy brows, crossing his forehead as if drawn there with a ruler. Willa's kin were all widow's-peaky, as were her progeny.

"That needle container looks full," she said. "I'll ask Jane for a new one. If she brings it we don't have to pay for it, for some reason." Willa remained mystified by the specific benefactions of Medicaid, to which Nick still had no idea he was beholden. They always held their breath when he ranted to Jane about welfare scammers.

Tig frowned at the container. "I *hate* that. Throwing away syringes every day."

"It's okay, honey."

"Yeah, Mom, except it's not. They're piling up somewhere. They don't just *vanish* when they leave this house in a hazardous waste container."

"I know. I guess some things don't make sense to recycle."

"Needles can be sterilized and reused. It is actually possible to do that."

Willa was in no position to argue with Tig, who did the most undoable things. Changing diapers, dressing the weeping wounds on his gangrenous extremities. "Tell me a story, Papu," she coaxed now as she rolled layers of compression bandages around his swollen legs, wrapping him like a mummy from the bottom up.

"Don't give me *skatá, Tell me a story Papu*. Changing the subject. I said I want to go tomorrow. You're taking me."

"Where do you want to go, Pop?" Iano brightened at the prospect of an outing.

From Nick's mumbled Greek response Willa caught one word that led to a disquieting guess. He confirmed it by saying, "Graveyard."

"I told you we can go tomorrow morning," Tig said patiently, "if you're feeling good enough to get in your wheelchair. If not, it'll have to wait for another day."

"Why do you want to go to the cemetery, Pop?"

"Whya hell you think a dying old *malákas* goes to the cemetery?"

Into the consequent silence Tig dropped this explanation: "To choose a gravesite."

A spasm of eye contact made the rounds: Iano to Willa; Willa to Tig, with a small shake of her head to convey *That's not happening*; Tig to Jorge with a little lift of the eyebrows that said *I told you*.

"We'll have to look into that, Pop," Iano said, unhelpfully. If they qualified for funeral assistance through Medicaid it might get them a pine box, but not a plot in Vineland's fancy cemetery. The family was still in arrears on Helene's funeral debt; Willa ignored that one on the grounds that Zeke should long since have broached this with Helene's parents, and in the meantime no one was going to repossess Helene. But the difficult Nick conversation had been undertaken by Iano and his sisters. Decisions had been made. It would fall to Willa to share these with Tig after they'd gotten Nick doped down for the night.

Everyone watched Willa perform the ritual of the morphine: crushing, diluting, meting out, as somber and elaborate as a tea ceremony. She handled the heavy narcotics because she didn't want Iano or Tig to feel responsible if something went wrong. Nick accepted the dropper under his tongue with the same heartbreaking eagerness as Dusty taking his bottle. Willa returned the morphine to its hiding place (as advised by Jane, in case of a break-in) behind a framed family photo on the shelf. Iano volunteered to stay with Nick. Tig went to check on the baby. Willa migrated with Jorge to the kitchen.

"You two haven't eaten either. I'll make us something," Willa said, staring into the woeful interior of her refrigerator: ketchup, mayo, a half block of cheddar. A leftover mash-up of something that would have been Dusty's dinner. A hand of speckled plantains someone had stuck in the fridge to rescue their lost youth. Because of the iffy electricity they weren't stockpiling a lot of perishables, but this was grim. She considered grilled cheese, then saw the lone heel of bread on the counter in its rumpled condom-like wrapper. She'd used up the loaf on sandwiches that morning.

"Something from nothing, looks like," she said. "Sorry, the cupboard's bare. I meant to get to the grocery today but I guess we played hooky instead."

What she'd done instead was turn over Iano's last paycheck in full to ACE and Visa, and go on counting on Tig for the rations that always turned up in their kitchen. Willa had noticed she was working less, but missed that the restaurant had all but closed. She stood with her block of cheddar in hand, ambushed by memories of the government cheese she'd subsisted on through her college years.

"I've got this," Jorge said, running water into a saucepan and lighting a burner on the camping stove. She admired his optimism.

"You shouldn't have to cook on your day off."

He smiled. "On my day off I can make what I want, and eat it." He handed her a grater and a plate and made himself at home, rooting around in the cupboards to find sugar and a bag of cornmeal. He adjusted the burner expertly, as if any normal household might have a twenty-year-old camp stove seated atop a defunct kitchen range. Willa didn't mind him taking over the situation. She was a little in awe of this tall, self-possessed young man with the velveteen head.

"Thanks for helping out with Nick," she said. "I mean, *thanks* doesn't touch it."

He lifted a shoulder, seeming a little defensive. "I'm not going to let Tig do that alone."

"No, but still. It's ugly stuff. A lot of guys would find something better to do."

She watched him stir salt, sugar, and butter into the water as it came to a boil. "It's just how it goes," he said finally. "I used to have another brother, the oldest one of us? He got messed up real bad, brain dead but not exactly. Man, you talk about mean, he was like . . ." Jorge shook his head, throwing a couple of wild punches at the air. "You don't realize how hard a dude can hang on without really having the lights on."

Willa recalled mention of a disabled relative in the Vineland Training School, but that was a cousin, still living, she was sure. "I'm sorry. I didn't know about your brother. A car wreck?"

"Something like that. Semivegetative state."

"Sorry." She regretted asking. *Something like that* might be an OD or a suicide attempt, some shameful violence. She made herself look at the barbed-wire tattoo circling his arm. A crown of thorns. "That must have been really hard on your family."

"On my mom, mostly. She and my sisters did all of it. I guess me and José Luis were finding something better to do."

"It must have been a while ago. You and José Luis would have been little kids."

"Sure."

"Tig says your mother knew my aunt. When she lived here."

"Yeah, I think so. Nice lady. Dreama, right?"

Willa nodded. His history in this neighborhood had taken no previous shape in her thoughts. He'd grown up, lost a brother there. "Where's she now? Your mother."

"San Juan. She went back for the cure I guess, after my brother died."

"Sounds like it worked out."

"She likes it, she hates it, you know. There's all these *viejos*, the aunts and uncles. We used to go every summer, for the whole three months by God. Mami's gonna be sure her kids are *Boricuas*. She's still on us all the time to come visit, but you know. It's harder when you get older. Maybe this year."

Tig appeared. "All quiet. Everybody's asleep."

"Even Dad?"

"Almost. He looks worn out. What did you guys do?"

"Just walked. A lot, maybe ten miles."

"*Mmm,* sorrullos," Tig said happily. She tied an apron around Jorge's middle to keep his shirttail out of the fire and then stood next to him watching the saucepan boil, leaning on him slightly like a friendly dog. Willa executed her assignment, grating a pile of yellow cheese onto a blue plate.

"So Tig," she said after a bit.

"So Mom." Tig turned to face her.

"I'm just going to say this. We can't afford a cemetery plot. Dad has talked with his sisters. They've all agreed on a different plan."

Tig nodded. "We'll have him cremated, right?"

"It seems like the best thing."

"I figured."

She *figured*? "Aunt Athena wants us to send his ashes back to Phoenix. They'll organize some kind of memorial service there."

Tig mulled this over. "Can you send human remains through the regular mail?"

"I hadn't really got that far," Willa confessed.

"Well, that all makes sense. Most of the family is back there. Some guys that worked with him in the plant might still be around, people that remember him in his glory days. That would be nice."

"So you're not upset?"

"I'm upset because you were going to tell him." Tig and Jorge exchanged the briefest of glances, letting Willa know this had been discussed. *She* had been discussed.

"Tell him what, we can't buy him a grave?" Willa stared, flabbergasted. "After twenty-six years you've decided to get on board with the little white lie?"

Tig didn't look at her. "There's times."

"Seriously. This is the occasion. And you think being honest would make *me* the bad guy?"

"Being *honest*? Like you've ever mentioned how he owes his life to Obamacare? But now you have to tell him he gets no say in what happens after he dies. That's cruel."

Jorge kept out of it. He was stirring cornmeal into the boiling water in a meditative way, thickening it into a yellow batter. Tig lit the other camp stove burner and heated oil in a skillet. Jorge took Willa's plate of cheese and stirred it into his batter.

"So you vote for lying," Willa said.

"I vote for letting Papu be happy. He won't know what we do after. Obvi."

The thought of sugarcoating things for Nick left Willa feeling marooned in a sea of resentment. Tig scooted deftly around her to reach into the fridge to extract the plantains. Willa watched her peel and slice them, and tried for the thousandth time to understand the lay of her daughter's moral land. "You're right," she said finally. "We can lie to Nick and let him be happy. Even if he's determined to make us all miserable."

"I don't think that's his goal. He just thinks he's right and we're wrong about basically everything. And the clock's running out on getting his point across."

Jorge rubbed oil into his hands and began rolling the steaming batter between his palms into fat little cigars. From her own restaurant days Willa remembered the asbestos hands of a practiced chef. If you built up a tolerance gradually, you could trick your brain into ignoring the signals of danger. Tig, meanwhile, dropped her plantain slices into the hot oil and fished them out with a fork as soon as they softened. When she completed the batch, Jorge used the same skillet to fry his cornmeal cigars. Willa felt like a voyeur. The efficient camaraderie of their restaurant life seemed as intimate as a marriage.

"You're both really kind to Nick, even when he says disgusting things. I honestly can't do it. I guess I don't see why we should let him off easy."

"You think he's getting off easy?" Tig spoke without turning around. She was standing on tiptoe, leaning onto a plate to press it down on the softened plantain slices. When she lifted it they were all squashed into little flower shapes. Willa's fascination was distracting her from the Nick question.

"No. You're right. He's smoked and eaten and sworn himself into a living hell. But still. Doesn't the meanness kill you? The 'spic boyfriend' and all that? I'm sorry, Jorge. I feel like I need to apologize for every minute you spend in our house."

He shrugged. "It's not you saying it. You have to hear it too." He held out a plate of golden corn fritters. "Careful, they're hot."

Willa took a bite and held it between her front teeth until it cooled enough to taste: crisp on the outside, sweet and melty in the middle. She made an appreciative noise with her mouth full.

"Yummy, right?" Tig said. "You're supposed to dip them in garlicky mayo."

Willa obediently got out the mayonnaise, found some garlic to peel and dice, and wondered what other miracles these kids would pull out of an empty larder. For the first time in Jorge's presence Willa thought of Toto, her daughter's first big love, wondering if she still missed him. Whether Jorge was living in his shadow, or slowly outshining it. Evidently he'd been some kind of genius, this Aristotle: engineering, chemistry, auto mechanics. Maybe it wasn't such a big leap from there to auto mechanic, gifted cook, and agreeable changer of diapers. Willa herself had a soft spot for poets and dreamers, but her daughter clearly liked men who were good with their hands.

Jorge finished the fritters and began to refry Tig's squashed plantains, dipping them in water before they hit the hot oil. They spat violently. Willa worried for his eyes, but Jorge was fearless. And tall.

"I appreciate what you're saying about Nick, but it's hard to reconcile that with the way you always correct your dad and me." Willa knew she should let this go. "And Zeke, my God. You two haven't stopped fighting since the day you learned to talk."

"Papu's not in charge of anything anymore. He won't even live long enough to vote again. But Zeke's probably around for as long as I am. He's a very big problem."

"Okay, but I guess my rule of arguing is the same as my rule of housecleaning. You start with the worst mess, and move on from there to less offensive clutter. You can't deny, Nick is the worst mess."

"You're a journalist, Mom. You feel this god-given duty to set people straight."

"Don't you? As a scientist?"

"I'm not a scientist. I'm a line cook."

"Then I'm not a journalist. I'm a nothing."

Willa watched Jorge put one of the twice-fried plantains into Tig's mouth as she tipped up her face like a baby bird. She held the morsel between her teeth and blew to cool it, exactly as Willa had done a minute before. Iano always found it amazing that she and Tig could put things in their mouth that were too hot to hold in their hands. He noticed these little things that made them birds of a feather, or something like that. He had some Greek expression about daughters never escaping their mothers.

"You *think* like a scientist," Willa persisted, holding out the cup of garlicky mayo.

Tig shook her head, chewing and swallowing as she pointed at the corn fritters. "The mayo is for the sorullos. These are tostones, you eat them with salt." She vigorously shook a salt shaker over the plate of plantains before offering it to Willa. Tostones were a miracle. Like sweet, hot potato chips, only better.

"In the department of setting people straight," Willa said, "I don't think you and I are all that different. Just saying." Willa caught a hint of a smile from Jorge, and she adored him for it.

"Thinking like a scientist," Tig insisted, "just means trying to figure out what 'straight' really is."

"And getting it on the record."

"Maybe. But people have to come around in their own ways, Mom. Only when they're ready. Most people will die first."

"That's cheerful," Willa said.

Jorge turned off the burner and conversation ended as they stood in the kitchen feasting on something from nothing. It dawned on Willa that Tig might think it *was* cheerful, about the deluded masses dying off with delusions intact. From Tig's point of view, this would be a happy prognosis.

⚹

For weeks it was touch and go as Nick's organs vied for last place in the martyrdom of an overspent body: heart, lungs, kidneys, blood vessels, brain, pancreas. Any treatment to boost one of them would rob from another, was how Jane explained it. The meds that eased the strain on his enlarged heart, for example, would play havoc with his kidneys, and vice versa. Drained by this internal conflict, Nick drifted into a long twilight sleep with a permanent bluish cast to his lips as if he'd nodded off while eating blueberries. Talk in the sickroom grew quiet as the family learned about things like the death rattle (Willa had thought this was an invention of gothic novels) and the phone calls they would need to make immediately after Nick passed. Ironically, a trip to the cemetery was the last thing on anyone's mind. But in early March the patient rallied back to consciousness for a last hurrah. They'd been warned to expect this, the evolutionary gift of one final surge of adrenaline to a beleaguered body to fuel an escape from danger. In Nick's case, "escape" translated into a demand to have his radio on at all hours, and a quest for cemetery real estate.

On the cool, clear, windless day when the outing seemed possible, Iano had a full day of classes and Jorge was working on an emergency transmission overhaul, so they rolled out as a party of four: Tig and Willa, Dusty and Nick. For the hour it took to get Nick dressed, properly oxygenated, and tucked into his wheelchair, the swollen legs lifted for him one at a time, Willa aimed for the same mind-set that gave her patience with Dusty. Nick was just another helpless, diapered human being in a stroller, surely worthy of her sympathy. Today there would be no arguments. Her vow lasted the length of the front walk.

Even through his layers of fog Nick had gathered that his political hero was on the rise, winning primaries like a house afire. Nick liked to explain how right he was, on a subject Willa could no longer avoid by rolling her eyes.

"Look, Nick, I'm just going to say this one thing. The guy doesn't do anything, he just brags about how great he is. He brags about shooting people on Main Street, for God's sake."

"*Mom*," Tig said.

"Probably should. Plenty a bastards out there need it."

"Really. Except he'd get his hands dirty. He's never spent a day of his life doing anything you would call work. I don't understand why you respect him."

"Respect him . . . he respects me," Nick said woozily. "Eat what I want, drive a big damn car and say what I want to . . . niggers and faggots . . . wear a biggest fucking gold watch. No dick-ass liberal telling me . . . ashamed a getting what's mine."

For thirty years she'd believed her father-in-law had no filters. Turns out, he could have been worse. "Not quite with you on the gold watch. But never mind."

"Pansy ass . . . don't want us a have it good. Keep a working man down whiney welfare scum . . . Mexicans everybody but the guy that did the work. Okay?"

Willa understood there was no fair fight to be had here. She was quiet for a full minute or so. Until Nick burst forth again. "Goddamn . . . born in Africa too lazy. . . . Go making a good deal for our side."

"You can't be discussing the president."

"*Mom.*"

"Don't want a guy like me . . . good life."

"Why would he want to hold you back, Nick?"

"Reasons . . . Eenie-meenie-minie-moe . . . favors for his kind. Special interests."

Tig must have noticed the steam coming from Willa's ears. "Mom, let's switch. You take Dusty's stroller. I'll push Papu."

Willa gladly obliged. She wasn't sure Tig could manage four times her own weight, but she did. Tig the mighty. She needed Willa's help only getting him up and down the curbs, her eyes flashing warnings throughout. Willa obediently kept quiet. Tig looked like a traffic beacon in a bright orange secondhand parka and a red wool scarf tying up her locks. Dusty was solemn as he gazed out from his swaddle of blankets at the cold, vivid day. Willa had often taken this route when she walked Dixie, but that had been a while. Today the giant, leafless trees lining Park Avenue seemed alive in some way they hadn't been for months, perhaps feeling some movement of the sap in their hearts.

Traffic in the cemetery was nil. They bypassed the gothic double stone arch and pedestrian entry, sticking to the paved roadway. This was Nick's first visit and he seemed alert to possibilities, pointing at areas he perceived as vacant, where the more demure markers lay flat in the winter-killed grass. This graveyard was Vineland's original, with ornate nineteenth-century monuments and some of the biggest trees Willa had ever seen. Landis himself was supposed to be in there somewhere. She assumed the ground had long since filled up, necessitating the newer cemeteries that had opened on the outskirts along with the shopping malls.

Even here, Nick was not going to go gentle. The cemetery turned out to be as ethnically segregated as the rest of the world, and some powerful racial radar was still operative behind Nick's deteriorated retinas. He had no interest in the ghettos of Italian or Hispanic headstones. Willa noticed Dusty's somber expression growing more distressed, and she worried she'd underestimated the cold. Tig was getting ahead of her, trailing an exhaust stream of Nick's incomprehensible ramble. When Dusty started to cry, Willa yelled to get her attention. "Hey, Tig? He's getting cold. Think I should head back?"

Tig pointed at a little chapel in the center of the grounds. "You could take him in there. It's usually open during the day."

Willa was relieved to find the door unlocked. She gathered up the bundle of Dusty, left the stroller outside, and hurried into a small, dim space of simple pews and stained-glass windows mostly covered with duct tape and cardboard. The plaster walls were water stained. A sign near the door pled for donations to help repair damage from Hurricane Sandy. Willa accepted her usual front-row seat on the crumble of civilization.

But Dusty's spirits improved the minute they sat down in a pew. At seven months he was getting more upright. He wanted to pull himself up holding on to her fingers, stand on her lap, and have himself a look around. She thought of Helene's funeral, the last time they had been in a church, and felt guilty for how far his mother had slipped from all their thoughts. Zeke was the only one who could keep her present for her son by recognizing bits of Helene in his looks and habits as he grew. Zeke might never be up to it. *Motherless* was in these little bones along with the calcium, and all the months he'd cried before they figured out a human needed to cry in someone's arms. Willa pondered the immensity of Dusty's loss while checking the temperature of his hands, which seemed fine, and holding her cheek to his cold face, crooning as she warmed him up. "You're okay," she said again and again, the wishful abracadabra of motherhood.

"Scam. Goddamn global . . . hoaxers." She could hear Nick grunting out the verbal turds of his argument as she approached. She had stayed in the chapel longer than really necessary, hoping the final resting place would be nailed and they could call it a day. She studied Tig's face for clues as she wheeled toward them.

"Did you find a good spot, Nick?" Willa asked brightly. "Show me where, so I know what to ask for when I go to the front office."

Tig widened her eyes at Willa, suggesting she might be overdoing it.

"Under them big trees. . . . gotta Metaxes . . . Christopoulos, Papadopoulos, whole damn neighborhood. Drink me some ouzo with them guys."

"That's great. A Greek section." Willa could just see the party, a nagging-free afterlife where husbands could eat, drink, and smoke without moderation.

"I been telling your . . . Aunt Jemima here it's cold. She didn't . . . jackasses say it's warming up. Chinese and them full of shit hoax."

"Let's switch," Willa said, handing off the stroller and pointing Nick toward the exit. "My daughter," she said loudly, "has studied atmospheric science. Actual physics. Did you know that?"

He grunted.

"Scientists measure the temperatures all over the world. With thermometers. I'm no expert but I know that much, the temperatures keep going up. We're having hurricanes where they've never been, stronger than ever before. Like the one that blew out the windows in the chapel over there. Seems pretty real to me."

"Plenty other reasons . . ."

"Okay. Whatever." *Please shut up*, Willa prayed. Meaning herself. *Let it go.*

"Rotation . . . earth went a little off maybe."

Willa shot a sideways glance at Tig, expecting a smirk, seeing something like physical pain. Of course this wasn't funny, watching a man struggle so hard for a lucid claim on his perennially illogical world.

"Or this other thing . . . guy onna radio . . . it's fish. All get together one part of the . . . ocean. Stirs up the hurricanes."

Willa's sympathy ruptured into laughter. "Oh, come *on*."

"Scientific fact," Nick assured her.

"Okay, Nick. Maybe it's a fish orgy. Maybe the earth slipped on its axis. Or possibly we burned stuff that put carbon in the air. Christ almighty. You're the one who knows chemical reactions. When you burn petroleum, where does the carbon go?"

Nick was nonresponsive.

"Into the sky, maybe?"

"Those other things . . . people. Think this, think that . . . lotta things. You don't know who's right. You can't say."

"Yeah Papu, actually you can," Tig piped up suddenly. "There's a rule about that. It's called Occam's razor."

"What?" He craned his neck around to look at Tig, suddenly at full attention. Willa felt acutely envious. This is what came of picking your battles.

"When there's a lot of different explanations for something," Tig said slowly and loudly in the manner of a teacher for the hearing impaired, "including supernatural and voodoo, you have to go with the simplest one. You look at *just* the evidence, nothing extra thrown in, and then go with simple."

Nick shook his head. "Nah . . . don't see that."

"Yes you do. Like, we're looking at a white horse out in a field. You say Tig, maybe that's a hologram being projected by aliens.

Maybe it's a zebra somebody painted white. Occam's razor says, cut the crap. It's a horse."

"Who'sis Occam? One your . . . spic boyfriends?"

"Oh for God's sake, Nick. She has one boyfriend, his name is Jorge. Come on, you can say it: *HOR-HAY.*"

Nick seemed to have drifted back to sleep. This did not deter Willa.

"Jorge does things for you that I'll *never* ask my own kids to do for me. And just so you know, he's kept our car going for us all winter. When you stroked out he got you to the ER." Willa's grip on the wheelchair handles would have crushed elderly bones. "You're going to waste your last breath *hating*, you know that? Hating on every single thing that's keeping you alive. Jorge, Jane, even your oxygen. Portion control. Nicotine patches. *Obamacare.*"

"You're . . . crazy bitch."

Willa stopped and lifted her hands in the air. "Okay, that's it. I'm a crazy bitch and I'm leaving you here. Right in the middle of East fucking Peach Street."

Tig stared at her. Willa stared back.

"Mom. *You* don't have to kill him." Tig made an exaggerated smiley face.

There in the street, for a millisecond, Willa caught sight of the world through her daughter's eyes: the global contempt for temperance and nurture, the fierce entitlement to every kind of consumption. How many Nicks there were. All wired to self-destruct.

"Wow. You're right. He's taking care of that, isn't he?"

Tig pushed on, singing a quiet little lullaby to Dusty. *Ashes, ashes, all fall down.* Willa took the chair and followed, listening to the secret song about Papu and the end of days.

14

⌇

End of Days

Someone's shot! On Landis Avenue."

It was the janitor Mr. Goby at the door to Cutler's office. Thatcher's first thought was to welcome the interruption. He would repent of it for many years after.

Cutler leaped up from his striped settee with an open hand raised as if in surrender. His lieges sat in astonished silence: Elocution, Classics, French, Bookkeeping, called there because they always agreed with Cutler. And Thatcher, who never would.

"Are the police summoned?" Thatcher asked. "Or a doctor?"

Goby stood slack jawed and rheumy eyed, staring at the little band of teachers perched on the ostentatious furniture. Thatcher had requested the meeting to discuss an early end to the spring term, because so many families now needed their sons to prepare fields for planting. April was the month for it. He was dispirited by losses one by one from his rolls, even Giovanna Persichetti, kept home to tend a baby sister who had fallen into a scalding laundry vat. Such realities meant nothing to Cutler. He was adamant to hold them all in until June, or mark them as criminal truants.

"Speak up, man," Thatcher pressed poor Goby. "Is someone hurt?"

"They say it's Landis."

"Landis hurt! Oh my heavens." Cutler went pale.

Goby blinked several times more. "They say it's Landis that shot a man."

"Oh." Cutler slowly sat down. "He must have had good reason."

Miss Hirstberger nodded her agreement, followed by Elocution and Bookkeeping.

"I'll go see what it's about," Thatcher said, glad for a reason to leave. The final reckoning had arrived: Cutler demanded he disavow Darwinism or find no letter in his mailbox April first, when contracts for the autumn term went out. Cutler accused him of obstinate self-isolation. This morning's contentious meeting was only proving it true.

Out in the street he realized he should have asked Goby for more particulars. But he could hear men shouting before he reached the corner of Landis Avenue, and from there no one could have missed the commotion in front of the newspaper offices. With a wicked pleasure Thatcher thought of his friend Carruth, who had just caught himself a fine haul of headlines if the captain had really made murder.

He worked his way through a crowd of stopped carriages and restive horses, a Friday morning's traffic brought to a standstill. Newsboys stood dumbstruck, momentarily eclipsed, among fur-trimmed ladies with shopping and children in hand. Thatcher stepped back from a pair of boys who carried a large pane of glass between them, distracted from some delivery and now angling themselves precariously into the throng. Polly would be inconsolable to have missed this. Carruth must be here, still invisible for the moment, although Thatcher almost certainly recognized his printer, Hank Wilbur, who had once joined them for a drink. Poor Hank—if Hank it was—seemed in a terrible lather, twisting his cap in both hands and shaking his head in the center of a great constabulary circle. Thatcher had never seen this many brass buttons and round domes in Vineland, all directing their gazes at the wretched Hank. A victim was being loaded into a cart; through the crowd Thatcher could see men tilting a long gurney into the shay. The driver whipped his horses and hied off down the avenue. The accused was nowhere in sight. Surely Goby had gotten it wrong. But it was hard to think of any other reason the ringmaster would absent himself from such a dandy circus.

Thatcher saw no one there in need of immediate help. He could just as well read the story tomorrow in *The Independent*. Or go home to hear Rose and Aurelia's version, which would be well established already, and thoroughly favorable toward the culprit if it was Landis. *He must have had good reason*, were Cutler's first words. Looking north across the street for his escape, he paused for the passing of a fancy buggy that happened to be the Dunwiddies'—one of their *several* fancy buggies, Polly would have corrected—with Leverett of the pointed boots and his dull, round father riding inside. Thatcher touched his hat but the Dunwiddies didn't see him, as such men rarely did. The Pussytoes and the Toadflax, botanical names that pleased him so well he'd shared them with Rose. She was furious. She truly believed he envied her friends' money and position, when in fact it was their slavering for these things that put him off. Thatcher did not pretend remorse for a disaffection that was mutual. Every hour Rose spent with the Dunwiddies was time outside her husband's understanding. Those hours were becoming many.

When the carriage had passed he found himself directly facing Mary's girl, the fuzzy little mullein. Selma. She crossed the road toward him with a basket swinging from her right hand and her left firmly clamped to Willis Chester. Of all people, Willis, his diminutive former pupil, was leading Selma by the hand across Landis Avenue. She was first to see Thatcher and dropped the hand, or rather swatted it away, lowering her eyes and flushing deeply as she curtseyed. "Mr. Greenwood."

"Mister Greenwood!" Willis echoed. "You ain't in the school-house!"

"Nor are you, Willis. We have missed you since the holidays."

"No sir, I lit out. I got me a proper job at the Keeley Bakery."

"Have you."

"Yessir. They needed extra hands with the holiday cakes and after it wasn't Christmas no more they done kept on with me."

"You must be doing good work."

Willis flushed with the pride of a gainfully employed man and pointedly restaked his claim on Selma, taking back her hand. Thatcher could not make this pair sensible in his head: Willis, Selma. Two children. Willis was taller than Selma by a thread, and Selma barely taller than a vigorous peony shrub.

"How are you, Selma? I recall your strong opinions on cakes. You and Willis must have spirited conversations."

Selma blushed nearly purple by way of an answer. Thatcher looked about for Mary, though he knew better. Maid and mistress were colleagues in the forest, but Selma would be sent alone to do errands in town. This was mostly the point of her employment. Today especially, this town was no place for those who did not fare well with hubbub, as only Mary could have put it.

"Are you coming from work, or going?" he asked them both.

"Going and coming," Willis said in a professional tone. "I'm done. My pa gets me up when he comes home from graveyard shift and I run our whole section upknocking the ones that's going in for early shift. They pay me five cents a head for it by the week, for the upknocking. And I still get to Keeley's before light to make the bread. So now I'm done, you see. Selma has a ways to go yet. We meet at the middle."

"Sometimes," she clarified.

"Me and Selma's getting married," Willis added.

"Married! How old are you?"

"Fifteen," they said together, unconvincingly. "Mr. Greenwood," Selma added, "Mistress Treat wouldn't know about it. If you please?"

Little towheaded Willis, whom Thatcher had wanted to feed outside his classroom like a stray dog, now the upknocker for his neighborhood, rapping windows in the dark and getting men shifted into the mill on time. Then making their daily bread. With matrimony now in his sights. The smallest seed could become a tree.

"I won't mention your engagement to Mrs. Treat," Thatcher said, knowing in fact he would. Selma and Willis seemed to be waiting for a dismissal. The crowd had grown even larger and more boisterous in the minute they'd been speaking. Nearly as an afterthought he asked, "Do you know if someone was shot?"

"Yes sir," Willis said. "It's Captain Landis and Mr. Carruth."

"Dear God. That can't be." Thatcher's knees nearly buckled. The irrepressible agitator. "Carruth *shot* him?"

"No sir. Landis shot Carruth."

"No," Thatcher said, still trying to blot from his mind an image of his friend rising from the Plum Hall crowd, raising a pistol, and shooting Landis dead. It hadn't happened, of course. But the reverse was incomprehensible.

"It's so," Willis insisted. "Hank Wilbur seen it happen. Landis marched right in the door and plumb shot the man."

"How do you know this?" Thatcher endeavored to breathe.

"We was right there yonder! I was waiting for Selma to come out of the dry goods and here comes Hank roaring down the stair crying 'Help, he's shot,' and all. He's still over there with the police-men right yet. Look, sir. Frank Ladd seen it all too."

"Are you telling me Landis and Carruth had a fight? Here, today?"

"No sir. Carruth wanted none of him but Landis shot him in the back of the head." Willis seemed to grow taller on the strength of his testimony. Thatcher stood dumbly shaking his head.

"That can't be."

"It was on account of a piece that come out in his paper yes-terday, they said. About the captain's wife being loony. Captain couldn't stand for it, is what they said."

Thatcher had read the piece in *The Independent*, a comic little ramble about a man giving his wife a pistol for self-protection, the woman shooting up the crockery. Carruth's normal satirical non-sense. No names mentioned. No cause for bloody murder. "Where was it?" he asked.

"Back of the head, Frank says." Willis rapped the rear of his own noggin.

"No. I'm asking you where it happened? If you say Landis shot Carruth, where did he do it?"

"Newspaper office. Landis walks in there asking, 'Where's Car-ruth?' Marches right on in the printing room and next thing you know, *bang*! Landis comes out of there hollering, 'I killed him, I was obliged! Oh, my poor, crazy wife.'"

This wasn't possible. Leaders of men did not behave this way. While Thatcher struggled to form a question, Willis appeared more than ready to get himself and his intended away from this mess of old men's making. "Wait, Willis. Where are they now?"

"Landis lit out, they say. Reckon he'll be in the jailhouse di-rectly."

"And Carruth?"

Willis pulled up his shoulders and rolled his eyes toward heaven.

≫≪

But he was not in heaven. Not quite. Every newspaper on the Eastern Seaboard carried an account of the shooting in its Saturday or Sunday edition, except Carruth's *Independent*, which predictably went quiet. The *Vineland Weekly* reported that after the mishap Carruth was resting quietly at home, with no serious ill effects.

"For God's sake. He took a half-ounce bullet in the brain!" Thatcher shouted. Rose cringed, Aurelia set down her teacup and stared. Polly watched cautiously from the settee, where she held a plate of meat and gravy on her lap. They now took their meals in the parlor because the dining room ceiling had fallen. Of greatest concern to Rose and Aurelia, amid this collapse, was the strain of making continued excuses to dissuade their new friends the Dunwiddies from calling on them at home.

The Brooklyn *Eagle*, the New York *Sun, Herald*, and *Tribune*, the Philadelphia *Evening Star*, and many more ran prominent articles about the shooting. Thatcher knew this only because the *Weekly* had reprinted generous excerpts from these sources, all describing the shooting as a fully defensible act. Yes, Landis had drawn his pistol on an unarmed man and shot him in the back of the skull. But the man with the pistol was aggravated. His wife was frail, and the renegade journalist's accusations against her husband were driving the lady near to distraction.

"In modern times," Aurelia read aloud in a queenly voice, holding the *Weekly* at arm's length to accomplish a focus, "wealthy and successful men must bear the covetous resentment of less industrious people. Their lurid false accusations follow these ideal men of our society right into their homes. It cannot be allowed to continue."

"You're quoting from the murderer's newspaper. You realize that, don't you?"

"Thatcher!" Aurelia cried, dropping the paper to her lap. "Captain Landis is not a *murderer.*"

"I'm sure you're praying for Carruth's recovery. Out of no good will toward a man shot in cold blood, but to spare Landis the title of murderer."

"You behave as if you *knew* this man Carruth," Rose scolded.

"What if I did?"

"Well, you don't. If you did, you wouldn't be so distressed. Please sit down, you are pacing like an Arabian."

"I won't be managed like your damned speckled horse," he snapped.

"Well at least you must eat something," she said, placating but not cowed. Then added, "Marvel isn't *my* horse, thank you."

This was Rose as he knew her lately. As the equestrian passions waxed, the yen for producing a baby had waned, along with any other use for Thatcher, it seemed. He stood at the window looking out through the infernal leaded panes. Mary had come out of her house wearing a long overcoat and a stout muffler the color of bricks. During his frequent visits he'd seen Selma knitting that awful thing in her idle moments all through the winter. A warm scarf for her mistress, the presumed act of devotion, would help break the news she was leaving Mary soon for Willis Chester. The cycle of idiocy and betrayal that humans called love was losing its thrall for Thatcher.

"Have some of Mrs. Brindle's saddle of lamb, it's quite good with her mint jelly."

He turned to look at Rose, who gestured at the heavy platter balanced on the étagère as if nothing here were out of place. God bless Mrs. Brindle, still laboring away in her basement kitchen, the only refuge still undamaged in this tumbledown house. Gracie had gone away, after months of complaints over the cold and damp and the melting plaster everywhere. But nothing could stop Mrs. Brindle. With an air of lunatic determination she continued to cook full meals, one after another, dutifully carted upstairs and presented into the wreckage. It was all she knew how to do, just as Aurelia knew only to worship her captain, and Rose to be disappointed in her husband. Every officer and yeoman performing loyal service on the sinking ship.

"Our journalism is too personal"—Aurelia was reading again— "growing worse and worse. If the tone of public opinion is not sufficient to correct this tendency, the press must seek protection from its own bad elements through more stringent libel laws."

"Aurelia, you read Talk of the Town every week, in that same newspaper. Every barn burned, every drunk staggering naked in an alley or child falling down a well. Is that not all rather *personal?*"

Aurelia's eyebrows reached into the territory of the lace cap. She returned to her reading. Polly ate in silence, uncharacteristically subdued. Scylla and Charybdis lay at her feet watching every bite move from plate to mouth. The beasts were visibly uneasy with the collapse of human protocols, and distracted by the proximity of food.

"Leverett says that man is a *fiend*," Rose now said to Thatcher in a quiet voice, suggesting she had darker knowledge to impart. "Mr. Landis has been trying to make business arrangements abroad, and he requires more workers from Europe. Lots of them I suppose, for new factories and farming concerns. But now he can't get them to come."

"I see. The peasants are wary of his false promises."

"Only because of this vile Carruth! These negative and oppositional reports he makes are frightening them away."

How his friend would rejoice to hear of his newspaper's reach, even across an ocean. This, truly, was the tumbling of Jericho's walls. Thatcher could not countenance the thought of this giant force of a man snuffed out. Not while the sun blazed its ordinary light and late March broke the buds on the trees. From the rumors that flooded Vineland that week, Thatcher gleaned only two facts he chose to believe: Landis was in the Bridgestone jail, and Carruth was still alive.

※

The house was not easy to locate. He found an associate of Carruth's at work in the *Independent*'s office, or at any rate saw him through the pane in the locked door, but the boy would not let Thatcher in. It was not Hank Wilbur but someone younger, leaning over a rack, setting type slugs with his youthful spine arched like a bow. No matter how Thatcher knocked and called through the glass, vowing himself a friend, he had no proof to offer. The boy straightened briefly, shook his head anxiously, and continued with his urgent project, perhaps an obituary for his employer. After several minutes the typesetter walked to the door and sadly pulled down the shade, leaving Thatcher to feel humiliated. And useless, as a friend. How could he have shown so little curiosity about Carruth's home and family? But it might have been Carruth's habit to avoid such talk, out of caution, as this young man was being exceedingly cautious now. Carruth had enemies, to be sure. How deadly they were, and how brazen, Thatcher could not have imagined.

He followed his nose. The parlor of the little house in the Italian quarter where he and his friend had drowned several sorrows was now full of Carruth, in the spirit of a premature wake. Even at this hour, late morning, men from the night shift crowded in to absorb the shock and commiserate. They spoke of their friend as if he were mayor of an alternate Vineland just around the corner, where invisible laborers had more determinate flesh and commanding voices, along with fatter pay. They sent Thatcher straight down the alley to a cottage with a bramble of leafless roses twined through its fences and a ginger-haired child beating a tin drum on its front step.

"Is Mr. Uri Carruth your father?"

The boy looked up at Thatcher with the deep-set eyes he recognized. The effect was startling: those great, weary eyes on a child not older than six. "I'm to ask who goes there," he reported.

"I see. You are the lookout. Very well done. You can run inside and tell your ma I'm her husband's good friend Thatcher. Or Mr. Greenwood. The schoolteacher."

The boy hesitated, perhaps overwhelmed by too much choice. The drumstick hung limp from his hand.

"I suppose you wouldn't want to be playing your drum inside. To give your papa a headache."

The moon eyes studied him. "Papa's gone away. He's here, but he doesn't know it." The boy disappeared, leaving Thatcher in grief. *Gone away.*

A pretty Mrs. Carruth in a tired blue apron ushered him in, and the whole household struck Thatcher at once. So much life was being lived in a single room that served as kitchen, parlor, nursery, and sickroom. A yellow pup sat by the butter churn with ears cocked to the stranger's arrival. The officious adolescent twins with identical white caps tied under their chins hovered about the bed; a younger sister sat near it with a bowl and a spoon; a second boy sat on the floor, this one drumless, only a little older than the lad outside. At the center of this small universe was Uri, propped up in a bed or chaise of some kind wearing flannel pyjamas, his lower body buried under quilts and his head so copiously bandaged he resembled a Rajasthani. Uri would have found the comparison amusing, if he were there. The eyes were open and vacant, unmoving, the gaze seeming fixed on something beyond the walls of this cottage. Thatcher's grief threatened to blind him. He managed to introduce himself to Mrs. Carruth, who was younger than he'd expected. She seemed both desolate and distracted as she pushed back curls of tomato-colored hair that strayed out of her cap onto her brow.

"Has he spoken at all, since the attack?"

The mournful looks all around told Thatcher more than he wanted to know.

"He can swallow a little," one of the twins offered. "You have to set the spoon just so on his tongue."

"Has a doctor seen to him?"

"Not so much as you would call it *seeing to*," Mrs. Carruth said. "They brought him here in a shay with some swaddling round his head and some idiot declaring he'll be fine in a day or two."

"Nothing more than that? No examination or treatment?"

"None. I was here with the boys and here came those men barging in the gate with Uri strapped on a gurney like a pig trussed for the spit. Think of it, sir. The boys having to see that. It was the first we knew of any harm done to Father."

Thatcher did think of it, struggling to fathom the miles of woe this family had trod together in seven days. Their great bear, the jokester and zealot who strode from this house each day with his cap set to a more reasonable world than the mess they'd inherited. In every conceivable way, they had lost their sole provider.

"Can I call someone in? I would gladly pay the doctor's fee." Gladly, he thought, and in practical terms, not easily.

"I thank you. Many have made the same offer but . . ." She trailed off, looking at her husband with a tenderness that struck Thatcher through the heart. Here was a marriage.

"I hate to ask, but the . . . bullet. Is it still with him?"

"Are you trying to spare us? Look at him. That's just how he came to us Friday last, only with some extra bandaging we've boiled and put to his head."

"You're boiling the bandages, then. That's wise."

"We're educated people, Mr. Greenwood."

"Of course. I meant no . . . Uri speaks highly of the children. How keen they are at reading and learning."

"Like their father."

"Like those who've reared them. A mother is often the greater influence." Thatcher had immediately noticed she was well spoken, with a hint of Irish in her vowels and a better claim on grammar than most of his pupils. He counted another sadness to add to his own lot: he would not be teaching science to these clever twin girls next autumn. To anyone's children, clever or not.

"The bleeding has stopped, I take it."

"It stopped soon after. But nothing else has come out, in the way of a bullet."

"A doctor should extract it. To relieve some of the pressure on his brain."

"Well, the doctors. They're all friends with Landis, you see. They won't come here to treat him."

"They had better," Thatcher said angrily, thinking of what he'd shouted at Aurelia. Some goodwill here would benefit their friend if they didn't want him hanging for murder. Landis was a free man, had paid the bond himself and walked out of Bridgestone with no charges against him so long as Carruth lay in limbo.

"Landis's fate is tied with your husband's recovery," he managed to say.

"I expect the doctors see a lost cause, and don't want to get tangled with it."

"It's not a lost cause. We'll get him back. I've never met a stronger man than your husband. That is the gospel. The Uri Carruth I know is not a man who gives up a fight."

She stared at him for a moment seeming put out, like a mother whose child is being difficult. Then abruptly turned away. "I'll make you some tea. You sit awhile there with your good, strong friend. It would be a pleasure to him if he could see you've come. Maybe he does see yet."

"He blinks," one of the twins put forward, bringing a chair for Thatcher. "At loud sounds. We're sure he hears them."

"Or would you rather a cup of warm broth, Mr. Greenwood? For a cold day? Do you think this winter will end?"

"Please don't bother. I haven't come to be a burden on your family. Only to take some of it away, if I could."

"If you could," Mrs. Carruth said without looking at him. She opened the stove and prodded the fire under the kettle. "If you had some magical potion for him to drink."

"Please allow me to be hopeful," Thatcher said, made miserable by the sound of his own selfishness. He took the chair that was set for him very close to the lifeless right arm of his empty friend. Thatcher reached for the hand, whether to shake it briefly or hold on to it he didn't know until he touched the flesh. It was not cold, but oddly insensible. He had to let it go.

"Men are known to surprise us in cases like this. Especially men like your husband and father."

All the children looked at him, expressing a range of doubts. They were remarkable and unnerving, those hooded eyes replicated so exactly in the progeny. Uri's legacy on earth would be these eyes, left to search out a more sensible world than the one they'd got. It was cruel to give them hope. Thatcher found he could do nothing else.

"I'm not a doctor but I worked many years among medical men, studying the humors and organs. Please believe what I say. Men like your father may have unexpected reserves."

15

⬭

Unexpected Reserves

The end came, with none of the signifying drama they'd been led to expect. Iano was on watch that night. He and Nick went to sleep, and only one of them woke up.

Now, a week later, Willa sat in the dining room feeding Dusty his lunch, listening to an asthmatic wheeze from the dog asleep at her feet that really might qualify as "death rattle," and trying not to look at a baby-food jar containing some of Nick's ashes on the other end of the table. It felt like an excessively rendered tableau of the Stages of Life.

Outside, the grass was greening. Willa might have felt cheerful if she hadn't been missing Iano. Two nights in a row he'd checked in by phone, but from the midst of a family clamor where he couldn't really talk. She'd been wistful, and wondered aloud how many years it had been since they'd slept apart. He reminded her: not that long. It was when she'd gone to Boston after Helene died. Willa recalled ruefully that *she* hadn't called home much either. It was lonelier to be the one left holding the fort. Especially this one, with a dead man's equipment lurking around. The oxygen compressor's powerful pulse had gone still, and the consequent silence kept startling her awake at night. Hospice was arranging for the pickup of the hospital bed, wheelchair, and other large equipment they had on loan, but not the unused needles, cannula or tubing, the pulse oximeter, vials, pill crushers, any of that. The baggage of terminal illness was mostly nonreturnable.

And human remains, Willa learned, were considered a hazardous material. Mailing them turned out to be legal but complicated, and ultimately unnecessary. Iano flew with the ashes back to Phoenix on Athena's husband's frequent flyer miles. Willa thought this sounded like a Greek mythology Mad Lib. But to Iano it was home and family. As the male heir of the Tavoularis clan, he had ceremonial duties.

The night before he left, Willa and Tig had robbed the urn, taking out a pinch of Nick they planned to bury in the Vineland cemetery. A promise is a promise. Iano could be oddly superstitious, so Willa insisted they keep their thievery on the downlow. The "urn" was a plain metal canister inside the cardboard box they'd picked up from the crematorium (payment due on receipt). Inside the canister, a plastic bag. "Talk about excess packaging," Tig had complained. "Do they think he's going to try to get out?" Once they finally got through to the goods, they were both struck with a squeamishness that surprised them. Surely the hazardous label applied more *before*, given the oozy wounds and anger-management issues. But some barrier between living and nonliving human substance rose up, not wanting to be crossed. It didn't even make sense that this was Nick. That such a very large man, when all was said and done—when *a lot* was said and done—could be reduced to a couple of heaping handfuls of gritty white powder.

Not that they touched it with their hands. Tig was the scientist, Willa reasonably pointed out in an effort to coax her on. She should just see this as so much carbon and calcium. "Nuh-*uh, you,*" Tig said, pushing the spoon at Willa. Eventually Willa mommed up and did the deed, reaching in with a teaspoon, nervously transferring some of the sand-like grit into a baby-food jar she'd washed and saved (because, as Tig said, she'd paid good money for it). A fine cloud rose from the plastic bag and they both held their breath, pretty seriously not wanting to inhale him.

For the burial of this secret stash of Papu they assumed they would need the cover of night. The dispensation of human substance was a closely watched business, they already knew, and poaching on cemetery ground could not possibly go down well with the landlords. They had a week to work out a plan before Iano got back.

Right then Willa was enjoying the smell of April drifting in the open windows after a long winter's fight to seal the elements out of her stupidly leaky shelter. She shoveled lunch into Dusty as fast as a baby-size spoon could do the job. There was no reconciling her memories of last fall—Aldus of the puny disposition and endless howls—with this jolly boy in the high chair who opened not just his face but his whole being to Willa's tendered grace. The mouth popped wide with every approach of the spoon. He was working on a rainbow coalition of Tig's pureed vegetable cubes—beets, pumpkin, green beans would be a guess—plus a spoonful of peanut butter as per instruction. It all felt wrong to Willa, but the pediatric gospel had reversed again: modern advice was to throw the kitchen sink at babies, foodwise, as soon as they could chew and swallow. Even the allergy triggers, early and often. Willa as a young mother had been ordered to sterilize everything within a hundred yards of baby, hold back on solids, and avoid potential allergens, ideally until voting age. And now the doctors said: bring on the peanut butter. Put the babies on the floor, let them eat dog hair.

She was scraping out the bowl when Iano called. She handed spoon and bowl over to Dusty, keeping an eye that he didn't give himself a tonsillectomy.

"How's Dixie?" Iano asked immediately.

"Fine. And so am I, thanks."

"Sorry, *moro*. How are you?"

"It's okay. I'm nervous about Dixie too." The plan was to bury her under one of the two big trees. Willa couldn't decide which Dixie favored—the beech where she always peed, or the oak where she didn't. This and other matters would be decided when the time came. Jorge and Tig had volunteered to dig the hole. Willa found all of it unthinkable. An inadmissible position, to a husband who'd just lost his father. "We're all good here. How are your sisters? How was your flight? You haven't told me anything."

He let out some air, a sound she knew. The release valve on the Greek family pressure cooker. "It's kind of a soap opera, to tell you the truth."

"Are they okay with the rest of us not being there?"

"Of course, they know what flights cost. Really it's the opposite, you're a saint now. '*Ianaki*, your wife that poor woman,' et cetera. Everybody feels guilty he died on our watch. That we had the hardest part."

Ianaki, little Iano. Willa pictured his diminutive sisters all stretching on tiptoe to fawn over him. "Well, we did. We took one for the team. They can be grateful."

"And how do they show this? By taking it out on each other. Triangulating, I guess you call it. Each one has to pull me aside for a secret bitch session about the others. What can I say? *Sisters*."

"Wish I knew." As an only child, Willa could hear people's complaints about their siblings only as a primal form of bragging. They had a tribe. They belonged.

"And the flight, *gamo to*. You don't even want to know."

Willa watched Dusty biting the plastic-coated bowl of his little spoon with an expression of deep satisfaction. Working his first teeth through the gums. "Well, your airplane took off, it landed, and we didn't pay for it," she said. "Sounds good to me."

"Because you weren't there. In a middle seat, with Tweedle One oozing over onto me from the window side and Tweedle Two, ditto, from the aisle. And *she* has a *dog*. One of those little rug mops, in a carrier at her feet. It never stopped yapping."

"You can't blame your seatmates for being big, Iano. I'm sure they were more uncomfortable than you."

"No, *moro*, I blame them for lifting the armrests to express their full privileges of billowing. They booked the aisle and window so they could use all three seats. They were a *husband and wife*. At thirty thousand feet I was caught in their marital crossfire. 'Will you stifle your stupid dog? I told you not to bring the dog!' 'What, leave him with your lazy nephew who already killed all my plants?'"

Willa smiled. "It's Dee and Dum."

"What?"

"Tweedledee and Tweedledum. They're from *Alice in Wonderland*." She pictured Iano between a giant couple in beanies, licking lollipops.

"My knees had no place whatsoever to go, they were jammed into the seat in front of me. So the guy sitting *there* turns around to give me a nasty look. I invited him to trade places with me, and that took care of *his* ass for the duration. Jesus. I couldn't get out of my seat, and of course like a fucker I had to piss the whole time, from Philly to Phoenix. Trapped like a rat in steerage."

This line of complaint was making Willa feel less guilty about her heartbreak over Dixie. "There's your free flight. A Tweedle sandwich."

"And a *dog*."

Willa rubbed Dixie's soft coat with her bare feet. The asthmatic seesaw paused for the release of an appreciative sigh. "So, I have some good news. I've finished the justification section for the historic registry application. Basically a thumbnail sketch of our man Greenwood, and why I think he's a person of historical interest. Chris has found a guy to come and put a date on the house for us. Some historic architecture specialist out of Philadelphia. No charge."

"Nothing is free, *moro*."

"But it is. I guess it's considered part of his research. A Mr. Peabody."

"Mr. *Peabody?* Isn't that Bullwinkle's dog? With the glasses?"

"Bullwinkle doesn't have a dog. He has a squirrel. It's not really Peabody, it's something close to that. He's coming, is what I know. Next Wednesday. Now I'm looking around this homeless shelter we live in and freaking out. I have hostess anxiety."

"You don't have to serve him tea."

"No. But I'll pick up all the clothes off the floor. And ask Tig not to dig up the entire yard until after he leaves."

"My genius wife. You're doing this."

"I am."

She was doing more. Willa had waited a respectful interval of hours before claiming the dead man's room as an office and moving in her desk, ostensibly to file the application for historic registry. She hadn't told Iano yet, in case it wasn't true, or Christopher for fear he might resent the incursion on his territory, but Willa had passed *application* right out of the starting gate. Now she was gaining on *book proposal*. Her desk was piled with draft outlines, printouts from internet searches, and copies of Mary Treat's letters, which she was combing for references to Thatcher Greenwood. From archived newspapers she was picking out sparse but tantalizing shrapnel: a crazy WWF-style verbal match in the town hall, titled Darwin versus Decency. A school scandal, an outburst at a murder trial. What she craved to find was direct correspondence between Thatcher and Mary. Willa was riveted by these two, both ahead of their time, joined (she imagined, somehow) against their world. It wasn't the idyll she'd thought. Mary's correspondence with her scientist friends suggested the gentle Victorians of Vineland, and America for that matter, had shit for brains. They resisted Darwin's logic and rationality in general, to an extent that struck Willa as nuts. A great shift was dawning, with the human masters' place in the kingdom much reduced from its former glory. She could see how this might lead to a sense of complete disorientation in the universe. But still. The old paradigm was an obsolete shell; the writing on the wall was huge. They just wouldn't read.

Dusty had turned over his plastic bowl and was using the spoon as a drumstick. Resourceful lad. "Why is Tig digging up the yard?" Iano was asking.

"To plant stuff. You know this."

"I thought that was over at the school for the disabled."

"Also here. She and Jorge offered our property for the same project."

"To the Feebleminders."

"They have a new name. *Freedom* Minders. Maybe that was it all along, and Tig was just yanking our chain. Whoever they are, they're showing up at all hours with shovels to dig up our lawn for vegetable beds. April would be the month for it." Through the window Willa could see at this moment a quartet of girls, two young, two older, one of them challenged, judging from certain physical cues so subtle Willa would be hard pressed to describe them. "You *know* about this, Iano. We talked about it. The night Tig told us she and Jorge were moving into the carriage house."

"We discussed digging up the yard?"

"Yes. We absolutely did."

Tig wasn't home yet. She worked only the lunch shift now, and took full charge of Dusty the rest of the time. But the diggers came and went on their own schedules. Through her wide network Tig was also arranging to get every remnant of Nick's medical supplies back into the system. Jorge's sister Sondra knew a full range of sick people who could use the lot. Willa was confounded. Millennials she thought she knew: the overmothered cyborgs helplessly sunk in their virtual worlds. From what planet came this new, slightly feral tribe of fixers, makers, and barterers, she had no idea.

"I was distracted," Iano said. "That night Tig told us about moving in with Jorge."

What he'd been was upset. "Why does it bother you so much? Your daughter is twenty-six. You and I were married at that age. We had Zeke."

"What are you saying, Willa? She's pregnant?"

"No! Just that it's normal for Tig and Jorge to want their own place."

"A filthy old garage in the backyard with no plumbing or electricity."

"It has electricity. They found wiring, they just need to update it. You should see the place, it's bigger on the inside. It has an upstairs." She laughed. "No stairs, per se. But an upper floor. You get to it through a little square hole, with a ladder."

"Sounds lovely."

Willa still couldn't put a finger on Iano's objection to the Tig-Jorge narrative. It certainly wasn't Jorge as a particular choice; in the realm of proving himself, the deal was more than done. Maybe it was just a father's duty to resist a daughter's drift toward another man. For whatever reason, Willa found herself in the stunning position of being Tig's favored parent and keeper of some large secrets, beyond the swiped Papu ashes. Tig was getting a phone. She'd submitted to this as a first step on her long road to becoming, maybe, eventually, Dusty's legal guardian. Their talks on the subject were taking on Yalta Conference dimensions, with one of the significant powers excluded. Willa had no idea how to get Zeke to the table, when every tentative Dusty conversation felt as if she were breaking down walls to storm the raw terrain of her son's broken heart. She settled instead for warning Tig of the infinite complications of parenthood. But the logistics of a new phone turned out to be simple: Tig could add herself to Jorge's family plan. This might be a modern equivalent to marriage.

Dusty was probing the straps and buckle that locked him into his high chair. Willa judged him to be about two minutes from jailbreak. She needed to wind up this call.

"Are you still in bed, lazybones?" she asked.

"Not in bed exactly. But not officially up. I haven't yet presented myself."

It was earlier in Phoenix by some inconstant number of hours. Sun-scorched Arizona did not do Daylight Saving, because why would they, and in years of calling home, Iano had invented a mnemonic for the relative time zone. In winter they skied with the Rockies, in summer they surfed with California. In April, who the hell knew.

"Do you have coffee, at least?"

"I do. I sneaked into the kitchen unapprehended."

"Athena must have a houseful. Did she put you in the basement on that brokeback fold out?"

"No, my rank has evidently improved. I'm upstairs, in Artemisia's bedroom. I haven't been in here before. It's kind of . . . ruffly."

"*Artemisia's* room? She's what, midthirties by now?" Last Willa had heard, Artemisia answered to *Art* and was running a salmon-fishing charter in Alaska.

"It's a museum. I'm not kidding. Dried prom corsages, posters, the altar is untouched. I'm bunking here with Boyz II Men."

"Seems like they'd figure out she's not coming back. And way over the ruffles, in any case."

"Don't tell my sister. She thinks the lesbian sea captain thing is just a phase."

"Ah. It so rarely is."

A five-foot twist of gristle, that girl Art. Some of the Tig genes had surfaced over there as well: tiny but mighty. They had one more pint-size cousin, an unfortunate boy. Takis. He'd been teased mercilessly at family reunions, the adults being worse than the kids, and Takis had grown up to show them all, achieving fame and fortune as a snowboarder. Olympic finalist, commercial endorsements, the works. He'd retired in his thirties with enough money to open a microbrewery in Boulder.

Iano had returned to the subject of his miserable flight. It was a little maddening but Willa understood she needed to hear this out so he could move on. The memorial service was later that day. "It's over five hours, this flight, and they feed you nothing. I'm crammed into a space the size of a dog kennel, I have to pee, and I'm starving."

"Iano, honey. This is common knowledge, that airlines no longer give you food. I offered to pack you a lunch. Remember?"

"I objected on principle. These airlines are supposed to be transporting humans. They used to do that. Now they don't. *Nobody* could fit comfortably in that space. What kind of passenger are they making these airplanes for?"

"Not the kind I like. Tall, dark, and handsome."

"The humans of the future. *Bots.* They're making airplanes for bots. Are those an actual thing?"

"I know they actually crawl around the web and try to steal your cookies."

"I picture them looking like spiders."

"I don't think they do. They're numbers. Codes, or something. So not real, as in taking up space."

"And not eating. You see, *moro*. I rest my case."

"I'll betcha money the Tweedles packed lunches."

"*Gamo tin panageia.* Tuna fish, fried chicken. Egg salad!"

"Wow. Hell is other people, with egg salad."

"And a yapping dog."

"Poor baby, starving to death in the bacchanalia. Did they share, at least?"

"No! If we had been on a raft, they would have eaten *me*."

"But you're so adorable. Mrs. Tweedle didn't share?"

"She was immune to my charms."

"Nope. Not buying that."

"Okay, she shared. A little."

Willa would let him complain until he was finished. Then he could turn to the family rites, a bone-grinding dance of survivors and the patriarch they couldn't quite love to the end. Willa would scrape off the food and liberate her charge. Soon she would hand him off to Tig and pull off her own escape, disappearing into the thrilling possibility of a book. The arrival of a hero in her house had blown Willa's passion for Mary Treat into a giddy disease state. These two iconoclasts living in one another's line of sight, anode and cathode, had some current flowing between them that Willa had accidentally stuck a hand into. Now she lay awake nights hearing their conversations, seeing them in Mary's parlor among her spider jars. Walking in the barrens. After a lifetime of meticulously detached journalism, this felt less like an assignment than an out-of-body experience. While executing all other duties—cooking, baby minding, even now, listening to Iano—Willa found herself fidgeting like a derby horse at the gate, impatient to get to her writing desk.

And Tig was likewise impatient to scoop Dusty into her arms when she came home from work every day. Willa could see it. Tig walked around with the starry-eyed, introspective glow of an expectant mother. Willa worried about what she'd set in motion the day she asked Zeke for power of attorney. He'd agreed a little too easily to custodial transfer, but of course he was overwhelmed, trying to recover a life for himself in Boston. It made sense for Dusty to stay where he was, until *something*. If Zeke kept avoiding the subject of what that something might be, and if it should someday come to pass that Tig's life was a better place for a child than Willa's, technically she wouldn't need Zeke's permission for another custodial transfer. But could not imagine proceeding without his blessing. And between those two siblings, little was blessed.

"Have a good funeral," she told Iano when he finally sounded ready to sign off. "And then fly straight home, I miss you. Take a deep breath, suck it up. Pack a lunch."

"Have fun with your what's-his-name architect, Mr. Peagraves."

"He's going to ride in here and save the day." Willa found she believed this. The house and its fortunes had felt different since Nick's passing. Or maybe it was just April, but life seemed possible here, one house down from the corner of Sixth and Plum.

A minute after Willa hung up the phone, a funny thought struck her: Tig would have fit on that plane just fine. Tig, Art, Takis, these anomalous, scrappy survivors, might be the lucky ones. They ate less and took up less space: the humans of the future.

⋊⋉

Peakesbury was the name. His game was disaster. Willa needn't have bothered with cleaning up, because the expert never went inside. He got out of his white pickup truck wearing clean, pressed khakis and a button-down shirt, and required less than an hour to wreck her world.

His tools were a clipboard, retractable tape measure, and a little trowel he used for scraping the edges of bricks, looking for identifying marks. Masonry happened to be his area of special interest. He followed his nose to a date, in very short order: 1880. He declared the house to have been built that year, or soon after.

"No," Willa said. "We're sure it's older than that."

Peakesbury looked from Willa to Chris, and back to Willa. He was too young and polite to say what he was thinking, but Willa saw it plainly: *Did I just drive an hour to talk to a couple of know-it-all shitwits?*

"I'm sorry," she said. "It's just that we have conflicting information. Why that exact date?"

"In 1683 the General Assembly fixed a size for common brick that conformed to the English-made product of the time. There wasn't a brick in New Jersey bigger or smaller than nine and a half by four and a half by three. Until 1880, when the Dunwiddie brickyard opened over by Union Lake."

Wow, Willa thought. She did ask.

He took a pen out of his shirt pocket, looked at it, put it back, and soldiered on. "So, Dunwiddie struck mud over by that lake and invested in machinery nobody else could afford at the time. He'd already made one fortune in glass factories. His new yard made bricks cheaper and faster than any other in this part of the country, and they turned out a little smaller. Nobody called him on it, because he paid off the authorities."

"So these are some kind of Mafia bricks?" Willa asked.

"He's quite a big name in bricks, Orville Dunwiddie," he said, dodging any hint of irony. "Later on his son Leverett took over the operation. The bricks themselves are worth something, to folks who really know their masonry."

She had to wonder how many folks really knew their masonry. Peakesbury knelt at the base of a corner wall and scraped lightly at the end of a brick. "Now, you see this mark on the end, a little impression of a D?"

Willa and Chris leaned over obediently to observe the D.

"That's the Dunwiddie stamp."

Chris had not yet said a word to this expert, even when Willa had deferentially introduced him as "our town historian" and the two men shook hands. She noticed he'd worn his best suit to this appointment, an antique white three-piece ensemble a tad more eccentric even than his everyday wear. Christopher, she realized, was starstruck.

"I see the mark," Willa said. "I'm not arguing with any of that. You obviously know bricks. But we've done a lot of research on a person who lived at this address; we're *sure* he lived here. And it was only for a short time, between 1874 and 1875."

"There is *no* mistake about those dates," Chris finally chimed in with his trademark hauteur, to Willa's relief. "That was a significant year in Vineland, 1875. As you undoubtedly know."

Peakesbury looked blank, and not too interested.

"Charles Landis and Uri Carruth. The murder of the century." Chris was rallying now. Willa decided to step aside and let the eggheads duke it out. "A resident of this house was involved in the famous trial. We have primary sources on that. Newspaper articles, that level of reliability. Our person of interest was a public figure."

"We know it was this house," Willa added, seeing a potential weak spot. "We even have a correspondence that mentions those two trees."

The expert ran a hand through his tidy brown hair and looked around the yard, as if for an escape route. Willa was starting to feel embarrassed for everyone present.

"I'm not saying the trees weren't there in 1875," he allowed. "And I'm not saying your man wasn't here. This *house* wasn't here.

These bricks at that time were mud in the ground. The plant that manufactured them did not make a brick before 1880."

"Our dates and identification for our historical personage are solid," Chris said, getting peevish. "We know it was not *after* 1880, because he left town in 1875. Prior to the fall of that year, and for most of the previous one, he was right here. So what do you suggest he was living in, a tent?"

Peakesbury looked at the house a little sadly, for such a long time Willa began to feel uncomfortable. The cockeyed chimneys, those horrible cracked walls. The man might as well have been looking up her skirt. Finally he spoke. "No, I expect he lived in a house. Something that got pulled down to make way for this one."

"Oh," she said.

"This would have been prime real estate at the time. If the house wasn't up to snuff, the owner wouldn't have hesitated to raze and rebuild, in order to stay here in the center of town."

"But he *didn't* stay here," Chris parried, failing to move to the next step of the logical progression, as Willa had. She'd relaxed her denial muscles and heard what the man was saying: Thatcher Greenwood lived in a house that got torn down. For whatever reason. Soon after he left Vineland, the walls came down. His castle hadn't stood.

"You've still got a late-nineteenth-century structure," the man offered, clearly seeing the need here for a consolation prize. "Not that addition of course, that's nineteen twenties. And I can't vouch that the rest of the structure is worth the expense of restoration. To be honest I'm going to vouch that it isn't, from what I can see standing here. Unless you've got some extenuating value. But 1880s is still historic."

"That's the nail on the head," Willa told him. "We've been betting on the extenuating-value clause. 'Structure associated with persons of historic significance.'"

She waited for the thunder and lightning, or worse, to burst into tears in front of these men. But they were paying no attention to Willa now, circling each other in the ring. There was no win here. The house hadn't stood. She'd put her faith in a resident who probably had been just as stuck then as she was now, had inherited some inappropriate wreck of a place and tried everything to keep it standing. He'd failed, and so would she.

She thanked the expert, took his card, and sent him away in his white truck. Chris seemed to want to hang around for a debriefing but Willa couldn't bear it. She pretended she had things to do inside, a baby to check on. She kept waiting for tears but what came to her instead was a weird, deathly calm. Beyond the mess of everyone's wants and needs lay a simpler calculus of what this house could be, and what it couldn't. She'd asked for a fact-finding mission and that's what she got, even if the facts blew up everything she'd counted on. Nothing is free.

꙰

They went to the graveyard by day. Tig pushed Dusty in a lightweight fold-up stroller she'd gotten in trade when she decided to get rid of the Cadillac buggy. And Nick of course fit handily in Willa's pocket. This family was learning to travel light.

After some reconnaissance they'd realized their illegal interment would be less risky in broad daylight than at midnight. Almost no one ever came into this cemetery, but cars passed steadily on Park Avenue and North Valley, and nocturnal shenanigans would likely attract more notice from people driving by. To normalize the appearance of their mission they brought a picnic, which they laid out on a blanket in the appointed spot. It had been Willa's idea to get a bottle of ouzo, which neither of them had ever tasted, and wasn't all that easy to find. They'd toyed with the idea of bringing shot glasses to throw down and shatter after the toast, Zorba style, but decided against it. This being not yet the afterlife, someone would have to pick up the pieces.

"His self-confidence was herculean," Willa said, lifting her juice glass and knocking it back. Ouzo was alchemical: clear as water in the bottle, but when poured into a glass with water it instantly turned whitish, like an ammonia-based cleaning fluid. That pretty well defined the taste also, though Tig had the better palate. She got cleaning fluid with notes of licorice.

"To self-confidence," Tig said, knocking back her shot, wincing.

They sat cross-legged on a plaid blanket staring at the baby-food jar of ashes that sat between them. Dusty also could sit unassisted now, making it a foursome.

"So was his vocabulary. Herculean," Willa said, raising an empty glass. "But I think I'm done with the fucking ouzo."

"Me too," Tig agreed, setting down her cup. "Here's to Papu's vocabulary, and fuck the Virgin Mary!"

"To the whore ocean! *Pou se gamoun ta psaria*, I think."

"Gamo to!"

Willa glanced at Dusty. He'd recently learned to manage a bottle himself and was doing that now, while watching them both with wide eyes over the plugged-in dome. "I'm sorry he'll never know Nick. But can you imagine? Sending him to preschool with that kind of language rattling around in his head?"

"Mom, you were almost as bad. We never told you, but Zeke had to go to the principal in fourth grade for telling the lunch lady no thanks, he didn't want any fucking green beans."

"*Zeke* did?"

"He swears to this day he didn't know it was a bad word. He'd heard it from you and Dad so much he just thought it was a regular adjective."

Willa, without a defense, picked up her tomato and cheese sandwich and finished it off. They'd stuffed a generous picnic into the mesh pocket on the back of the new little stroller, which weighed ounces instead of pounds, easily lifted with one hand. It felt like the end of an era, being done with that ostentatious stroller. In the same trading session Tig had ditched the Gucci diaper bag and all other baby items that were more showy than functional. The car seat they'd retained, but not the baby monitors with TV cameras or the mobiles with literal bells and whistles. In the exchange, along with a good deal of cash, Tig procured a wardrobe of lightly used clothes, as Dusty had suddenly outgrown every stitch he owned. Also a bale of cloth diapers, because Tig was sick of throwing shit away. Willa thought she would sweep the motherhood medals if she stuck that one out, but something told her this wasn't just a show of sincerity to impress Willa. The process had a life of its own, and at this stage of her nonpregnancy Tig was nesting, in her antimaterial way. Preparing for a baby on her own terms. And really, after everything she'd done for Nick, how bad was baby shit?

Dusty emptied his bottle, threw it down, and lifted his arms to be picked up. Tig swooped up the boy and lifted him in the air, making him shriek ecstatically. He worked his arms and legs like an earnest little swimmer mastering the air. Tig cooed nonsense as she lowered his face toward hers, touching his button nose to her own. He reached for the handles of her hair and she swooshed him upward again, both of them squealing. Willa remembered the days in a grief-drenched Boston apartment where she'd first watched her son with his son, waiting for the chemical magic that would rivet them together for life. Waiting for this.

Willa lay on her back and looked up at the sky through tree branches that glowed with a faint green haze of a leafiness soon to come. It reminded her of the heartbreaking, awkward furze on a thirteen-year-old boy. The end of something that everyone agrees must end. She had no earthly idea where she was going to live now. What would become of her family. The only one with an assured destination was Nick. After a while Tig put Dusty down on the blanket, got out the hand trowel they'd brought, and carefully lifted a divot of grass. She pushed the baby food jar into the slot, exactly as if she were planting a large seed. Willa started to help replace the sod, but Tig stopped her.

"Hang on." She reached into the back pocket of her jeans. "I told him this would go with him. You've seen it, right?"

She handed over a small slip of photo, not exactly square. It had been cut down from a larger size, maybe to remove other people or to make it fit in a tiny frame. It was creased, had been bent. Extremely worn. "Where did this come from?"

"He used to keep it in his cigarette lighter. Remember that gold one he had with the little sliding compartment on the side?"

"Oh, yeah. I do."

"After we made him quit smoking, he kept it different places."

"Like where?"

Tig shrugged. "The drawer in his nightstand, in a wallet he never used. When we rearranged everything to bring in the hospital bed he kind of freaked. He kept asking me to hide it someplace or another. Finally I stuck it in with his morphine stuff, the pill crusher and all. He liked it being in there. I figured you would have seen it."

All of this astonished Willa: That he'd had such presence of mind at that late stage, and managed to maintain an arena of privacy. Mostly, that she'd missed it altogether. The photo was a black-and-white portrait with the yellowy-brown cast of antique chemicals losing ground against time. Taken in Greece, she could tell by the whitewashed stone wall behind the couple. Who but the Greeks pursued that obsession with whitewash? The background was a haze of yellowish clouds but the subjects were clear enough: a tall man with an arm around his tiny bride, gripping her as if gale force winds were expected. But smiling, both of them. Her head was enlarged by a hat or a headscarf—or a crown. If this was a wedding portrait, Willa realized that's what it would be, the *stefana* made of leaves and flowers. She and Iano had worn these, in the only trace of orthodoxy they'd allowed into their wedding. In the old days the couple wore them for a week, but if Nick wore any headgear in this photo it was drowned under the mane of black curls. Willa held the photo as close as her eyes could focus. The little bride in the vise grip of her man looked fiercely happy. Small but undominated. She looked like Tig. And the young man, so exquisitely undamaged. Tall, dark, and handsome.

She handed the photo back to Tig with salt burning her eyes. Tig stared at her.

"Mom. Are you *sad*? About Papu?"

"He's . . ." The words caught. When Nick died, she'd called the proper authorities and watched the body roll out of the house on a gurney without feeling much of anything. On Wednesday when the architecture expert took the wrecking ball to her future, no tears arrived. Nothing got to Willa anymore. She shook her head to clear this away.

"He looked just like Iano," she said finally. "I never knew that. I wish I had."

"Seriously? You didn't see how much they looked alike?"

"Not at *all*." Willa had a disorienting recollection of Tig making a face at the goth girl in reference to Iano's putative attractiveness. *Antwack*, if she remembered correctly. Her beautiful Iano, just another old guy.

Tig kneaded grass and sod back in place over the burial, leaving no visible trace, and quietly began packing up their picnic. She'd kindly offered no judgment on Willa for failing to see the resemblance, absolving the evergreen human crime of denying the past and seeing oneself as original. Willa looked around at an April day struck through with clear light. It felt like more than she deserved.

"As long as we're here, I'd like to look for somebody. A grave."

"Who, Mary Treat?"

Willa was startled. "You knew she's buried here?"

"I know where she is."

With Dusty back in the stroller they bumped over the grass to the paved road that snaked through the grounds. Outside the cemetery's tall iron fence the traffic steadily passed, but in here the grounds were all theirs. They followed the road into the oldest section, where gravestones took more liberties: obelisks, corbels, ogees. A few unapologetic phalluses. Statues of angels. Many names were all but erased from the stones' rain-washed faces. Tig led the way, going off-road again to enter a section of smaller markers, and suddenly there was Mary.

"Goodness." Willa sat down beside the marker. It was as modest as the woman herself, not even a headstone exactly, just a small stone column about knee high and equally wide with a slanted top engraved with the name and dates. MARY A. TREAT, 1830–1923. The weathered granite was discreetly mottled with aureoles of yellow and green lichens, channeling the soul of a woman who loved ferns and mosses. Willa laid her face against the stone. After months of cat and mouse, thinking she'd nearly touched Mary before losing her again, this was as close as she was going to get.

"Is that what you call a plinth?" Tig asked. She, standing by, and Dusty in his stroller had their heads tilted in a similar quizzical aspect that made Willa laugh aloud.

"What?" Tig asked, startled. "Is that a dumb question?"

"No. Not at all. Technically this style is called a pulpit. What's dumb is that I actually know that."

She knew because decades ago in her more commercial days, she'd done a brochure for a monument company. And her brain seemed resistant to the life-changing art of pitching things out. Willa had written hundreds of articles about thousands of things and probably could still list most of them. None had laid any lasting claim on her heart. She pressed both hands against this cool stone, feeling the roughness of the lichens. Mary had lived her discipline. Both of them had, she and Thatcher, with an integrity that led them to give up, practically speaking, their lives. Born under the moon of paradigm shift, they got to be present to a world turning over on itself. Willa ached for a devotion like that, something to move her beyond herself. Out from under the soggy cardboard box she might be holding over her head—a visual Tig had lodged in her mind that Willa would pay good money to erase.

"Over here is another Treat," Tig said. "I *think* it's Treat. You can make out 'eat,' almost, and it sort of matches. Husband?"

Willa got up to look. "Husband. Sort of."

Now *here* was a conspicuously uneasy his-and-hers setting. The matching monument was set much more than an arm's length away. More like the proverbial ten-foot pole. And it really didn't match. It was slightly bigger, all square angles, no lichens, and a flat top that took the full brunt of eroding rains. The J. TREAT was almost gone. No date had been engraved. Willa knew Joseph had died just a few years after running off to New York in pursuit of free love and a bigger audience. Victoria Woodhull spurned him, he devoted a few last years to revenge-shaming her, and died without friends. Mary would have been obliged to buy this plot for the two of them. Probably she told her relatives, "Okay. But not too close."

And then she outlived him by more than forty years. While most people who knew her probably pitied her for lacking the protection of marriage, she lived adventurously and committed her voice to the page so well that Willa could hear it plainly.

Tig sat on the ground a little distance away to admire Mary's real estate, with Dusty on her lap and an accommodating family stone for a backrest. Willa joined them. Dusty was drifting. After lunch and bottle came nap.

"How did you know where this grave was?"

"I know people here." Tig grinned.

Willa knew she came here often. It made sense she would have noticed the name when she happened on it. For a beautiful ten minutes or so they were quiet, with nothing required to complete the space between mother and daughter. Willa relaxed her focus and took in the view of all that even ground, the immense trees with their arms lifted, the motley garden of stones at their feet bearing an aspect of afterthought. Little flags posted here and there signaled flashes of patriotism that had flared and burned out.

"I know you come here a lot," Willa finally said. "I guess I've wondered why."

"It's comforting. All these dead people."

"That might not be a conventional position."

"I know. But I'm not superstitious. I just . . . like seeing all these lives. Most of them started in this town, and ended here."

"They're rooted."

"Yeah. Literally. Most of the coffins have degraded, especially the older burials. Before people got all defensive about trying to keep their bodies out of the carbon cycle."

Willa had to smile. Only her daughter would see embalming as *defensive*. "So you think we should have dumped Papu out of the jar? To get him recycled?"

Tig looked at her. "Would that be okay with you?"

"Of course. If we can even find that spot again. We can liberate him."

Tig was pleased. "Pine box with a body inside, no preservatives. That's how most of these people went down. So now they're part of those trees. Isn't that where you want to end up, Mom? In a tree like that?"

Willa looked at the oak over their heads. Its trunk was a monument to resilience and its branches to tenderness, touched at their tips with the faint rose color of baby oak leaves. Who would not want to end up in a tree like that?

"Plus," Tig said, "it reminds me to be patient. Seeing all these people that have passed on. I get frustrated sometimes, waiting."

"For people to die?"

"Yeah. To be honest. The guys in charge of everything right now are *so old*. They really are, Mom. Older than you. They figured out the meaning of life in, I guess, the nineteen fifties and sixties. When it looked like there would always be plenty of everything. And they're applying that to *now*. It's just so ridiculous."

Willa could see the reason in this, unnerving as it might be. "I get that your generation is waiting for their chance. I remember feeling that way too. But there's no guarantee, unfortunately. Like, poor *them*." She pointed at the family stone facing them: Frank and Emma, both born 1859, produced four children who all died in 1888. And so did Frank.

"Oh yeah. The Keurigs. I've noticed them before."

Willa imagined this Emma whose husband and children, the youngest an infant, she tried desperately to nurse through some fever. Then followed in a cart to this spot, buried them, and went home to her empty house, perhaps to be avoided by her neighbors as a typhoid pariah. "Not much comfort there."

Dusty was sleeping sideways across Tig's legs in a pose of spectacular relaxation, head dropped back, mouth open. Willa thought of the days when he fought sleep as if death lurked inside it. Tig had one hand resting on his belly, and seemed to be contemplating the tragedy of the Keurigs. "The thing is, Mom, the secret of happiness is low expectations. That's a good reminder, right there. If you didn't lose your husband and kids all in one year, smile! You're ahead of the game."

"Wow. That's what I raised you to believe in? Low expectations?"

"What did you want me to believe in?"

"I don't know. You can be anything you want. Hitch your wagon to a star and all that jazz."

Tig didn't smile. "I saw you and Dad doing that, hitching your wagon to the tenure star, and it didn't look that great to me. You made such a big deal about security that you sacrificed giving us any long-term community."

"I think there are other ways to put that."

"But not simpler."

Three words. Willa wanted to get up and walk away from this censorious child and parenthood altogether, the Möbius strip of torment. Their day had been nearly perfect. Naturally it had to blow up. She stood up so quickly her vision briefly washed out. Brushed off her jeans, listened to her throbbing head: *Walkaway walkaway*. She'd just been accused of vagrancy, it seemed. Or a refusal to dig in. She dug in.

"And you think you can be a parent," she said, standing over her diminutive daughter with the baby on her lap. Looming, really, which felt aggressive. She sat down again. "I guess your plan would be to live somewhere perfect and give Dusty roots."

"No place is *perfect*. Don't be so touchy."

"Well, it's been kind of a week, Tig. I just found out our house is slated for demolition."

"Mom. The permafrost is melting. Millions of acres of it."

Willa tried to see a connection. "And I'm just worried about my house. That's your point?"

Tig shook her head. "It's so, so scary. It's going to be fire and rain, Mom. Storms we can't deal with, so many people homeless. Not just homeless but placeless. Cities go underwater and then what? You can't shelter in place anymore when there isn't a *place*."

Willa tucked her hands between her knees and declined to believe these things.

"The Middle East and North Africa are almost out of water.

Asia's *under*water. Syria is dystopian, Somalia, Bangladesh, dystopian. Everybody's getting weather that never happened before. Melting permafrost means we've got like, a *minute* to turn this mess around, or else *it's* going to stop *us*."

"Well shit, Tig. And you want to raise a kid?"

"I don't want to get pregnant. But he's already here." She stroked the cloudburst of his hair with a feathery touch. "I didn't mean to hurt your feelings, Mom," she said quietly. "You and Dad did your best. But all the rules have changed and it's hard to watch people keep carrying on just the same, like it's business as usual."

"*All* the rules. Really?"

Tig nodded almost imperceptibly, like a seed head bobbing on its stem. She didn't look at Willa but out at the graves. "People can change their minds about little things, but on the big ones they'd rather die first. A used-up planet scares the piss out of them, after they spent their whole lives thinking the cupboard would never go bare. No offense, Mom, but you're kind of not that different from Papu. You want a nice house that's all your own, you want your kids to have more than you did."

"I'm human, Tig. We live, we consume. I think that's just how we have to be."

"Of course you think that. When everybody around you thinks the same way, you can't even see what you're believing in."

"Most of us can't see past our noses, but for some reason you can?"

Tig grinned. "Just that special."

"Seriously, I'm asking."

"I don't know. I've got less of a stake. You and Dad kept turning your hamster wheel, and so did Zeke, but I never thought I had much of a shot. Especially with Zeke telling me ever since I was born that I'm a pea-brained midget loser. It makes you kind of sober about your prospects."

Willa's heart constricted at the thought of a daughter incurring damage while she looked the other way. Siblings teased, that was normal. Every mother secretly had a favorite but Willa had been careful not to let that show. Tig always seemed impenetrable, even superior. One after another these defenses rose to Willa's mind, and she understood this was how it worked, refusing to see past your nose.

"I always thought if I was good at anything," she finally said, "it was being a mother. And what I hear you saying is that I've let you down completely."

Tig considered this, looking at the boy in her lap. "A person can succeed and fail at the same time. Maybe letting me down was your way of getting me to be me."

"Fierce." Willa nodded. Not that she'd wish quite *that* on any child. Or the mother involved.

"I was going to say adaptable. You know what's funny, sometimes the stuff you hate for yourself you admire in other people. Like Jorge. I love that he's a grown-up, and I know it's because he wasn't sheltered. He got zip in the dad department."

"I've wondered about that."

"Yep, same old story, the disappearing dad. So their mom had to be like, pack your own lunchbox, *m'ijo*. Not that they were destitute. I mean, she bought that house. But Jorge was *eight* when he had his first job. He worked for his uncle, selling beers to tourists on the Playa Condado."

"Well thanks, I feel better. I didn't hire you out as a barmaid in second grade."

Tig laughed. "You wanted us to be happy. I know you did. Not *that* self-sufficient, but self-sufficient. Good workers, good at relationships. All the same things we want for Dusty. But he needs a different kind of mom. The reward system in his lifetime will be totally different. He'll have to learn how to be happy with what he's got."

"To expect nothing, in other words. And get it."

"He doesn't get a choice. He got born in the historical moment of no more free lunch. Friends will probably count more than money, because wanting too much stuff is going to be toxic. We didn't ask for this, it's just what we got."

"Thou shalt not want."

"Something like that. Waste not, want not."

"If you're right, then Zeke is right too. If you can't borrow from the future you have to steal from now. You're offering me this Mad Max scenario of pirates taking everything they can grab, and I just can't accept it. It's too horrifying."

"Seriously, Mom? It's here. One percent of the brotherhood has their hands on most of the bread. They own the country, their god is the free market, and most people are so unhorrified they won't even question the system. If it makes a profit, that's the definition of good. If it grows, you have to stand back and let it. The free market has exactly the same morality as a cancer cell. Even Zeke knows that's true."

"I think he's trying his best to apply morality to the process."

"Which is like trying to reason with a cancer cell. He *knows* this, Mom."

"So you get to the bottom of the barrel and then what? Teach Dusty to steal?"

"Or pick up something people were throwing away, and use that."

Willa recalled Zeke's earliest warning about Tig teaching Dusty to Dumpster dive. "I appreciate the sentiment. Secondhand clothes are one thing, but secondhand food, not so much. Or secondhand gas for your car."

"You can't see it because you don't have the right eyes. There's stuff going to waste right in front of you. Always. We're, like, *swimming* in wasted stuff."

Dusty was stirring. His nap had kept them from raising their voices, and for that Willa was grateful. The danger of screaming had passed. "I just spent a winter feeding a family on lentils and sleeping in a sleeping bag. Conserving toilet paper. I'm so tired of thrifty. You show me what I'm still wasting and I will cook it for goddamned dinner."

"You're still wasting, Mom. Everybody is."

Willa said nothing. Dusty opened his eyes and blinked up at the trees and sky. Then looked at Tig's face. He smiled, she smiled. The simplest of things.

"Be specific," Willa said.

Tig stared through the iron fence at the street beyond it, for such a long time Willa began nursing a wild idea that she'd won the argument.

"Okay," Tig said. "In thirty seconds four cars went by with one person in each of them. That's at least twelve trips to wherever those cars are going, all going to waste. Times a hundred and twenty, that's way over a thousand rides per hour."

"In theory. They're not exactly useful to *me*."

"It could be arranged. People do it. In Cuba it's an official job. *El Amarillo*."

"'The yellow'?"

"'The Yellow Guy,' I guess you'd translate it. They can be men or women. They wear this yellow outfit and stand at major inter-sections. Everybody recognizes them. It's just an example. Of mak-ing an invisible resource actually useful." Tig interrupted herself to lift Dusty up and sniff his bottom. "Pew, *mister*!"

She rifled through the stroller pocket for a fresh diaper and a plastic bag of damp washcloths, then laid Dusty down on the forgiving grass. Willa watched. In her many years she'd never changed a cloth diaper. Not one.

"So the yellow guy is what, like an Uber dispatcher?"

"No, it's simpler than that. Like a free, countrywide transit service. Anytime you need to go somewhere, you walk to the nearest *Amarillo* and tell him where you're headed. If you're driving a car with any empty seats, you see the yellow suit and you stop. It's the law. He asks where you're going and matches passengers to destinations."

The bottom was wiped and the change accomplished with little fuss. Willa had imagined onerous pins, but Tig used diaper covers with snaps to hold everything in place. "It's a pretty cool job. The pay is good." She wrestled Dusty back into his overalls and sealed away the stinky stuff in a bag. "It requires people skills, you know? It's not just first come, first serve. He'll give priority to a pregnant woman, or somebody with an appointment that's time sensitive. It has to be fair, so everybody stays happy. They all get where they're going, and every car is full. All the time."

"But what if you just want to go somewhere by yourself?"

"You get over it. That's so last century, Mom. Anyway, that's how I met Toto. Remember I told you I was hitchhiking, when I rode with him to Bayamo?"

"Yellow Guy set you up?"

"Uh-huh. It's like Tinder, with practical benefits. I knew so many couples that met in cars, on their way to someplace they both had to be."

"Still. Seems like people would want to be more in charge of their destiny."

"Oh, right. *Destiny.* They'll remember how in charge they were, next time another hurricane puts the Garden State Parkway underwater."

Willa thought of the sad little sign in the yard of the bankrupt farm: *Dear Mother Nature, Please Spank Sandy.* "You're right. They won't see any human-caused connections. They'll just be mad."

"Uh-huh. Until they get here." Tig was buckling Dusty into

the stroller, preparing for departure. "Then they finally start to soften up a little bit."

They made their way back toward the spot where they would try to relocate the time capsule of Nick they'd just buried, and invite him to join the nutrient cycle. Tig was in a generous mood now. When they reached the easier going of the paved roadway she put an arm around Willa and they pushed the stroller together.

"Poor Mama," she said, leaning her springy head against Willa's shoulder. "I know. It feels like the end of the world when you can't have the things you always wanted. But it's not the end of the world. There's some other place to go."

"Sorry to tell you, but that's a very old chestnut. My mother used to say when God slams a door on you, he opens a window."

Tig gave this two seconds of respectful consideration before rejecting it. "No, that's not the same. I'm saying when God slams a door on you it's probably a shitstorm. You're going to end up in rubble. But it's okay because without all that crap overhead, you're standing in the daylight."

"Without a roof over your head, it kind of feels like you might die."

"Yeah, but you might not. For sure you won't find your way out of the mess if you keep picking up bricks and stuffing them in your pockets. What you have to do is look for blue sky."

16

⚭

Blue Sky

Once, for nearly a fortnight, Thatcher slept in a tree. It was during the war when he'd run away to travel with a regiment on the move. The march stalled in a rivershed while they waited for orders to continue toward Boston, where troops and supplies were slowly being moved south by rail. In the meantime the men were encamped, but Thatcher had no official place yet in the regiment. Other tagalong boys, some much younger, ran from one tent to the next making bargains, running errands, or carrying out small missions of larceny for the privilege of rolling up under a cot in a blanket crawling with lice. Whatever dread of night birds and crickets was driving them to those dens, it did not trouble Thatcher. He found an accommodating oak with a wide crotch of limbs radiating from an old injury where the tree had been topped by a violent storm or lightning strike. There he built his squirrel's nest of leaves and his single blanket, and slept as well as he had ever in his father's house. He hadn't thought of the tree for years, but he thought of it now. Possibly some instinct was warning him to make ready to run.

He stood in the parlor near the window. Rose sat in one of the small, armless chairs opposite the settee. Husband and wife were applying every faculty to avoiding an argument. Outdoors a summer was greening. Thatcher observed it with physical longing, but the ornate leaded windows of this wretched house could not be thrown open.

Rose was upset because Mrs. Brindle had finally given her notice, as any sentient being could have predicted. Rose was upset by any number of things. Her new blue day dress had not fitted properly and had to be sent back to Mrs. Clark for alteration. Someone was mutilating the shade trees on Landis Avenue! Under cover of night the vandals carved vulgar threats against the captain, directly into tree bark where they were impossible to erase. The newspaper Rose held in her lap reported this crime on its front page. She had just read the article aloud, appalled by the crime and expecting Thatcher to be even more so, given his fondness for trees. Landis had posted a reward for information leading to the apprehension of the culprits.

But Thatcher felt sympathy for the tree mutilators. Or at least for the cleverness of these insurgents whose broadsides could not be whitewashed over by morning. What appalled him was that Landis maintained the privilege of posting any sort of reward. The overpowering pretense of normality in this newspaper and the town was driving Thatcher mad. The opposition paper had ceased publication, of course. The only mention of its editor in the *Weekly* for many weeks had been the occasional small note that Carruth was resting comfortably at home, expected to make a full recovery.

And now the great bear was dead. Now there could be a murder trial. Rose and Aurelia allowed no discussion of the subject, because it led only to shouting and tears. Both women prayed for Landis to be found innocent, because *everyone* relied on Landis. Their friends the Dunwiddies retained connected business interests, and would suffer losses if their partner were forced to divest under distasteful circumstances.

This was making it difficult for Thatcher to break the news that he now must. He set his fingertips on the windowsill and through the cage of lead and glass looked out at the house next door. Mary knew already. Knew, praised his courage, and trusted him to do the job well. Had put her arms around him and let him weep like a child he had never been, for Thatcher had no memory of having wept in the shelter of human arms. Now he had. On her worn settee among the ferns he had lost himself in grief for the death of his friend, and so much else.

He turned to face his wife. "Blast Landis's trees, Rose. I'm to testify at his trial."

She glanced up quickly: blue eyes, cloudless sky. "What trial? Oh! How on earth, Thatcher, *you*? What a privilege."

"No. Against him."

She shook her head slowly, looking only at the air before her.

"I'm testifying on behalf of the murdered man. Uri Carruth."

"Why would you? He is *dead.*"

"Exactly. I was contacted by the lawyer seeking to prosecute his killer."

"You never spoke of it. You've kept this from me?"

"You wouldn't let me! Damn it, Rose, you're not even listening now."

Her eyes flared like a struck match before she looked away. Thatcher had rarely sworn in her presence, let alone damned her.

"He's asked me to make a statement before the jury."

"Why *you*? What do you have to do with any of it?" This without looking at him.

"He learned through Carruth's family that I was a friend." He watched this register as a faint rush of color to her throat while her body remained still. "We became acquainted last fall through business at the school. I never mentioned it because I doubted it would interest you. Since the shooting I've visited him at home. As often as I could."

Still she did not look at him or speak. Only her hands moved, pressing the fingertips of one into the palm of the other, perhaps for reassurance she was not dreaming.

"He was never *resting comfortably*, he was in agony. He died of an infected brain. The poor man, Rose, and that family. He has a young wife and five children who depended on him completely. Who loved him. You can't think how they suffer."

Thatcher had been astonished to be summoned by a lawyer, a man named Thomas, for the request of his testimony. A murdered man did not generally need a character witness. Carruth was shot, unarmed, in the back of the head, Thatcher had pointed out. Surely Landis could make no case for self defense. But in effect, Thomas explained, that case was being made. The counsel for Landis planned to press an argument they were calling "defense of insanity." They meant to prove Carruth's actions as newspaper editor made Landis temporarily insane, so he could not be held accountable for the shooting. Thatcher listened to all this in the oak-paneled office and felt as Rose probably did now: like a person dreaming. No man could plead *insanity* as a defense. Had any such case been argued before? To his knowledge, Thomas said, it had not.

Finally she spoke. "What do they want you to say in court? For that *poor man*."

"That Carruth was a kind and honest citizen who intended no harm."

"He did cause harm. You can't deny it."

"Sometimes people stand on principle, Rose. Pressing new ideas against old, defending one group of men against the actions of another. It causes rancor, if that's what you mean. It brings shame, or it should. But not the necessity of violence. Not *insanity*."

"Who are you calling insane?"

"No one. I'm a pawn in this game. You're always first to say how unimportant I am. But at least I will be the pawn who tells the truth."

He sounded angrier than he felt, for speaking with Rose made him hopeless, but his words had the effect of a scolding. She looked down at her hands. With her little shoulders back and her head tilted low, she looked like nothing so much as a lovely child.

"I'm sorry, Rose. I know my appearing in court will place you in an awkward position with your friend Louise. You've only heard one side of this from the Dunwiddies. But you'll find there are other people . . ." He stopped short of saying *in Vineland*, as he no longer vouched for anything this town held for them. Certainly no employment. "You will find other friends," he managed to say.

"But you don't understand," she said quietly. "It means everything to our future for Landis to remain free. If he is convicted he will see the collapse of many assets that he and the Dunwiddies hold jointly."

"Yes, I expect he will. And why should I care about the Dunwiddies?"

The child lifted her chin. "Because Mother and Mr. Dunwiddie are to be married."

"What?" Aurelia and the Toadflax. The dream he'd dared to dream.

"I wasn't to tell you until another week on. We have hardly told anyone, except Mrs. Clark, of course. Mother will need a dress. But they want it to be very quiet and proper without a fuss."

"Of course. Mrs. Clark." In the *Scala Naturae* of his household, Thatcher wondered how far he stood below Mrs. Clark the dressmaker. "And when Aurelia becomes Mrs. Dunwiddie, will she move into his domain?"

"Perhaps, although. Well." She clasped one hand with the other.

"As you know, Mother is the rightful owner of *this* house. She inherited it when Father passed away." Still Rose refused to meet his eyes, and in the avoidance he sensed something more complex than anger. Rose, guilt stricken, was a new sight before him. With a falling sensation Thatcher understood he was about to learn more than he wished to know.

"I see. So there is talk of Dunwiddie rebuilding this house. He would have the resources to try it. I suppose that would please Aurelia. The domain will move here." He tried to make sense of this reordering of his small universe. "I don't quite understand where that leaves us, Rose."

"Where it *leaves* us," she said. And nothing more. It was a statement. Now finally she looked at him directly, the pale eyes like windows thrown wide. He saw the gathering of self-protective outrage that would see Rose through to the end of whatever she wanted.

"What are you suggesting?"

"That I would also like to move into that domain."

"You and Louise are friends . . ." He felt himself thrashing about foolishly. "No. You don't mean with the, with *Leverett?* Are you fond of that man?"

She reacted with a brightening of her whole countenance. Maddeningly, she *smiled*. As if this were a parlor game of guessing, and Thatcher had got it right at last. He took a few steps, put his hand on the back of the settee, and stopped there, allowing his stunned heart to settle. He nodded, seeing what any sentient being could have predicted. Thatcher would soon have to leave this place, and Rose never would.

※

"I can only speak as a scientist, because that is what I am." Thatcher wondered how many more times he would be made to say this, and how a truth so obvious could cost a man so much. Carruth had known better friends than Thatcher, but none with his education, Thomas had explained. None with the gift of sounding so impartial.

The courtroom was not as large as Plum Hall, and less oppressive than the high school auditorium, with banks of reassuring sunlight streaming through its windows. The area before the judge's bench, where Thatcher now stood, was separated by a sturdy fortification of railings from the crowded pews where spectators murmured and perspired in their morning coats. An upper gallery spanning the back of the room was packed with women and children, to judge by the skirted knees and small faces pressed between the balusters. None had paid fifteen cents to be there.

"As a methodical man, then," Thomas said with a little smile, "you will give us a trustworthy impression of the late Mr. Carruth. First, tell us how you were acquainted."

"The same way anyone in Vineland might have known him. He sometimes attended meetings and lectures where I also found myself. First, at a meeting of the school where I was employed. Next, at a Plum Hall lecture. We happened to leave at the same time, we spoke in the street. He was congenial."

"You formed a friendship."

The murderer sat with his lawyers at a small round table not five yards away, hands folded on the green table linen. Thatcher felt repulsed by the sight of him. "We met on only a few occasions, sir. I regret there were not more, and never will be."

"Why is that?"

"The regret? Because I enjoyed his company. I admired him. He was the rare man who put others ahead of himself. He dedicated himself to the aid of working men whose lives were damaged by dishonest promises. He told me he'd had two brothers killed in the line of loyal duty, both to overseers who were careless of their workers' safety. He was from the Badger State, he said. But decided he would not be a badger."

"Meaning what?"

"I suppose he meant he would not hide in a burrow, even if bravery should cost him. Which it did, terribly." Thatcher made himself look at Landis, but the man seemed absent. He turned then to address the stone-faced jurymen in their solemn rectangle of benches. "Now the third brother is dead."

"Do you mean to say he was belligerent?" Thomas asked.

"He was honest. Determined to tell the truth. A newspaper-man."

"Would you say he was mean spirited?"

"The opposite. He was probably too kindhearted."

"Not the sort of man, then, who would deliberately drive an-other man mad."

The other lawyer interrupted then, and while spectators shifted in their seats and pined for fresh air, the legal men had a wrangle as to whether and how anyone might speculate on a dead man's motives. Thatcher had watched this lawyerly two-step for days, and its absence of heart had nearly broken him. Now, on the last day of argument, he was called to speak *impartially* on behalf of his murdered friend, with the hope of influencing a jury that must be woefully confused, if not lulled to outright torpor. Thatcher knew no more of the law than they did; he was only a scientist. As he'd said.

Thomas was allowed to rephrase the question.

"Can you comment on the possibility of any man causing an-other to become violently insane?"

Thatcher felt in danger of suffocation. "It might be possible, or it might not. The question seems beside the point." He now gave himself a good look at Landis, who avoided his gaze. The man looked pathetic. No velvet waistcoat, no gold watch or fob, all grandiosity reined in by his keepers for the theater of this trial. Thatcher allowed himself a rush of anger, as a drowning man might take hold of a timber. "Look at this man! Lord and mayor of our town. He decided to shoot another man because he did not like hearing the truth. I understand I am not meant to comment on the morality of that act. But every person here knows it was murder. It was heinous!"

Thatcher looked around the room, completely uncertain how any words, measured or furious, could break him out of this cell. "I believe I am called here to speak of our times. From a darker era of fear and magical thinking, we move toward an age of reason. Landis was beloved, is still beloved, because he claims he can protect us from mythical beasts that prowl the swamps at the edge of our understanding. Perhaps he does protect us. Some of us. But in this courtroom he alleges he has lost his capacity to make out the difference between myth and fact. He declares he is mad."

The men in the benches and ladies in the gallery looked on, probably sore afraid. "Madness is a disorder of the brain," Thatcher told them. "Not a spell or enchantment, to come and go at a whim. Natural laws apply not only to the beasts of the field but also to us, whether we like them or not. They do not cease to apply when we find them no longer convenient. If Landis is mad today, he will also be mad tomorrow and the day after."

The jury regarded him warily. Thatcher mustered his best imitation of power and might. "You came to Vineland looking for what every man wants: a safe home. After you make your judgment today, nothing can be the same. You will find a man guilty of murder, or innocent. If you decide on the latter, you cannot go on seeking shelter from a man who has no capacity for reason."

He turned from the jury, closed his eyes for a single second, and opened them on the heaven-sent vision of the court recorder dragging open the sash of a window. Through that breach Thatcher drew light and breath, and there was his answer, this would be the last of it. He was finished with declaring himself to a public without ears to hear his language. *Without shelter, we stand in daylight,* she'd insisted once, and he had thought only of death. Simple man. He might sleep in a bed of cactus thorns or a tree under the stars, but he could choose the company he kept and it would not be this fearful, self-interested mob shut up in airless rooms. They would huddle in their artifice of safety, their heaven would collapse. His would be the forthright march through the downfall.

17

❧

The Downfall

It began as a family celebration, with Zeke driving in from Boston. Jorge's sisters and their kids would also be invited, of course, and Tig's employers and coworkers at the restaurant, who also had kids. From there it expanded to include friends, which meant almost nobody would be left in the vicinity to report them when the partiers made too much noise. By a quick count Willa estimated more than a hundred big and little people in their yard, on a Thursday evening no less, for the neighborhood cookout-potluck that was Dusty's first birthday party. Jorge had set up a borrowed sound system in the doorway of the newly wired carriage house. Sondra and Lara made a cake, and some kids from the training school brought a concoction they called "Worms and Dirt," chocolate cake and icing mashed to a mud-like texture, laced with gummy worms, obviously a hit.

Tig moved through the crowd making sure plates were filled and everybody knew somebody. Jorge operated the keg, and was taking his commission, Willa noticed. She was keeping an eye on

Dusty as he got passed around among the guests. Tig had dressed him for the fiesta in a Che Guevara T-shirt and a baseball cap he kept pulling off and throwing on the ground. He'd attracted a cadre of training school kids who followed him around picking up the little cap and replacing it on his head, always backward. Willa tried not to hover as he cycled through the arms of dozens of people she'd never seen before. Dusty bore up to the socializing better than Willa did—hullabaloo was not her gift—but when he started getting cranky she swooped in and took him to the picnic table under the big oak. She sat on the bench facing out, watching the crowd, while Dusty crawled around finding acorns that she dissuaded him from eating.

The sound system pulsed and people kept arriving to fill a yard that was already congested with debris from the ongoing house project. Willa watched a toddler wander into Tig's garden and pick green tomatoes. She watched Iano at the grill talking with an older guy in a do-rag, so wrapped up in conversation he was ignoring whatever he'd put on the fire, and completely missed the two dogs that came out of nowhere and ran off with a package of hot dogs. The playlist kicked out a *bomba* and she watched scores of bodies simultaneously struck with undulating rapture. Whatever else they were holding—plates, babies, conversation—they *moved*, hips and shoulders, as if this were some Holy Roller church of sexual revelation. She thought of something Tig had told her once about Cubans: that they'd perfected all the kinds of fun that didn't cost anything. Willa couldn't recall the exact list, only that it was sultry enough to end in a need for good child care.

Zeke emerged from the crowd, walking toward her carrying a plastic cartoon glass full of beer. "Hey. Is this the misanthropes' table?"

"Join us. The birthday boy was getting a little overwhelmed."

From the careful way he sat down next to her, and because she knew him so well, Willa realized Zeke was working on getting plastered. At his son's birthday party. Some instinct—either hope or defiance—made her pick up Dusty and set him on Zeke's lap, while deftly relieving him of his beer.

"Thanks, I needed this." She took a quaff. Then examined the cup. "Wow. The Powerpuff Girls come of age. Where in the heck did you get this?"

He shrugged. "Somebody gave it to me. I couldn't find the Solo cups."

"Your sister vetoed them. She asked people to BYO drinking glass."

"Wow. The recycling Nazi."

"I've noticed people are keeping track of their drinks, though. Instead of leaving them all over the place and starting a new one. I'll be glad tomorrow when I don't have to pick up a thousand plastic cups with two fingers of beer in them."

"That was the best deal of the party, when we were kids. Sneaking the leftovers."

"Oh for the good old days." Willa studied the Powerpuffs, with their little white socks and big, angry eyes, preparing to deliver their trademark whoop-ass. Tig had been quite the fan. "You weren't thinking of driving back to Boston tonight, were you?"

He seemed to be there now. Not quite here, at any rate. "No," he said after a pause. "I brought some work I can do from here, so I can stay through the weekend."

Zeke was no longer self-employed, his start-up had unstarted, and he'd been hired by a real firm. He remained passionate about microfinance and his new area of interest, brokering carbon credits, for which Tig was trying pretty nobly to give him the benefit of the doubt. Behaving kindly toward her brother was another condition Willa had placed on becoming Dusty's guardian. Zeke was the natural father, and no arrangement could function unless some bridges were repaired. This threatened to be a deal breaker for Tig. "All bridges burned," she'd reported, to which Willa curtly suggested she build some new ones with whatever scraps she could find. That being her specialty.

But Willa carried the burning on her conscience. Since her talk with Tig in the cemetery, she'd accepted that their history transgressed the norms of sibling teasing. Tig had been fierce, it was true, but Zeke was older, and cast his charm so easily over others. She could beg Tig to forgive and Zeke to atone, but that maternal currency was exhausted long ago, and probably misspent. Now Willa had only Dusty, and no decision she made for him could be grounded in favoritism or reparation. It was a King Solomon situation.

Zeke now looked close to tears, as he stared down into the crown of Dusty's wild head. The little baseball cap had been successfully ditched, along with the attendants, and he was squirming to get free of Zeke's grip. Dusty no longer consented to being held on a lap for long, and yet Zeke held on. Willa reached over to wrest away a long splinter of wood he'd managed to pry off the edge of the seat.

"I'm sorry, honey. All this celebrating, and nobody's giving her much thought. I am. I promise."

Zeke lifted his mournful gaze to her, surprised. "Thanks, Mom. It's just, *damn it*."

"Yeah, damn it. She should be here. To see her beautiful boy turn a year old. It's wrong, and it's never going to be right. All we can do for Helene is what's best for him."

"I know that. Everything you're doing is . . . I'm really thankful. I was thinking when I'm more stable financially, like in another year or so, maybe I could take him part-time in Boston. I could get somebody to come into the house. Like an au pair."

Willa exhaled. "That's a subject that calls for clear heads. Right now isn't the time." At other times, she had certainly tried to open this conversation. She suspected it was terror of his own failure that made Zeke so evasive about Dusty's future. And now this, out of nowhere. "I don't think Michael and Sharon are going to want an au pair in their spare bedroom. You need to think about getting your own place."

"Oh. So, I've been meaning to tell you. I'm moving in with Priya."

"With *Priya*?"

He widened his eyes without looking at her. "Sorry you don't approve."

"Approve? Two hours ago I'd never heard of this girl. Now you're moving in?"

"We've been dating awhile. She has a nice apartment, I'm over there a lot, so it's the logical next step. I didn't want to tell you until I knew we were, you know. Serious."

Willa could just see this Priya: cool, accomplished, raven haired, with the traditional overbearing family and consequent work ethic. Maybe there was a nice boy lined up for her from the home country, and Zeke was her one act of rebellion. Willa was girlfriend-profiling, she did realize, but nothing she'd heard yet was off-type. Priya worked in finance, she was on the fast track, the gift she'd sent for Dusty was expertly wrapped in silver polka dot paper, obviously an in-store job. Probably ordered by phone, between meetings. Willa could see it right now on the gift table, lording it over a motley tribe of reused bags.

Mothers and sons. She sighed, knowing she would have to try harder than this. Just talking about the girl had switched some lights back on for Zeke; Willa had watched it happen. So she could get herself on board. Anyway, a little professional polish couldn't hurt this ramshackle family.

Abruptly she looked at him. "Okay, but where the hell *is* she?"

With a beer-slurred reaction time he looked confused, then defensive. "Boston."

"You know what I'm saying. Why isn't she here?"

"She sent a gift."

"But couldn't find the time to come and meet her partner's son."

"She will."

"Zeke. This matters. Your sister turned out about a hundred people today who all count for something in this little boy's life. And you couldn't even bring *one?*"

"Mom, don't tell me how to do this. I'm taking it slow, okay? You have no idea how hard this is for me."

"I'm sorry. I guess I do. You're scared."

"Getting attached to somebody again is like, *Jesus*. I don't even know the words. Driving way over the speed limit. Honestly, I didn't want her to come. It's just going to take time."

"Honey, I know." She put her arms around both her boys, the sad one and the restless one who needed to climb onto the table. It would take time, and no clocks stopped for a child. With or without Zeke, everything would keep moving.

She looked up to see Jorge headed toward them with a plate of Worms and Dirt.

"Hey! Junk food for the birthday boy." Jorge set the plate down on the picnic table, and Zeke swiveled around to face it with Dusty still on his lap. Jorge moved quickly ahead of Dusty's two-fisted grab to pick out the M&M's that lay half exposed in the cake-crumb mound.

"Nice move, dude. Stealing candy from a baby."

Jorge regarded Zeke with a neutral eye, for a moment whose length surpassed neutral. Given the combined blood alcohol numbers there, plus testosterone, Willa made ready to grab the child and run.

"Choking hazard," Jorge said finally. Then tossed the whole handful into his mouth, chewed, and swallowed.

"I'd look out for the worms too," Willa gently warned Zeke.

"They're soft, but I'd pull them apart first. He's never had anything like that before, as far as I know." Or chocolate, or very much sugar. After the first tentative fistful, Dusty set himself to the earnest labor of stuffing his face with cake. Zeke's attention remained fixed on Jorge.

"So what are you now, an EMT?"

"Nope. Still turning and burning 'em down at Yari's, same as your sister. And overhauling engines."

Jorge surprised Willa by sitting down on the bench opposite, knees spread wide, elbows on the table. Until this moment she'd thought of Jorge as conflict averse. He was definitely lubricated, but Willa didn't believe in so-called Dutch courage. In her experience, cowards who drank were still cowards and nice guys mostly stayed nice, if a little stupid. These two were going to be themselves, just maybe a little more so, while she sat here hoping it would come to no one's undoing.

"So, but here's the thing," Jorge offered. "I've had to do the Heimlich at the restaurant, two times, and I'm going to tell you, man. A brother could shit himself."

Zeke seemed to be recalculating his position. "I hear that." He poked through Dusty's disappearing dirt pile and found another red pebble, which he ate.

"One of the times it was a baby," Jorge said. "Not a *baby* but a little kid, like around three. Ho-ly mother. Little dude turned blue, I thought we were going to lose him right out there at table six."

"Wow," Willa said. "But you saved him?"

Jorge looked off to the side, an uncomfortable hero. "Just luck. I didn't know how to work it on a kid so I kind of had to guess. After that I asked Sondra to show me. She's had to take all those EMT classes. To take care of her *viejos*."

"*That's* who that is," Zeke said. "Sondra. I recognized her when she said hello, but couldn't remember how I knew her. That's her over there talking to my dad, right? The beauty queen in the Daisy Dukes?"

"Hey, horndog. That's my *sister.*"

"O-kay," Willa interrupted. "So how *do* you do the Heimlich on a child? That's something I should probably know."

Jorge turned to Willa with a solemn, slightly unfocused look. "It's not too hard. I'll show you sometime."

His protectiveness of his sister had smacked her across the heart. What she once would have dismissed as machismo now struck her as something she'd failed to teach her son. Zeke's habitual gallantry made his treatment of Tig all the worse. Willa sat with this revelation while watching Dusty polish off his pile of cake, working around the gummy invertebrates. Some instinct must have warned him off. The ill-fated Che on Dusty's white T-shirt was getting buried in a shallow grave of crumbs.

"Where did this little shirt come from?" Willa asked.

Jorge shrugged. "She gets his clothes from everywhere. Mostly for free."

"I know, but I never saw this one before today. I was wondering if she brought it back from Cuba."

"Seems like the place for *el Che,*" Jorge agreed, *"en la ropa de bebé."*

"But there wasn't any Dusty at the time."

"He existed," Zeke corrected.

"Well, I mean, you were expecting him." Willa thought about it. "She came back in February, he was born in July. But she hadn't been in touch with any of us for almost a year. She wouldn't have known." Willa thought of Toto's young children and wondered how well Tig had known them. The tangle of heartbreak that might lead a girl to buy a tiny shirt. Willa tried to brush off some of the mess, which only made matters worse. "If she did bring this from Cuba, it would have been for some theoretical baby."

"Putting away Che for the future family," Zeke said, laughing. "That's exactly the kind of batshit hope chest my sister would have."

"Hope chest?"

"An ancient rite," Willa explained. "Girls used to stash away clothes and linens in a chest, to prepare for their future as wives and mothers. If Zeke and Tig heard the term from me, I promise I was using it ironically."

Zeke grinned. "Tig heard it plenty. You know. That old joke, 'You still *hope* you'll grow a *chest* some day.'"

Jorge narrowed his eyes at Zeke, working out the crude insult implied. "She'd be the one to have a batshit hope chest," he finally agreed, "'cause the lady has got some serious batshit hopes." He observed the effect of *the lady* on Zeke, and winked at Willa. "What can you say? She keeps it one hundred."

※

"*We* lived in a garage," Willa reminded Iano. "We didn't have much more than they do. And we were deliriously happy."

"Your brain edits out the misery from your past."

"Okay, I probably don't have perfect recall. But we weren't miserable."

"We were married."

"So? You going all old-school on me here?" She looked at him, still in his teaching clothes but out of his shoes, holding a half-empty glass of wine. "What's your worry, legality, permanence, what? Are you thinking Jorge's going to run off and abandon your deflowered daughter? Because honestly, I'm not sure what more this family could have done to scare him off."

"He can't run away. The garage isn't our property, it's his."

Willa felt proprietary toward the little ivy-covered carriage house, and constantly forgot it wasn't hers. Or refused to believe it,

even that first day when Pete condemned their house in a word—
shambles—and assigned the stip house to the neighbors.

"You know what? It's Mary Treat's. The house where she lived
is gone, but that building would have been there in her backyard."

"Tig and Jorge are shacking up in Mary Treat's garage. Is this
significant?"

"I don't think Mary had a vehicle. What's interesting is that it
was constructed as a provisional dwelling. And it's the only structure still standing."

Iano reached for the bottle to refill their glasses. For Willa's
birthday he'd surprised her with a bottle of wine and some excellent Thai takeout, which they were eating out of the cartons as they
sat on the back steps admiring the upheavals on their property.
Yesterday's party had left no major scars, but the place was a mess
in its own right. Pallets of old bricks were stacked on both sides of
Tig's garden. The double doors of the carriage house stood open to
ventilate a newly installed and refinished floor. Tig and Jorge had
gone out somewhere with Dusty while the fumes dissipated, leaving the elders there to speculate on the nature of their attachment.

Willa thought she and Iano had been happy in their garage life
because it felt impermanent; they'd expected their poverty not to
last. Now, as Jorge and Tig set up their own tiny home, she wondered if their sentiments might be the opposite: they were happy
for a circumstance that had a good shot at enduring. Tig's batshit
hopes notwithstanding, she believed material desires were toxic.
She aimed to be immune to the ambitions and disappointments
that had maimed her parents' existence and now were stirring up
a national tidal wave of self-interest that Willa found terrifying. It
was pretty clear there would be no stopping the Bullhorn, or someone like him. Here was the earthquake, the fire, flood, and melting
permafrost, with everyone still grabbing for bricks to put in their
pockets rather than walking out of the wreck and looking for light.

Iano persistently didn't get Tig's view of the world, thinking she refused to invest in the future, but Willa knew that was untrue. The girl had drawn out a detailed plan for the garden she wanted to make on the property, just for instance, including an arbor with grapevines. She'd made a convincing case that she could provide for a child. They were eating from the small garden she'd already planted there, and a bigger one that belonged to whatever they called their commune at the training institute. These kids were well connected.

For Willa's birthday Tig had given her a handmade card. Zeke had eaten breakfast in sunglasses and then spirited himself to someplace with good Wi-Fi for the day, so he'd probably forgotten it. With the celebration budget thoroughly blown the day before, Willa expected no more. A year ago, in the excitement of a grandchild's birth, she hadn't registered the future cost of this near collision of his birthday with her own. But she'd never liked being the center of attention. This was the party she would have preferred all along. She watched Iano wave mosquitoes away from their ankles, thinking only very briefly of the encroaching Zika virus, and decided that if sexier feet than her husband's had ever met the earth she didn't want to know about it.

"I think it's because of what happened with Zeke and Helene," he said, and Willa had to row backward through several tributaries of thought to get to his meaning.

"Oh, your worry about Tig and Jorge? I can see that. He seems about as emotionally resilient as they come, but tragedy can strike, there's no doubt. Some things would have been easier for Zeke if they'd been married. But he also would have assumed her debts. I don't think he would have come out ahead financially."

Iano didn't respond. She studied his face for clues. "You don't mean financially. You're scared of her getting hurt that much. But honey, that's just life. Love is the big risk." She set her glass on the step and put both arms around Iano. "Look at this. Me, telling Zorba not to be afraid of living boldly."

"I'm trying to turn over a new leaf, *moro*."

"Oh, dear God. Don't do *that*."

Iano had taken a contract to teach summer classes for almost as much money as he made the rest of the year. The university had to incentivize, since few faculty members wanted to hang around Philly in summer. Willa and Iano were very much hanging around. They'd taken a lease on an apartment that was walking distance from campus in an old building with loads of antique charm, which was real-estate lingo for no elevator, window air conditioners, and a minuscule kitchen. Its principal attraction was that it would allow Willa and Iano to live within their means. But she was starting to see advantages beyond decent shelter: a world of close neighbors, greengrocers, a movie theater, a Macedonian bakery that made bougatsa. Also a vintage tiled bathroom with a giant claw-foot tub. When Tig had looked at her pictures of the apartment she'd kept scrolling back to that tub, betraying a hint of material envy. She mentioned she might try to find one online, from the salvage yards.

Willa and Iano had a week to wait before they could move in, but already the house was coming down around them. They'd struck a deal with Pete to do demolition and dismantling, taking most of the materials in exchange for his labor. Architectural salvage was a new big thing in the East Coast housing market, and this old house was a mine of stuff Pete could use or sell. Hardwood flooring, fixtures, most of the interior moldings, even the big warbly panes of antique glass were in demand. Tig thought this was dreamy, a whole house getting recycled. She looked forward to the extra space they'd have for her garden when the house was gone, and a nice view of the streetscape. Plus, very much more sun. The house had been casting a lot of shade.

Initially Tig had insisted the carriage house was fine as it was, but gradually allowed a few improvements, such as plumbing. With expert help they were putting in a sink, shower, and toilet and hooking it into the sewer main. In the words of Pete Petrofaccio, who remained mystified by the Tavoularis specifics, "With a baby, you need your plumbing." Tig and Jorge also pulled up some hardwood flooring, laid it down on joists, and had refinished it this morning, when by all rights at least one of them should have been hungover. A big improvement over the previous dirt, this floor was expected to help with the ant problem. Willa worried about termites under a wood floor, but Tig explained the ants would keep away termites. These ants, she said, are here to stay.

Mr. Petrofaccio planned to have the whole house taken apart and hauled off by summer's end and foresaw no problem selling all the salvageable materials, right down to the doorknobs. He was keeping a ledger and would reimburse them for everything he netted beyond his fees. He'd found a motivated buyer for the famous Dunwiddie bricks. The unexpected windfall still felt surreal to Willa. When a house no longer provided shelter, it turned out to be worth exactly the sum of its parts.

⚹

With so many folders and papers spread out on the table between them, it could have been a board meeting. Dusty at the head of the table would be the CEO in the high chair. Tig had cut up chicken and vegetables into tiny bits and was putting these onto his tray a handful at a time, which he shoved into his mouth open handed.

One of the last moving chores was to sort through the boxes rescued from upstairs. It had to be done today, before Zeke went back to Boston, so Willa corralled the kids and sat them down. Few other obstacles remained standing between herself and the exodus. They'd sold nearly all the furniture. Tig's wizardry on

Craigslist made it a snap. Willa was finding it easier every day to let go of things she'd considered family treasures, including this dining table that had served them for years. It was too big for any of their future homes. The Knox family crib was one of the few things that would stay in the family, along with its current resident, location TBD.

The departure no one could talk about was Dixie's. She would not rise again. Every few hours Willa carried her outside to urinate and have a look at the sky, and when food was placed in front of her she managed to eat, a little. Willa knew this wasn't a life. Soon they would put her down and bury her under the tree. The one where she peed. Willa could see that for most thoughtful creatures, this was a positive choice.

Now they were sorting through the boxes she'd kept for the kids since they'd first put crayon to paper to articulate their souls. Only the more exceptional works were supposed to have made the cut: drawings, poems, various certificates of excellence. The kids had made the choices themselves, and named these archives their Forever Boxes. If Willa once had a notion of holding them to one large cardboard box apiece, that philosophy of restraint had gone the way of Prohibition.

Willa had a raft of her own boxes too, containing among other things a print copy of nearly every article she'd written or edited over the decades, clipped from the original publication. After she started working full time for a magazine it got simpler, she just saved every issue. Of course she knew every word was archived electronically somewhere, and she could find it online if she really wanted to read an article about sailboat building she'd written twenty years ago, which she definitely did not. But giving up the physical record of all that work felt like a kind of death. Online wasn't enough. She wanted it to *weigh* something.

She'd set up each of them with a small "keep" box and trash

bags for the rest, and now she watched her offspring dispassionately stuffing their entire past into garbage bags. Almost nothing was getting kept. "You're not even looking," she accused. "What is that right there you're throwing away?"

Tig held up a drawing, essentially a stick figure with arms and legs growing directly out of the egg-shaped head. The mouth leered a half-circle smile; the eyes bore pupils, whopping curved lashes, and astonished eyebrows.

"Ohhh," Willa lamented. "Your Humpty Dumpty phase. I loved those drawings. This child psychologist friend of ours said they were way ahead of normal development for your age. They count IQ by the number of body parts a three-year-old includes in a drawing, and you put in everything."

Tig aimed the drawing at her brother. "Hey Harvard, looka here. *Genius*." Then she stuffed it in the bag.

"You're not even saving *one*?"

"No, I don't have room for crap like this. What are you going to do with all that stuff you're keeping, Mom?"

"Just . . . don't worry about it. I'm archiving it."

Willa carried on with her hoarding. She still had boxes she'd brought from her mother's house when they emptied it out, and never took time to look through before now. She was finding the predictable yellowed clippings: recipes, advice columns with tips on stain removal. Also many files of family trees, results of a genealogy hobby Darcie and Dreama shared, which had kept the twin sisters connected and internet savvy into their seventies. Willa had never taken much interest. Now she saw they'd found relatives in the region, not in Vineland but nearby. She vaguely recalled they had family in Pennsylvania, drawn north from West Virginia via the so-called hillbilly highway into the steel belt after the war. That family history suddenly seemed like something she ought to hold on to. This craving was not letting up. Anything in her mother's handwriting she saved. Willa wanted her also to go on weighing something in the world.

The kids were ruthless. "Another one for the *archive*," they began to taunt in unison, while throwing their own things away faster than they could look at them. Zeke had a head start, since most of his latter-years cache had been lost to water damage back last winter. He'd been angry at the time, but now seemed more than ready to let it all go. The balm of the new life, Willa thought. *Priya* sounded like it might be Sanskrit for "Darling, forget about your messed-up family."

Once he had lunch down the hatch, Dusty needed more entertainment to keep him from climbing out of his chair, and Tig had a basket of toys at the ready. He examined each article she handed him for an unpredictable number of seconds before throwing it on the floor. The toys were mostly combinations of household things: a wooden spoon and spatula connected with a big rubber band; two potholders pinched together with a hair clip. Dusty went straight to the connectors and tried to work out how to pull the things apart, just as he was drawn to cabinet latches. Now that he was crawling and cruising, he expressed a powerful bent to get at the world and deconstruct.

The potholders hit the floor and Tig gave him a big plastic vitamin bottle, emptied of vitamins and partly filled with pea gravel. Dusty shook it, widened his eyes at the large noise, and looked around to make sure everyone was clear about authorship.

"Nice," Zeke observed. "A redneck rattle."

"Excuse me. It's not an oxycontin bottle."

"Okay, stop," Willa said, not at their argument but the artifact Tig was about to throw away: a child-manufactured book with a red construction paper binding held together by acorn brads. "What is that?"

Tig held it up so Willa could read the handwritten title: *CLUB OF WORLDS*.

"It was this stupid thing we'd do, take turns making up a world. When it was your day you were the president, and everybody else had to agree with your world."

Zeke took the book from her and read aloud. "November 6, 1999. Today's President: Antsy Tavoularis. World of today is Tree World. The citizens"—it's spelled *cizitens*—"are turtles frogs and bugs. Trees are king. Nothing is allowed to get killed."

"Oh, my, God!" Tig erupted. "Delouse Cameron! Remember how she got all up about the snakes? She said if there were snakes you would have to kill them. I told her it was my day and she couldn't kill the snakes."

"Yeah, you just thought it was okay to kill *her*."

"We kicked her out," Tig explained to Willa. "Not that day, but later. She was so boring. Every single time it was her turn she'd make *Walmart* World. We told her that wasn't a Club World, there already was a Walmart and you could just fucking *go* there."

Willa understood this was probably an exact quote.

"Her thing was in her Walmart you'd buy whatever you wanted without money."

"Are you saying 'Delouse'?" Willa asked. "That can't be a real name."

"It was Dee Louise. Zeke the big meanie came up with Delouse."

"*I* was a meanie? You pulled out a big old hunk of her hair."

"Okay, but she had like a hundred pounds on me and she started it. The girl was douche. I mean, will you please. *Walmart World?*"

Dusty threw the vitamin bottle rattle on the floor, to spectacular effect.

"Why don't I remember this girl?" Willa asked. "Where was I?"

"It was in CC club. That after-school club at school, which we so knew was a rip-off, Mom. It meant we got to spend two extra hours *at school*."

"With all the other kids whose parents had nine-to-five jobs. You poor things."

Tig reached down to pick up the rattle and hand it back to Dusty. "We never even knew what CC stood for. Mom, you called it the Continuous Crap club."

"Sorry. You did bring home a lot of, let's call it 'handiwork.' And you never wanted me to *throw anything away*." She raised her eyebrows at them. "Come to think of it."

"Delouse wasn't in CC club," Zeke said. "That was the first year we got to be latchkeys. You were in third, I was in sixth. They always came over even though their Mom was a stay-at-home. She just wanted to get rid of them."

Tig squinched her face, trying to remember. "Are you sure about that?"

"Yes! They lived down the street. Her little brother was the Mouse Trap."

"Oh God, yes. The Mouse Trap."

Willa felt much as she did when trying to follow a conversation in Spanish or French. "Why would they be at our house unsupervised when their mother was at home?"

"Sometimes we went over there. But it was more fun at our house. Obvi."

"Delouse was fourteen or something," Zeke explained. "Technically she was supposed to be babysitting us, but after we kicked her out of the club she got all pissy and never came back. But we let the Mouse Trap stay."

"He was so weird, Mom. He hid in cabinets. He would go into, like, one of the kitchen cabinets, he'd move the pans around so he could get his whole body in there. And then he wouldn't come out for two or three hours."

"Seriously," Zeke confirmed. "I think he was trained. The Camerons were some kind of survivalists."

"Why didn't I know you were playing with the children of survivalists? Did they have firearms?"

The look between Tig and Zeke suggested firearms weren't the half of it.

"Amazingly you survived." Willa took the book from Zeke and paged through it. She found considerable repetition of something called Chess World. "What's this?"

"That was Zeke. He was almost as boring as Queen Walmart."

"So in your world, people were chess pieces?" Willa recalled a serious chess period: he was president of the school club, went to state meets. Whole phases of her children's lives, these passions that had seemed to be their purest marrow, had faded away one after another. And character persisted.

"Kind of like that," Zeke evaded. "It was complicated."

"On his days you had to play chess," Tig clarified, "and whoever won got to be King Bossyface."

"That sounds reasonable. A meritocracy."

"No-o," Tig corrected, "because Zeke *always* won. We probably played five thousand games of chess and he won every single time. See, what I finally figured out was that he taught me how to play, and I think he held back on some of the rules. He'd just whip out some exceptional new move whenever he needed it to win."

"Absolutely false."

"Okay, I'm keeping this," Willa said. She archived the Club of Worlds.

With the Forever Boxes conquered they moved on to a pile of things they still had to decide about, mostly valueless: the prickly pear cactus Tig made of cardboard and toothpicks for a science fair, to demonstrate "Adaptation to the Arid Environment." (This had survived four moves?) Dorm room posters that no one needed to pull out of their cardboard cylinders. Willa trashed an armload of these with a prideful flourish. Then retrieved one, because it felt suspiciously heavy. She picked the tape off the end and pulled out a Navajo rug.

"Whoa," both kids said when she rolled it out on the table.

"Wow," she agreed. "I haven't thought about this for as long as you two have been alive. If I'd accidentally thrown it away, I never would have missed it."

"You spent the whole afternoon saving crap," Zeke observed, "and then tried to throw away a couple thousand dollars."

"Probably more," she had to concede. "You know what these are worth now?"

"Where'd you get it?"

"It sounds crazy but it was no big deal at the time. One of our trips through Navajo land when Dad and I were in college, driving from Colorado to Phoenix to see his folks. I guess Navajo weaving was undiscovered, or we just happened to be at the right place. I guarantee you we couldn't even have paid a hundred dollars for it."

Tig ran her fingers over the lines of color, vivid dark reds and cloudy grays, reading the craftsmanship in a way Willa couldn't. "It's really, really beautiful," Tig said.

"I think we intended it as a Christmas present and then decided to hang on to it ourselves. And then I guess we thought it was too nice to use."

"You could sell it," Zeke said. "Or does that make me the enemy of the people?"

Willa looked from one to the other. "I don't know. It's been in the family a long time. Do you want it? Either of you?"

They both shook their heads. "I agree, it's too nice to use," Tig said. "I mean, it shouldn't go on the floor. And we don't have any space to hang it on the wall. You should take it, Mom. For your new place."

"We have even less wall space than you do. And I'm not going to walk on this."

Zeke said nothing. Willa couldn't help thinking of Helene's designer taste, and the fact that he was about to move once again into a woman's life. About whom Willa knew nothing, except that her son didn't go for arts-and-crafts types.

"Well, this is a conundrum," she said. "A museum-quality piece, but it's so valuable nobody wants to take it."

Tig laughed. "Give it to your pal Chris, for *his* museum. He'll take anything."

"Ha ha." Willa was used to defending Christopher, whose xeric charm was lost on her family, putting it mildly. But it was a thought. He might know a collector who'd pay top dollar.

Willa had gotten to one last shoebox of her mother's things, which looked safe to pitch out: recipes copied in her mother's handwriting. She thumbed through them, remembering her mother in a steamy kitchen with hair plastered to her temples, canning and pickling things by mystical means Willa had refused to learn. Maybe Tig would want some of these recipes. "Zucchini relish," she read aloud. "Okra Dilly." Then she stopped, read silently, put her hand over her mouth, and burst into tears.

"Mom! What is it?"

Tig gently took the scrap of paper from Willa and read aloud. "I was something that lay under the sun and felt it, like the pumpkins, and I did not want to be anything more. I was entirely happy. Perhaps we feel like that when we die and become a part of something entire, whether it is sun and air, or goodness and knowledge. At any rate, that is happiness; to be dissolved into something complete and great. When it comes to one, it comes as naturally as sleep."

Both kids stared at Willa. They looked so alike.

"It's from *My Àntonia*. By Willa Cather. Mama's favorite book."

"It's okay." Tig handed it back. "You should keep this."

"No. It's not okay. She wanted me to read this at her funeral. And I didn't."

"It was a nice funeral, Mom," Zeke said. "You just forgot."

"I forgot. She gave this to me, I don't know, ten years before she died. I didn't want to think about her *funeral*. So I stuck it in a box, and I completely and absolutely forgot. It's one of the only things she ever asked me to do for her, and I didn't do it." This grief ran so deep Willa could hardly name it. Not just for her mother's loss, or the funeral that wasn't perfect. She'd failed to keep order.

"You had too much else on your mind, Mom."

"No." Willa wiped her face with the back of her hand. "It was here in this box, with these completely unrelated things that weren't important to me, inside other boxes of completely unrelated things. I had too many things. Just too much goddamn stuff."

They sorted in silence awhile, clearing the table for good and all.

"Watch out there, buddy," Zeke suddenly said in Dusty's direction.

Dusty had managed to get the cap off the plastic bottle, remarkably, and now had the look of a boy with contraband in his mouth.

"Good thing it *wasn't* an oxycontin bottle," Zeke said, while Tig scooped him out of the high chair and had him on her lap in a flash. She expertly dug a finger into his mouth and produced a couple of wet black lumps.

"Nope, nope, here you go," she crooned gently. "Shhh. Give those to Mama."

The rock eater wasn't pleased to give up his cache. Willa watched him screw up his face in a tantrum, and it took her a moment to register that Zeke was staring at his sister as if she'd slapped him. He turned to Willa looking bewildered, a confusion salted with wariness, or anger. "Mom, he's going with you to Philadelphia. Right?"

Tig sat perfectly still with Dusty in her arms, looking at no one. The *mama* had been a slip, natural and unintentional. Tig slid her eyes to meet Willa's. The look could have torn her heart from her chest if Willa hadn't been prepared.

"No, Zeke. Dusty is staying here. With Tig."

He said nothing for a long moment. Then he got up and left the dining room, and a minute later, the house. They heard his car start in the driveway, heard it pull out, and that too could have knocked a mother down if she hadn't been braced for it.

It took forever for either of them to speak. "The hard thing with Zeke," Tig finally said, "is he has to always win."

"You're right. And also to be sure he's doing the right thing. For Dusty, in this case. I'll call him later. You'll have to trust me to handle this. I can walk him through it."

Tig shook her head. "He would have to figure out how to see it as his win."

"I think he will. Because it is."

Willa studied the wide-eyed face of this child who expected nothing and mostly got it. She'd had no use for anything Willa ever tried to give her, it seemed. But maybe this. "Sometimes the right thing isn't a thing but a person."

"And that's me?"

"And that's you."

Willa bumped down the sidewalk feeling like a tourist of the laughingstock class, pulling two rolling suitcases—huge and huger—with extra items attached on top with bungee cords. Here was the flotsam of a family, everything too precious or too worthless to sell on eBay. She turned south from Landis onto Seventh, glad to get away from traffic that was sparse at this hour but loaded with empty passenger seats. Ever since the Yellow

Guy revelations, that troublesome confederacy of ghost riders had been visible to Willa.

She'd given Christopher a heads-up on the impending donation but hadn't told him about the Navajo rug, as a strategic choice. She was trying to unload one weird batch of stuff here, without much to sweeten the pot.

She hadn't been in the door a minute before she unrolled the rug.

"Two Gray Hills!" He fondled the texture with frank approval. "Willa, this is worth a mint. You have to keep it."

"I can't. Our apartment in Philly is microscopic. Believe me, I thought about it. But we won't have anyplace to hang it, and it's too good to use on the floor."

"Oh, definitely. We'll display it on a wall here, in the main room. How ever did you get your hands on a piece like this?"

"Kind of by dumb accident. We were paupers at the time. We got it for a song."

"Well, it's worth the whole opera now."

"But it doesn't exactly belong here, does it? A rug from Navajo land?"

Willa was being coy. This museum had relics aplenty from the western territories, notably a velvet-upholstered chair made of Texas cow horns. What did not belong here? The antique silver services, the cameo collection laid out on a swath of velvet, the arcane photos and personal papers hanging out upstairs with Charles Darwin, all vestiges of a citizenry who'd called this place home. Chris Hawk in his tailcoat and neatly trimmed beard was president of the club, and it would always be Vineland World.

He hefted everything onto a table under one of the portraits of the founder, and started unpacking. Willa tried not to cringe as Chris carefully lifted and stacked papers, sorting through the mess. "We've got some genealogical documents there," she offered. "A record of the Appalachian diaspora after World War II. My family was part of that." Unfortunately it was sandwiched between children's drawings, the complete works of Willa Knox, and words from a novel that had allowed her mother to die in peace, lost for a long interlude in a box of recipes. Willa's lifelong service to the duty of proper order now seemed like an idiot's game. School papers and photos had been labeled by year, her own articles filed away with research attached, and in the end she'd pitched everything into a couple of suitcases like an evacuee from a wrecked cruise ship.

"Somewhere down the line this will be useful to somebody," he reassured her. "After you break out with the biography, there will be interest in your earlier work."

Was Christopher cracking his first joke? She watched him tuck his white hair behind his ears and lean over the suitcase like a pirate surveying the booty. "I'm just sorry for the mess," she told him, but in this place of flotsam far in excess of her own she was starting to feel a whole lot less embarrassed. "I tried to keep things in categories but we're on deadline, with the house coming down. At the last minute it got chaotic."

"Oh, it's fine. Chaos gets me out of bed in the morning. I'll get it all cataloged and labeled. Your name will be attached to everything."

"A family in memoriam."

"You're still alive. Most of you. You'll be coming back to Vineland often, I assume."

"Probably every other day. I have to see the little boy. And I've got a million hours of research to do in here." The pricey rug was her down payment on Christopher's future services, and his willingness to cede some territory. Already he'd happened on a surprising Mary Treat lead from a historical society in Jacksonville, Florida, and turned it over to Willa without delay. She was counting on no reversal of fortunes with the book she'd confessed to be writing, but it was getting her out of bed in the mornings. And not exactly a biography, either, but something breaking into her thoughts as a string of intimate conversations in a light-filled parlor, in a class-room smelling of chalk and ammonia, in a forest clearing where a heron stalked the banks of a blood-red creek: words luring her across an unexpected bridge at the end of the world she knew. She needed to be still, to listen and be taken. The prospect of living apart from Dusty had opened a physical grief that shocked her, but it was ebbing behind Willa's itch for time and solitude. In a zero-sum apartment she was trading crib space for desk space. A Greenwood-Treat correspondence existed somewhere, she knew this in her bones, and she would be the one to find it. Taking custody of these other lives felt as large in its demands as birthing a child. Holding other eyes inside her line of sight, other futures and risks, would mean making something new—even if *new* was impossible because they were all made of just one set of molecules. Possible or not, she'd have room to find out, having jettisoned the nonsense Chris was busy appraising.

"If you need to sell that rug as a fund-raiser, that's fine. A do-nation is a donation. Don't feel obligated to expand your collection into the western territories."

"Oh!" He stood upright and focused his eyes on Willa with a hint of dazzle. "I have something new to show you." He disap-peared into his office.

Willa watched dust motes track the banks of light coming in through the tall windows. The Landis portrait glared down at her: desperate eyes, snowy beard. This would be an "after" in the Dorian Gray–like series. His hair and beard were said to have turned white in a single year after he murdered one of his public critics and got away with it. Tricky, the getting away with it.

Chris returned and handed over a large postal envelope, very old, addressed to Mary Treat, not on Plum but Park Avenue, with no hint of a return address beyond an elaborate postmark made in Provo, Utah. Willa emptied its contents onto the table and felt anxious for the brittle state of the pages that fell out. Pencil sketches. She fanned them out with her fingertips and studied what appeared to be a series of botanical illustrations, all drawn by the same hand and classified: Sego lily, *Calochortus nuttallii*. Goldenrod, *Solidago elongata*. Saltbush, *Obione truncate*. Willa felt an ardent need for something more personal here than Latin names, but found only minimal notations. The milk vetch, *Astragalus iodanthus*, offered this small note: "appears to thrive in hostile conditions." The most interesting of the drawings was unlabeled but obviously a giant redwood tree, drawn in detail from its broad, burled trunk to its narrowing upper branches. Willa felt she shouldn't touch anything but did anyway, turning over the redwood portrait to find a tantalizing inscription on the back, not quite verse:

Unsheltered, I live in daylight. And like the wandering bird I rest in thee.

"Who did she know in Provo, Utah?"

"No idea." Chris was pleased with her agitation, she could tell. He turned back to poking through the entrails of her family history. "I'll send you a receipt for your donation," he promised. "When I've gone through everything and can attach a dollar amount. The Tavoularis-Knox collection will be a nice addition."

"Okay, but I really should apologize for bringing it to you like this." Should, but couldn't. Under the gaze of the old mad man on the wall in his kingdom of dust motes, she felt unapologetic. "It's the state of the union at our house. We're a shambles."

☀

Willa walked home toting her two empty suitcases with ease, one inside the other. From the corner of Sixth and Plum she spotted

Tig and a half-dozen teenage girls sitting cross-legged in a semicircle on the grass in front of the carriage house, all watching Dusty. Naked as an old-time circus strongman, wearing nothing but his bulky diaper, he was working hard on a solo stand-up. Willa stopped to watch from the sidewalk with her luggage in hand, like some homeless lady, because she didn't want to intrude and break his concentration. This act took everything he had: first raising himself bottom-up with fingers and toes gripping the grass, then letting go and lifting his arms, slowly bringing himself upright. When the girls applauded he beamed at them, and that small distraction cost him: he fell down on his padded bottom.

But he went right back to it, trying again. He would do this over and over until he had it, and today or tomorrow he would walk. Willa remembered all this. She'd watched her kids master these first small tasks with an application of effort that seemed superhuman, but of course it only amounted to *being* human, a story written in genes. First they would stagger, then grow competent, and then forget the difficulty altogether while thinking of other things, and that was survival.

18

⚭

Survival

Of all seasons in the Pine Barrens, summer was consummate. The pair rested in a glade he had never seen before, kept in reserve by Mary. It was her favorite place. The fluted green columns of pitcher plants rose all around them with ruffled hoods lifted and mouths slightly agape, nearly smiling as they digested their minuscule prey. Mary and Thatcher drifted likewise in their thoughts, with their eviscerated lunch bucket lying nearby. Mary sat on Thatcher's coat spread over the damp ground. He had insisted. Thatcher lay on the moss with his head resting on Mary's lap, unwilling for now to consider any place beyond this one.

They'd been conveyed that morning as usual by the steadfast Foggett, but without Selma, who had given her notice two days before with more tears than necessary and some biting of knuckles. The girl had presented herself in such a state of emergency, it seemed likely she and Willis were already now married and on to the procreating stage. It was a season of precipitous ends and beginnings.

Mary was terminating the lease on her house and moving into rooms at the back of the Campbells' manor on Park Avenue. She would enjoy the company of her friend Phoebe, and in a few years would put by enough money to purchase her own home. Mary had already chosen the lot for it, also on Park Avenue, where she could have a small house built precisely to her needs. She had already drawn the plan for the garden. This home had long been a dream of Mary's, but inertia and a duty toward Selma—and, she confessed, the pleasure of visits from a neighbor—had held her in place. Freed of those duties and pleasures, and with Joseph securely gone, she could sally forward into life.

Thatcher's house, which was never his house, was now the legal property of Orville Dunwiddie. Aurelia had married without fuss, as promised. On this very day she and her daughters with all conceivable fuss, he imagined, would be tyrannizing the Dunwiddie servants who had come to pack up the flatware and corsets, completing the move into the Dunwiddie dominion. Scylla and Charybdis would be Dunwiddie hounds. Aurelia and Rose could not be happy about that, but their other choice was to watch Polly throw herself down on the threshold and rend her clothing. If Rose could have horses, Polly would have her dogs. The eventual fate of the house on Plum Street remained at large. Rose and Aurelia would need more time to understand what Thatcher had known for a year: that no money could save a structure so thoroughly flawed.

Rose seemed to have less difficulty abandoning a marriage. The lawyer Mr. Thomas, in gratitude for Thatcher's services at the trial, had directed him to the friendliest possible judicial channels. Thatcher would have to offer Rose sufficient grounds, swearing among other things that he'd failed to provide for her properly, which was certainly true. But a marriage without issue could be closed like a book, and with Thatcher soon gone from Vineland, the path for Rose would smooth itself. After a sufficient pause she would begin referring to herself as a widow, and so would everyone else. Unblemished, she could marry again.

"I find myself shockingly relieved," he told Mary, who had listened with sympathy to his full accounting of the wreckage. "Only now I have to bring up something difficult. It concerns you."

"Then it can't be very difficult."

"Delicate, then." He closed his eyes briefly and listened. Water flowed through the ground underneath the moss. "In order to dissolve the marriage, I have to declare I was unfaithful to my wife. It's a formality. Everyone says what they're required to say in these cases. I needn't be specific. But in a town full of gossips. Well. I worry."

She said nothing. He saw she was smiling.

"I'm worried about *you*, Mary. Your reputation. What if someone thought of you as . . . the party involved?"

"Me! The poor little crone discarded by Joseph Treat when he trotted off to New York in pursuit of the glamorous Woodhull. Did a year in Vineland teach you nothing?"

He laughed. "That is probably the general opinion."

"Well, I can tell you this. My household allowance of scandal is used up. I am now invisible."

Thatcher thought Mary was not invisible, but as free as any woman could be. And in the grip of fresh discoveries, always. Yesterday after more than a year trying she had succeeded in watching a queen of her captivating *Polyergus* ants take over a colony of the species they enslaved, the *Formica*. The ascendant queen invaded the *Formica* nest, found the host queen, and licked her aggressively until she died. Thereafter in less than a minute a transformation took hold of the invaded colony. Every worker became subdued, without exception. "I did not see any visible communications among the members of the colony." Mary seemed freshly struck with the wonder of what she'd seen. "But the effect was instantaneous. All of them were stupefied and subservient to their new leader. It must be a chemical signal given off by the dominant queen."

"You could call it the Landis effect."

"Oh, *Landis*." She seemed neither amused nor very bothered.

"He is walking free, Mary. A murderer."

The jury had found him innocent by reason of insanity. Having watched the charade, Thatcher was not very surprised with the verdict, only at the number of days the jury required to reach it. Evidently it took some doing to boil a human conscience down to cornmeal pap. The twelve men went into their sealed inner room and locked the door. After two days they sent out a note: *Eight for acquittal, four for conviction. We see no way to bring all parties together.* Naturally, a minister was summoned to get them all on their knees. *And when they arose,* the newspaper reported, *two of the four went over. Seeing this result they tried it again and another juryman was gathered into the fold, leaving one poor fellow alone and unprotected. What could he do?*

"Landis is finished, regardless," Mary said. "He doesn't have the power of a *Polyergus* queen."

Thatcher felt Mary was optimistic. But this was true: the man he'd seen in the courtroom was a punctured flask. Getting stripped of his gold watch and forced into mock humility, even for the span of six days, might prove fatal to his potency. If the man is only a man, his rule will be resisted. The utopia would ravel at the seams and show itself as a costume covering naked greed.

Thatcher would not be in Vineland to see it. In less than a week he would be on the train to Boston to join an expedition to the western territories. The director of the Harvard herbarium was dispatching men to collect and classify plants previously unknown to science. They would be traveling for months, conditions would be rough, the pay only adequate, and Thatcher could imagine nothing he would rather do. Darwin embarking as a young man on his *Beagle* voyage could not have felt more eager. Mary had written the director to recommend Thatcher for the position, but insisted he'd been hired on his merits. Perhaps. Thatcher also knew Dr. Asa Gray owed his friend a favor.

As a parting gift she had just now given Thatcher her neat little vasculum for his collections. It might be the only material thing he'd coveted in years, apart from sturdy shelter. Somehow she knew, even though he'd never spoken his longing aloud. Nor did he tell Mary now that he could see her soul. It was a giant redwood: oldest and youngest of all living things, the tree that stood past one eon into the next. He would see them in California, not as drawings in a book but as living forests. He would see sego lilies and cactus trees, and species not yet known, impossible sights he'd never thought himself worthy to claim. Asking was not in his nature. Given the choice, he might have stayed in his burrow like a badger. He certainly had not gone looking for Mary but was led to her by a pair of hounds, not very willingly, and for that he had Polly to thank. She'd demanded he go, just as she later bullied him through his rehearsals for the debate that ruined him in Vineland. And at the end, urged him to stand up for his friend Uri.

"Do you know," he told Mary, "my little sister Polly was on my side entirely in the Landis trial. She believes he is a murderer and should pay the price."

"Your sister is still young enough to see the world honestly."

"And no longer my sister. It's the greater share of my regret in ending the marriage, to be honest." He laughed. "Do you know what she asked me? The girl is not timid. She asked me to please consider, after Rose and I are quite finished with all our divorcing, whether I might want to marry *her*. In a few years' time. When she had finished with all her growing up, is how she put it."

Mary did not laugh. "And will you, then?"

"Oh, Mary, dearest. Polly will meet some stallion by and by, young enough to take her on and get himself handily broken." Thatcher felt a little sad at the prospect, sincerely hoping it would be the stallion broken and not the rider. "Polly is nearly twenty years younger than I am. Rose is younger by only half that, and even *one* decade was a gulf I failed to navigate."

"And I am older, by nearly the same decade."

He looked at her closely. It was an odd vantage from which to inspect a face: he saw mandible and earlobes, the tender cheek, stray vines of chestnut hair at her temple, and no gulf. "It's different. Rose and I never were friends. We had no opportunity for that." He wondered that she would mention her age. "Mary, here is an odd thing I want to ask. Do you think of me as a son?"

The jaw tilted upward. She was looking at trees or the sky. "I never had a son," she said directly. "I don't know how I would think of one. Why, do you think of me as a mother?"

He smiled. "I never had a mother. I don't know how I would think of one. But I don't expect a son feels such desires as I do. I sometimes feel I ought to take the pins from your hair and make my home in it, like a bird in a tree."

"Oh dear," she said, as Mary would, and rested a hand on the buttons of his vest.

"The other share of my regret is that I cannot come back to Vineland, even to visit. How will I see you?"

"You'll find me an unrelenting correspondent. You will grow very tired of hearing from me."

"Try your best to exhaust me." He took hold of the hand on his chest, kissed it, and returned it to its place. "You will fail."

"This winter I will be in Florida. Phoebe's cousin William has offered me the use of his little cottage on the Saint Johns River, in the swamps between Jacksonville and the coast. It is a piece of divine providence from the sound of it, this cottage. It comes with the use of a flatboat. All perfectly isolated in the forest, not another soul for miles."

"Mary Treat. How many women has God made like you?"

She chose not to answer, or did not know. "I'm taking the cottage for the whole winter. Dr. Gray has written me about collecting an aquatic iris reported to grow in the Saint Johns that he thinks may be unclassified. When your expedition is finished, you would do well to join me there."

They both went quiet, imagining a river of irises. Thatcher lay watching the sky through the leaves, white clouds skipping across small lenses of light. Here was a world, where he'd asked for nothing. He would escape with his life before the dust had settled on the collapse of his falling house.

Acknowledgments

Mary Treat was a nineteenth-century biologist whose work deserves to be better known. She comes to this novel as a construction from her journals, published writings, and correspondences with Charles Darwin, Charles Riley, and Asa Gray. *Unsheltered* is a work of fiction, but most of its nineteenth-century characters and events are real, if often implausible: the Venus flytrap self-sacrifice, the female vote of 1868, the shenanigans of Charles Landis, the murder on Main Street, all true. The Greenwood family is fictional, and Thatcher's relationship with Mary Treat is my invention. Among the novel's twenty-first-century characters, any resemblance to persons living or dead is coincidental.

I'm thankful to the Vineland Historical and Antiquarian Society and its expert curator Patricia Martinelli for archives generously made available to me, and in one of the most electric moments of my life, letters from Charles Darwin dropped into my bare hands. *Abrazos* to Renzo Zeppilli for doors he opened in Cuba, and to Nathaly Pérez for patient guidance into a world so nearly unfathomable to the capitalist-reared brain. I'm grateful to Terry Karten and HarperCollins for twenty-two and thirty years, respectively, of literary partnership. Sarah Brown made efficient work of historical fact-checking. Doug Johnson was the copy editor I've always wanted. Three illuminating books guided my hand as I wrote: *This Changes Everything*, by Naomi Klein; *The Bridge at the Edge of the World*, by James Gustave Speth; and *The Book That Changed America*, by Randall Fuller. George Eliot kept nineteenth-century voices in my ear. And let us all thank Willa Cather for *My Àntonia*.

My deepest debts are to the friends who keep showing up for the years it takes to coax a book onto the page. They've all made it better. For reading, again and again: Judy Carmichael, Steven Hopp, Sam Stoloff, Terry Karten, Caroline Eisenmann, Felicia Mitchell, Jim Malusa, Sonya Norman, Lily Kingsolver. For shelter, personified: Judy Carmichael. For the steadying advocacy that makes anything possible: Sam Stoloff and the Goldin Agency team. For believing from the beginning: Frances Goldin. For teaching me modern Greek in ancient times: Dimitris Stevis. For the years we survived together among the wild things: Rob Kingsolver and Ann Kingsolver. For everything else, most of what I know and all I want to be: Steven, Lily, Camille, Reid, and Owen.